EXTREME MAKEOVER

EXTREME MAKEOVER
APOCALYPSE EDITION

DAN WELLS

TOR

A TOM DOHERTY ASSOCIATES BOOK
NEW YORK

This is a work of fiction. All of the characters, organizations, and events portrayed in this novel are either products of the author's imagination or are used fictitiously.

EXTREME MAKEOVER: APOCALYPSE EDITION

A Tor Book
Published by Tom Doherty Associates
175 Fifth Avenue
New York, NY 10010

www.tor-forge.com

Tor® is a registered trademark of Macmillan Publishing Group, LLC.

The Library of Congress Cataloging-in-Publication Data is available upon request.

ISBN 978-0-7653-8562-8 (hardcover)
ISBN 978-0-7653-8563-5 (trade paperback)
ISBN 978-0-7653-8564-2 (e-book)

Our books may be purchased in bulk for promotional, educational, or business use. Please contact your local bookseller or the Macmillan Corporate and Premium Sales Department at 1-800-221-7945, extension 5442, or by e-mail at MacmillanSpecialMarkets@macmillan.com.

First Edition: November 2016

Printed in the United States of America

0 9 8 7 6 5 4 3 2 1

This book is dedicated to Dan Wells the actor,
Dan Wells the race car driver, Dan Wells the snooker player,
and Dan Wells the Australian rules footballer.
Sometimes you try to find someone else,
and all you can find is yourself.

Contents

PREFACE

In the early nineteenth century a powerful bacterial neurotoxin was identified in spoiled meat, earning it the name *botulinum toxin,* or "sausage poison." The resulting condition, known as botulism, destroys the nervous system's ability to communicate with muscles, rendering all soft tissues—including the heart and lungs—completely immobile. A mere ninety nanograms can kill a two hundred pound adult in a matter of minutes. It is the most acutely toxic substance known to man. And in 2014, nearly five million beauty-conscious customers voluntarily injected it into their faces.

People don't like the way they look. More than two-thirds of women in the United States are trying to lose weight; more than half of American teenage girls have quantifiable eating disorders, with symptoms occurring as early as kindergarten. Beauty products and cosmetic surgeries account for more than $426 billion in annual global sales, rising at a rate of nearly 100 percent per year: men implant hair in some places and laser it off in others; some women have their breasts enlarged, others have their breasts reduced; fat is vacuumed out of abdomens; collagen is injected into lips and eyelids; wrinkles are masked and puttied and stretched and poisoned.

In a culture where we can be anything we want, only one thing is certain:

Nobody wants to be themselves.

PART ONE
NEWYEW

1

"The yew," said Carl Montgomery, "is a majestic tree." He wheezed with the effort of speaking, and paused to take a slow, deep breath from his oxygen tank. "Yggdrasil was a yew," he said, "the tree that holds up the world."

They were gathered in an opulent conference room: Carl, the CEO of NewYew, Inc., and all of his executive staff. Lyle Fontanelle, the chief scientist, was always surprised at the sheer ostentatious luxury in this part of the building. The offices had been constructed and furnished in the early days of the company when business was booming, orders were rolling in, and Carl used to say that "people are dying to give us their money!" This was technically true: their sole product at the time had been paclitaxel, a chemotherapy drug, and their customers were all cancer patients. That had been before Lyle was hired, but Carl had often confided to him that the secret to his success had been the ability to treat cancer without curing it: "Sell a cure for something," he would say, "and you've destroyed your own market; sell a treatment, and you've gained a customer for life." Given that his customers' lives depended quite literally on the treatment he sold them, Carl's philosophy had been remarkably accurate.

Lyle liked to tell himself that he would not have worked for NewYew during those days—that he would not, when confronted with fabulous wealth, compromise his principles. He was not a mercenary. He was a scientist.

NewYew's fortunes had changed in the 1990s, when scientists developed a way to synthesize paclitaxel without the need to harvest its namesake tree, the Pacific yew. A simple, unrestricted process meant that more companies could manufacture it; more manufacturers meant wider availability and lower prices; good access and low prices meant that more patients could use it. The patients were happy, the doctors were happy, even the environmentalists were happy because the Pacific yew was no longer in danger.

Carl Montgomery had not been happy.

Without a monopoly to sustain it, NewYew suffered a huge financial hit and was forced to rebuild itself; they had the equipment and the infrastructure to manufacture consumer chemicals, so they simply repurposed them from chemotherapy to cosmetics. They recruited Lyle, an up-and-coming chemist from Avon, and got to work. The only real difference, as far as Carl was concerned, was that now his lobby portraits were supermodels instead of little bald children—so, if anything, the offices looked even nicer than before.

As with most evolutions, this one had produced a number of vestigial appendages—holdovers from the old company that didn't really apply anymore, such as the name of the company and the tagline "The Healing Power of Yew™." Carl even went so far as to insist that the Pacific yew be included in their cosmetics formulas, though his executives fought him on it every time. On the morning of March 22, Lyle Fontanelle rolled his eyes and prepared to have the argument again.

"Yggdrasil was an ash," said Lyle. "I looked it up."

"And we can't use yew in a hand lotion," said the lawyer, a man named Sunny Frye. His real name was Sun-He, and he was Korean; Lyle had been working in makeup for so long, he could pinpoint a face's origin with uncanny accuracy. Sunny continued patiently: "The yew tree has no moisturizing or antiaging properties whatsoever. We've gone over this before. It adds nothing to the product."

"So don't use very much," said Carl, virtually motionless in his chair. It was an overstuffed office chair of soft black leather, blending deliciously with the rich brown mahogany of the conference table, and Carl rarely ever moved from it—or, truth be told, in it. He was seventy-nine years old, long past retirement age, and in Lyle's opinion he had no business trying to run the company. On the other hand, Lyle had to admit that the alternative was probably worse: the next in line of succession for the position of CEO was the company president, Jeffrey Montgomery. He was Carl's son, and almost willfully useless.

Carl sat unmoving in his chair. "We don't need to use very much yew, just enough to put it on the label."

The room full of executives sighed as politely as they could. There were four of them (not counting Jeffrey, who was playing games on his phone in the corner): the vice president of finance, the vice president of marketing, the chief legal counsel, and, of course, the chief scientist. Lyle had long harbored the secret dream of changing his business cards to say "chief science officer," but for nearly ten years and counting he'd been too afraid to actually do it. He wasn't sure which was scarier—being mocked for the *Star Trek* reference, or realizing that nobody cared what it said on his business cards.

Carl plunged onward, feebly waving a wrinkled hand for emphasis. "The yew is a glorious tree, and our customers associate it with health! We treated cancer for thirty-five years with the yew tree, can't we leverage that somehow?"

"It *would* be a brilliant marketing move," said Kerry White, leaning forward eagerly. He had been hired as vice president of marketing only a few months previously, so this conversation was relatively new to him. "Think of the commercials: 'The company that saved your life is going to save your skin.'"

"We ran that campaign four years ago," said the VP of finance, a skeletal woman named Cynthia Mummer. "It didn't play."

"It didn't play," said Carl, "because we didn't have yew in the products!"

"Okay," said Lyle, "can we . . ." He wanted to show off his newest idea, and struggled to find a good segue. "Can we make it a pun?"

"A pun?" asked Kerry. "That's your contribution?"

"Our whole company name is already a pun," said Cynthia.

"But I mean a pun on what Carl just said," said Lyle. "That we have yew in the products. 'You' in the products."

"We know what a pun is," said Cynthia.

"Just let him explain it," said Sunny. Lyle was grateful and indignant at the same time: he needed Sunny's support every time in these meetings, but he didn't want to need it. Why couldn't they let him stand up for himself?

"I've been researching some biomimetic technologies," said Lyle, "and I have something I want to—"

"What's biomimetics?" asked Kerry.

"Bio-mimicry," said Lyle. "It's like a smart product, that can adapt itself to match your body."

Cynthia nodded. "We have biomimetic lipids in our teen skin care line. It's one of our best sellers."

"Oh yeah," said Kerry, "my wife loves that lotion."

"Your wife uses teen lotion?" asked Cynthia.

"If you've been researching biomimetics," Carl growled, "what have you got? We don't pay you to sit on your butt all day—that's why we have Jeffrey. You we pay for research and development. So: have you developed anything?"

"Actually I do have something I'd like to show you," said Lyle, lifting up his briefcase to set it on the table. "It's the burn cream we've talked about before—it's, ah, showing some interesting promise as an antiaging lotion. It's not ready for the public yet, by any means, but the early results are promising and I want to dedicate a bigger piece of the budget to following it up."

"Why do we need a burn cream?" asked Cynthia icily. As CFO, she would have the strongest say in whether or not he got any more funding. Lyle swallowed nervously and opened his briefcase.

"It's not really a burn cream," said Lyle, pulling out a folder and a stack of glossy photos. "The technology comes from a burn cream, from some medical research published a few years ago, but like I said, I think we have some pretty neat options for using it in cosmetics, in antiaging especially. The key component is plasmids."

"Oh," shouted Jeffrey, "like in that game!"

"No," said Lyle, "like in the bacteria."

"You're putting bacteria in a hand lotion?" asked Kerry. "I know there's no such thing as bad publicity, but that's pushing the limit."

"It's not actual bacteria," said Lyle, flipping through the folder. "Bacteria is where plasmids come from, but then they take them out and sell them separately." He found a photocopied page in the folder and held it up, displaying two grainy, black-and-white images of what may or may not have been skin. "This is from a test at Boston University, using plasmids to rebuild burned skin—they go into the cells and accelerate collagen production, so the skin heals faster and more fully."

"Wait," said Kerry, excited, "this is like a collagen injection in a lotion? That we can market the hell out of."

"Then why are you working on a lotion?" asked Carl, "and not a lipstick? Can we do it in a lipstick?"

"Most lipsticks just make your lips *look* fuller," said Kerry, "this one would actually make them *be* fuller. I can see it now—"

"Wait," said Lyle, "it's not . . . it wouldn't work like that. I mean, we're not talking magical plastic surgery lips or anything."

"What are we talking?" asked Sunny.

"It doesn't enlarge anything," said Lyle, "but it has the potential to be a pretty amazing wrinkle reducer."

"Antiaging is huge," said Cynthia. "The baby boomers are so old their children are getting old; we could do a lot with a new wrinkle reducer."

"It's a very clever system," said Lyle, pleased to have their positive attention. "Your skin is primarily composed of collagen, and other proteins, and as you get old your skin stops producing quite so much of it, and that's what makes it sag and shrivel. The plasmids help you heal from a burn by producing more collagen—or more accurately, by tricking your cells into overproducing it. When you apply it to healthy skin, it creates extra collagen and fills out the sags and wrinkles. Here, I think I have some of our test photos here. . . ." He riffled through his folder. "Every other anti-aging product on the market, from Botox to makeup to everything else, is all just covering the problem, or stretching the problem, or doing something to hide it. But a lotion that directly stimulates your skin cells to build more collagen is actually solving the problem—not just hiding the wrinkles, but reversing them."

"Rejuvagen!" shouted Kerry. "The first skin care product that actually reverses the aging process, exclusively from NewYew!"

"That's not bad," said Carl, pointing an unsteady finger at Kerry.

"Thanks," said Lyle uncertainly. He found the photo he wanted and placed it on the table. "This is one of our early test subjects. We were testing the healing properties on a small abrasion here, on her cheek, but you can see her whole face pretty well."

"Wait," said Sunny cautiously. "You said it goes into the cells? What do you mean by that, exactly?"

"Well, it's a plasmid," said Lyle, "so it—"

Carl cut him off. "I don't care how it works, I care if we can protect it, economically and legally. You say this came from a university study—is the research public domain?"

"The university study was an academic proof of concept," said Lyle. "The technology is fully public, and the plasmids themselves are pretty common. I ordered these off the shelf from a chemical supply place."

"But how invasive is it?" asked Sunny. "If it messes with the cells directly we'll probably have to run it past the FDA, and that could take years. If you think we can really use this, a portion of the budget will have to go toward that."

"The FDA will never pass it," said Cynthia sternly, picking up the photocopied page and pointing to the blurry text. "Lyle forgot to mention that this is gene therapy."

"Gene therapy?" asked Carl.

Sunny laughed. "The FDA has never approved gene therapy in a consumer product, Lyle, why didn't you tell us up front this was a gene thing?"

"I said it was plasmids," said Lyle, looking around the room. "What else would I be talking about?"

"Nobody knows what plasmids are," said Kerry.

"I told you," said Jeffrey, "they were in that game."

"A plasmid is a circle of DNA," said Lyle, ignoring him. "They're a very small, very efficient way of transcribing genetic information. The one I'm using attaches itself to your DNA to prompt the creation of HSP47, which is a heat-shock protein—"

"This is genetic engineering," said Sunny, shaking his head. "There's no way the FDA would even get near it."

"It's not exactly a weird technology," said Lyle defensively. "I told you, I bought these by the case from a lab supplier. They're everywhere."

"They're everywhere in labs," said Sunny, "not in consumer products. That's a pretty huge difference."

"Let me see your test results," said Cynthia, looking at the photos. Lyle slid his folder across the table, but Sunny shook his head.

"The tests don't matter," said Sunny. "It could be the most effective antiaging product in the world and we still wouldn't be able to sell it."

"But it is," said Cynthia, looking up from the file. She was smiling, but Lyle thought it looked surprisingly predatory. "The most effective antiaging product in the world. Look at his notes in the margin: 'A seventy-six percent reduction in deep wrinkles. Complete reversal of fine lines. Full results in two weeks, visible results in a matter of days.'" She looked at Carl. "This is a gold mine."

"It's a gold mine we can't touch," Sunny insisted. "At least not without another ten years of FDA testing. Seriously, Lyle, *we* shouldn't even have been testing this without good legal coverage."

"The subjects all signed the release forms," said Lyle, "and I passed them all on to you."

"But you didn't tell me they were for genetic engineering!" said Sunny. "What if something goes wrong?"

"Now ease up a bit," said Carl, leaning forward. The others in the room stopped and looked at him—Carl never leaned forward unless he had something very important to say. "If this lotion is as good as Cynthia says, what are our options?"

"With gene therapy?" asked Sunny. "Nothing. Wait ten years for FDA approval, or scrap it and reformulate."

"How closely did you look at this photo?" said Cynthia, placing it back in the center of the table. Everyone leaned in to examine it.

"Cute," said Kerry. "Is this a teen product?"

"That's a forty-three-year-old woman," said Cynthia, "after just three weeks of treatment. With a face like that she could get picked up by a pedophile."

The room was silent. Carl stared at the photo. "Lyle," he said slowly, "are these results typical?"

Lyle couldn't help but smile. "The woman in that photo had a fairly youthful face to begin with—there's more going on there than just our lotion—but yes, in general, that level of wrinkle reduction is typical of our test cases. I've had several of them call back to ask if they could get more. This product has the potential to be a best seller like we haven't seen since . . . paclitaxel, really. Everyone's going to want this."

Carl stared at the table in front of him frowning in thought. At last he spoke, without looking up. "Sunny, you're going to find a way for us to sell this."

"But—"

"If you do," said Carl, "I will personally buy you a Caribbean island, and I will do it with the loose change this product puts under my couch cushions."

Sunny paused. "It *could* be huge . . . but only if there's a way to make it work legally."

"Find a way." Carl looked at Kerry. "I want a name, I want commercials, I want bottle designs, I want everything."

"Absolutely," said Kerry.

"And you," said Carl, pointing a yellowed finger at Lyle. "I want this in production by next week."

"That's impossible."

"Not a full run," said Carl, "we don't even have a bottle yet. But I want sample runs and stability tests. Call Jerry at the plant and set it up."

Lyle grimaced. "I have one more test scheduled for next week, but . . . yeah, I can probably get it done. Two weeks would be better."

Cynthia raised an eyebrow. "You've tested everything from litmus to rats to human skin. What else do you need?"

"I'm still refining the formula," said Lyle. "The woman in the photo is from batch 14E, and the newest is 14G. The tweaks were minor, though, and one test ought to do it. It's already scheduled through HR: adult males, eighteen to forty-five."

"Skin care for men is the next big thing," said Kerry.

"None as big as this," said Carl. "Run your test, Lyle—I want this product guaranteed for every gender, every age, every race, every everything. If you've got skin, you're a customer." He folded his frail hands and stared at the executives sternly. "A lotion that literally makes your skin younger—and does so this effectively— has the potential to be the biggest cosmetic breakthrough since breast implants, and with a wider appeal. I want a bottle of this lotion in the hands of every man, woman, and child in the coun- try—I want women to bathe in it, and I want schoolgirls to feel old if they don't use it. Am I clear?"

The executives nodded.

"Good," said Carl. "Let's go change the world."

2

"This is ridiculous," said Susan.

She was a student from NYU, working as Lyle's research assistant to help pay for college. She was an excellent chemist, a hard worker, and at least a decade too young for Lyle, who consequently spent most of his time not looking at her, talking to her, or being near her. Thinking about her, on the other hand, occupied a great deal of his mental energy.

Lyle kept his eyes on his computer. "Hm?"

"An earthquake in Mombasa," said Susan, stabbing her computer screen with her finger. "Ten hours ago: it leveled the city. They have no homes, no food, nothing."

"That's awful," Lyle murmured, not really paying attention. Susan was an impassioned activist for almost every cause she encountered, and he didn't have the energy to keep up with them all. His fingers clacked on the keyboard, filling in the final details on his most recent report. Sunny was still trying to find a loophole that would let them actually make the antiaging lotion, and he needed all the details Lyle could give him.

"It's because we're racist," said Susan.

"Now . . . wait a minute," said Lyle, turning fully to look at her. Her hair was long and blond, streaked with natural highlights; Lyle had spent enough time working on hair dyes to know a natural highlight when he saw one. He tried not to think about

Susan as the model on a box of hair dye. "The earthquake happened because we're racist?"

"America hasn't helped them yet because we're racist."

"It's only been ten hours."

"We can get there in ten hours."

"So maybe we're slow," said Lyle. "That's not the same as racist."

"We can be fast when we want to," said Susan, "but Kenya's
not a major trading partner, so screw them—we'll toss a few volunteers and water bottles off a cargo plane, but we'll save the good
stuff for the next time Japan gets a tsunami. We only help when
it helps us, or when it helps our image." She stared at Lyle, and
held up her finger for emphasis. "But image means nothing."

"You realize you . . . work for a cosmetics company?"

"You can change what people look like," said Susan, "but you
can never change who they are."

"I . . ." Lyle looked at her face, identifying almost subcon-
sciously her shade of lipstick: plum pink. He lost his train of
thought and glanced at the clock instead. "It's 2:08," he said
quickly. "We need to get ready for the test."

"14G?" asked Susan, forgetting her tirade almost as quickly
as she'd started it. She rolled her chair across the floor to Lyle's
desk and looked at his computer. "What's new in this batch?"

Lyle became acutely aware of the proximity of Susan's knees
to his own. "Some pretty interesting stuff, actually." He looked
up and gave her what he hoped was a dashing smile. He was
pretty sure it didn't work, and stopped. "I've added a retrovirus
to help regulate the process."

"Really?" asked Susan, leaning in closer to look at his screen.
Lyle pursed his lips and thought about flat things: *walls, cabinets,
tables*. He swallowed and slid his own chair a few inches away.
"I thought the formula was bacterial."

"The plasmids are bacterial," said Lyle. "That's where the DNA
is. The retrovirus is how we get the DNA out of the plasmid and
into the host cell." He wanted to say more, eager to impress

Susan, but this was the part he didn't know as much about; he was a chemist, not a geneticist. He thought for a moment, then repeated the blurb from the supplier's brochure. "It uses an RNA transcriptase to unzip the host DNA, inserts the DNA fragment stored in the plasmid, and zips it back up again. They came from the same supplier; they're engineered to, um," he tried not to look at her, "fit together." He started to gesture with his hands, then turned a little red and fell silent.

"Cool," said Susan, peering closer at the screen. She was almost as interested in chemistry as she was in social justice, and arguably better at it. "This is . . . well, it's groundbreaking."

Lyle turned red and pretended to busy himself with some papers. "Well, it's certainly interesting, and we have high hopes. I mean, Carl said it's going to change the world, but what does he know, right?" He was practically bursting with pride. He'd probably get on the cover of *Scientific American* again, and Susan thinking he was brilliant was the cherry on top of the whole thing. He glanced at the clock, and jumped up with a shout, "It's 2:15! I'm late!"

"Need any help?"

Lyle frowned, his mouth half open for words that never came. Of course he wanted her to come, he wanted her to go everywhere with him, but he wasn't supposed to want her to go anywhere with him. "I . . ." He didn't know what to say.

Susan gestured at her computer. "I finished color matching the lipsticks you asked me about."

Lyle stared for a moment, trying not to think about her lips, then turned to gather up his samples. "Sure, you can do the photos."

Susan picked up the trays and spatulas and headed cheerfully down the hall, Lyle following several steps behind. *Kerry gets to look at beautiful women every day,* he thought, *with photo shoots and commercial shoots and who knows what else. He gets paid to look at beautiful women. Is it really so bad that I look at this one? One who's wearing* a lab coat, *for crying out loud? It's not like she walks around in a swimsuit all day.*

Hmmm, Susan walking around in a swimsuit all day. . . .

"Dr. Fontanelle!" Lyle shook himself from his daydream and realized he'd walked past the door. He smiled nervously, wondering if Susan knew what he'd been thinking about, but she seemed as cheerful as ever. He walked back into the room and smiled at the six men seated on the other side of the long, narrow table. HR had managed to grab a batch of outside volunteers with a pretty good mix of skin types: an Asian, a Latino, and four Caucasians, one of whom had red hair and intensely fair skin, and another who was heavyset and greasy. It should be a good test.

"Sorry," said Lyle, "just got a little distracted. I assume you've all read the packet and signed the release forms?"

"We get paid for this, right?" said one of the subjects, a tall, skinny man with dark black hair.

"Naturally," said Lyle, collecting the row of proffered papers and checking to see that each release form had been fully filled out and signed. Susan followed him, placing a small Styrofoam tray and a mini plastic spatula in front of each man.

"Good," said the tall man—Lyle saw on his paperwork that his name was Ronald—"because that's why I'm here. To get paid." He seemed nervous, and Lyle laughed silently. Test subjects were so twitchy sometimes.

"Good," said Lyle, and looked at the group. "Well. I'm pleased to tell you that this is a very late-stage test, and the product you'll be sampling is essentially ready for production. Your skin is in very safe hands, and in fact we think you'll be pleasantly surprised. Now, we've given each of you a tray and a spatula; next we'll give you a— Susan?"

Susan was on the end of the row, rubbing lotion onto the back of a subject's hand. A very handsome subject, Lyle noted with some irritation. The man glanced at Lyle, then looked up at Susan and flashed exactly the kind of debonair smile Lyle had tried to

make earlier, in exactly the kind of way that made Lyle know
he had failed. His teeth were more perfect than some of the models they'd used for their teeth-whitening ads.

"You'll give us a Susan?" the man asked, grinning devilishly.
Susan smiled back. "If I'd known that, I'd have signed up weeks
ago."

"Susan," Lyle whispered, walking toward her, "we can't actually touch them. That's what the spatulas are for."

"He doesn't mind," said Susan, and gave the man a stunning
smile.

Lyle rolled his eyes. *She's flirting with him.*

"I don't mind at all," said the man, smiling back.

Lyle successfully avoided groaning. "No," he said, "I mean it's
actually illegal—if you're not a licensed cosmetologist you're not
even allowed to touch another person's face, and the hands are . . .
essentially the same thing, so." He pulled Susan gently away.
"Let's just not touch anyone, anywhere, just to be safe."

Susan raised her eyebrow, staring at him.

"Give them all some lotion," said Lyle, gesturing at the other
men. "Just a squirt from the bottle, straight into the tray." Susan
saluted, and Lyle frowned. "Now, gentlemen: use the spatula,
or your fingers—you can touch your own face without a cosme-
tology license, of course—and spread it around on your arms or
your face, maybe somewhere you have some fine lines or wrinkles. . . ." He watched as the six men poked and sniffed at the
lotion and slowly began smearing it on their skin. "Careful of
your eyes, of course," said Lyle. "It's perfectly safe, but that doesn't
mean it feels good in your eyes."

"We want to test it over time," said Susan, "so we need you to
come back in three weeks so we can see if there's any progress."
She finished giving each man some lotion, and picked up a
camera. "I'll be taking some 'before' photos so we have something solid to compare it to when you come back."

The nervous guy looked up. "Do we get paid now or at the
end of the three weeks?"

"Both, Ronald," said Lyle. "Don't worry, you'll get paid. I just have some quick questions first." Lyle looked at the sheaf of papers and saw that the handsome man's name was Jon Ford. "Mr. Ford, let's start with you: Do you ever experience any . . ." He paused, realizing what the question was about, and felt a surge of mischievous satisfaction. "Do you ever experience any itching, perhaps a contagious skin rash of some kind, or an epidermal fungus?"

"Do I have to answer?" asked Ford, scowling in disgust.

Lyle stifled a smile. "I'm sorry, this is for science. Now, please tell us the exact nature of the problem."

3

Ronald Lynch waited by the service elevators in the dirty back room of another office building, just a few blocks away from NewYew. He'd worked in this building for years, but he'd never once entered through the front doors. Corporate espionage was a little more complicated than that.

The elevator dinged, and the doors opened, revealing a heavy-set man in an ill-fitting suit, leaning calmly against the back railing. He didn't move, but raised one finger and beckoned for Ronald to step in and join him. Ronald did, and the man nodded.

"Floor seventeen," said the man. Ronald pushed it, and the doors closed. "I'm Abraham Decker," said the man, and offered his meaty hand to shake. "Chief scientist. We've never met, but I've read your reports. You do good work."

"I came straight from the product test," said Ronald. "They wouldn't let me take a sample, but I—"

"Straight?" asked Decker.

"Well, I . . . meandered a bit first," said Ronald. "Obviously. Nobody followed me."

"I don't think they understand what they have yet," said Decker. "We need to be extra careful with this one."

Ronald frowned. "Seemed like a pretty standard test to me."

"It's a whole new technology," said Decker. "It's so cutting edge we'll need new legislation just to manage it."

"For a wrinkle reducer?"

"For genetic engineering," said Decker.

Ronald looked at his hand in shock, wondering what he'd just rubbed on his skin, but before he could ask any more questions the elevator dinged again and the doors slid open. Decker heaved himself up from the railing and walked into the hall, Ronald close behind, and after a few short turns they entered a massive corner office, bigger than Ronald's entire apartment and furnished like a mansion. This, more than anything else, is what finally started to make Ronald scared. He didn't mind reporting on product tests: rival companies were always going to spy on each other, and Ronald figured somebody was going to get paid to do it so why not him? He honestly kind of liked the excitement. But he'd always dealt with intermediaries—burner phones and anonymous envelopes of cash—but this office was a whole new level of intrigue. This was a place for high rollers; this was a place for people who were ambitious and proud and ruthless. This had to be the CEO.

Ronald started to realize that this was a much bigger deal than he'd expected.

"Have a seat," said Decker, plopping down on a couch by the wall, and gesturing for Ronald to join him. A few moments later another man walked in, tall and stern and flanked by two dark-suited giants whose skills, Ronald guessed, had little to do with cosmetics. They arrayed themselves in front of Ronald and stared at him a moment.

"Ira," said Decker, "this is Ronald, one of our informants in the product testing program." Ronald stood up to shake his hand, but the beefy man on Ira's right pushed him back down. Ronald swallowed and tried to smile.

"How do you do, sir?"

"Welcome to Ibis Cosmetics," said the man. "My name is Ira Brady, and I'm the CEO. You're our man at NewYew?"

"Yes, sir," said Ronald. "At least for today, sir. They were testing a new kind of hand lotion with some kind of antiaging—"

"I know what they were testing," said Ira. "What we don't

know is the interior layout of the building. You've been in a part of NewYew none of us has visited." He started pacing as he talked, gesturing broadly with his hands. "What floor did they take you to? How many doors did you pass through to get to the room where the test was held? How many turns did you take, and in what directions? And perhaps most importantly . . ." He turned back toward Ronald. "Did you happen to see any laboratories while you were there? And could you tell us accurately how to find them?"

"You're going to steal the lotion," said Ronald.

"Of course I'm not going to steal it," said Ira, "that's illegal. But a technology like that is bound to be stolen eventually, and I suspect that it may, through circumstances beyond our control, end up in my hands. Now: describe the building."

"An herbal supplement," said Sunny, grinning. He threw a tennis ball at the floor, bounced it off the wall, and caught it again. "We can get away with anything in an herbal supplement. The FDA could care less about them."

"*Couldn't* care less," said Lyle. "The FDA *couldn't* care less, not *could*, that doesn't make any sense." Sunny was one of the few people at NewYew whom Lyle considered a friend, though even so, most of their interaction was business related. Now that he thought about it, Lyle didn't interact much with anybody else at all.

"Could, couldn't, the point is that they don't care." Sunny bounced and caught the ball again. "Listen to this: the FDA regulates the kinds of drugs and formulas and whatever that we're allowed to sell, because they want to make sure those formulas are safe, right? You come up with something new, and they spend years and years testing it to make sure it doesn't do anything it's not supposed to do. But! Herbal supplements are different. The FDA keeps an approved list of 'natural' ingredients that they've already vetted, and as long as you stick to those you're fine; they know those ingredients don't do anything wrong because they don't do anything at all, by definition. It's just ground-up flowers and crap. The approval process for herbal supplements is zero days, because they literally don't bother to look at them. If they're labeled right, we don't even have to submit them."

"It's a little more than ground-up flowers," said Lyle.

"Totally," said Sunny, throwing his tennis ball again, "but as long as nobody knows that, we can do whatever we want."

Lyle tried to catch the ball as it bounced back to Sunny, hitting it at the wrong angle with his fingers and knocking it away. He swallowed, feeling stupid, while Sunny laughed and picked it up. "Listen," said Sunny. "We label this new lotion of yours as an herbal product, we release it, we market it as this wonderful antiwrinkle lotion, but we never make any claims of structure or function—we never tell anyone, officially, what it does or how it does it."

"But . . ." Lyle grimaced, queasy at the thought of giving up so much credit for his design. "I've been working on this for a year—for more than a year, if you count some of the early research. This is one of the most groundbreaking innovations in the entire health and beauty industry." Lyle paused, trying not to say his next thought out loud, but somehow said it anyway. "I was going to get on the cover of *Scientific American*."

"Is that what you're worried about?" Sunny shook his head, waving his hands in a smoothing gesture. "We can still make that happen, we just have to wait a while. Take this same formula, tweak it a little in case anyone takes a good look at it, and submit it for FDA approval. It takes a few years, but if it's as safe as you say it is they'll eventually stamp it through and we can launch the technology officially. NewYew stays on the forefront of cosmetic innovation, you get the nerd accolades you crave, and meanwhile we're earning money hand over fist with the exact same product under a different label."

Lyle shook his head. "That's sounds amazingly dishonest."

"You're adorable."

"It's not just a moral issue," said Lyle, though the amorality did tickle at the base of his spine; Sunny was a shark, certainly, but this seemed uncharacteristically vicious. Even so, Lyle had learned over the years that appealing to the other executives' morality was rarely a useful tactic—he had to hit them somewhere else. "Think about the marketing. You're saying we're going to make money hand over fist with a product we're not even allowed to advertise effectively. 'This product is awesome, but we can't tell you why.' I don't think 'Seriously, just trust us' is a very good retail slogan."

Sunny shrugged. "Word of mouth."

"Word of mouth," said Lyle with a snort.

"Yes," said Sunny, "word of mouth, but we're not going to just sit back and hope the right mouths start saying the right words. We're going to manipulate the word of mouth—we're going to create it." He threw the ball again, missed the catch, and lost it under his desk. He dismissed it with a wave and looked back at Lyle. "Carl wanted a solution, so here's the solution: a secondary marketing campaign. The company never talks about the plasmids or the collagen or the gene therapy aspects in the least bit—I know that delays your tell-all in *Scientific American*, but bear with me here. We don't say a word. But we feed the right info to some science Tweeters and some 'independent' bloggers, and they start making some noise and talking about this revolutionary new science behind the product. Some hotshot reverse engineers it, and writes a big article about the unique combination of biological agents blah blah plasmids blah blah all-natural biomimetics. Our primary marketing stays as clean as a whistle, while our secondary marketing has all the good stuff, by pure word of mouth, in such a way that NewYew itself stays completely unaffiliated."

Lyle raised his eyebrow. "So the scientific breakthrough I spent a year on is an accident from combining the wrong ingredients. Instead of a genius, I'm a buffoon."

"It's not an accident, it's a . . . positive side effect." Sunny put on his best placating face, which only made Lyle feel more patronized. "We'll say it's all part of the something something flower we use in some of our herbal stuff, what is it . . ." He flipped through the file on his desk. "Meadowfoam. That's on the FDA-approved list of herbal ingredients. Everybody uses it."

"These plasmids don't come from meadowfoam," said Lyle, "they come from Rock Canyon Labs. We have official invoices for the sale."

"No," said Sunny firmly, "I think you're remembering wrong—we're using those plasmids to develop a new gene therapy product to help burn victims. It's still in testing, and we're submitting it to the FDA for approval."

"But—"

"Lyle." Sunny looked at him, unwavering. "Let me be very clear about this: anything you say in public or in e-mail will agree with this story. It has to."

"You're asking me to lie."

"Technically I'm telling you to lie. As far as this company is concerned, your new lotion is an herbal supplement with no genetic technology whatsoever."

"Sunny," said Kerry White, walking into the office, "I've got new bottle copy for you to review." He handed Sunny a sheet of paper and leaned against the wall. "Hey, Lyle."

Lyle pointed at Sunny, eager to have a new ally in the war against Sunny's plan. "Have you heard about this?"

"About the secondary marketing?" asked Kerry. "I think it's brilliant. Hey—tell me what you think of this as a name: Rebirth. Or maybe ReBirth, with a capital 'B.'"

"Why a capital 'B'?" asked Lyle.

"So we could trademark it," said Sunny, his head down over the page from Kerry. "Legal thing."

"Never mind the 'B,'" said Lyle, shaking his head, "you can't possibly be okay with this marketing plan."

"I came up with the marketing plan," said Kerry. "I'm the marketing guy."

"But it's lying!"

"All advertising is lying. Women buy our makeup because they want to look like the women in the ads—never mind that those women have perfect genes and half a dozen eating disorders and we still Photoshop their pictures anyway. People accept lies in advertising—they expect them. This is the same thing."

"It's not the same," Lyle insisted. "Implying that a product will make you look like a supermodel is one thing, but specifically concealing the fact that a product will alter your DNA is kind of . . . well, it's pretty ridiculous, don't you think?"

"It's safe, though, right?"

"Of course it's safe, that's not the point—"

"Then don't worry about it."

"He's not worried about the safety," said Sunny, "he's very nobly worried about the credit. Apparently there are people who actually read *Scientific American*."

Lyle ignored the jab. "What I'm worried about is explaining our product approval process to a federal court. I'm no lawyer, but I'm pretty sure that 'we mislabeled it on purpose so we could make more money' will be seen as less of an explanation than a confession."

"We're not mislabeling it," said Kerry, "we're just being careful."

"Is that what we call lying these days?"

Sunny waved the paper Kerry had handed him. "Listen to this, Lyle, this is exactly what we're talking about; absolutely nothing in here is a lie. 'ReBirth uses a biomimetic herbal formula to support your body's natural ability to produce collagen, giving you beautiful skin that looks younger and feels healthier.' You see how they do that? It never claims anything specific—it doesn't say your skin will *be* younger or healthier, it says your skin will *look* younger and *feel* healthier. That's unprovable, and that makes it un-dis-provable. And completely defensible."

"What about the collagen?" asked Lyle. "You said it produces collagen."

Kerry shook his head with a smug smile. "No, we said it 'supports' your body in making its own collagen. 'Supports' is the magic marketing word—it sounds great and it makes people feel good and it doesn't mean anything. Everything supports your body's ability to make collagen—eating breakfast supports your body's ability to make collagen. I, personally, politically, support your ability to make collagen. If we're being strict on the definition, burn wounds support your ability to make collagen because they force your body to heal itself."

Sunny bent over his desk and signed the paper. "This copy is approved, and I'll research the trademark for ReBirth. Even if the trademark's free, though, I doubt we could get the URL for it, so think of something else we can use for the website."

"Will do," said Kerry, taking the paper. He slapped Lyle on the back. "This really is a great product, Lyle—you've outdone yourself." He walked out, and Sunny reached under his desk for the tennis ball.

"You going out to the plant?" asked Sunny.

Lyle nodded. "I sent them the recipe and a sample bottle yesterday. They should have a test batch ready to go—but I want to go on record that testing is not finished, and we can't consider this a final formula until the follow-up visits for 14G are analyzed and approved."

"The wheels of progress are turning," said Sunny. "We've got to move fast to keep up."

"I wish the wheels of progress would wait for next season," said Lyle.

"The wheels of progress are greased by money," said Sunny, "and this project has so much money in it these wheels are the greasiest they've ever been. They're practically frictionless."

"Friction provides control," said Lyle. "We need it to steer."

"We're fine," said Sunny. "We've launched a hundred other products together; we could do this in our sleep." He grinned and threw the ball. "What's the worst that could happen?"

NewYew had many production facilities, but their primary site—and specifically for Lyle's purposes, their small-scale testing laboratory—was in Upstate New York. Lyle made it there in just under five hours.

"Jerry!" He waved his hand, trying to catch the foreman's attention. "Jerry!"

Across the bright white factory, a man in a white plastic coat raised his head, smiled, and waved back. He nodded to the man next to him, handed him a clipboard, and jogged over to Lyle.

"Welcome back, Doctor." Even at this distance they had to shout. "I wondered when you were coming."

They stopped by a rack on the wall, and Lyle pulled on a white jumpsuit and a clear plastic hat. "How far are you?"

"No real production, obviously," said Jerry, "just a sample run. We've ordered the materials for a larger run but they won't arrive for a few weeks." They started walking again, and the foreman led Lyle through the factory. "Sounds like they're in a hurry on this one." Jerry smiled. "What is it?"

"Antiaging," said Lyle, following him up a white metal stairway. "You followed the instructions to the letter?"

"Of course."

"All the proportions are correct?"

"I think you might want to adjust them, but yes, we followed your initial recipe exactly."

Lyle frowned. "Adjust what?"

They stopped by a churning metal barrel full of loose, white goo. "I'd add more lecithin," said Jerry, "the consistency's all wrong."

Lyle peered in. "Is this it?"

"Yep."

Lyle stared at the vat of lotion. *I should pull the plug,* he thought. *The product's not ready, the marketing campaign is unethical, the entire thing is being handled wrong.* He watched the white lotion swirl around, catching the light in bright, almost iridescent patterns. *That doesn't look right. . . .* He pulled off his right glove and dipped his fingers in, scooping up some lotion and rubbing it between his thumb and forefingers.

"Actually you're not allowed to do that anymore," said Jerry, and held up a small, long-handled ladle. "New protocols to keep the batches clean; we just started them last month."

"That's good," said Lyle, "that's good. And I need to get out here more." He closed his eyes, feeling the consistency. "You're right, it's off." Lyle could feel it precisely: too much rice bran oil, not enough lecithin. The product would function just fine, but the wrong consistency would make it feel greasy, and that would turn off most of the end consumers. The texture had to be perfect, or the function didn't matter.

Jerry carefully dipped the ladle in the lotion and dripped some onto his own hand. "We tried to match the viscosity by mixing in the sample you sent us from corporate, but going up to this scale changed it too much." He examined the lotion, feeling it on his fingers. "See what I mean? Too oily."

Lyle nodded: it was too oily, and he knew exactly how to fix it. He wiped off his hand. "Let's get to work."

5

Susan was wearing a skirt when she came into work, just barely shorter than her lab coat, and Lyle, walking behind her, had to try very hard not to imagine that the skirt had disappeared altogether. He quickened his pace to walk next to her.

"One small blob for each man in the test," he said, pulling a plastic bottle from his shirt pocket. The bottles were simple plastic tubes, filled from the test batch at the plant; the labels were handwritten with a black marker: "14G." "We get their thoughts, we take copious photos, and they get their money on the way out. Easy."

Susan nodded. "Is it against the rules to fraternize with a business associate?"

Lyle stopped short. "What?"

Susan stopped and turned back to face him. "Like, if I meet someone at work and I ask them out on date—would I get in trouble for that?"

Is she coming on to me? Lyle smiled. "No, I don't think that's a problem at all."

"Great," said Susan, "because I'm going to ask test subject one for his phone number—he was way too cute to pass up."

Lyle steadied himself with a hand on the wall, then slowly started walking again. "I see." He walked into the testing room and stood silent for a moment before finding his voice. "Welcome . . . back, to the . . ." He paused.

Test subject one wasn't there. Five men and one empty chair. "Where's the other guy?"

"How should we know?" said the skinny one. Lyle couldn't remember his name: Ronald something?

"Of course, I just . . ." Lyle looked at Susan. "Do you know where he is?"

Susan shook her head. "I wish. Restroom, maybe?"

One of the other subjects raised his hand. "He wasn't here when they led us in from the lobby."

Lyle frowned. The test results would still be valid without all six men, of course—this was only a minor test to appease his conscience, after all—but it would appease his conscience a lot more effectively if the subjects didn't drop out halfway through. He handed the folder to Susan, pausing to pull out the ID forms the subjects had filled out last time.

"Give them the questionnaires and get started," he said, forcing his voice to be cheerful. He still felt Susan's unwitting rejection like a punch in the gut. "I'll give him a call; maybe we can reschedule."

Susan put her hand on the forms anxiously. "Oh! I can call him if you want."

Lyle pulled the forms away gently. "Don't worry about it; I can handle it." He turned and left the room, flipping through the papers as he walked back down the hall. *Jon Ford.* Even the man's name was handsome. Lyle grumbled and sat at the desk in the lab, picking up the phone and dialing Ford's number.

"Hello," said a voice, "Jon's phone." The voice was male and kind of goofy.

"Is this Jon?"

"No, man, this is Trav. Jon's sick."

Crap. "Really?" Lyle closed his eyes. *Don't let it be the lotion.* "What's wrong?"

"Flu or something—he was puking all night the other night, and crapping like a weasel. You from the shop?"

Lyle sighed in relief. *It's not his skin.* He paused. *Wouldn't hurt to ask a few more questions, though.* "No," he said, "I'm not from the shop. Tell me, 'Trav,' do you know if Jon was experiencing any . . . dermatological symptoms?"

"Dude, are you the doctors? Because I told your nurse, I don't know what kind of insurance he has."

"Yes," said Lyle quickly, "I'm a doctor, but I'm not looking for the insurance information. I need to know if he had any problems with his skin—a rash or a welt or a reaction of any kind."

"No, man, nothing like that, it was just the runs and stuff. Should he be taking something?"

"We'll have to get back to you," said Lyle. "Thanks for your time." He hung up without waiting for a response.

Nothing wrong with his skin—we're fine. He opened the files on 14G, pulling up the records for the previous product tests; Susan could finish the final test on her own, and Lyle was in no hurry to see her again. He could start the paperwork now, and plug in her results when she returned.

Susan returned about thirty minutes later. "I went ahead and finished the test," she said, rubbing her hands. "This lotion's great, by the way—they couldn't stop raving about it. We could probably use some of these guys in an infomercial if we had a good stylist to clean 'em up. You call the hottie?"

"Huh?"

"Test subject one, the cute guy who didn't show up—you called him?"

"He's sick," said Lyle, looking back at his screen. "Some kind of flu."

"Gross," said Susan, then paused. "Can I have his number?"

"No, you cannot have his number, he's a test subject."

"But you said that wasn't a problem."

"I didn't think you meant . . ." He paused.

"Yes?"

He glanced at Susan, just barely, and looked back at his computer. Susan's jaw dropped.

"Oh! You thought I meant—" She covered her mouth and

stepped away. "Oh my gosh, I am so sorry, that is not what I meant at *all*."

"Yes, well . . ." Lyle looked down at the computer. "I think we're done here."

"Not at *ALL*."

"Thank you, Susan, I got that; not at all." He stood up. "Start a final report for the test: five out of six subjects loved it, sixth subject unavailable." He stopped and scowled. "Carl's going to hate that. I'm going to have to track this guy down and get a final testimonial."

"Are you going now?"

He walked out without speaking, down the hall to the elevator, desperate for fresh air. His one chance to tell Susan about his feelings had snuck up on him, and he wasn't ready, and he'd blown it. She had no interest in him whatsoever, plus now she thought he was a creepy jerk. The elevator dinged, and he stepped in.

Susan's voice floated down the hall. "I'm really sorry about the dating thing, Lyle! That's not what I meant at *all*!"

The doors closed.

"One of our test subjects died."

The executives stared at Lyle in shock.

"It happened last night," Lyle continued. "Jon Ford—the same guy I told you about a few weeks ago, with the flu and the dehydration."

Kerry rolled his eyes. "Not this guy again."

"He died of a stroke about twelve hours ago," said Lyle. "Try to show a little tact."

Cynthia raised an eyebrow. "That's terrible." She paused. "How was his skin?"

"His skin was fine," Lyle snapped. "This is not about his skin, this is about his life, which is over now, and about his recent activities, which include using our product."

"That's ridiculous," said Kerry, "obviously it wasn't related."

"Of course it's not related," said Sunny, "but this is still a very big deal for PR, and thank you, Lyle, for bringing it to our attention. All our competitors have to do is point to a dead guy in our testing history and go 'Ah? Ah?' and suddenly the public thinks we killed him. It doesn't matter how stupid the connection is: if the connection is ever made at all, the damage will already be done."

Cynthia frowned. "You say his skin was fine? No dermatological symptoms?"

"Yes, his skin was fine," said Lyle, "great, actually, though I hope that's not your plan for a PR strategy: 'Man dies with great skin, story at ten.'"

"How many test subjects were there?" asked Kerry.

Lyle drummed his fingers on the table. "Six."

"No," said Kerry, "the full number—every test you've ever run."

Lyle had the number memorized. "A hundred and twenty-eight human subjects, ranging from two to twenty applications each."

"So this man who died, he only used it twice?"

Lyle nodded, seeing where Kerry was going. "Technically only once; his flu started before the second test and he never came back." He did some quick calculations in his head. "We've recorded more than a thousand total applications of the product, in its various stages of development—that's some pretty weighty evidence saying how safe it is."

"So we're fine," said Kerry. "The guy took our test, ate some bad food, and had the most poorly timed stroke in history. This isn't about product safety, it's about image control: who knows about the connection, and who stands to profit from it? Is it likely to hit the news at all? Can we do some preemptive whitewashing?"

"This is never going to make the news," said Carl gruffly.

"This is a very tight industry," said Sunny. "Everyone in health and beauty is in bed with everyone else, and we've all got grudges and feuds and more catfights than a junior high cafeteria. If word *can* get out, it *will*, and it will spread like wildfire through everyone that matters."

"It wouldn't hurt us to slow things down," said Lyle. "We need time to gather two things: evidence that this wasn't remotely connected to us, and quantifiable proof that we did our due diligence to follow up just in case. On the off chance that this ever does get back to us, we'll know we've done our part."

"And other people will know we've done it, too," said Kerry, "which is the more important thing."

"Then consider this day one of emergency mode," said Sunny,

looking around at the others. "We've already banned all mention of 14G or ReBirth in company e-mail, to avoid the electronic paper trail if we ever get investigated for mislabeling; that ban stays in place. Verbal and paper communications only, and the papers will be shredded. Dust off your alibis and start shoring up your CYA files: you need to account for everything you've worked on for the past year, and it better not have anything to do with a plasmid lotion. The only official company project in the realm of gene therapy is Lyle's burn cream, which has yet to be submitted to the FDA and, to be clear, has nothing to do with anything."

There was a knock on the door, and a man poked his head in; it was Marcus Eads, the head of internal security. "Excuse me, Mr. Montgomery, but I think you need to see this."

Jeffrey stood up, but Carl shouted him down. "He's here for me, idiot." He glanced at Marcus. "Is this about the stolen ID card?"

"Yes," said Marcus, hurrying to the conference table. He set a handful of papers in front of Carl; Lyle could see they were photo printouts. "The receptionist's ID card logged four different uses between 2:54 and 3:17 a.m." He pointed at the photos. "This man came, walked the halls for a bit, and left."

"Whoa," said Lyle. "We had a break-in?"

"Last night," said Cynthia. "Try to keep up."

Carl scowled. "If he showed up so clearly on the cameras, why didn't your men do something about it! Were they asleep?"

Marcus shook his head. "This image is the only frame of security footage he appears in. He knew exactly where our cameras are, and he avoided them like a ghost."

Sunny whistled lowly. "So he had help on the inside."

"Fire the receptionist," said Carl. "And make sure to interrogate her first."

"Already on it," said Marcus.

Cynthia stood and walked behind them, staring at the photos. "That's the door to the lab wing," she said, pointing at the photo. She looked up at Lyle. "Is anything missing?"

"No," said Lyle, "everything's still there. My assistant moved a couple of— Holy crap. The lotion!"

Everyone looked at him.

"There were two bottles of lotion missing when I came in this morning," said Lyle frantically. "I thought Susan must have moved them, but she's in Mexico for another week! I didn't even think about it." He pointed at the photo. "He stole two bottles of ReBirth!"

"Find a face," said Carl coldly, turning to the security officer. "Find a fingerprint, find a piece of hair, find anything you can. I want his name on my desk by this afternoon, and his head by tomorrow." Marcus nodded and left. Carl turned back to the executives. "I don't have to tell you how much we stand to lose if ReBirth gets out early. I want this man found and I want whoever sent him destroyed."

"He knew our security system and he knew exactly where to go for the lotion," said Cynthia. "How did they even know about it?"

"We had a hundred and twenty-eight test subjects," said Sunny. "One of them must have talked."

"Wouldn't the plant be easier to break into?" asked Kerry.

"Yes," said Lyle, "but it doesn't have everything—a few samples, and the formula if you know where to look, but my office has the formula, the research, the test results, the whole thing. And now this guy has them, too." He looked at Sunny. "This kills our little corporate deception—whoever has those files can prove beyond a shadow of a doubt that we put the plasmids in there on purpose."

"Find him," Carl growled. "I want his head on my desk by morning."

7

Lyle scanned the produce section, looking for brussels sprouts. He found them, filled a bag, and put it in his basket.

The entire company was in a holding pattern, too wary to continue with the lotion but too greedy to stop. Until they knew who'd stolen it, and why, they didn't dare to move. Only Lyle had kept working on it, careful building an iron-clad case for his own role as the inventor of the technology, ready to submit to the FDA the instant he got Carl's approval. What else could they do? And it's not that he was proud—this was about the principle of the thing. The science he'd done to create it. He'd spent too much of his life on products that made you "look younger and feel healthier." He'd wasted his entire professional career making rich people attractive, and what had that gotten him? What did it matter what they looked like if they were still the same inside? And why bother with false beauty at all if someone like Susan could look better than all of them without even trying? NewYew was doing everything wrong, and if they'd only listen to Lyle—if they'd only let him tell them what to do—

Why do I need them to let me? Lyle asked himself. *Why can't I just do it?*

The plasmids were supposed to be his thing—his big break into the world of real science. He could get work in a lab, or maybe a university; he could mold young minds and spark new ideas and really make a difference in the world. He was a smart guy—last year he'd reformulated NewYew's entire line of eye shadows using a method no one had ever tried before, creating colors that kept their shade and thickness longer than anything else on the market. It was an astounding feat of chemistry—he'd even written a paper on it, which had landed him an interview in a *NOVA* documentary. He was relatively famous in the industry, but that was the first time people outside of it had cared. The first time he'd gotten any widespread recognition. It was the greatest thing that had ever happened to him.

And NewYew was taking it away. He wanted to do it honestly, scientifically, with papers and prizes and maybe an interview in *Newsweek*. Burying it in a hand lotion like this, and then keeping it a secret from the world . . . that didn't advance science at all. It didn't help anyone but NewYew.

Lyle picked up a package of steaks and poked at the plastic, watching the meat rebound back into shape. *That's what people really want,* he thought. *Plumpness. We want to have fat skin and skinny fat. We want six-year-old skin on twenty-year-old bodies, with hair colors that don't exist in nature.* He put the steaks in his basket and then, because they were right there, a package of sausages. He was hungry. He moved on.

I need to sell my shares and retire, Lyle thought, not for the first time. He took a jar of peanuts from the shelf. *If we ever get past this theft thing, and ReBirth goes global and we all get rich, I'm going to sell my shares and buy my own lab and get back to basics.*

Lyle got in line at a register, and when he reached the front the cashier looked up at him in relief.

"Oh good, you came back. Here it is."

"What?"

She handed him a credit card. "You've got to be more careful with that, you could get your identity stolen."

"This isn't mine." Lyle looked at the name: *Christopher Page.* The name sounded familiar, but he couldn't place it. "This isn't mine."

"You were just here," said the cashier, "you just bought

some . . ." She pointed at his groceries in the basket, confused. "Some brussels sprouts. Are you buying more?"

"Excuse me!" said a man, puffing breathlessly as he jogged up to the register, "I forgot my credit card." Lyle looked at him and shivered.

He looked almost exactly like Lyle.

The cashier looked at the newcomer, then at Lyle, then back again. "Whoa," she said, "that's freaky."

Their clothes were different, of course, and their haircuts, and the newcomer was heavier than Lyle, though not by much. What matched were the faces—the same shape of nose, the same color of eyes, the same general form to the features. The eyes were the same shape, as well, and the same deep green, but the newcomer's were solid while Lyle had a heterochromia in his right eye—a small patch of amber on the green iris. He saw it in the mirror every day; he'd had it since he was born.

It was disconcerting to see his own face, so close yet so un-cannily different. They didn't look like twins, maybe not even fraternal twins, but they could certainly be mistaken for brothers.

Lyle held out the card. "I take it you're Christopher Page?"

"Thanks," said the man, then stopped, staring at Lyle's face. "Are you . . . Dr. Fontanelle?"

Lyle peered at the man more closely, his stomach suddenly queasy. "Do I know you?"

"You don't 'know me' know me," said Page, "but we met last month, at the NewYew building. I was in the lotion test."

"Are you brothers?" asked the cashier.

"We're not . . ." Lyle paused, still staring at Page. "I'm very sorry, I don't remember you. Were you in the 14G test?"

"I've lost a ton of weight since then," said Page, slapping him-self in the stomach. "Pretty great, huh?"

"How do you not remember him?" asked the cashier. "He looks exactly like you."

"It's the weight," said Page again, smiling at the cashier. "You didn't see me before—I had a face like a side of beef. Take that all away and I . . . well, I guess I do look kind of like you, Dr. Fontanelle. That's an honor. I'd never noticed before."

"Wild," said the cashier. "Thirty-two dollars and forty-eight cents."

Lyle absently handed her his credit card, never taking his eyes off the uncanny mirror image in front of him. Christopher Page, his memory finally informed him, had been the large man, the greasy-faced man. He remembered the name because they'd paid special attention to the way the lotion reacted to his oily skin.

It had only been a few weeks—nobody lost weight that fast. Lyle's scientific curiosity took over, and he spoke without thinking: "Did you have a . . . bypass? Like a surgery?" He immediately felt guilty for asking such a forward question.

Christopher smiled proudly, evidently too proud to be offended. "Nope, just exercise. I've lost fifty pounds."

The cashier handed Lyle his card and bags, subtly pushing him out of the lane. "Thanks for coming to Pathmark."

Lyle followed Christopher to the front wall, staring. "You've lost fifty pounds in three weeks? That doesn't happen with just exercise."

"Well, I've been working on it for a while," said Christopher, "it's just that it finally kicked in for some reason. I could barely fit in my chair at the product test, but now look at me!"

"That's . . . great."

"Here," said Christopher, digging eagerly into his back pocket, "here's my business card, I sell HVAC systems. You want anything done, I'll give you a great deal."

"Yeah," said Lyle slowly, "thanks." *Losing all of that weight must have exposed more of the underlying bone structure,* he thought. *He looks completely different.* "Have you been sick?"

"Not really," said Christopher, shaking his head. "Pooping like a champion, I guess, and drinking like a man in a desert. I ride an exercise bike for twenty minutes every morning—that's thirsty work."

Lyle snapped to attention, staring at the man's too-familiar face. *Jon Ford's friend had said the same thing about him: heightened thirst and increased defecation.* Lyle kept his face passive. "Have you had any pains? Trouble breathing? Numbness on your left side?"

"Not at all."

Lyle pursed his lips, nodding. *It's probably nothing. I'm just creeped out from thinking he looked so much like me, and it's getting to me.* He picked up his bags. "I've got to get going, but it was nice to see you."

"You've got my card," said Christopher, calling after him. "And let me know when that lotion comes out—I'll tell all my friends!"

8

It was Susan's first day back from spring break: fifteen days in Mexico. Lyle was imagining her, all excited and tan and, if he was lucky, still clinging to a relaxed beach dress code. He'd worn his best shirt and gotten to work early. Susan staggered in half an hour late, her body hidden under a pair of baggy sweats and her hair wispily escaping from a pair of old pigtails.

"Holy crap," she said. Her voice was deep and sluggish, like she had a cold. "This is what I get for burning all my sick days on this vacation. I totally shouldn't be here today."

"Oh," said Lyle, scooting his chair just slightly farther away. He registered his disappointment at her appearance and pushed it aside, changing tactics on the fly. *Now I can help her; show her what a nice guy I am.* "I'm sorry to hear that. Is there anything I can do for you?"

Susan put her head on her desk. "Kill me."

Lyle scooted closer. "Did you eat something bad in Mexico?"

Susan's voice was muffled by the desk. "I have no idea. Ate something or picked up a bug. I thought I was being careful."

Seeing her this close he could tell she was heavier than before—not fat, but she'd definitely gained weight. There was something weird about it, though; the weight hadn't appeared in the places he'd expected.

That's what fifteen years of staring at skin will get you, he thought, feeling guilty. *Someone has a bad day and you get all judgmental.*

"Look," he said, "you don't look bad."

"What do you mean I don't look bad?"

"I . . ." He paused, unsure. "I mean you don't look bad."

"Who said anything about me looking bad? How did that become a topic of conversation if it isn't true and no one was talking about it?"

"I didn't mean—"

"I already told you I'm sick, okay? I'm sorry I don't look like your stupid makeup models for your stupid photo shoots! You're supposed to eat a lot when you're sick, and I'm sick, and I wasted my whole vacation, and I feel like a whale and my—" Suddenly her voice cracked, a high-pitched break in the low, congested tirade, and she broke down in tears. "My voice cracks and I'm breaking out in zits all over the place and all I want to do is eat more!"

Lyle stared at her, his mouth moving uselessly as he tried to consider what to say. *How did my chance to seem sympathetic go so horribly wrong?*

"I just want to go home," said Susan, putting her head back down.

"Yes," said Lyle quickly. "Go home. That's exactly what you should do."

"I can't," she growled, facedown on the desk. "I don't have any sick days left."

"I won't tell anyone," said Lyle. "I'll count it as a full day, and you can go home and rest and come back whenever you feel better."

Susan rolled her head to the side looking up at him suspiciously. "Seriously?"

"Seriously. This is a lab, for crying out loud—I can't have a sick person in here anyway. Here—we'll make it official." He pushed his chair back to his desk, rooted around among the papers, and held one up in triumph. "I need a supply run—one bottle each of every hand lotion you can find. Use the company card, but don't go until you feel better; I don't have to start this test until May anyway, and it's the perfect excuse for being out of the office." He shrugged. "Just get better."

"Are you sure?"

"Go," he said, holding out the paper and nodding. "If you're not better by Monday just give me a call."

Susan stood up and wiped her nose on the cuff of her sweatshirt. "Thanks, Lyle." She smiled feebly. "I'll call you on Monday." She took the paper and walked to the door, then stopped, turned, and looked back. "You're really sweet."

She left, and Lyle tried very hard to keep his heart rate down. *This is childish,* he told himself. *I'm being childish and stupid. Where am I, in junior high? I'm an adult. I shouldn't be mooning over girls like some kind of sick puppy—I should be ignoring them or, if I like them, I should be asking them out. I should be asking her out. There is no earthly reason why I shouldn't just ask Susan out on a date, like two adults . . .*

. . . who work together, in a direct managerial situation, and who graduated high school more than a full decade apart. For all I know she wasn't even born when I graduated high school.

Lyle turned to his computer, clicking the mouse idly through a series of spreadsheets, not paying any attention to them. *I think she's just too tense. I can't date her, maybe, but I could give her a quick neck rub some time, right? Nothing serious, just something to ease the tension. I could use that spa lotion we put out a few years ago—the coconut stuff. That would b—*

Lyle froze: mid-word, mid-thought, mid-action.

Susan had used 14G.

He could see it clearly in his mind: he'd left the test to call Jon Ford, stayed to research something, and when Susan came back from the test she was rubbing her hands and saying "great lotion, by the way." She'd used it. Two of the test subjects were experiencing completely random, unrelated results—sickness and weight loss—and now Susan was sick, as well. And she wasn't losing weight, but she was gaining it. No one was reporting these results because they made no sense individually—they couldn't possibly be connected to each other or to the lotion—but seen together they formed a pattern. A senseless, meaningless, inexplicable pattern, maybe, but a pattern nonetheless.

What other results had gone unreported?

Lyle opened his filing cabinet and ticked through the folder until he found what he wanted: the liability waivers for all 128 test subjects, complete with their full contact info. He started at the beginning, with formula 5A—the first one he'd done human testing for—and started calling.

Two hours later he'd called twenty-one women, asking the same questions and getting the same general answers: they felt fine, they didn't like being asked about their weight, and the test was so long ago they couldn't recall any kind of poor reactions to the lotion. On the positive side, most of them said they remembered liking it. Lyle sighed and put the phone back in the cradle, grimacing and stretching his arms above his head. *Maybe I need to start at the other end,* he thought. *Talk to the recent subjects who can still remember their results. But if the results are so innocuous you can't remember them, isn't that just as telling?*

Lyle stared at the stack of papers—there were still 107 names to go. He braced himself for the task, knowing he had to just dive in and do it. He reached for the stack when suddenly the phone rang, startling him. The ID screen said it was the receptionist. He picked it up.

"Hello?"

"Hi, Dr. Fontanelle, I have a William England on the phone for you."

Lyle cocked his head, holding the phone against his shoulder, and reached for the papers. *That's one of the 14G subjects.* "Sure, put him through."

"I warn you, he sounds pretty angry."

"That's fine, put him through." The phone clicked, went dead, then clicked again. He could hear breathing. "Hello, Mr. England, how are you today?"

"I'm very upset," said the man; his voice was curt and angry. "Is this the guy who did the testing?"

"Yes," said Lyle. "My name is Lyle Fontanelle." He found William England's form and laid it out in front of him: thirty-eight years old; an address on Long Island. "What seems to be the problem?"

"I know I filled out a waiver when I came in for your little test," he said, "but that waiver is completely void if you fail to give us full disclosure on the product you're testing, and I want you to know I have every intention of suing you if I am not fully recompensed."

"Why? Just tell me what's happened."

"As if you didn't know. You told us we were testing a hydrating lotion—a moisturizer—and then you slipped us a skin-bleaching crème. That's completely unacceptable! I am very proud of my heritage and my color, and I do not look lightly at this at all—"

"Wait," said Lyle, "a skin-bleaching crème? Did the lotion bleach your skin?"

"Don't pretend you didn't know about this," said the man on the phone. "You were running the test—even if you gave me a skin bleacher by accident, you're still liable for it. Your whole company is."

Lyle searched frantically on the form before him, finally finding the skin type information: William England had marked "Asian." "Wait, Mr. England, you're Asian?"

"Of course I'm Asian."

"I just . . . I remember we had a man with Asian skin in the test, I just didn't connect it with your name."

"I am not interested in your racist assumptions about my name, Mr. Fontanelle. I want to know what you're going to do about this. My face is white—I'm practically Caucasian!"

"How white?" asked Lyle, reaching for a pen.

"What does it matter how white? Just fix it!"

"But there's a lot of range in Caucasian skin," said Lyle. "Are we talking white-white, or tan, or kind of pinkish? What is it?"

"Kind of . . . average color, I guess. Just . . . white."

Lyle scribbled notes furiously. "When did this start?"

"A week or two ago, I guess. Pretty soon after the test."

"Is that the only change?"

"Change?"

"Have you had any other symptoms? Flu, weight loss, weight gain . . . anything else?"

"Why, is there a problem? Should I see a doctor?"

"There's no problem," said Lyle quickly. "Listen, I want you to call me if you notice anything else strange, okay? Anything at all."

"Oh, I'm calling all right, I'm calling a lawyer."

"There's no need for that, I'm just . . . I just want to know what you experience so I can tell you if it's our lotion or not. I'll go through every record we have, every sample bottle on our shelves, and figure out exactly what happened. Okay? But I need you to call me if anything changes."

William England sighed. "Okay. But I wasn't kidding about the lawyer—if you can't give me a good answer, and soon, I will go public and I will sue."

"Just a few days, Mr. England, that's all it should take."

"Fine," said the man, and hung up. Lyle dropped the phone in the cradle and whistled. This made no sense—everyone in the most recent test was reacting, but they were all reacting differently. There was no trend; no way of knowing where the reactions were going, or where they might be coming from.

I need more information, thought Lyle. *If any of the earlier tests had reacted this strongly, I would have heard about it; I need to start with 14G. The men. Is there something about men specifically? But no—Susan was sick, too. Everyone who touched that batch of lotion. . . .*

Lyle froze. *I touched that lotion. I touched it in the plant, and again here in the office. I used it a few times. Am I going to get sick, as well?*

Am I going to die, like Jon Ford?

Lyle turned to the next sheet of paper: a man named Tony Hicks. *I have to call them all.*

He picked up the phone and dialed.

"Congratulations!"

Ira Brady, the CEO of Ibis Cosmetics, raised the lotion bottle in a mock toast. It was a small plastic cylinder about four inches tall, maybe an inch in diameter. The white sticker on the side said "14G," carefully written in thin black marker. "Thanks to this product, Ibis is set to create a new future for the cosmetics industry!"

The executives cheered. Ira had ordered steaks, and the beer was flowing freely. Ronald smiled in the back of the room, just happy to be included.

Ira continued. "Our . . . let's call him a subcontractor . . . dropped off the information late last night. We have the full specs and formula, including all of their lab results, and this sample of the lotion. I've been through all of it, along with Dr. Decker, and I assure you: it's every bit as valuable as we anticipated."

The executives erupted in cheers again, and one of them cried out: "Pass it around!"

Ira smiled and tossed the sample bottle to the man. "There you go, Gordon—everybody feel free to try it. Now, normally we'd have to do months of safety testing on a product like this, especially something with an experimental ingredient, but in this case our dear friends at NewYew were kind enough to cover all of that time and expense for us." The room erupted in a round of applause and laughter, and Ira had to shout to make himself heard. "If we move quickly on marketing and legal, we can have this on the shelves in just four months, and beat NewYew out of . . . oh, a couple of billion dollars."

The man on Ronald's right handed him the bottle of lotion, slightly slimy from so many sampling hands. Ronald passed it along; he'd already tried it, and the bottle was running low. Better to give everyone else a chance. *I want everyone in this room to understand exactly what I helped them get.*

Ronald's phone buzzed, vibrating in its belt holster, and he wiped his hands carefully on a napkin. It was a new phone, the best his latest Ibis check could buy, and there was no sense getting steak sauce all over it. He pulled out the phone and yelped in terror.

"It's NewYew!"

The noise abated slightly as some of the executives stopped talking to look at him. Ronald stood up, holding the phone above his head. "Mr. Brady, it's NewYew! They're calling me!"

The room fell silent, suddenly tense.

"Answer it," Ira hissed. Ronald held it up to his ear, but Ira shook his head. "On speakerphone."

Ronald nodded, fiddled with the buttons, and set the phone on the table. Nobody breathed. "Hello?"

"Hi," said a man on the other end, "this is Lyle Fontanelle from NewYew, am I speaking with Ronald Lynch?"

Ronald swallowed, looking at the others in the room. "Yeah, this is Ronald."

"Excellent, how are you, Mr. Lynch?"

"I'm good. How are you?"

"I'm great, thank you," said Lyle. "I'm sorry to bother you, but I'm calling to follow up on the product test you participated in a few weeks ago. Have you experienced any oddities or complications with your health since that test?"

"Oddities?" Ronald looked around the room again, shrugging nervously. "I'm not sure what you mean."

"Increased appetite or thirst; unexplained weight loss or

weight gain; flu symptoms such as vomiting or diarrhea or intense abdominal pain. Dermatological effects such as skin bleaching, or a discoloration of the skin or hair. Deformation of bone or muscle mass—"

"Wait," said Ronald, "are you serious?" The other men in the room were frowning as the list went on; Ira was giving the phone a look that could shatter stone. "Is any of that stuff likely?" asked Ronald.

Lyle sighed. "No, I'd actually say it's unlikely, but . . ." He paused. "Let's just say I'm concerned."

"Concerned!" said Ronald. "What do you mean, concerned?"

"We have reason to believe that the product you tested is causing . . . unexplained biological phenomena," said Lyle.

The other men in the room were now frantically cleaning their hands, wiping them off on napkins and suit coats and whatever they could reach.

"Mr. Lynch," said Lyle, "are you there?"

Ronald found his voice. "I'm . . . fine," he said. "N-no side effects."

"That's great to hear," said Lyle. "Honestly. I don't mean to scare you, but if anything develops, I need you to call me immediately. Can you do that?"

"Um . . ." Ronald's head was thick and foggy. "Yeah. I can call you."

"Thank you for your time, and good luck." The phone hung up, and the room erupted in angry, terrified shouts.

"Bloody hell!" shouted Decker. "Every one of us touched that stuff! What's going to happen?"

"I don't know!" cried Ronald.

"Be quiet," said Ira. The men were still frantic, and Ira shouted again with shocking authority. "Be quiet!"

The room went quiet.

"Whatever happens," said Ira evenly, "you report it to me directly. You don't talk to anybody else—not your wife, not your doctor, and definitely not NewYew. Is that clear?"

The men nodded.

"We're going to find out what's going on," said Ira. He paused for a moment, his eyes bouncing back and forth as his mind raced through the various ramifications. "We're going to make ourselves safe, and we're going to find out what this lotion really does." He looked at each man in turn, his eyes practically blazing with purpose. "And I promise you, whatever it does, it's going to do it for us."

10

"Mr. Fontanelle?"

Lyle looked up; the man was tall and wide framed, looming over him in the hospital waiting room. He wore a short-cropped beard, dark black, but Lyle could see the telltale silver where the roots were a different color. *I wonder if he uses our dye?*

"Hi," said the man, "I'm Dr. Allgood. I understand you're a friend of Jon Ford's?"

Lyle stood and shook the doctor's hand, his fake story practiced and ready to go; he wanted to keep NewYew's connection to the story secret for as long as possible. "Just an acquaintance, really. I met Jon while working on a paper about flu epidemiology. I was devastated to hear about his death, but I'm a little ashamed to say that the scientist in me was intrigued by the transition from flu to stroke. I was hoping you might be able to let me look at his treatment files."

Dr. Allgood sighed. "I'd love to—everyone here was completely baffled by his symptoms, and we'd appreciate an outside opinion, but medical records are protected and we can't just—"

"Oh!" said Lyle, trying to sound like he'd just thought of it. "You need permission, of course. I've got it right here." He held up a clipboard containing Jon Ford's liability waiver, the New-Yew name and logo hidden by the clip at the top. If the doctor looked at it closely the ruse would be lost, but Lyle was gambling that he wouldn't. What nonlawyer had time to study legal forms? "He signed a full release when I first included him in my research." Lyle held it out for him to take, but Allgood waved it away.

"Leave a copy at the desk on your way out. Come on back to my office and I'll show you the file."

Lyle smiled and followed Dr. Allgood through the back halls of the hospital, nervously nodding at the occasional nurse. *What if someone recognizes me? What if they link me to NewYew?*

What will we do?

"Normally I'd have to make you wait while we try to collect everything," said Dr. Allgood, "but you're in luck today: Mr. Ford's files are sitting on my desk as we speak."

"You're still going through them?"

"Like I said," said the doctor, "it's a very confusing case, and we still haven't deciphered exactly what he had. It's not really our job at this point, but I don't like not knowing, you know?"

"Exactly."

They reached Dr. Allgood's office, a smallish room lined floor to ceiling with books and shelves and filing cabinets. It felt more like a cave than an office, though the desk in the center was relatively clear. "Here you go," said Allgood, stepping behind the desk and pushing an open folder toward Lyle; it was stacked with an inch or more of multicolored papers and reports.

"Wonderful," said Lyle. The two men sat down on opposite sides of the desk, and Lyle scanned through the first page of the file: standard admissions information, a description of symptoms, and so on. Jon Ford had been checked in just a few hours before his stroke, nearly comatose, by a friend named Travis Meyer. The symptoms were consistent with a severe flu: fever, intense head and muscle aches, lethargy, and extensive fluid loss through runny nose and diarrhea. *Nothing new there.* Lyle flipped to a new page, where the admitting physician had jotted down that the fluid loss had left Jon extremely dehydrated and recommended an immediate IV. He turned another page and found the results of a blood test: A+ blood, with a high white cell count, but that was standard for a flu patient. Beyond that it all looked good—good cholesterol, good minerals, good everything. Lyle leaned in closely, examining each line of the printout in detail: *iron's fine, potassium's fine, red cells are low . . . wait.* His estrogen levels were incredibly high. Lyle frowned at the number on the page. *High estrogen in a male subject suggests a much older man, maybe fifties or sixties, but Jon was barely twenty-five. Was he getting old prematurely? Could an antiaging product somehow turn around and literally accelerate aging?*

Dr. Allgood spoke. "What did you find?"

"The estrogen," said Lyle, looking up. "What was that about?"

Dr. Allgood laughed hollowly. "If you're anything like us, you immediately assumed it was a premature aging shift, but wait 'til you see the autopsy report." He reached over to the folder and sorted through it quickly, pulling out a thick subset of papers clamped together with a paperclip. "Page four, somewhere in the middle. When they made the Y incision through the soft tissues of the chest, they found mammary glands."

Lyle jerked his head back up. "Mammary glands? He had breasts?"

Allgood nodded. "Normally they don't cut through those, obviously, but how were they to know? They were grossly underdeveloped, and there was nothing in his medical history about intersexuality."

Lyle looked back down at the autopsy report, scanning through it desperately. "You've got to be kidding me. Did he have anything else?"

"Immature ovaries, a semideveloped uterus, and a corresponding weakness in all his-her male sexual characteristics, primary and secondary. Medically speaking, he was neither really male nor female, just a halfhearted attempt at both."

Lyle couldn't help himself; the first thing he thought was *Susan was so into this guy.* He shook his head to clear it and looked back at the notes, but Susan's interest in Ford kept coming back to mind. It didn't make sense.

"I've met Jon Ford in person," said Lyle. "There was nothing feminine about him. He was manly and handsome and . . . manly."

Allgood shrugged. "His testosterone was just as high as his estrogen. Now you can see why we were so confused."

"He never told me anything about this," said Lyle.

"He was probably pretty sensitive about it, for obvious reasons."

"Then why did he agree to a medical test?" asked Lyle.

Allgood scratched his beard. "I don't know. A cry for help, maybe? He wanted to be discovered?"

Or he didn't know about it when he signed up, thought Lyle, *because this is another crazy, impossible side effect of that damned lotion.* Lyle stared at the papers, trying to think. He riffled the big file with his thumb. "Is this a full medical history?"

"As close as you'll get without a lot of extra legwork; we've got a description of every visit he's ever made to this hospital, but he may have been to others."

"Did he have any previous blood work?" asked Lyle. "A blood test from last year, or even older than that?"

"He's been a patient here a couple of different times, according to the file, I'm sure he had a blood test at some point."

"Are those results saved somewhere?"

Allgood nodded, picking up his phone. "Sure, I'll make a request."

Lyle went back to the files while Allgood spoke to his assistant. The rest of the autopsy report was fairly standard, though apparently his kidneys had been thrashed. It wasn't until the final page that Lyle found another surprise.

"His cause of death wasn't the stroke?"

Allgood finished his call and hung up the phone. "No, we stabilized him after the stroke, and then his kidneys killed him a few hours later."

"Renal failure," said Lyle, reading the line again. "What was wrong with his kidneys?"

"He had an acute hemolytic reaction," said Allgood. "You saw the low red cell count?"

"Yeah."

"Something was killing them, and the hemoglobin this released into his system was very slowly destroying his kidneys. We should have seen it, but so many of the symptoms overlap with the flu."

"What if it wasn't flu at all?" asked Lyle. "Just a prolonged kidney failure that looked like a flu?"

"That's the thing," said Allgood, "this kind of kidney failure isn't usually prolonged—red cell destruction typically happens in one big swoop, like you'd get from a bad blood transfusion. The antibodies from one blood type attack the red blood cells of the other, and the whole body falls apart. That could even explain the stroke, if enough of the dead cells got into a bottleneck in his brain."

"So is that it?" asked Lyle. "Did he get a transfusion?"

"Not in our hospital," said Allgood, "and nowhere else that his friends or family were aware of. So it has to be something else, we just don't know what."

"There's no way he could have gotten foreign blood into his system?"

"Not as far as we can tell. We couldn't even find any needle marks aside from our own, and we know we didn't do it."

Lyle sighed and rubbed his eyes. "This doesn't make any sense."

Allgood laughed again, a dry, humorless cough. "Tell me about it."

Four hours later Lyle was back in the hospital lobby, staring listlessly at a mirrored wall. He'd gone through everything in the folder, found every scrap of evidence he could, but none of it led anywhere. *All I need is just one clue*, he thought, *just one clue that can tie all the symptoms together—not just Jon Ford's but everyone's. Why had William England's skin turned Caucasian? Why had Pedro Trujillo's bones elongated? Why had Christopher Page lost so much weight?* If there was a common trend, he'd have something to work with—if *everyone* was losing weight, or if *everyone* had bone deformation—then he could at least identify the direction of the problem, if not the cause. As it was he had nothing: no trends, no hypothesis, nothing.

Lyle thought about Christopher Page's face in the grocery store—his own face—and shivered at the remembered shock of looking into his own eyes, familiar and foreign at once. He looked across the floor at his reflection in the mirrored wall—a man on an identical bench, tired and scared, the hospital bustling unnoticed behind him. Who was he, really? *Who is Lyle Fontanelle? A chemist. A developer. If I'd never taken that first cosmetics job, would I be here now? Would I be somewhere else? Or would I be someone else—another Lyle altogether, living another life?*

Lyle's reflection stood up, and walked toward him.

"Holy—!" Lyle jumped back in shock. The reflection scowled angrily, pointed, and started running straight at him.

"You did this to us!"

In the seconds before he was tackled, Lyle had just enough time to realize two things: first, there was no mirror at all, simply another bench lined up beside another identical pillar.

Second: the other Lyle had a Mexican accent.

11

The new Lyle smashed into the old with horrific force, tackling him to the ground and knocking the wind from his lungs.

"This is all your fault!"

Lyle gasped for breath, struggling to crawl away; he almost managed to inhale before something solid slammed into the side of his head, and his vision exploded in white stars. He fell on the floor, blind and deaf. His lungs ached for air, and he gasped a ragged breath. Somebody pulled the other Lyle off of him, and when his hearing returned he could hear the same voice again, with the same Mexican accent, ranting angrily.

"He did this to me. You see my skin? You see my arms? He did this to me!"

"Please calm down, sir, just tell me what's wrong."

Lyle saw himself standing about ten feet away, held tightly by a pair of hospital orderlies. The haircut was different, but close; the clothes were the same general color as Lyle's. At a distance you might not be able to tell them apart.

It's Christopher Page, thought Lyle. *But no, he doesn't have an accent.*

"I do not look like this," the man growled. "He ruined my bones, my skin, my whole life!"

"Wait," said Lyle, clambering to his feet. He stared at his other self. "Who are you?"

"You know who I am!" the man shouted. "I am Pedro Trujillo—you used me like a rat in a lab, testing your poison, and then you called me on the phone. Don't pretend you don't know me!"

"Pedro Trujillo," said Lyle, realization washing through him like nausea. "You can't be Pedro Trujillo—you're nearly five inches taller than he is. And you're white."

"I know I'm white!" Pedro screamed.

One of the orderlies looked at Lyle. "Is this a . . . relative of yours?"

"No, he's a . . . business acquaintance." When Lyle had called him before, the same day he called the others, Pedro had mentioned intense leg aches but he hadn't blamed Lyle or NewYew for any of it. "Pedro," said Lyle, "why didn't you tell me about the skin bleaching?" *That's two subjects with a similar symptom— the first match I've found yet. But what does it mean?*

And why does he look like me?

"The skin change is new," Pedro spat, "but I know that you did it—that's why you called me, to see if it had started yet. When my skin changed, I knew you must have done something to my legs, as well."

"What are you talking about?" the orderly asked. He looked at Lyle. "What is he talking about?"

I need to play this off, thought Lyle, *I need to calm him down and keep this quiet. No one's mentioned NewYew yet; if he says anything about NewYew this entire thing could explode.* "Mr. Trujillo," said Lyle, walking toward him, "I promise this is just a misunderstanding, and I'd be more than happy to offer some kind of compensation—" Lyle reached his hand toward him, a gesture of peace, and then stopped, frozen, staring at Pedro in shock. Now that he was closer, he could see that his eyes were green, with a small patch of amber in his right iris. Pedro had heterochromia.

Exactly like Lyle.

"That man gave me poison," Pedro shouted. "He tricked me into using some kind of chemical, and it's destroying my body. I demand that you call the police and have him arrested!"

"Your eye . . . ," said Lyle, but Pedro shouted him down.

"Call the police! This man is trying to kill me! He is!"

"Excuse me," said another man, stepping purposefully into the circle. He wore a very expensive suit. "I'm Dr. Whitaker, I'm the hospital administrator. Would you gentlemen like to continue this discussion in my office?"

"It's . . ." Lyle paused, too shocked to speak. *Pedro has my eyes—not just the same color, but the same irregularity. How is that possible? And what does it mean?* "We have to talk," he said at last, pleading to Pedro. "We need to go somewhere and talk, we need to figure out what's going on—"

"That was fast," said Pedro, looking over Lyle's shoulder, "the police are here."

The hospital administrator glanced at another orderly. "Hold them both." The orderly put a hand on Lyle's arm, his grip light but solid, and the administrator stepped toward the police. "I'm Dr. Whitaker, the hospital administrator. Can I help you?"

"I'm Officer Woolf," said the first policeman, "and this is Officer Luckesen. We're looking for a man named Lyle Fontanelle." He held up a photo. "His secretary told us we might be able to find him here. Have you seen a man matching this . . . description . . ." His voice trailed off as he looked at Lyle, then at Pedro, then back at Lyle again. "What's going on?"

"*He* is Fontanelle," said Pedro, pointing at Lyle. "I don't know who called you, but thank you for coming!"

"Nobody called us," said Officer Woolf, confused. "We've been looking for him all day."

"I'm Lyle," said Lyle, waving politely. "What's this all about?"

"You've been connected to a robbery in Brooklyn," said the second policeman, Officer Luckesen, stepping forward to grab Lyle's free arm. "We're going to have to take you in for some questions."

"I haven't been to Brooklyn in . . . forever," said Lyle, confused. "I definitely didn't rob anyone there. Or anywhere."

"He's crazy," said Pedro. "He's some kind of mad scientist—look what he did to me!"

Officer Woolf looked at the administrator. "What's he talking about?"

"He attacked . . ." The administrator paused, looking at Pedro and Lyle to get his bearings. Finally he pointed at Pedro. "This one attacked the other one. I haven't determined exactly why yet, but he's raving about . . . well, you heard him."

"They were doing some kind of test," said an orderly. "They were both talking about it."

"He is using me as a lab rat for chemical weapons!" Pedro shouted.

There was a small crowd gathered now, keeping a respectful distance but listening actively. Lyle could tell the administrator was upset by the upheaval in his lobby. *He just wants to get this over with,* thought Lyle. *If I give him an easy out, I might be able to keep this quiet.*

Lyle beckoned the administrator closer, and leaned toward him and the policemen confidentially, whispering so that Pedro couldn't hear. "I don't want to press any charges for the assault. Pedro is a relative of mine—you can see the resemblance—but he's completely delusional. The family suspects paranoid schizophrenia. I mean, you heard what he said: I used chemical weapons to make him taller?" He looked at the administrator innocently. "I'll just go with the police to sort out whatever misunderstanding we have about fingerprints, and meanwhile maybe you can get this man in to see a counselor."

Officer Woolf chuckled, and Lyle held his breath in hope. *It's working.*

"If you can make people taller, sign me up," said the officer. "I'll join the NBA and get away from these lunatics." He looked at the administrator. "You need help with the, uh, crazy guy?"

"I'm sure we'll be fine," said the administrator softly, glancing quickly around at the periphery of onlookers. He was in familiar territory now—treating an overexcited patient instead of breaking up a fight. "The less commotion the better."

"Let us know if you need anything else," said Officer Luckesen.

The policemen directed Lyle gently toward the main doors, and Pedro shouted triumphantly behind them.

"Make him pay for it! I can testify against him—we all can! He's a Frankenstein!"

Lyle followed the policemen to their car, trying to force himself to stay calm. "So what's this all about? Who got robbed?"

"It's a house in Brooklyn," said the officer, climbing into the driver's seat. "A very expensive one, with very little evidence, and the detectives eventually resorted to a DNA test. I'm afraid your name came up as an exact match."

"I swear," said Lyle, "I haven't been to Brooklyn in ages. I don't know how my DNA could possibly be there—" Lyle stopped abruptly, frowning. "I don't even know how my DNA got into your database. I've never been arrested or processed or anything."

"That's no real surprise," said Woolf. "It's an FBI database, and they pull in a lot of noncriminal records. Have you ever had a background check, like for a job? One that included a blood test?"

"Yes, New"—Lyle shook his head—"my current employer runs checks on everyone they hire."

"There you go—a lot of these big companies sell those files to the FBI; helps offset the cost of the background check."

"I see," said Lyle, nodding. "That's kind of creepy, knowing that's out there."

"It's a lot creepier having your house broken into."

"You've got to trust me on this one," said Lyle, leaning forward. "Your test must be wrong. Look, when did the robbery happen?"

"April fourteenth; it was a Saturday night."

"Perfect!" said Lyle. "Saturday nights I'm usually at work."

"Sure you are."

"I am," said Lyle. "Almost every week." He wracked his brain, trying to remember if this was one of those weeks. "We've got an electronic security system that logs our ID cards—it should know exactly when I got there and when I left."

The officers glanced at each other. "Those can be faked. And that's a conveniently specific alibi."

"My face will be on the cameras," said Lyle.

"Cameras can be faked, too. You could get somebody who looks like you—that guy from the hospital, maybe—to be on camera for you."

"But what if I'm on the camera and that other guy robbed the house?" asked Lyle. "You could have the wrong guy."

"DNA evidence doesn't work that way," said Officer Luckesen. "It's not perfect, but it's a lot harder to fake than a camera."

Lyle snapped his fingers. "The security guard! Saturday night is such a weird time to be at work, the security guard usually comes in and talks to me for five or ten minutes. He gets bored. He'll definitely remember me."

Officer Woolf sighed. "We'll call from the station to check, but you're going to have to get processed regardless."

Lyle's cell phone rang, and he looked at the officers. "Can I get that?"

"Go ahead."

"Thanks." He pulled out his phone and checked the number; it was the hospital. *Probably something about Pedro.* He thumbed the screen. "Hello, this is Lyle Fontanelle."

Dr. Allgood's voice boomed on the other end. "I'm sorry this took so long, but I have that blood test you requested."

"Which?"

"One of Jon Ford's old tests, from a visit three years ago. Do you have a fax number I could send it to?"

Lyle looked at the policemen in the front seat. "I'm actually not sure if I'll be able to get to a fax machine anytime soon." He pulled a folded paper from his jacket pocket and fumbled in his pants for a pen. "I've got a copy of the other blood test here, could you just read me the results and I can jot them down for comparison?"

"Sure thing," said Allgood. "Line by line, here we go: Name: Jon Ford. Age: twenty-two. Blood Type: O negative. Red cell count—"

"Wait," said Lyle, staring at the paper spread awkwardly on his knee. "His blood type is A positive."

"No," said Allgood. "It's right here on my printout: O negative."

"The notes in the file said A positive."

"What in the . . ." Lyle heard papers rustle and shuffle, then a low whistle. "Saints and angels, you're right. Our last test with him was A positive."

"Are you sure you have the right Jon Ford?"

"The patient numbers are identical," said Allgood. "The address and phone number match. It's even the same insurance policy number, he just has . . . two different blood types."

"How is that possible?"

"It isn't," said Allgood, sounding eager, "but it *is* consistent. A positive is anathema to O negative; if he had enough A positive in his bloodstream it would attack the old blood and cause all the problems we talked about—the stroke, the hemolysis, the renal failure. It's amazing he lived as long as he did."

"But you said he hadn't had a transfusion," said Lyle, "you specifically checked into it."

"Oh, goodness no," said Dr. Allgood, "a full transfusion of A positive blood would have killed him in hours; we had him for almost a full day, and he was sick for quite a while before that. No, to react the way he did, the foreign blood would have to be introduced very slowly, over a very long time, or you'd get a sudden shock that overwhelms the system."

"Was somebody trying to kill him?" asked Lyle.

"If they were, they hid it really well. I told you before, we couldn't find any needle marks except the ones we made, and the first one of those was the A positive blood test." The doctor whistled. "It's almost as if it was all internal—like his body just decided out of the blue to make the wrong kind of blood. Maybe his DNA got confused; I don't know."

Lyle gasped, thoughts flashing in his mind like a hail of bullets. *Blood type. DNA. Heterochromia.* "I'm going to have to call you back." He ended the call without saying goodbye, staring at nothing. *Skin bleaching. Bone deformation. Weight loss.* Lyle's mind staggered as realization dawned. *I couldn't find a trend in the test subjects' symptoms because they're not trending in a single direction, they're normalizing toward a central point.*

Me.

Lyle rubbed his face, stared blankly, then rubbed it again.

"You okay back there?" asked Officer Woolf. "What was that all about—you said something about somebody trying to kill someone?"

Lyle ignored him, running through each case in his mind: *Christopher Page was big and heavy, so he lost weight until he matched me. Pedro Trujillo was short, so he gained weight and mass and height until he matched me—and then his skin color changed to match mine, as well. William England has darker skin that got lighter; Tony Hicks had very light skin, practically white, that got darker. I bet if I call him back his hair color's changed, as well.*

They're all becoming me.

It was something in the plasmids—he was sure of it. *Changing DNA is their whole job; it wasn't supposed to be this dramatic, but somehow it was.* Lyle sat motionless, his jaw hanging open. *Everyone who's handled the lotion is turning into me. That's why I'm the only one who never changed—or perhaps I've been changing all along, but I was changing into myself and didn't notice. Except—*

He paused.

Except I don't have A positive blood. I'm O negative, which is a universal donor—that's why the men turning into me aren't having the same blood reaction that Jon Ford had. But then who was Ford turning into?

In a flash Lyle remembered the autopsy report: half-formed ovaries and mammary glands, high levels of estrogen, and even a semideveloped uterus. *Susan applied Jon's lotion directly—the first day of the test she rubbed it right onto his hands, skin to skin. He was turning into Susan.*

So then who is Susan turning into?

"Hey, buddy," said Officer Luckesen, practically shouting at

him. "Wake up. Hey!" He banged on the protective grate between the front and back seats, and Lyle jerked out of his reverie.

"I have to make a phone call."

"You have to answer my question," said the policeman. "Who
were you talking to, and what did you say about somebody trying to kill someone?"

"I was wrong," said Lyle, "nobody was trying to kill anybody.
It was all an accident."

"Accidental death still sounds like the kind of thing you ought
to tell us about."

"It was an acute hemolytic reaction, but drawn out over time,"
said Lyle. "That's why none of us saw it. His body was literally
giving itself a blood transfusion cell by cell over the last five
weeks. Do you realize how impossible that is?"

"Who are you talking about?"

"I need to call a lot of people," said Lyle. "We have to deal with
this immediately. What if Susan has the wrong blood type, too?"

"Who's Susan?"

"Just let me make a phone call," said Lyle, bringing up his
phone. "I have to call and find out how she is."

The cops slammed on the brakes and dove out of their seats,
bolting around to the back. Lyle found Susan's number and hit send
just before the cops swarmed through the rear doors and tackled him.

"Put down the phone! Do not touch that phone!"

"I'm just calling a friend!"

Ring.

"That's her," shouted Lyle. "Just let me talk for five seconds!"

Ring.

"Calm down," shouted Woolf. "You're talking about killing
people and giving people blood and we cannot allow you to
make a phone call until you answer our questions!"

The phone on the floor clicked softly, and a woman's voice
spoke. "Hi, Susan's phone."

Lyle shouted. "Is Susan there—*oof.*" One of the officers hit him in the gut, and he doubled over as much as he could with two policemen holding him down.

"What do we do?" asked Woolf.

Luckesen shook his head. "I have no idea."

"I'm sorry," said the woman on the phone, "Susan's not available right now. She's in the hospital."

"I told you," Lyle wheezed, gasping for breath. "Find out if she's okay."

Woolf adjusted his grip on Lyle, keeping one hand tightly on his wrist while reaching down with the other to pick up the phone. He held the phone to his ear.

"Hello, ma'am, this is Detective Woolf, NYPD. Do you know a man named Lyle Fontanelle?"

Lyle couldn't hear the answer.

"I see. Does your friend Susan know anyone named Lyle Fontanelle?" Pause. "No, I don't know anything about Susan, it's . . ." He glanced at Lyle. "It's kind of a weird situation; we witnessed some suspicious behavior and stopped it while the phone was already ringing. Tell me, ma'am, why is this Susan in the hospital?" There was another pause, and the officer's eyes went wide. "Seriously?" Pause. "Seriously?" He pulled the phone away, glanced at it, then held it back to his ear. "I may need to call back tonight or tomorrow with some more questions. Will you keep this phone on you? Thank you." He hung up and looked at Lyle. "Who is Susan?"

"My assistant at work," said Lyle. "I'm the vice president of Research at NewYew Incorporated. Chief science officer. She's a lab intern."

"Looks like you might need a new intern pretty soon," said Woolf. He looked at his partner. "Susan has leprosy."

12

Sunny sat down next to Lyle on the bench outside the police station, rubbing his eyes with one hand and clutching his coffee with the other. "I've cleared up the robbery issue: they're convinced, for now, that you were at work when the crime was committed, but the investigation is ongoing." Sunny twisted his neck, stretching until it cracked quietly. "They're somewhat more concerned about, and I can't believe I'm saying this, alleged chemical weapons testing." He looked at Lyle. "What in the bright blue hell do you do on your weekends? Is there anything else I should know about?"

"You and the entire executive staff," said Lyle. "Can we go?" He had already called the hospital again, asking about Susan; her body was sloughing tissue from the chest and groin, which they had preliminarily diagnosed as leprosy. Lyle knew better. "We have a lot to do."

"Yeah, we can go," said Sunny. "Just give me a minute with this coffee first, okay? I'm a corporate legal counsel, not a divorce lawyer—I'm not used to these emergency police station visits at four a.m. And in Brooklyn, no less—why'd you have to get arrested in Brooklyn?"

Lyle stood up. "I know who it was."

"Who what was?"

"The guy who robbed the house was named Tony Hicks. He was one of our test subjects for 14G."

Sunny frowned. "The last ReBirth test? How do you know it was him?"

"Because he has a criminal record," said Lyle. "And my DNA." Lyle identified Sunny's Mercedes and walked toward it. He stopped at the curb and looked back; Sunny was still standing by the police station doors. "I need your help on this, Sunny. You know they don't listen to me."

"Who has your DNA?" asked Sunny. "And how?"

"It's the lotion," said Lyle, "it's ReBirth." Lyle lowered his voice, glancing nervously at the police station. "We killed Jon Ford, do you realize that? The allegations of chemical weapons testing are not far off. Do you have any idea what ReBirth is doing?"

"I might," said Sunny, walking toward the car, "if you'd cut the histrionics and just tell me."

They climbed in the car, and Lyle scanned the parking lot nervously before saying it out loud for the first time. "It clones people."

Sunny raised an eyebrow. "You're joking."

"I'm deadly serious," said Lyle. "Somehow the plasmids in the lotion are getting into the test subjects' DNA and changing it, literally overwriting it, so that your DNA becomes my DNA. You become a clone of me."

"Why you?"

"I don't know," said Lyle, "obviously it has to get the DNA from somewhere, I guess it just got it from me because I was the first person to touch it."

Sunny started the car. "You're insane, Lyle. You're talking about this lotion like it's alive."

"It is alive, in a way—it has self-replicating genetic matter, so it's just as alive as any virus or bacteria."

"But it's not sentient," said Sunny, pulling onto the street, "it's not some kind of blobby lotion monster that's going to eat everyone."

"I'm not saying that," said Lyle, frustrated. "I'm saying that it is cloning people—right now it's cloning me. By my count there are currently six people who share my DNA, walking around right now in New York City."

"Probably not walking," said Sunny, "it's six in the morning."

"You're not taking this seriously."

"That's because it's ridiculous! You can't expect me to believe something like this, Lyle, it's . . . it's unbelievable. It is not mentally possible to believe it."

"I'll prove it to you," said Lyle, pulling out his cell phone. "I'm going to call the hospital."

"Whoa," said Sunny, catching Lyle's hand in his own, "let's not involve any hospitals just yet, okay? The last thing we need is for this story to go public, whether it's true or not."

"Don't worry," said Lyle, pulling his hand free, "that's exactly why I'm calling." He dialed Bellevue and hit send.

"Bellevue Hospital, how may I direct your call?"

"I need to reach a patient admitted last night," said Lyle. "Pedro Trujillo."

13

"I don't believe it," Kerry whispered.

The full executive staff sat in the conference room, staring slack jawed at Lyle and Pedro standing side by side. They were almost indistinguishable.

"I don't believe it," Kerry said again.

"I haven't fully figured out how it happened," said Lyle, "but I'm working on it."

"So he looks like you," said Cynthia, dismissing the idea with a wave of her hand. "That doesn't prove anything. He could be wearing a disguise, trying to bilk us out of a few million in fake damages."

"He's not the first one I've seen," said Lyle. "Plus, look at this." He leaned forward, opening his eyes as wide as he could. "See this, in my right eye? That's called a partial heterochromia—a patch of one color in an iris of a different color. It's a genetic trait, encoded in my DNA, and look at Pedro's eyes"—Lyle pulled Pedro forward, pointing at his face—"he has the same thing. He doesn't just look like me, he *is* me, genetically speaking."

"But what are you going to do about it?" Pedro demanded, pulling away.

Carl frowned. "You say the lotion did this? Your lotion?"

"It's hard to believe, but yes," said Lyle. "It didn't start happening until the most recent formulation, 14G. My best guess is . . . well, I honestly have no idea. We added a retrovirus in that batch, but they're supposed to regulate the plasmid activity, and this is exactly the opposite of that." Lyle shrugged. "ReBirth is supposed to be producing collagen, and I don't know why or even how it started doing this instead. I don't even know *what* it's doing instead."

"I don't care *why* it happened," said Pedro, "I want to know what you're going to do about it!"

"Obviously we'll make what reparations we can," said Sunny, "but we're going to have to work together on this—this is new territory for all of us—"

Carl leaned forward, and everyone stopped to look at him. Even Pedro grew hushed.

"Get Marcus in here," Carl rumbled.

Cynthia opened the door and Marcus Eads stepped in, followed by two suited men from the security staff. Carl pointed at Lyle and attempted to smile warmly. "Please take our friend here to my private lounge upstairs. Get him some breakfast, and treat him well." The men moved toward him, but Lyle shook his head and pointed at Pedro.

"I'm the real Lyle; you want him." He glanced at Carl, suddenly uncertain. "Don't you?"

The men looked at Carl, who frowned at the two Lyles, then nodded. The suited men led Pedro into the hall, but Marcus hung back. Cynthia closed the door, and Carl spoke in a low voice.

"Keep him here for now," said Carl, "and keep this as quiet as possible. I don't want one word of this to get out until we're good and ready for it."

"Bellevue Hospital knows," said Lyle.

"Everyone in the whole hospital?"

Lyle grimaced. "A handful of orderlies, the hospital administrator, and anyone else Pedro may have talked to. A crowd of people from the lobby. I don't know if any of them understand what's going on, but they did hear some of the details."

"The Brooklyn police know about it, too," said Sunny, "though again, they don't know everything and they probably don't understand the full implications of it."

"Then we keep it that way as long as we can," said Carl. "If they don't hear about it again, they won't think about it again. Now, let's be very frank here: what kind of fallout are we expecting from this? How many people?"

Kerry's face was white with fear. "I . . . I've been using it. So has Carrie."

Jeffrey laughed nervously. "You're talking in the third person now?" He looked at Lyle. "Is that normal?"

"Carrie's my wife," said Kerry.

"You married someone with your own name?"

"It's spelled differently!"

"I've used it," said Lyle, "long before anybody else, which is probably how it got imprinted with my DNA. Six test subjects used it; one of them is dead now. My assistant Susan used it; she's currently in the hospital."

"This can't be true, though," said Kerry. "There's got to be another explanation. I mean, I started using it . . . ," Kerry counted in his head, "two, maybe three weeks ago. And I don't look anything like you."

Lyle leaned in close to him, peering at his face. "You have the heterochromia. And your hair's coming in lighter."

"It is?"

"I can see it, too," said Cynthia, walking to Kerry's chair. She stared at him, fascinated. "You have black hair, but all the roots are brown—about the color of Lyle's."

Lyle picked up Kerry's hands, examining them closely, then looked back at his face. "The human body completely replaces its own skin about every three weeks. Odds are good that all of your skin is mine by now."

"It's not the same color, though," said Cynthia, "it's darker than Lyle's."

Kerry swallowed nervously. "I tan," he whispered. He looked at Lyle pleadingly. "I started last week. My wife said I looked kind of pale."

"So he has your skin and he's growing your hair," said Sunny, "but he doesn't look like you. Pedro could have been your twin—why is Kerry different?"

"Because bone and muscle take longer," said Lyle. "Change his skin and he just has different skin. He won't look like me until his body has time to rebuild the muscles on his face, and the bone structure underneath. Those are the features we recognize."

Carl growled. "How long does that take?"

Lyle shrugged. "Normally it doesn't happen at all—you'll keep your same bone cells all your life if they don't get injured. They don't replace themselves like skin cells. But if something tells your body to regrow them, like an injury or some kind of . . . insane hand lotion, a healthy adult can fully rebuild bone tissue in about six weeks."

"Pedro did it in four," said Sunny.

"This process is very aggressive," said Lyle, nodding. "That's why most of the subjects—the ones who had to make major changes in order to align with my body type—have experienced flulike symptoms and dehydration. Your body's using water and raw materials at an incredible rate; that's not a comfortable process."

Kerry paled further. "My wife has the flu."

Lyle paused. "I'm very sorry."

"She's a woman, though," said Kerry, "does that mean it'll happen differently?"

"Are you not listening to me?" Lyle snapped. "Your wife has my DNA! She's turning into me, dammit, she's turning into a man!"

Carl swore.

"No!" shouted Kerry, jumping to his feet. "You're wrong—there's got to be another explanation!"

"You want proof?" Lyle cried, striding to his chair. He opened his briefcase and pulled out a thick file, slamming it onto the table. "This is the autopsy report for Jon Ford—he had Susan Howell's estrogen levels, he had her ovaries, and if he'd lived another week he'd have had one of the best pairs of breasts in New York."

Kerry stared at the wall in horror. "Carrie's going to be . . . a man?"

"At least her name will still work," said Jeffrey.

"How does it kill?" asked Carl. "What kind of damage are we looking at?"

"The only immediate danger is blood type," said Lyle. "I have O negative blood, which they call a 'universal donor'—it's not ideal for everybody, but it can be given to anybody without serious consequences. Everyone turning into me is probably fine—"

"There's nothing fine about it!" shouted Kerry.

"I mean physically." Lyle stopped, stammered, and corrected himself. "I mean they won't die. I don't have any genetic diseases, and I don't have a dangerous blood type. Aside from the heterochromia I'm as genetically average as you can get. But if the lotion gets imprinted on someone else, I don't know what's going to happen."

"*Can* it imprint on someone else?" asked Sunny. "I mean, how does it work, exactly?"

"I don't know how it works," said Lyle. "I'm still trying to piece it all together. Jon Ford was the first case, and he turned into Susan; the lotion he used came from a new sample bottle I made in my lab, completely untouched until Susan squirted it into the trays for the testers."

"So Susan imprinted it when she passed it out like that?"

"She can't have," said Cynthia, "or the others would have turned into her instead of Lyle."

"After she passed out the lotion, she scooped it off of Jon Ford's tray with her fingers and applied it to his hands directly," said Lyle. "She touched it first, but his was the only lotion she touched."

"She's not allowed to do that," said Sunny. "We have clean procedures—"

"Of course she's not supposed to do it," snarled Kerry. "I think we're past the point where that matters!"

"The rest of the test subjects didn't start showing symptoms until weeks later, so they were probably affected at the follow-up visit." Lyle frowned. "But they were using clean samples applied directly to their trays. We never touched the lotion, so I don't know how—" Lyle's eyes went wide. "The plant. Those samples came from the plant, from the big batch we made as a test run. I went out to check on it, and Jerry showed me around, and I . . ." Lyle exhaled sharply, like he'd been punched in the stomach. "I touched the whole batch. I stuck my fingers right into it to test the viscosity."

"You're not supposed to do that!" Sunny repeated. "Why do we have clean procedures if nobody's going to follow them?"

"The entire batch is imprinted on me," said Lyle. "Everything that's come out of it, every bottle we've filled, has my DNA. We have no idea how many of the plant workers have touched it—I know Jerry did, at least. He drizzled some on his fingers right after I sampled it."

"I'll call the plant," said Marcus, pulling out his cell phone. The executives watched him in hushed silence. "Hi, this is Marcus Eads from corporate. May I please speak with Jerry Maldonado?" Pause. Marcus looked at Cynthia. "He's out sick? A flu? Yeah, that's going around. Tell me, do you have any other employees from the chemical floor who are out with the flu? Or anything else?" Pause. "Can you please e-mail me a full list? Thank you." He hung up. "Jerry's out, and three others. They think it's just a bug going around."

"It might *be* just a bug going around," said Cynthia. "We need to know for sure exactly how many people are affected."

"I'll visit them all in person," said Marcus, opening the door. "What do you want me to do if they're . . . Lyle?"

"Make sure they stay inside," said Carl, "and don't let anybody see them. Give them paid leave, give them bonuses—whatever it takes to keep them quiet. We'll figure something out."

Marcus nodded and left. The rest sat in silence. Lyle shifted uncomfortably, drained and frightened.

"Obviously we have to destroy it," said Cynthia.

"Obviously," said Lyle.

"It's too dangerous," said Sunny, "it's an out-and-out chemical weapon. I suppose that means I lied to the cops this morning."

"No one will ever know," said Carl. "We destroy the lotion and we hide all the evidence—Kerry, I want a plan for spin control; we need to tamp down leaks, we need a way to find and stop any leaks that get out—"

"Is there any unimprinted lotion left?" asked Kerry abruptly.

"What?" asked Lyle. "Why on earth would you want more?"

"To save my wife," said Kerry. "She's turning into a man—into Lyle, no less. No offense, Lyle, but . . ." He sat forward, pleading with the others. "If you can just give me a tiny bit of blank lotion, just a tiny bit, I could find something with her DNA—a hairbrush, maybe—and imprint it, and turn her back into herself. I won't even ask to save myself, just please let me save Carrie."

The room was silent.

Jeffrey laughed softly.

"Shut up, Jeffrey!" Kerry shouted. "Why are you even here, you worthless idiot!"

"Sorry," said Jeffrey, "I was just thinking. I was just wondering if she's hot."

"What the hell kind of question is that?"

"I was just thinking," said Jeffrey, "if you're going to turn her into somebody, you may as well turn her into somebody hot, right?" He paused, looking at a room of shocked faces. "I mean, look at these posters on the walls—face models, bikini models, all long legs and nice racks and . . . well, come on, I can't be the only one who thinks about this, right? They're gorgeous, that's why we take their pictures in the first place. So I'm just saying, if you're going to turn your wife back into a woman, why not . . . turn her into one of them? That redhead by the

window, maybe—or that Asian girl from the moisturizer ads."
He laughed again. "That's just what I was thinking, though. It's
nothing. I'm sorry I said anything."

The world seemed to tilt on its axis.

"Interesting," said Cynthia.

"Oh no," said Lyle, shaking his head, "no no no no no. Absolutely out of the question."

"It's kind of . . . the ultimate beauty product," said Sunny.

"This is completely wrong," said Lyle. "It's immoral, it's
illegal—"

"It's just like cosmetic surgery, really," said Kerry. "You pay
money, we give you a new body. It's like my wife's nose job last
year, only . . . easier."

"It's not just a nose," said Lyle, "it's your entire body—it's your
identity! We can't ask people to give up their own identity!"

"We don't have to ask," said Cynthia, "they're going to be
begging us."

"It's wrong—"

"Oh, grow up!" Cynthia snarled. "This is our business, Lyle:
people give us money, and we make them look like somebody else.
People want to look good, Lyle—they want to be beautiful! Look
at the redhead Jeffrey pointed out—that photo's on one of our hair
dye boxes. Not just her hair, her entire face. And the women who
buy that hair dye don't just want her hair, they want her cheekbones and her nose and everything else. That's the illusion that
makes advertising work—that a product will change who you are.
Nobody buys hair dye because they like their hair; nobody goes
to a plastic surgeon because they love themselves for who they are.
So get off your high horse and start acting like you know your
job!"

"But I—" Lyle stammered.

"You've been in this industry for twenty years, Lyle, don't pretend this isn't the same thing you've done every single day of it."

Lyle closed his mouth, stunned. *That's not true.*

Is it?

"All we need is a tiny vial of ReBirth," said Kerry. "Pedro turned into a six-foot gringo with just a tiny sample, right? So we barely need any to make it work. We fix my wife and then we fix everybody else. You want to look like the model on the box? NewYew can do it—just pick the age and the size and we'll make it happen, and we'll even give you the perfect hair color to go with it. Like a bonus prize in the same package!"

"Of course all our models would have to have O negative blood," said Sunny, "for safety reasons."

"Don't pretend like this is safe," said Lyle.

"And they would need perfect skin," said Cynthia. "No more futzing around with oily and flaky and combination formulas— you just rub on some lotion and your skin is perfect, right down to a genetic level."

"But you'd need the models' permission," said Lyle, "and there's no way any of them would give it."

"For enough money they'll give us anything we want," said Cynthia. "Just ask Jeffrey."

Jeffrey turned red.

"It's illegal," Lyle insisted, searching for anything he could think of to stop them. "The FDA wouldn't give ReBirth a second look back when it was just a moisturizer. You think they're going to allow it now that it clones people? Are you insane? The first advertisement that goes out is going to get this entire company seized by the government—and we can't rely on the secondary marketing plan you came up with before, because the only way to sell this is to tell people exactly what it does. This is not just some boring technology nobody needs to know about— the technology is the whole story. We can't not tell people what it does, but if we do tell people we could be charged with . . . I don't know, war crimes for all I know. Bioterrorism."

"We'll go offshore," said Sunny simply. "The company, the manufacturing, the whole deal, and then we just import it. There are virtually no restrictions on lotion imports under current law—we could flood the country with it."

"But we still couldn't sell it," cried Lyle. "We'll bring it in and they'll seize it all and we'll be right back where we started!"

"Except the price would go through the roof," said Cynthia. "This could fetch hundreds of dollars a bottle, maybe thousands, and that's when it's legal. Think what a black market would do for it."

"You're talking about running drugs," said Lyle.

Cynthia's face grew cruel. "We are talking about running everything. This is not just a beauty product, this is *the* beauty product. Anyone who uses it—anyone, bar none—will look like a model. Cosmetic surgery is the most common category of surgery in this nation, maybe in the world, and now we can do it in two seconds with no pain, no surgery, and no complications— just rub on some lotion, drink a lot of fluids, wait four weeks. You thought the market for the old formula was going to be big? This new version won't just outsell our competitors, it will make them obsolete—there will be no reason for anyone to ever buy from anyone else again. ReBirth is going to buy us the world."

Lyle swallowed. "It's too easy to misuse," he said lamely. He was running out of arguments. "You put the wrong lotion on one morning and suddenly you're accidentally someone else."

"Every cosmetic product has a safety warning," said Sunny. "We'd just make this one . . . stricter."

"And it would work for men, too," said Kerry. "I'm already excited to try it—on purpose, I mean. For every woman out there who wants to look like Angelina Jolie, there's a man who wants to look like Brad Pitt."

"What about . . . ," Lyle shook his head. "I can't believe we're even talking about this."

"We need unimprinted lotion," said Carl. "All we have for sure is Lyle lotion, and nobody wants to be Lyle. Lyle doesn't even want to be Lyle."

Cynthia looked at him. "Do you have any?"

"I won't give it to you," said Lyle, straightening up. "You want to clone the world, you do it without me."

"Then what about your little girlfriend?" asked Cynthia. "The one in the hospital? She's already turning into you; if you destroy ReBirth, there's no way to save her."

Lyle went pale.

"Is there any blank lotion?" she repeated.

Three bottles, Lyle thought, *sitting right on my desk. But I can't give it to them. What they're planning is wrong—it's not just wrong, it's stupid and dangerous and illegal. It's evil.*

But . . . Susan.

Lyle looked at Cynthia—really stared at her, examining her in detail. Not her face, but her mind. *She's horrifying,* he thought. *A person like her should never have access to this kind of power. But that's always the way: scientists invent the future, but accountants control it. I can't let her have ReBirth. I can't let any of them have it.*

But can I even stop them? Lyle looked around, glancing at the door as casually as he could, hoping they didn't see it; hoping they didn't guess what he was thinking. *I could run, but then what? If I run to my office they'll stop me from leaving the building, and if I leave the building instead they'll just search my office and find the lotion. They'll get it either way; they're offering me a chance to save my job. To save Susan. Isn't it better that I stay? Isn't it better to be here, where I can watch them and keep things under control? It's just like when the lotion got stolen—it's better to help NewYew get it out first than to let some unknown criminal have it—*

Lyle swore. "The theft last month—whoever stole it has this technology."

Everyone swore.

"What was in the stolen bottles?" Cynthia asked, rising quickly. "Was it you, or was it blank?"

"I'm not sure," said Lyle, "I don't remember—I have to check."

"Then go!" shouted Carl. "Don't just stand there like an idiot!"

"We save Susan," said Lyle, not moving an inch. "Whatever else you do—whatever else *we* do—we save Susan first."

"Of course," said Cynthia. "All we need is her untainted DNA."

"We can go to her house," said Lyle, standing up, "we can ask her roommate for something of hers—a hairbrush, like Kerry said, or a—"

"Nobody can know," said Carl. "We'll save Susan, but we'll do it in secret."

Lyle nodded. "The blank lotion's in my office."

14

"Good," said Carl, nodding at the slide show. Kerry was presenting new product ideas for ReBirth, and Carl nodded again, as giddy as Lyle had ever seen him. "I like it. What else?"

"I think you'll really be pleased with this one," said Kerry, walking to the computer. He looked more like Lyle every day. His wife had already found new DNA to change herself, but Kerry was waiting. He was still trying to decide who he wanted to be.

They'd put ReBirth on hold after the theft, unsure what the thieves were planning to do and how they should respond to it. Now all such concerns were gone: a moisturizer they could delay, but a DNA overwriter was too big to take any chances with. They were pushing forward as fast as they could, hoping to launch on the first of July. There was too much money at stake, and the executives were going wild.

Kerry tapped a key on the laptop and the slide changed to show another row of images, mock-ups of hypothetical product, each bearing the image of a buxom woman. "Breast augmentation," said Kerry, grinning like a maniac. "Boob jobs in a bottle! We identify a range of models with our standard quality baseline—good skin, attractive, O negative blood, et cetera—but specifically calibrated in a full range of breast sizes. You want to be bigger, smaller, perkier, whatever, we can do it in one application: no surgery, no stress, and no judgment."

Carl nodded, and looked at Lyle. "Will this work?"

Lyle threw up his hands. "We'd have to be incredibly careful to make sure our models are all naturally beautiful—the lotion doesn't copy your body, it copies the genes that produced your body, which means our customers are never going to be getting exactly what's on the box. Models with breast implants are right out, obviously, but that's not the only way these women have artificially altered their bodies. What about exercise? Models tend to have excellent metabolisms, prone to good health and limited weight gain, and yes, our DNA lotion can copy that, but they also have strict daily regimens of diet and exercise. Pedro and the others looked like me because I don't do anything to change my body, but these models do—their look is half genes and half very hard work. ReBirth can't just give that to someone."

"So we start selling exercise equipment," said Kerry, pulling out a pen and jotting down the idea. "We could sell fitness kits: some ReBirth, some weights, and a Pilates program all rolled into one package. 'An exercise program designed to make your body beautiful, and a body designed to make your exercise as effective as possible.'"

"That's a step in the right direction," said Lyle, "but there's so many other ways to use this technology to help people. If we can give people a healthy metabolism, why not take it all the way and give them a healthy heart? Healthy kidneys? Let's find people with good bones and strong circulation and imprint *that*—give our customers a way to improve their actual lives instead of just their appearance."

"Never sell a cure when you can sell a treatment," said Cynthia. "A magical lotion that protects you from heart disease is great for you, but then what do we sell you in the next fiscal quarter? How do we keep our business growing? We need something temporary and/or disposable."

"I've got just what you're looking for," said Kerry, tapping the keyboard. The slide changed to show a glamorous couple on the streets of Paris, the Eiffel Tower shining brilliantly in the background. "Fantasy kits," said Kerry, barely controlling his excitement. "Ma and Pa Kettle from Nowheresville, Wisconsin, decide they want a vacation, something really special like an anniversary, so they buy this kit and rub on the lotion and *bam!* Suddenly they're young, dashing sophisticates on a weeklong cruise on the French Riviera. And here's the kicker: each fantasy kit includes a couple of bottles of blank lotion, so they can imprint themselves first, and then when they're done with the high life they go back to Nowheresville and put on the 'them' lotion and turn back into themselves. They get the best of both worlds, and when they're ready for another fantasy they come right back to us and buy another one."

"I love it," said Cynthia. "It would be even better if we could do it with actual celebrities."

"Can we get celebrities?" asked Kerry.

"Only the ones desperate for attention," said Sunny.

"And those are never the ones you want," said Jeffrey.

Carl looked at Lyle. "Will it work?"

"It's biologically feasible, yes," said Lyle, "but do we really want to sell unimprinted lotion? That could get out of hand incredibly quickly—it's like giving the gun to the retarded kid."

"Wow," said Sunny. "I thought *we* were crossing the sensitivity line."

"It's an old science fiction story," said Lyle. "You know the one I'm talking about, right? Nobody?"

"Some of us had dates in college," said Kerry.

"There's a scientist who invents a death ray or whatever, and his friend tries to convince him not to tell anyone, and the guy insists he's just there to make the science, and he's not responsible for what anybody else does with it. So the friend gives the scientist's mentally disabled son a handgun, like as an object lesson."

Sunny raised his eyebrow. "What kind of sick bastard gives a mentally disabled child a handgun?"

"That's exactly my point!" said Lyle. "You can't just give someone a power they don't understand and then say it's not your fault when they hurt someone with it. If we give people blank ReBirth, we are giving them a power they can't possibly hope to control. I don't even think we can control it."

"So let me get this straight," said Cynthia. "You think our customers are mentally retarded?"

"It's a metaphor."

"It doesn't matter," said Sunny, "because we're already on it. The standard retail model is too uncontrollable, like you said, so Carl had me working on alternatives all night." He glanced around the room. "This is jumping the agenda by a couple of bullet points, but Carl's approved the plan so we may as well announce it: we're building our own clinics. Just a few at first, in some of the major cities, which incidentally gives us a period of limited supply where we can boost the price due to heightened demand. Instead of buying this stuff at Walmart you come in to a private NewYew center, make an appointment, and a trained professional oversees the whole procedure under the safest possible conditions."

"We'll need to contract a new design team for the look and feel of the clinics," said Kerry. "Something as classy as possible, to justify the prices we're going to charge."

"I like it," said Cynthia. She looked at Lyle. "Does that mollify you?"

Lyle nodded, grudgingly. "I have to admit that yes, clinics are a very good idea. The tighter we can control this substance, the better."

Carl nodded sagely. "The clinics give us higher visibility, as well, which doubles as advertising. Sunny's team is already shopping for high-profile locations we can buy."

Lyle raised his eyebrow. "You want to ask if this is scientifically feasible, as well, or can I object on some other grounds?"

"Please, Lyle," said Cynthia, her voice mocking. "Tell us all the things we're doing wrong."

"You need to get off your damn high horse," growled Carl.

"You think you know better than everyone else in the room—you think you are better. You're as deep in this as everyone else: you keep telling us we're evil for thinking of product ideas, but so far you've signed off on every single one of them. You could turn us in to the cops in a heartbeat—you've got more than enough evidence to get us all locked away for the rest of our lives—and yet you haven't done or said a thing. You want to protest, but not enough to actually stop us. Just enough to mollify your conscience and still get the payout at the end."

"I'm here because you promised to help Susan," said Lyle.

"And your part in that plan," said Sunny, "is to modify her DNA without her knowledge or consent. The morally murkiest part of this entire project."

"It's the only way," said Lyle. "That doesn't mean I'm happy about it."

"Of course you're happy about it," said Cynthia. "Because you get to make a decision for somebody else." Her eyes were cold. "Because you always know better."

Lyle felt queasy. *This is wrong,* he thought, then grumbled and closed his eyes. *But it's also right. I think? I'm trying to save Susan, I just wish we didn't have to be so . . . invasive about it.* He looked at the other executives, softly discussing the theft and their plans and their horrifying line of ReBirth products. *They're the reason,* he thought. *We're not robbing Susan's home to save her, we're robbing it to protect them—so they can come out of this fiasco clean, and sell their products and make their zillions of dollars. If I wasn't stuck with them I could really help people. I could get out there and use this product for good. It rewrites your genes, for crying out loud: we could completely abolish genetic diseases. Don't they care about that? We could be world-saving heroes, but all we're doing is making them rich. And we still don't know who stole it, or what they've got planned for it—*

Lyle stopped, frozen.

We don't know who stole it. He looked around the room. *They don't know who stole it. We're all on pins and needles, waiting to see*

where the lotion surfaces, but until it does . . . they don't know any-
thing.

So if it turns up somewhere good—a hospital, for example, using it
to save lives—they'll assume it was part of that original theft. If I can
sneak a blank sample, I can give it to someone who'll us it properly, and
the original theft will cover my tracks.

Lyle smiled. *They want to work in secret? It's time I had a secret of*
my own.

15

Susan looked horrible; her face was dull and thick, her body covered in bandages and bristling with needles and sensors. Her skin was discolored and ill-fitting—tight in some places, sagging in others, like a set of clothes made for somebody else. She'd been unconscious for nearly four full days. Lyle checked her pulse: faint, but steady.

The hospital still thought it was leprosy—some new, devastating strain that their standard treatments couldn't solve. Lyle had talked to the doctors, trying to learn everything he could, and while the hospital had noticed a rise in her testosterone he was fairly certain they didn't suspect she was changing gender. He glanced up at Sunny and Cynthia. "Are we ready?"

Cynthia nodded grimly, pulling out a bottle of ReBirth. "How does this work?"

"Is that blank?"

"Of course it is."

"You're sure?" asked Lyle. "This isn't going to do any good if it's already imprinted on someone else."

"It's one of the same samples we took from your office," she said. "No one's touched the lotion. We haven't even opened the bottle."

Lyle nodded. "All right, then, let's get this over with." He wheeled the bedside table from the wall to Susan, and pulled on a pair of disposable gloves. "Give it to me."

Cynthia handed him the bottle; he wiped it down carefully and set it on the table. He reached into the pocket of his suit coat and pulled out two plastic bags: a large one with a Styrofoam sample tray, and a smaller one containing a dull white powder. He set the tray on the table and picked up the powder bag, examining it carefully.

"That's Susan's skin?" asked Sunny.

"They're called epithelials," said Lyle, nodding. "Relatively large pieces of skin, recovered from a pedicure kit our thief found in her bathroom."

"How does this work?" asked Cynthia.

"You've got me," said Lyle. "I'm pretty certain what's going to happen when I do this, but I still don't know how or why."

"You're going to imprint the lotion with Susan's DNA," said Cynthia, watching his face, "which will turn it into some kind of . . . magical Susan lotion."

Lyle laughed drily. "That's the idea. I think it's the retrovirus."

"You said the retrovirus was supposed to prevent this from happening."

"Yes, but it's the only explanation I can think of. Retroviruses are designed to read DNA—that's what makes them so good at regulating plasmids, which is why we put them in there in the first place. They attach to a strand, read it, and decide if it's doing what it's supposed to be doing." He opened the bag gingerly, and poured the dull powder onto the sample tray. "I think the retrovirus in ReBirth is not just reading the DNA but remembering it, and then somehow forcing all the future DNA it encounters to match that initial template."

"Can it do that?" Sunny asked.

"No." Lyle shook his head. "No, it can't. Retroviruses transfer information, but they don't store it. It should be impossible." He poked at the powder with a gloved finger. "And yet it works, consistently and predictably." He picked up the bottle. "Are you ready?"

"Stop asking and just do it," Cynthia snapped.

"Okay, okay," said Lyle, "it's just . . . Okay, I'll do it." He popped open the plastic cap. *This can imprint on anything,* he thought. *This much of it, all in one place, could overwrite the DNA of everyone in this hospital. Be very, very careful.* He tipped it over the tray and squeezed gently, holding his breath while a thick blob of creamy white lotion oozed out onto the skin rubbings. He squirted out a pea-sized drop, then carefully closed the lid and slipped the bottle into his pocket.

"This is when it's dangerous," said Lyle. They both stepped back. "It's reading Susan's DNA and . . . doing whatever it does to imprint it. If you touch it now, you'll be Susan inside of four weeks."

"I'm not getting anywhere near it," said Cynthia, taking another step back. Sunny moved with her. "You're the one who has to apply it."

Lyle watched the drop of lotion, some terrified, primal part of him expecting it to start slithering across the table. Obviously it didn't.

"How long does it take?" asked Cynthia.

Lyle shrugged. "I have no idea. We know from the way it's behaved in the past that a DNA contact in one part of a lotion sample will eventually spread to the entire sample, so obviously the information is being transferred from one . . . thing . . . to another. Again, probably the retroviruses." He reached out with a gloved fingertip and stirred it gently, rubbing the lotion around in the skin cells. "Do you realize how frightening this is? How stupid we're being?"

"Don't start this again."

"We don't know how this works," said Lyle, "but we're selling it to every John Q. Public with a credit card. In two months this will be in our clinics all over the country—all over the world—and yet here we are, the people who made it, and we're almost too scared to breathe." He picked up the tray with his clean hand, still stirring with his other, and stepped toward Susan. "Ready?"

Sunny and Cynthia nodded.

Lyle scooped the lotion onto two gloved fingers, reached out, and slowly rubbed the lotion onto Susan's chest, just above the sternum. One of the areas most visibly affected by her "disease." He massaged the spot for a few seconds until the lotion was completely absorbed, and then stepped back.

"Done."

"Good," said Cynthia, and gestured toward the red hazmat container on the wall. "Now for the love of all that's holy, put that stuff away—do you want to kill us?"

Lyle gestured toward the plastic bag the tray had come in, keeping his hands away from everything. "Open it for me."

Cynthia looked at Lyle, then handed the bag to Sunny. "Open it for him."

"Are you kidding? What if he gets some on me?"

"Just open it!" Lyle snapped. Sunny opened the bag wide, keeping his fingers far away from the mouth of it, and winced as Lyle slid the sample tray into it. Lyle used his clean glove to peel off his contaminated glove, being careful not to let the lotion touch any skin, and dropped it in the bag. He carefully removed the other glove, sealed the bag closed, and placed the entire thing in the hazmat container.

"Well done," said Cynthia. "Time for the next phase. Have you talked to Marcus?"

"He's on the move," said Sunny. "We have a few of them already."

"A few of who?" asked Lyle.

"Loose ends," said Cynthia, scrolling through her messages. "Your friend Pedro and all of our other security leaks are taking a vacation overseas."

"Voluntarily?"

"For now."

"So we're kidnapping people?" asked Lyle. "How low are we going to go?"

"We can't just turn them back the way we turned Susan back," said Sunny, "because they, unlike her, know it was the lotion that did it. Several of them have already stated an intent to sue the company. NewYew could break in half. Then instead of us controlling ReBirth you'd have no one at all, or worse yet someone like Pedro."

"I'm starting to think that would be better," said Lyle.

"Just step lightly," said Cynthia, narrowing her eyes. "Now that we have the blank lotion, and the means to make more, you're a lot less important than you think you are. Don't make us send you on vacation with them."

They opened the door and walked into the hall. Lyle followed them slowly, his feet heavy, his breaths deep and hungry.

I have to stop this, he thought. He patted the bottle in his pocket. *I have the lotion, and I have my plan, and all I have to do is follow it. Just take the lotion to a doctor and tell them how it works. Get the lotion out there where someone can use it for good, and chop the legs out from under all these sinister master plans.*

Not here, though. No corporation can have it, not even a hospital. I'll take it to a charity, where money will never enter into it, and tell them everything. Someone who'll use it to help the world instead of himself.

All I have to find is a good man.

16

220 DAYS TO THE END OF THE WORLD

Lyle hurried through the darkness, clutching the bottle of ReBirth tightly in his hands. The lid was taped shut, and the bottle was sealed in a plastic bag, and then the whole thing was sealed inside another bag, but he was still worried. This was not a part of the city he liked visiting during the day, let alone at night. *One bad mistake,* he thought, *one stupid accident—anything from a mugger to a slip on the sidewalk—and I'm ruined.*

He slowed without stopping, checking the address he'd scribbled on a piece of paper. He was close; just one more block. He heard footsteps in an alley and voices on the other side of the street; he was practically running now.

Where is it?

And then there it was—a simple storefront, humble but well maintained, with the words YEMAYA FOUNDATION painted across the glass in large letters. There was a light on in the back. Lyle jogged to the door, tried it, then knocked loudly when it didn't open. He glanced around nervously, seeing thieves and killers in every shadow. A figure moved inside the building, coming toward the door, and Lyle swallowed, holding his breath in a panic.

A tall man opened the door, long haired but clean shaven, wearing a brightly colored dashiki shirt. The stranger spoke in a warm, deep voice. "Are you the man I talked to on the phone?"

"Yes," said Lyle, pushing the stranger back as he rushed through

the door. "I'm sorry I couldn't give you my name, but . . .
well, it's a very long story."

"Don't be afraid," said the tall man. "We are all brothers." He
made some kind of gesture with his hands, then closed and
locked the door. "Please join me in the back. I've prepared some
rooibos tea; it will help calm your nerves."

"Um, thank you," said Lyle, following the man.

It had been unsurprisingly difficult to find a charity willing
to accept an unidentified medicinal substance, especially since
Lyle had refused to give his name to any of them, or to explain
where the substance had come from or what it did. Secrecy was
too important, and he didn't want to share too much information until he was 100 percent sure he'd found the right place.

He desperately hoped the Yemaya Foundation was the right
place, because at this point it was pretty much the only place left.

"Are you Dr. Halley?" Lyle asked.

The man nodded. "I use that name for legal purposes only;
please call me Kuvam."

"Dr. Kuvam, I can't thank you enough for—"

The man stopped, turned, and shook his head. "'Doctor' is
too limiting. I prefer 'guru.'" He led Lyle into the back room,
lit not by electric lights but by some kind of oil lamps. The walls
were hung with brightly colored fabrics edged with tassels,
and there was no furniture. Kuvam gestured at the floor, covered
with exotic pillows and homespun blankets in fierce orange and
blue. A small Bunsen burner sat in the center of the blankets,
heating a clay pot suspended above it. Lyle paled at the fire haz-
ard, and stepped carefully around it.

"You are a doctor, though, right?" Lyle asked. He smiled
nervously and sat on one of the pillows, hesitantly, as if expecting them to burst into flames. Or insects. He looked closer at
Kuvam and saw, in the light, that he was tanned and leathery,
like a man raised in the wilderness. "I mean, you are a licensed
medical doctor?"

"Of western medicine, yes," said Kuvam, "and of many more

besides. I've studied acupuncture in the mountains of central China, and lived for five years in the jungles of the Amazon learning their deepest, most powerful herbal secrets. They called me White Fingers, and taught me how to speak with my ancestors."

"That's . . . great," said Lyle. "What kind of medicine do you practice, exactly?"

"The Yemaya Foundation is dedicated not simply to wellness but to wholeness." He gestured as he spoke, making circles and waves with his hands. "True wholeness comes not from the individual but from everything—from our interaction as a society, and our integration as cells in the vast organism of Earth. My name, Kuvam, means 'Sun,' and it is through the sun that we gain life and power, yet it is only through us that the sun gains light and power. We call this bioluminescence—life creating light." He picked up the clay teapot and poured Lyle a bowl of red, sharp-scented liquid. "Your light is very weak. Drink."

Lyle accepted the bowl delicately. *What on earth have I gotten myself into?*

Kuvam lounged back casually on the pillows, his face breaking into a wise, fatherly smile. "I can see that you're not convinced. Know then that I studied medicine first at Harvard, and then at Johns Hopkins. For ten years in that hospital I tended the sick as a resident internist, not merely healing but teaching so that others might heal, as well. On the day my financial debts were paid in full I left and began a new life, a greater life, as a student of the world. My western education was inherently narrow, blinded as we are by our faith in observable science, but if those are the credentials that move you, then I do not deny them."

Lyle nodded. As much as he hated to admit it, a man like Kuvam might be the only person he could safely give the lotion to: a man with a solid medical background, capable of understanding ReBirth's potential, but at the same time loose enough and liberal enough to share that potential with everyone. Mastering western medicine gave Kuvam the first credential, and turning his back on it gave him the second. *The third point in Kuvam's favor,* Lyle mused, *is his overwhelming ridiculousness. No one will believe that he created this technology. When I finally have a chance to stand up and take credit for ReBirth, the world will be ready to accept me.* "Thank you," said Lyle. "I'm sorry for interrogating you like this, but I need to know that you'll understand what I want to give you."

"Indeed," said Kuvam. "I suppose that depends on what it is."

"This is where it gets strange," said Lyle, setting down his bowl of tea and pulling the well-wrapped lotion from his pocket. "I work for a company that . . . well, you're going to know who they are sooner or later no matter what I do, successful or not, but for now I think it's safer for you—legally—not to know. Plausible deniability. So I work for them, as a scientist, and a few months ago I invented—well, I should say it was mostly an accident—but I invented a technology that turned out to be incredibly powerful. World-changingly powerful. The medical potential alone is . . . well, it's staggering, it's completely mind-blowing, but all this company wants to do with it is make money, and . . ." He looked at Kuvam, eyes pleading. "I need a Robin Hood."

Kuvam nodded. "You need someone who can bring this technology to the common man."

"Yes," said Lyle, "but it's more than that. You're already more or less okay about stealing this, so I hope you won't balk when I say that the technology itself is illegal—we've broken the law even by testing it, let alone trying to sell it. But once it comes out and people see what it can do, we think everyone's going to want it so much they'll just go with it and look the other way— or they'll shut us down and we can make our zillions selling it like an illegal drug. Which is horrible, in so many ways, but it gives us an opportunity—a tiny little crack of a window of an opportunity where you and I might be able to make this work. You see, because there's no chance the government would ever approve this product in advance, we haven't taken any steps to protect it in advance. Not legal protection, I mean. And now another company—we don't know who—has stolen it, so the race is on, and whoever gets it to market first wins: they'll have the only binding evidence of origination, which means they'll get the patent and the exclusivity and the legal right to sell it for whatever they want. Instead of curing diseases it'll end up in resort salons, giving breast enhancements to millionaires' girl-friends, and the people who need it—the poor people, the sick people—will never see a drop. But if you can find a way to use this technology in a big, public way, saving lives the way it really, morally needs to be used, you can kill their exclusivity. If it comes from a charity group like yours it won't be owned by a corpora-tion, and anyone will be able to sell it to anyone."

Kuvam stared at Lyle, sipping a bowl of tea. Lyle waited for an answer, but Kuvam simply stared.

"I . . . ," said Lyle, "I don't know what you—"

"Tell me what it does," said Kuvam.

Lyle shrugged, looking at the wrapped bottle in his hands and laughing. "I know this sounds impossible, but . . . it overwrites DNA."

Kuvam raised an eyebrow.

"Right now it's blank, but as soon as it touches human tissue it will read the DNA and imprint itself with that pattern. Then whoever touches it after that will be 'infected' with that DNA. That's really the only word for it. The new DNA would spread from cell to cell, changing the genetic makeup to match, say, my DNA instead of yours. You'd still be you—you'd have your own personality and your memories and all of that—but you'd also be me. Sort of. You'd be you, but in an exact copy of my body."

Kuvam was silent again, his brow furrowed in thought. Lyle let him think, hoping he would understand. *Will he freak out? Will he accuse me of lying? Even if he believes me, will he see the potential for healing, or will he get caught up by the prospect of money?*

Kuvam nodded slowly. "So if I have a congenital disease, and I use lotion imprinted on someone who does not, I would then be free of that disease."

"Exactly," said Lyle, relieved to hear him grasp the idea so quickly. "You won't be you anymore, but you won't be sick and dying, either."

"What about extra mass?"

"Sloughed away or excreted as waste," said Lyle. "One of our . . . accidental tests was a woman, and as the gene shift took effect her body simply rejected everything that didn't match the new template—she lost her hips, she lost her breasts, she lost so much tissue the hospital thought it was leprosy."

"In that case," said Kuvam, "it should also cure cancer."

Lyle straightened, staring.

"Cancer cells would be overwritten," Kuvam continued, "returned to their original, healthy state, and the tumors would be rejected by the body as remnants of a foreign template."

Lyle leaned forward, eager and excited. "Yes! Yes! This is exactly what I'm talking about—a cheap, accessible cure for cancer. I told you this could change the world!"

"What does it do for age?" asked Kuvam.

Lyle frowned slightly. "Why would it do anything for age?"

Kuvam smiled. "Embracing the truths of natural healing does not mean that I have abandoned the truths of modern science. I have many former colleagues on the cutting edge of medical research." He sat up straighter, leaning forward. "Your biological age is determined not by chronology but by the expression of your genes—they exist in different states during the different stages of your life. As a child your DNA told you to grow, to form neural connections, to lose your infant teeth; when you reached puberty those same expressions of DNA changed, and started telling your voice to deepen, your facial hair to grow, your sexual organs to mature. In your thirties your metabolism changed, giving you that slight paunch around the middle, and in your fifties it will change again, and again in your sixties, and on and on until you die. We assume that our body ages over time, but in fact our body ages only because our genes tell it that it must."

Lyle whispered. "You didn't learn that in the jungles of the Amazon."

Kuvam nodded sagely.

"But that would mean . . ." Lyle sat back, losing his balance and almost falling off his pillow. He glanced nervously at the Bunsen burner and continued. "If age is carried genetically, then . . ." He held up the bottle, feeling cold and lost and small. His voice was a whisper. "What is this going to do?"

"It's going to save us," said Kuvam, reaching out to take the bottle from Lyle. Lyle resisted feebly, but Kuvam pulled it from him with surprising strength. "With this we shall eliminate not just illness but age; not just disease but death itself." He held the bottle up, examining it reverently. "With this we shall usher mankind into a new and enlightened era."

Lyle stared at the bottle, its plastic wrapping bright in the lamplight. *This is it,* he thought. *I grab it and run, or I let this lotion loose upon the world.* He looked at Kuvam. *Do I trust him?* He grimaced. *Do I have any other choice?* The guru's supply wouldn't last long, but it didn't have to—all he had to do was get it out there so no one else could own it, and the free market would take it from there. *Even if he does something crazy with it, we'll only have to deal with him for a week or two and then the damage will be done and ReBirth will be public domain.*

Lyle cleared his throat. "Will you do it? Will you help people with it?"

Kuvam nodded. "I accept this charge humbly, my friend." He cocked his head, still staring at the bottle. "What do you call it?"

Lyle whispered, "ReBirth."

Kuvam smiled. "Of course."

PART TWO
MAKEOVER

17

NEWSCASTER: We take you live this morning to the Regional
Cancer Center in Trenton, New Jersey, for continuing coverage of what doctors are calling a medical miracle. Donna
Pickett has spent the last seven years in a vicious battle with
breast cancer, becoming something of a celebrity last month
when she publicly rejected modern medicine in favor of naturopathic treatment. Still unable to leave her bed in the cancer
center, she brought in an alternative doctor named Guru Kuvam and began some kind of treatment with him. Last night
the story took a surprising—indeed, a shocking—turn, when
Donna awoke from her latest bout of cancer symptoms not
only healed, but seemingly decades younger. In many ways, the
sixty-year-old woman is the spitting image of her twenty-
eight-year-old daughter, Melissa.

DOCTOR: I don't know what to say. After seven years of cancer
and chemotherapy Donna was a shell—she was bald, she was
frail, her skin was damaged. She looked like she'd been living
on the streets, or in a desert. Now . . . well, I don't know what
to tell you. If she hadn't been in our hospital, connected to
our machines, I wouldn't believe this is even her. I still don't
know if I do believe it, because it's not just the cancer: I performed her mastectomy myself, four years ago, and yet . . .
well, look at her. They grew back. It's like Donna disappeared
and Melissa's long-lost twin showed up, except Melissa doesn't

have a twin. That's really Donna. I . . . I don't know what to say.

MELISSA: I'm just so happy to have my mother back—just so, so, happy. It's like she's been given a new life, a new start. I can't thank the Yemaya Foundation enough for giving us this incredible chance.

NEWSCASTER: The Yemaya Foundation itself, and its mysterious Guru Kuvam, may be the most interesting facet of this bizarre story. Originally a medical charity based in a crumbling Manhattan neighborhood, the Yemaya Foundation has recently turned into something of a New Age religion.

KUVAM: What you see in Donna Pickett is not merely new health but new life—literally a new body to replace her old one. Through the love of her daughter, and through her own efforts at self-healing and mind-body communion, Donna has been born again, and through her example we, too, can achieve our highest standards of human perfection. [Kuvam holds up a small plastic bottle.] This is the secret—a special lotion that is nothing less than a secular reincarnation. Through this, we have the power to shed our forms and gain new strength—new life—in each step of our immortal cycle. We must take this as a sign, a message not from gods but from our own selves, our collective consciousness, that the next step is not just for Donna but for the entire human race. Set aside the things of the past, and set your eyes not on our limits but on our potential. Today is the first day of the new human race.

18

"Bastard," said Cynthia, staring at the TV. "Pig-brained, half-witted, self-righteous little bastard."

"He can't be the one who stole it," said Jeffrey. He looked around at the other executives. "Can he?"

"We need to kill him," said Cynthia. "We need to rip his lying lips right off his tree-hugging face and shove them down his throat."

"We're not sunk yet," said Kerry, absently stroking his biceps. He'd searched for weeks for a new body—something to replace Lyle's unwanted DNA—and finally settled on an Italian underwear model. "I know it looks bad, but everything has a good marketing angle. We just have to find it." Kerry's new body was nearly seven feet tall, with a naturally fast metabolism and a genetic predisposition for lean, well-defined muscle. His wife had become a half-black, half-Korean bodybuilder with full lips and rich brown skin. Lyle still had no idea what they'd paid for the DNA, or how they'd convinced the models to sell in the first place. He had visions of them locked up in the company's new headquarters on São Tomé, imprisoned with the rest of the security leaks.

That's where I'll go if I'm not careful, he thought. *Or maybe Cynthia will gut me first and hang me from her office window.*

"A good angle?" asked Cynthia. "We just lost the race to the market—we can't get a patent, we can't get exclusivity, we can't get anything. Find a good angle in that."

"We can still turn this our way," Kerry insisted. "Even if this guy popularizes the lotion, we're still in the best position to supply the lotion. He's practically doing us a favor."

He moves differently, thought Lyle, watching Kerry closely. *It's the same Kerry, thinking the same old thoughts in the same old way, but he moves like a completely different person—different muscles moving different bones, rotating against each other with a completely different set of joints. He's . . . smoother than Kerry used to be. More flowing. Changing his body has changed the way he interfaces with the world.*

How will that change his brain?

"We need to find him," said Cynthia, "and figure out how he got our product, and then we need to make him regret it with every breath he takes."

"We don't even know it's our product," said Jeffrey. "It's probably just a passing thing with this lady—the cancer went into remission or whatever, so she cleaned herself up and they call it a miracle."

"Mastectomies don't go into remission," said Sunny. "This is definitely our product."

"You need to stop moping about what went wrong and start looking for what went right," said Kerry, flexing slightly. "We have our own hospital girl, for one thing: why can't we just use that?"

"Because it's come and gone," said Sunny. "We cured her, sure, but nobody knows it was us because we were trying to be so careful. And now she's been released from the hospital and it's old news. Besides, all we did was heal a sick girl, and people do that all the time. This guy brought a cancer patient back from the brink of death, with a twenty-year-old body to boot."

"We gave Susan a twenty-year-old body," said Kerry.

"Nineteen," said Lyle. "Those epithelials were older than we thought."

"You're looking at this wrong," said Carl, his giant face filling the screen on the wall. He was in São Tomé, overseeing the establishment of the new headquarters, and was attending the meeting through a webcam. "This guru isn't competition, he's free advertising. Thanks to him every cancer patient in the world wants our product."

"I told you to focus on health," said Lyle.

"Lyle has a point," said Kerry. "All of our applications are cosmetic, and this guy's saving lives—we look kind of shallow in comparison."

"I think you missed the point of my point," said Lyle.

"It's all in the presentation," said Carl, "and we have a month to make them work. I want every presentation at the launch event to focus on the 'whole body health' aspects of the product, and I want all the press releases rewritten to reflect the same kind of touchy-feely crap."

"It's too late to change the products and the packaging," said Cynthia.

"We don't want to change those," said Carl. "Those are going to the clinics, and those are just stores, and in stores people make decisions based on good old-fashioned self-interest—we tell them a product will make them beautiful and they buy it. All we're changing are the press releases, to make sure we look just as altruistic as this hippie Kuvam."

"We have to start running the commercials now," said Kerry. "We made them vague for legal reasons, and now that might work in our favor—people might see them and think the cancer cure was connected to us, which we will never confirm, of course, but if they think it that's a point in our favor."

"That's only jumping the gun by two weeks," said Sunny. "I say we do it."

"Is that too far before the launch?" asked Cynthia. "We need this launch to be huge."

"We have a whole month to think of something huge," said Sunny. "I think we need something as big as this cancer lady— bigger, if we can do it—so we can announce it a day or two before and tell people there's more news coming at the NewYew mystery event."

"We have four weeks until then," said Cynthia, nodding. "That gives us just enough time for the lotion to have full effect. Any ideas?"

"Another disease would be good," said Kerry, "people are eating that up with this cancer lady."

"And she has to be hot," said Jeffrey.

"Attractiveness will definitely help," said Sunny, "and the age thing is another good one. This Guru Kuvam hit all three major selling points with his cancer girl; he really knew what he was doing."

"Maybe we should stop trying to change the direction of the cancer lady stunt," said Cynthia, "and simply change the scale."

Lyle raised an eyebrow. "What, like we take an even older woman, with a worse disease, and make her even younger and healthier?"

"Think bigger," said Kerry. "Guru Kuvam healed one woman. Why don't we heal the whole cancer center?"

"We'll never get permission from everybody," said Sunny, "plus we'd need willing DNA donors, and then the patients would have to agree to that, too. We don't have time to arrange even half of that."

"I've got it," said Jeffrey, scrolling through something on his phone. "We'd lose the hot chick angle, though I guess the mom's kind of hot, but check this out: there were two twins born last month, two little girls, and one's completely healthy and the other's on life support: she was born with one kidney, one lung, no liver, and only half a heart. Family's going to pull the plug tomorrow."

"Unless we get to them first," said Kerry eagerly. "We turn the sick girl into a clone of the healthy one, we put their little faces up on the screen, and we tug on every heartstring in the country. Saving an old lady in Jersey is one thing, but saving a cute little baby is something everyone can get behind."

"The family might say no," said Sunny.

"We'll take over their hospital expenses," said Cynthia.

"More importantly," said Lyle, glancing sidelong at Cynthia, "we'd be saving their daughter's life. That's kind of a big deal to us normal humans."

"How could they say no?" asked Sunny. "The babies are identical twins, so they're already clones of each other; we'd just be fixing a . . . manufacturing error."

"Just don't present it to them that way," said Kerry. "Maybe we'd better let me do the talking."

"Whatever you do, do it now," said Carl. "We don't have much time to prepare for this, and apparently we have new competitors popping up almost every day." He picked up his phone. "While you work on that, I'm going to call Marcus and figure out who leaked our product to Kuvam." Carl narrowed his eyes. "And when I find him, I'm going to let Cynthia kill him with a pair of pliers."

19

Lyle put down his pen and rubbed his eyes; they felt raw and red from overuse. There was no time for his regular job anymore—all he did, for hours every day, was trawl through page after page of genetic tests and medical histories in search of congenital weaknesses. If ReBirth was to be loosed upon the world, the least he could do was make sure they were selling clean DNA.

It was the kind of work Susan would have been ideal for: long and slow and detail oriented, exactly the kind of thing you hire an intern for in the first place. As far as Lyle could tell Susan was still a "guest" in São Tomé, but he had no idea what that entailed. It drove him mad not knowing, but he couldn't spare the time to do anything about it; there were only three weeks left until the launch of ReBirth, and he had stack after stack of small-print DNA results to examine. Saving the entire population from a deadly drug was more important, at the moment, than saving one girl from a vacation.

Lyle looked back at the printout in front of him, poring over the genetic charts, but his eyes watered from fatigue, and he blinked the tears away. He was too tired, and his eyes were too strained; he'd been working since five in the morning, almost sixteen hours ago. He pushed his chair back and stood up squinting and rubbing his eyes. He could start again in the morning.

He walked to the elevator, wracked with doubts. *Am I doing the right thing? No. Definitely not. But am I doing the best thing I can, given the situation? I didn't want it to get this far, but I made a little compromise here and a concession there and now we're filling hundreds of thousands of bottles of ReBirth, which we're planning to sell illegally, and Susan's been kidnapped and a dozen other people with her and I think I helped start some kind of a cult. I didn't mean to.*

Heh. I wonder if the judge will accept that in court. "I'm sorry I broke a dozen laws and endangered millions of lives. I didn't mean to." He stepped out onto the sidewalk with a slow, resigned sigh.

The night sky was clear, and the streets were still warm. The subway entrance was just a block away, but Lyle stopped on the sidewalk and stared up, wondering. *What are Pedro and Christopher Page and all the others doing right now? They look like me, but do they really? What if they eat better, or exercise more, or get more sun—are they healthier than I am? Are they more handsome? What about their clothes? I don't know what looks good and what doesn't, and I haven't really dressed all that well since that girl in college helped me shop for clothes . . . what was her name? Paula? I liked Paula. I think I loved her, but she never loved me back. I've never known how to be in a relationship. It's a skill I never learned . . . but the other Lyles have it, or some of them, at least. Somewhere out there is a version of me that dresses better, looks better, and has a girlfriend. He probably has a wife and children. He definitely makes better choices.*

If I'm not the best me, who is? And what am I supposed to be instead?

A limousine pulled up to the curb, right next to Lyle, and the back door swung open.

"Dr. Fontanelle, please join us."

Lyle peered inside the dark limo; there were several figures, but their faces were shadowed. "Who are you?"

"Your brothers."

"I don't have any brothers."

"Brothers in mind," said the voice from the car. Two men stepped up behind Lyle—strong men with grim faces and iron grips. They had his arms almost before he knew they were there, and it was too late to run. They pushed him firmly toward the car.

"What do you want?" asked Lyle, bracing himself on the sides of the doorway. "Show me who you are."

"I told you," said the voice, "we are your brothers." The mysterious speaker pressed a button to bring up the lights, and Lyle gasped in shock: the back of the limo was full of five people, all identical.

All Lyle.

Lyle's own face smiled at him coldly. "Now get in the car."

Lyle was too shocked to resist; the big men pushed him through the door and he fell onto the seat, clutching it desperately, righting himself and staring at their faces in horror.

"But," said Lyle, "you're all gone!"

The other Lyle raised his eyebrow. "You know about us?"

"You're the . . ." But no; the men in São Tomé knew fully well that Lyle knew about them. These weren't the test subjects, and they weren't the factory workers. *Who else had the lotion?*

The answer came as quickly as the question: *These are the thieves.*

The men outside closed the door with a thump, and the limo pulled away into the street; Lyle looked up just in time to see another copy of himself standing on the sidewalk, clipping on his security badge. He checked his belt and found the badge missing—they'd stolen it from him when they pushed him into the car.

"You're the ones who stole the lotion," he said.

"I take it from the vagueness of your accusation," said the lead Lyle, "that you don't know any more than that."

Lyle shook his head.

"We've been watching you with some interest, Doctor. You and the rest of your company. When you abducted our contact we thought you'd discovered us, but it seems our fears were unfounded. For a company in possession of such power, you're far less dangerous than we'd expected."

"Your contact?" asked Lyle. "What are you talking about—

we didn't abduct any—" He stopped. *We* have *abducted people,* he corrected himself. *Everyone accidentally affected by the lotion: the test subjects, the plant workers, and now Susan. One of them was a contact for the thieves? Which one?*

"You're an excellent scientist, Dr. Fontanelle," said the lead Lyle. "As you can see, we've all sampled your product and found it extremely compelling. There is a use for a thing like this— many uses, few of them legal. All of them powerful."

"What do you want?"

"Isn't it obvious, Doctor? We want Igdrocil."

Lyle looked back at him, wondering what, if anything, his expression gave away. Igdrocil was the imaginary herbal ingredient Sunny and Kerry had dreamed up for the label; it was their shorthand way of saying "the part that overwrites your DNA," without coming right out and saying it, or even understanding it. Igdrocil was what made the lotion work.

Lyle just had no idea what it was.

"You want to make your own lotion," said Lyle.

The man nodded. "Being you is a profound experience, but hardly the most useful thing in the world. All we can really do as you is replace you, which we have now done, but our sources tell us you have very little power or freedom in the NewYew hierarchy these days. Even Jeffrey, the great embarrassment, has more say in the boardroom than you."

"How do you know all this?"

"Because we look exactly like you, and because we are not idiots." The man glowered; Lyle had never seen his own face look so frightening. "If we can go anywhere you go, and talk to anyone you talk to, we would have to be extremely incompetent not to have a fairly good idea of exactly what you're doing, and when, and why. More importantly, we have much grander plans to pursue, and much grander people to impersonate."

Lyle swallowed. "The president?"

"Eventually, yes, though presidential power is mostly ceremonial. But the director of the CIA, perhaps? Or Senator Moore, the special liaison to the Department of Homeland Security? These are positions with real, immediate power, which can help us cement our position for the future." He smiled. "I assure you that we have thought this through very, very carefully."

Lyle's mind reeled, thinking about the terrifying ramifications of such a plot, but he had more pressing concerns. He forced himself back to the present—back to the stony faces of his five solemn kidnappers. Maybe he could talk his way out of this? "You're right," he said, "I'm practically a figurehead these days—I don't know what you expect to accomplish by replacing me."

"They must keep you around for something."

Lyle shrugged, surprised to find himself nearly overwhelmed with emotion. "I think they just don't trust me to leave. Plus they still don't understand the science."

"Do you understand it, Dr. Fontanelle?"

Lyle shook his head. "I know what it does, and I think I know how, but I still haven't figured out why." He looked around the limo. "You don't understand it, either, do you? You definitely didn't understand it when you stole it, or you wouldn't have turned into me. I'm guessing you used it by accident the first time—" He stopped abruptly, staring at the lead Lyle. "But now it's been weeks, and you still look like me. You stole the formula when you stole the lotion: you can make your own." He looked around in confusion. "Why are you still me?"

The lead Lyle frowned. "We have an older formula: 14G."

"14G is the final," said Lyle. "We haven't changed it since then—the active ingredients are exactly the same as what we're putting in stores next month."

"That can't be," the man hissed. "We've tried it a hundred times—a thousand times! You think we want to spend our lives as you?"

"Have you kept it clean during manufacture?" asked Lyle. "Have you kept it away from your own DNA? Did you imprint it properly?"

"Yes, of course!" the man shouted. "We know all of that—we've been listening in on you for weeks, dammit, we know how it works! But it's not working!"

"That's what my replacement is doing," said Lyle, "isn't he? He's going through my files in person to try to figure it out."

"Your replacement is going to get us blank lotion from the manufacturing plant," said Evil Lyle. "It's a temporary measure, but we have plans that can't wait any longer. He's also going to look for the latest formula, though if what you say is true he's not going to find anything."

"It's true, I swear it."

"No matter," said Evil Lyle. "That's why we have you."

Lyle nodded; he'd been expecting this ever since they'd shoved him into the car. "You want me to make you more."

"It would certainly be easier than stealing it from NewYew every time we need it."

"But I don't know how," said Lyle. "When we make it in our plant it works fine, but if you can't make it work, then I understand even less about the lotion than I did when you shoved me into the car. There's no reason for ReBirth to do what it's doing."

"I don't care *why* it works," said Evil Lyle, "I just want it to work!"

"But 'why' is the most important part," said Lyle. "I can't make it do something unless I know why it does it. That's like asking me to repair an engine without knowing anything about combustion or electricity."

"Which in this analogy are chemistry and genetics," the man growled. "You know all about chemistry and genetics!"

"Not for ReBirth," said Lyle. "The engine was a bad analogy: let's say instead that combustion and electricity are the principles that should work but don't. ReBirth is like opening the hood of a car and finding the engine replaced by a rock, or an alligator. It's obviously functioning on some kind of scientific principle, because it's predictable, but until I know what that principle is I can't do anything to fix it."

The limo was silent; the five men stared at him, and Lyle forced himself not to squirm under their gaze. *They're weighing me,* he thought. *Like a worm right before it gets stabbed with a hook.*

The lead Lyle looked at the others, face solemn, then back at Lyle. "You will simply have to do your best."

"And if I still can't figure it out?"

Evil Lyle reached into his suit coat and pulled out a gun. "No one will even know that you are missing."

"Fine," said Lyle, putting out his hand to stall them. "I . . . need my lab."

"We've prepared a lab for you."

"My notes," said Lyle, "my equipment—"

Evil Lyle shook his head. "Our agent can get everything you need out of your office."

Lyle eyed the gun, searching for a way out. Even if he escaped, he couldn't just go to Carl and the board—as soon as they found out there were other copies of him, loose and with nefarious plans, they'd pack him off to São Tomé for "containment." Part of him didn't mind that—it longed for it, in fact. It would be an end to his troubles, an end to his fears, just a lifetime of blissful house arrest in a tropical paradise, lounging on a beach with Susan . . . and nine or ten other copies of himself. No. He wouldn't do it—it wasn't worth it. Even without the other Lyles, he knew he couldn't just sit there doing nothing while this technology—*his* technology— was used and abused by one misguided group after another.

Lyle looked at the other Lyle, at all five of them. "Okay," he said, "I'll help. I need to figure it out anyway, and if you're really willing to give me the support I need, you're my best chance of doing it." He looked out the window. "Where's your lab?"

"We're here," said the lead Lyle, and the car pulled to a stop.

"Here in Manhattan?" Lyle frowned. "We've only gone a couple of blocks."

Another pair of burly thugs stepped up to the doors and opened them. "Welcome to your new home," said Evil Lyle. "You're the new chief scientist at Ibis Cosmetics."

20

Susan Howell was a prisoner—there was no other word for it. They were treating her nicely enough, with plenty of food and a fairly luxurious room, but that didn't mean anything. A room you can't leave, no matter how nice, is a prison, and the person trapped inside was a prisoner.

She had one window, and she'd tried getting out that way, but it was barred from the outside. Looking out between the bars she could see a wide, green lawn, ringed by giant maple trees— sugar maples, by the look of them; her parents had several in their yard on Long Island. Was this Long Island? She'd been unconscious when they brought her here, and they'd told her it was a tropical island, but what kind of tropical island had sugar maples? And it smelled like Long Island: hydrangeas and sea salt and money. This was definitely Long Island, and fairly far east. The Hamptons, maybe. She'd grown up in the Hamptons, with her one-percenter parents. She'd know it anywhere. But who kept people prisoner in the Hamptons?

It didn't matter what they were doing, and it didn't matter why. She was a prisoner, and she hated it.

When the time came, she would destroy them.

An hour after dinner the door opened again, revealing one of the thugs—a tall, thickset man with receding hair and a coiled wire behind his ear. His name was Larry, or at least she thought it was—he had a twin somewhere in the house, as well, and she couldn't be sure which one this was. She'd seen them together once, and was so surprised to discover there were two of them that she couldn't help but ask why they'd both gone into the evil corporate thug business. They'd scowled and refused to answer, so she assumed it was a touchy subject—which only made it more intriguing.

Larry gestured to her, beckoning her to the hallway, and her eyes widened in surprise.

"A trip outside my room? What's the special occasion?"

"Hurry, please."

"You're talkative today." Susan slid off the bed and walked to the door. "Is this exercise time, or something? Take me out in the yard, let me lift some weights, maybe get a prison tattoo?"

"Meeting," said the thug. "That way." He pointed down the hall, and Susan stifled her disappointment.

The thug led her into a large room, filled with couches and chairs and little tables with vases on them. It was also filled with people, and Susan instantly recognized some of them: there was Cynthia Mummer, the CFO at NewYew; there was Sun-He the lawyer, and Jeffrey the president, and . . . there was Cynthia again, and . . . there she was again, and . . .

"What on earth?" said Susan.

"Ah," said one of the Cynthias, "our final guest has arrived. Please, Ms. Howell, have a seat."

Susan looked around the room in shock, counting in her head: *Three, four, five . . . five Cynthias. Four Sun-Hes. Two, three, four Jeffreys. Most of them look as shocked as I am. What's going on?*

And where's Lyle?

"Please," said the same Cynthia who had spoken before. She didn't look frightened like the others; she looked calm and cool and in charge. "Have a seat, Ms. Howell, and I'll explain everything."

Susan stared at the woman, weighing the risks of punching her in the face, but decided it wasn't worth it—all five of the thick-necked thugs were here, and it looked like they'd brought a few friends. . . . *Wait.* She looked at the thugs again, suddenly aware of similarities she'd never noticed before: Larry the thug wasn't just a twin, he was an octuplet. What was going on?

Susan opened her mouth, shut it, and took a step toward the nearest sofa. One of the other Cynthia Mummers was sitting on it, and Susan stopped, balking at the idea of sitting next to her. *Who are they? What's going on?* The thug who'd brought her shoved Susan down onto the sofa, and she shivered at the close proximity to the unsettling doppelgänger.

"Sure," said the Cynthia on the sofa, "you get the hottie and I get this. I can barely stand to look at myself."

Susan stared at her. "Ms. Mummer?"

"Is that her name?" The Cynthia raised an eyebrow. "Interesting. No, my name's Tony. Tony Hicks." She stuck out her hand. "Nice to meet you. I hope you're making good use of that body."

"All right," said First Cynthia, standing in the middle of the room. She was definitely the one in charge. "Let's get started."

Susan looked around the room and noted all the exits: two large windows, two hallways, and a door in the back. All were being guarded by thugs.

"For many of you," said First Cynthia, "this is the first time you've seen the others. It may come as a shock, though presumably not as shocking as the first time you realized your body was changing into someone else. I'm here to explain what that change means, and to make you an offer." She held up a small plastic bottle; Susan recognized it from the lab at work. "How many of you have seen this before?"

Some of the people tentatively raised their hands, including the Tony/Cynthia on the sofa next to her. Susan didn't move, refusing to play along, but she identified the bottle immediately as Lyle's new antiaging lotion.

And Tony Hicks . . . , she thought. *I know that name. . . . He was one of the men in the lotion test.*

Is that what this is about?

"This is a bottle of ReBirth," said First Cynthia, "NewYew's newest product and, to be frank, a technological wonder the likes of which the world has never seen before. Through various circumstances, some accidental and some not, each of you has been exposed to ReBirth, and it has altered your DNA to turn you into somebody else. The exception, of course, is Ms. Susan Howell, who started turning into someone else and was instead turned back into herself."

"That's your real body?" asked Tony/Cynthia. "Wow." She scooted closer. "You, uh . . . busy later?"

Susan grimaced and scooted away.

"On July third," First Cynthia continued, "just a few weeks away, NewYew will be launching ReBirth as part of a massive global event. It's going to revolutionize the beauty industry and, as I'm sure you can guess from personal experience, the entire world. It can replace a person's entire body with a new one— one that's younger, healthier, more attractive. Age and illness will be a thing of the past. ReBirth will usher in a world where race and appearance are no longer barriers but a means of personal expression. Imagine a world where biological prejudice is not only absent but completely meaningless. How many of you would like to help that world become a reality?"

One of the Sun-Hes raised his hand. "Are you going to let us go or not?"

"Straight to the point," said First Cynthia, flashing a practiced smile. "Let's say we did let you go: where would you go *to*? Back to your family, to try in vain to convince them you're you instead of me? Back to your jobs, which you can't prove are actually yours? You're not yourselves anymore; letting you go would be, perhaps, the cruelest thing we could do."

Susan exhaled sharply. "So you're locking us up because you're nice? Listen, lady, we're not that stupid—we know when we're being screwed, and right now you are definitely screwing us. Let's drop the act, okay?"

First Cynthia studied her, frowning, then raised an eyebrow and nodded. "All right then, let's put this in very simple terms. You look like us because you are our insurance policy. ReBirth is a revolution, and revolutions are rarely peaceful, and while many of our executives have moved overseas some of us will be required to stay behind and oversee the launch event. There's a strong chance that in doing so we will be arrested."

Susan's jaw dropped. "You want us to go to jail in your place?"

"Exactly the opposite," said First Cynthia. "If you choose to help us, and follow our plan, none of us will go to jail at all."

"Why would we help you, though?" asked Susan. "You've kidnapped us, you've locked us up here, you've . . . done some kind of crazy crap to our bodies. I'm the only one here who's still me, and I hate you—I can't imagine what the unwilling post-op Tony must be feeling. We should be throwing you in jail, not helping you stay out of it."

"Valid points," said First Cynthia. "And I suppose it is possible that some of you might actually want to hurt us instead of help us. But that's only because you haven't heard my offer yet." She held up the bottle again and looked around the room. "Let's start with a dose of ReBirth, completely pure. You've seen what it can do—it changes your entire body, from the inside out, into anyone you imprint it with. Give us the help we need, and you'll have your very own sample to imprint on any body you want."

Tony/Cynthia leaned forward, suddenly interested; Susan glanced to the side and saw several more of the clones perk up to attention.

One of the Jeffreys shook his head. "Are you kidding? You think you can just reset us back to the way we were and pretend this never happened?"

"I'm not talking about resetting you," said First Cynthia. "The unfortunate truth is that getting your old body back is probably impossible at this stage—though the presence of Ms. Howell is, of course, proof that it can be done."

"Wait," said Susan, finally sorting through the confusion. "Is that how you cured my leprosy? You turned me into a . . . clone of myself?"

"Technically, yes," said First Cynthia. "We even turned you into a younger clone of yourself. That body is only nineteen years old."

Tony/Cynthia gave her an appraising look, and smiled lecherously. Susan gagged and scooted farther away.

"Think of it," said First Cynthia, turning back to the main group. "With this lotion you can turn yourself into *anyone* you want—anyone at all. Tall, short, black, white, male, female, there's literally no limit. You want to play for the NBA? You want to be a supermodel? You can do it—you can do anything you want."

"No," said Susan. "This is wrong."

First Cynthia laughed coldly. "You're a lot more like Lyle than I expected. Did he rub off on you, or did you rub off on him?" She smiled harshly. "Or was it just general rubbing?"

Tony/Cynthia snickered, and Susan felt her face grow hot. "You can't do this to people," she said. "You can't take them away and lock them in a prison and then bribe them with their own bodies to help you do something even worse."

"That's easy for you to say," said Cynthia, "but like you said, you're the only one here who's still herself. What about the guy next to you?" She pointed at Tony/Cynthia. "You think he likes being a bony old witch like me? You think he likes being a woman at all? Ask him how much he wants to change—ask him what he'd do for a chance to start over."

Susan looked at Tony/Cynthia; he/she fidgeted in the sofa, frowning.

"This is wrong," Susan told him/her. "No matter what you get out of it, it's wrong."

"Don't decide yet," said First Cynthia, "because I'm about to sweeten the deal." She reached in her jacket pocket and pulled out a stack of cash. "In addition to your new body and the new life that comes with it, each and every one of you will receive a cool million dollars."

Excited murmurs filled the room; Susan heard Tony/Cynthia mutter, "Now we're talking."

"One million dollars," First Cynthia repeated, "in cash. You can go anywhere, do anything, be anyone. And in return, all you have to do is stay here for two, maybe three weeks; eat our food, and pretend to be us. It's as simple as that."

Tony/Cynthia raised his/her hand. "I'm in." Several more people raised their hands in agreement. "We're all in."

"But what about me?" Susan asked. "Are you going to turn me into one of . . . you? And what about Dr. Fontanelle—I notice there aren't any copies of him. Is he one of the ones that's already fled the country?"

Did he even try to help me?

"He's still here," said First Cynthia. "But he doesn't need protection. He's the one who created ReBirth—the government won't lock him up, they'll try to use him. But thanks to you, they won't get anything out of him."

Susan glared at her. "So I'm a hostage."

"Lyle is attached to you, Ms. Howell; it is a hopeless, brainless infatuation. And so as long as we have you, he will never work against us."

21

Ibis had prepared not just a lab for Lyle, but an apartment. He had state-of-the-art equipment, most of it new; he had a bed, a kitchenette, a sitting room, and a bathroom amply stocked with Ibis shampoos and cleansers and moisturizers. They made his skin feel tight—the pH balance was off. The lab itself was brimming with state-of-the-art equipment, most of it so new he still had to calibrate it, and they gave him an ample budget to acquire any item or ingredient he needed—assuming, of course, that his request passed the scrutiny of the Cabal of Evil Lyles. The minifridge was neatly stacked with soda pop and beer. The CEO's personal secretary had been instructed to order in any food he wanted to eat, since his phone would only call her. Even the lightbulbs were new.

He had everything he could possibly need, but nothing that he actually wanted.

Lyle had spent the weekend examining Ibis's records of their failed attempts to re-create ReBirth. Each batch had been meticulously catalogued by a man named Abraham Decker, who seemed to be Ibis's chief scientist, and he had done good work. The ingredients had been followed exactly, the measurements were precise, and even the order in which the ingredients had been combined had been followed exactly, even for the inactive ingredients that shouldn't have had any impact on the function of the product. The records were like the scriptures of a cargo cult, faithfully following every meaningless ritual they could think of in the desperate hope that something, anything, would work. Nothing had. Each batch was the same as the last: a wonderful moisturizer with a regenerative effect on wrinkles and burns and scars, but no DNA copying in sight. The later batches started varying the rituals in carefully calibrated ways, trying slightly different measurements or slightly different procedures, but none had been successful. The mystery behind it all, the Igdrocil—the thing that made ReBirth work—wasn't working.

If only I knew what Igdrocil was, thought Lyle. *The retrovirus is the only new ingredient in 14G; the batches before that didn't copy DNA, and the batches after that did. I always assumed they had to be the culprit. But Ibis's batches with the retrovirus were completely inert.* Ibis even used the same supplier, Rock Canyon Labs, but it still didn't work.

Lyle read the Rock Canyon documentation again just to be sure everything was the same, though he'd read it a hundred times already. The sole purpose of the retrovirus was to regulate the function of the plasmids—they could work on their own, but if they worked too much the retrovirus would shut them down. It was their only function. So it didn't make sense that the retrovirus would be causing the copying, and now, thanks to Ibis, Lyle had proof that it wasn't. It had to be something else. But what?

It was 8:10 a.m. Lyle called the secretary, his only allowed contact. "Hello, Mr. Sachs," she said. It was the code name they'd given him, to help keep his presence a secret. "How may I help you this morning?"

"I need to talk to Abraham Decker."

"I'm afraid he's unavailable at the moment, can I take a message?"

"Do you know when he'll be back?"

"I'm afraid he's unavailable," she repeated. "I'd be happy to take a message, and Decker will call you at his earliest convenience."

"I don't know what you think I'm doing in here—"

"I've been fully briefed, Mr. Sachs."

"—but I can't do it without the right information. Decker's papers are great and all, but I need to talk to the man himself."

"I assure you that I will pass that message along as soon as I can," said the receptionist. "Is there anything else I can do for you?"

Lyle grit his teeth, growling in frustration. He looked around the laboratory, as if searching for something else to force her to do, just as punishment. He closed his eyes instead, sighing. "Breakfast would be great—fresh fruit, yogurt, the good probiotic stuff." He breathed deeply. "And an assistant. I've got a lot of work to do."

"I'll pass that request along to Mr. Brady. Is there anything else?"

"That'll be fine, thanks." He hung up the phone with a resigned slump of his shoulders, put his hands on his hips, and stared at the lab. "We've looked at everything that's *supposed* to be in the lotion," he said out loud. "Maybe Igdrocil is something else—something that's not supposed to be there at all, that's not on the ingredients list or anything else." He nodded. "The best way to figure out what that might have been is to re-create my own lab as closely as possible, make a batch myself, and see if it gives me any ideas." He looked around again, realized he didn't remember his own office layout with the kind of specificity he needed, and frowned. After a moment he picked up the phone.

"Hello, Mr. Sachs, is there something else I can do for you?"

"I need to talk to your double agent," said Lyle. "Whoever's in my real office back in NewYew."

"As I told you before, Mr. Sachs, Mr. Decker is not available at the moment."

Lyle stopped in surprise. "Wait—you mean Decker is the one who replaced me? He's the one in my office?"

The secretary paused, the silence stretching out to the point of discomfort. "I'm sorry, sir, I'll have to call you back." She hung up, leaving Lyle once again alone.

22

"There's been another robbery," said Sunny.

Abraham Decker looked up from Lyle Fontanelle's desk. *Don't look at the filing cabinet. Don't look at the filing cabinet.* "A robbery? Of ReBirth?"

Sunny nodded. "And another salvo from Kuvam: he's curing a child of cystic fibrosis. A whole group of kids, apparently. It's like he's manufacturing cultists. Carl's called an emergency meeting, but I wanted to talk to you first."

Decker ventured a guess, and tried to sound more certain than he felt. "Have you finally decided to market ReBirth medically?"

"That's part of what I'm here to talk to you about," said Sunny. "You've got to stop fighting this all the time—you've got to stop fighting *us*. Cynthia's already calling for your head."

"But I'm supporting everything," said Decker. He'd only been with NewYew for a few hours, and already his position was in danger of collapsing—not because of his own actions, but because of Lyle's. "I've vetted your genetics reports, I've signed off on all the new product designs; I mean, I'm the one who made the stuff, Sunny. I support you." He worried that he'd overdone it, and backtracked a little to sound like the real Lyle. 'I'm just . . . also suggesting other avenues."

"But it's too much," said Sunny. "You kick and you scratch and you resist us every step of the way, and that's not the kind of behavior that wins you friends. When problems show up, like this new robbery, we look around and take stock of our enemies and you're always on that list. I stand up for you when I can, but . . . you're not making it easy. You've got to calm it down."

"You think I'm the one who stole the lotion," said Decker. This was too soon. He hadn't even stolen anything yet, and they already suspected him—which means they suspected the real Lyle. What had he done that Ibis didn't know about? "I haven't done anything to betray you—I've walked the line the whole way, every time—"

"They already suspect that you were the leak with Guru Kuvam," said Sunny. "And now, with a whole case missing—"

"A whole case?" Decker's blood froze. *I didn't steal a whole case!*

"I'm not saying you took it—"

"I didn't take it," said Decker.

"I'm not saying you did—"

"No, I'm serious," said Decker, "I didn't take it. Was it blank?" Sunny nodded. "Thirty tubes. Sixty ounces."

Decker closed his eyes. "Mother of Mercy. Sixty ounces, loose—worse than loose, they're in the hands of someone with the kind of resources to break in and take whatever they want. Why didn't you—" He stopped himself before saying "Why didn't you tell me someone else was stealing ReBirth?" *I thought we were the only ones—our surveillance didn't indicate that anyone else even knew about the product. What's going on?* He took a breath to recenter himself. "What is someone going to do with sixty ounces of blank ReBirth?"

Sunny shook his head. "I don't . . . Look, Lyle, I don't know who took it. I'm not saying it was you—"

"Yes you are!" said Decker, now even more nervous. His charade as Lyle Fontanelle had just begun, and now it was crumbling before he even had a chance to use it for anything. "You've said three times you don't think it's me—if you really don't think it's me, then why won't you let it drop?"

"Listen, Lyle, I am sticking my neck out for you, okay? I came in here because you're my friend, or you used to be, and I don't know what you're doing but it's stupid, Lyle, it's reckless and its dangerous and it's stupid. They're serious about this, Lyle. You know they have Susan."

Decker sat back in his chair, forcing himself to look . . . not calm, because Lyle was never calm, but . . . not frantic, either. Nervous but not guilty. "What are they going to do?"

"They're not going to do anything, if you start being smart about this. Now, we don't have much time left, but I'm going to leave for the meeting and you'll have a minute or two to do whatever you need to do—I'm not saying you need to do anything, but if you do . . . I don't know. Marcus and his men will be here in about four minutes. If you need to . . ." He stopped. "I don't know. I'll see you at the meeting." He opened the door, stopped, and turned back. "Be smart about this, Lyle."

He left.

Decker sat, motionless, sorting through the implications of the conversation. *They think I stole something—which I did, just not the thing they think I stole. But it doesn't matter what they think I stole because if they find the ones I actually stole I'm as good as dead. If not for Sunny I would be dead—it's good to know Lyle has at least one friend in here.*

It's going to make betraying them so much easier.

Decker walked quickly to the filing cabinet, opening the third drawer and pulling it out as far as it would go. In the back was a small cardboard box with ten small vials of blank ReBirth, half an ounce each. Future shipments would be smaller, but for now these half-ounce vials were being prepped as a launch event bonus: 200 percent more, absolutely free, but only if you buy now. *Buy now.* Decker shook his head. *The size of these vials is really kind of terrifying all on its own. It's simply too much ReBirth to be in any one place.*

He laughed nervously. *I'm even starting to* sound *like Lyle.*

He sat down at his desk, pulled his tape dispenser and tissues within easy reach, and opened the box. The vials glinted in the light—thin glass cylinders with narrow plastic lids. He wrapped each one in tape to keep them sealed, then in tissue paper to keep them from clinking, and then looked down at his socks. Did he dare? Even having them on his desk was frightening; to put them so close to his skin, where a single crack could contaminate him in a heartbeat, was terrifying. They were still blank—that is, they were supposed to be blank—but how could he be sure? What would even happen if he imprinted a new vial—would it carry Lyle's DNA, or Decker's, or some unholy combination of both?

It didn't matter: NewYew had started checking bags, to make sure nobody took any lotion without permission. Hiding the vials was the only way to get them out of the building. He slid each little packet down into his socks, shivering with a sudden cold sweat.

With the last vial safely in place he stood and examined his pants, making sure they hung properly around his calves. The vials were completely hidden. He stepped, testing the way the pants raised and the socks moved; it looked good. *This might work.* He looked at his watch and smiled. *Just in time.*

Decker broke down the thin cardboard box and folded it into a tight wad, hiding it in his pocket—if they searched the office, he didn't want them to find even that. He grabbed Lyle's laptop and phone and left the office, heading down the hall to the elevator. There was no sign of Marcus Eads or the rest of the security team. *And now?* he thought. *Now I play the game, better than Lyle ever played it. Sunny wants a team player, and I can be the best damn team player they've ever seen. I don't care about Lyle's medical hobbyhorse at all—I can drop that in a second, and toe the company line and do exactly what they want. I can be a better Lyle than Lyle was.*

The elevator dinged, not the up light but the down, and when the doors opened Decker looked up, saw the passenger, and froze in midthought. It was Lyle, another Lyle, standing there in the same suit, the same face, the same haircut. Their eyes met— the same eyes—and for just a moment the other Lyle seemed as shocked as he was, and then the doors closed and the other Lyle disappeared again.

Decker stared, frozen in place, and a moment later the elevator opened again. Empty. Decker shivered.

Who else is here? He can't be the real one, and he can't be from Ibis— we don't have anybody else at NewYew right now. It's too big of a risk. The elevator hung open and empty, while Decker's mind roiled in terror. *Does NewYew have other Lyles? Of course not. They didn't even trust the one they had, and all the accidental copies were locked down in São Tomé. Then who could it be?*

Realization dawned just as the elevator doors began to close, and Decker shot out his hand to catch them.

It's the other thief—the one who stole sixty ounces. The other thief is a Lyle.

And I can't expose him without making my own face a liability. They'd never trust another Lyle again.

He stepped into the elevator, hit the button, and turned to face the door. He watched it slide closed, just as the other Lyle had watched it slide closed moments before: the same position, the same clothes, even the same stance. Decker shivered.

Déjà vu.

23

Lyle had mixed twenty-seven batches of ReBirth in the last week. He had followed his recipe; he'd changed his recipe; he'd ignored his recipe completely and freehanded the entire thing. He'd made good lotion every time, but it didn't copy DNA.

After determining that the retrovirus wasn't doing the copying, his next best theory was that the functional lotion had become contaminated with something else, perhaps something in his laboratory at NewYew, and so he had mixed a series of batches (numbers three through twelve) without any of his standard clean protocols—he didn't wash his hands, he didn't keep the tools or beakers clean, he didn't protect the ingredients. On Wednesday a message came through from Abraham Decker containing a full list of the other chemicals and substances present in his laboratory, complete with photos of the laboratory layout. Lyle wanted to talk to Decker in person, but the Ibis Lyles assured him it was too dangerous at the moment; Decker was struggling to maintain his cover, and even sending the lists and photos had put him in danger of discovery. On the weekend, maybe. Lyle buckled down, waited for the weekend, and mixed more batches. Numbers thirteen through twenty-seven were various attempts to re-create specific contaminations from Decker's list of ingredients, trying to see if any of them, or groups of them in combination, could reproduce the accident that had created ReBirth. None of them had.

"What I need to do," said Lyle, "is analyze the lotion in action." He talked to himself all the time now, for there was no one else to talk to. The Ibis Lyles had refused his request for an assistant. "If I could watch it under a microscope, and really see what it's doing and how it's doing it, I might be able to make it work." He reached for the phone to call the secretary, but stopped when he heard the lock on the door click open. Someone was coming in. He looked up and watched himself walk through the door, his own face in his own beige suit.

"Hello, Lyle."

Lyle felt the familiar queasiness that always seemed to hit him when he saw one of his copies. He set down the phone. "Which one are you," he asked. "Brady? That's the CEO, right? Ira Brady?"

"We call him Prime now," said the other Lyle. "Our real names are potentially dangerous these days, and we needed a good way of differentiating who was who."

Lyle raised his eyebrow. "So Brady is Lyle Prime? As in, the first? The original? Shouldn't that be me?"

The other Lyle shrugged. "It's really more of a seniority thing, but . . . there you go. Sorry."

Lyle shook his head, sitting at his desk. "Well, great. First I'm not the only me, and now I'm not even the real me."

"At least you're still you," said the other Lyle. "The rest of us who are you are actually somebody else, from our point of view. You have to admit that's worse."

"You'd think so, but I don't know," said Lyle. "This is still pretty mind-blowingly weird."

The other Lyle walked toward him, extending his hand. "I'm Abraham Decker, by the way. I'm you at Ibis—and that's always how I used to explain it, even before this whole . . . mess. You were the head chemist at NewYew, and one of the best in the business, and I was the head chemist at Ibis—kind of in your shadow, I guess. Now I'm you at NewYew and you're me at Ibis. In a weird sort of way."

Lyle looked at the man's hand and grimaced, feeling another

wave of queasiness. "I'm sorry. No offense, Mr. Decker, honestly, but it's just too strange to shake my own hand."

Decker/Lyle nodded, dropping his hand and backing up toward another desk chair. "I understand completely." He grabbed the chair by the chemical counter, pulled it forward a bit, and sat. "And please, there's no 'mister' necessary, everybody just calls me—well, I was going to say that everybody calls me Decker, but these days everybody calls me Lyle. Even Prime and the others, as part of the charade."

"I'll just call you Decker," said Lyle, smiling ruefully. He knew the man was here to talk about the lotion, to answer the questions Lyle had been pestering Ibis with for days, but now that he was here Lyle saw his chance to ask about other news—about NewYew, and ReBirth, and the world outside. The product launch event was only a few days away. What was really happening out there? "You were finally able to get away from NewYew?" he asked. "They don't have you under surveillance?"

"I've managed to gain a level of trust," said Decker/Lyle, "probably more than you've had in several months, actually."

"They trusted me," said Lyle, though even as he said it he felt a flicker of doubt.

"They're holding your intern hostage," said Decker/Lyle.

"Susan?"

Decker/Lyle nodded. "Everyone knows you had a thing for her, so they're holding her hostage to keep you from talking. Cynthia explained the whole thing to me in a very uncomfortable meeting. You have information that could bring the entire company down, and they don't trust you to keep quiet, so they're using Susan as an . . . insurance policy."

Lyle shook his head; he'd suspected they might try this, but to have it confirmed, and so coldly, was a shock. He looked at Decker/Lyle harshly. "You have to keep quiet. Don't let them hurt her."

"I don't care for her one way or the other," said Decker/Lyle, "that's the irony here. But I do care about their trust, because it's the only way I can get the information and the access that I need."

"So you're playing along."

"All it took was to stop bickering," said Decker/Lyle, shrugging. "I don't attack their ideas the way you did, and every now and then I suggest a few of my own in the same vein. They love me now."

"This just keeps getting better and better," said Lyle, throwing up his hands. "I'm not the only me, I'm not the original me, and now I'm not even the *best* me." He could just imagine this impostor in the boardroom, laughing at Jeffrey's jokes and cheering at each new plan to turn his lotion into vast, heaping piles of illegal profits. *More effective than me, but far, far worse.* "At least I'm not living a lie. Or compromising every principle the real Lyle ever stood for."

Decker/Lyle raised his eyebrow. "You mean scientific advancement?"

"I mean saving lives."

"I told you, I won't let them hurt Susan."

"I'm not talking about Susan," said Lyle, "I'm talking about everyone—saving lives in general."

Decker/Lyle smirked. "When have you ever stood for saving lives?"

Lyle stared at him, his mouth hanging open. "I . . . what do you mean? I've always stood for saving lives."

"Just 'lives' in general?" asked Decker/Lyle. "Is that a charity I'm not familiar with? The Saving Lives Foundation?"

"I mean helping people," said Lyle angrily.

"Well, okay," said Decker/Lyle, "but again: which people? I don't want to be a jerk about this, Dr. Fontanelle, but I've spent years trying to emulate you, first in my own job and now in yours. You've never been involved in any charity organizations, you didn't contribute to any relief efforts or nonprofits in anything more than a token capacity, and even then only when it was your own company's new flavor of the week. Tossing a couple hundred bucks at the Haitian hurricane or the Salvation Army doesn't make 'saving lives' one of your core principles. I've been playing your role . . . accurately."

"My life is not a role."

"It is for me."

Lyle blustered, waving his arms as he searched for the right words. He had always thought of himself as a good man, an honest man, a man who helped his neighbors and did what was right and made the world a better place, but now that he was confronted about it—by himself, no less—he couldn't think of a single example. "I am not . . ." He gave up on examples. "I am a good person."

"I'm not saying you're not."

"I have never stood for *destroying* lives," Lyle said, punctuating his declaration with a point of his finger, as if this was the clinching piece of evidence. "No one can say that I'm a destructive or a bloodthirsty or even a careless person. I help people."

"Not hurting people isn't the same as helping them," said Decker/Lyle.

"But what NewYew is trying to do *will* hurt people," said Lyle. "That's what I'm saying, and that's what you're helping them do, in my name. And in my whole"—he waved his hand over Decker/Lyle—"body."

"That's where I disagree with you," said Decker/Lyle, leaning forward. "They're not going out of their way to help people, no, but they're not hurting anyone, either. They're going to bring an amazing product—your product—to market, and yes, they're going to make a mind-boggling amount of money doing it, but that doesn't make them evil. They're not stealing from anyone, they're not oppressing anyone, they're not even deceiving anyone. They're better than Ibis in a lot of ways, and while I'm only working with them as a ruse, I still feel some pride in what we're doing. You're giving the scientific presentation at the launch next week—well, I mean I am, but it's you. It's both of us, in a way."

"They would never let me speak at an event," said Lyle.

"Not the old you," said Decker/Lyle, "but you said it yourself: I'm better at being you than you are."

All of Lyle's anger and frustration seemed to come together then in a single point, his anger at NewYew for misusing his technology, at Ibis for imprisoning him, at himself for failing twenty-seven times to re-create his own discovery. At this calm-voiced, amoral, fun house–mirror version of himself that twisted his own words and called him a monster. Before he even knew what he was doing he was out of his chair and grasping the evil Lyle by his own lapels, yanking him from his seat, shoving him to the ground, and then he was punching him, smashing his fists into his face— into his own face, except every time he hit the face looked less like his own, mussing its hair, cutting its skin, streaks of blood welling up on its cheek, and suddenly the other Lyle was punching back, his own enemy fist lashing out at his own face, his real face, and felt his brain pulse and thump and rattle as he beat himself senseless. A moment later more hands appeared, bigger and stronger hands, and the Ibis thugs were pulling them apart. Lyle regained his footing, shrugging off the thugs' meaty hands, and when they saw that he was no longer trying to lunge forward they let him go. He stood panting, wiping the blood from his cheek with the cuff of his shirt. The Decker/Lyle stood across from him, wiping blood with the flat of his hand, flanked by a thug of his own. Another Lyle, untouched by the fight, stood in the doorway.

"Are we done with our little tantrum?"

"I don't want to do this anymore," said Lyle, and suddenly he felt like crying. He panted again, gasping for breath. "I don't want to do it."

"Are you Prime?" asked Decker/Lyle. The third Lyle nodded, and Decker/Lyle walked toward him. "I need to get cleaned up. NewYew's touring the Manhattan Center in three hours, prepping for the product launch. I can't show up looking like I've been in a fistfight."

"We'll find some way to cover for you," said Prime, helping

Decker/Lyle to the door. "A fake mugging, maybe, or a fall down the stairs."

"I don't want to do this anymore!" said Lyle again. "Doesn't anyone listen to me? I'm not going to give you ReBirth, I'm not going to live in your little lab, I'm not going to do any of it! The deal's over."

"You didn't come here because of a deal," said Prime. He let Decker/Lyle out, and closed the door again behind him. He looked back at Lyle. "You came here because we brought you here."

"But you can't make me work."

"We can't," said Prime. "But we can offer you incentives not to fail us. As it happens, you've written a very threatening letter to the president."

Lyle felt queasy. "I did?"

Prime nodded. "A very detailed letter, of the kind the FBI loves to follow up on."

"They'll know it's a fake."

"The envelope contains fragments of your hair and epithelials; the handwriting was harder to copy, but it's surprising how much of your movements were already right here in our hands." He held up his hand, turning it slowly from front to back. "Not muscle memory, of course, but simple muscle structure—the size of our fingers, the distance between our knuckles. It changes the way we write, Dr. Fontanelle. It changes us further and further into you. I assume that we also owe you our growing love for brussels sprouts."

"Food preferences aren't genetic," said Lyle.

"Not directly, no," said Prime, "but having your tongue means we have your specific distribution of taste buds—some are larger, some are smaller, certain areas of the tongue have more or less than before. And there's just something about a brussels sprout that . . . really hits that combination just right, doesn't it? A little butter, a little salt, that delectable bitterness buried deep in the leaves."

"Just stop already," said Lyle. "I'm sick of helping every two-faced, money-grubbing, walking conspiracy theory that thinks my hand lotion can rule the world."

"Give us the lotion," said Prime.

"Why don't you just buy some?" asked Lyle. "The launch party's in three days—the stuff's already been shipped to the clinics. Stand in the audience and you might even get a free sample."

"It's not enough to *have* ReBirth," said Prime, "we have to be able to *make* it. That's the only way we can control it, instead of being controlled by NewYew. This isn't just a beauty product, Dr. Fontanelle, it's the greatest weapon of espionage ever created. Instead of being you I could be a senator, a president; my friends and I could be the presidents of every political superpower on earth. NewYew isn't even selling blank lotion; they're keeping it locked up in their clinics, and if we can't make our own we'll have to go into those clinics and take it. Do you want to be responsible for any accidental deaths that might arise from that scenario?"

"That's not how responsibility works," said Lyle.

"Tell that to your guilty conscience when you see the first bodies on the news," said Prime, and his voiced turned to steel "Give us a working formula."

Lyle stared at him, running through a hundred different scenarios. None of them looked good, but one of them had potential. . . .

"So," said Prime. "What is your next step?"

To get out of here, thought Lyle. *To get out of here and run away and ꞁe done with this forever.* He blew out a long breath, and stooped to ᵗck up a chair knocked down in the fight. "I need to analyze the ᵗion—the real lotion—while it's working. I need to watch what ⁱoes, while it does it, and see if I can figure out why."

ᵗAnd what do you need for that?"

ᵗI need a genetics degree, for starters." Lyle shrugged. "Mostly ᵗheed better equipment: better tools, cleaner water. I want to start filtering my own."

Prime nodded. "That's the spirit. Give us a list and we'll get it for you as soon as we can."

"As soon as you can," said Lyle. He breathed heavily, still catching his breath. *Decker is their only chemist, and he's too busy to vet my list for them. They won't see what I'm trying to do. A few days to get the ingredients, and a few more days to get everything ready. . . .*

I just hope I can get out in time.

24

There was one day left; Susan had been counting them. One more day until NewYew unleashed its latest product on the world. One more day until ReBirth would be shipped across the globe.

One more day until the company she used to trust used her as a pawn to exploit the entire nation.

She needed to stop them, and today she had a new plan to escape. She'd tried before, of course—she'd tried almost every day—but they'd stopped her every time, and she was growing increasingly desperate. They'd removed every weapon from the room, and everything they thought she might use as a weapon, but the definition of "weapon" was changing, and they'd missed one. This was a luxury estate, and the private bathroom was well stocked with everything she needed to stay clean and presentable: shampoo, body wash, a full suite of makeup—all NewYew products, naturally—and a bottle of lotion. She picked it up, closed the bathroom door, and sat down on her bed. She was already dressed and ready to run.

"Hey!" It was early, but there was bound to be at least one Larry awake. There always was. "Hey, meatheads! Somebody get in here!" *No sense being polite*, she thought, *they all know I hate them.* She paused, listening for footsteps or an answering call, but there was nothing. She squeezed a glob of lotion into her hands and rubbed them together as she shouted. "Somebody come—"

"Shut up!" said a deep voice from the hallway. The speaker

rapped sharply on the door for emphasis. "Go back to bed, you idiot."

"There's a rat in my room," said Susan, examining her hands. "I need you to come kill it."

"A rat?"

"In the bathroom," said Susan. "A pretty big one, too. I don't know how it got in."

The voice paused, then laughed harshly. "Your bathroom is your problem. I'm not coming in there to get stabbed."

"Stabbed with what? You took everything I have. And I really have to pee."

"So kill the rat yourself," said the Larry, "it makes no difference to me."

"It will make a very big difference to you when I pee on the floor and they make you clean it up," said Susan.

"All right!" said the Larry. "Fine, I'll come take a look at your rat. But if you try anything stupid so help me, I will beat you like a dirty rug."

"You have my word," said Susan. "I won't touch you."

The lock on the door clicked and jiggled, and she watched as the knob turned and the door swung open. The thug was wearing a dark suit, as always, stretched tight across his chest and shoulders. *I can see why they wanted so many of this guy,* she thought, *his upper arms probably outweigh my entire body.* The thug stepped in cautiously, watching her. Susan squeezed out some lotion, rubbed it on her wrists, and nodded toward the bathroom with a smile. "In there."

"I know where the bathroom is." He closed the hall door behind himself, locking it carefully; his keys were on the end of a retractable lanyard, and they zipped straight back to his waist when he let go. He looked at her suspiciously, then walked to the bathroom door. "I'm going to have to close the door when I go in, to keep it from coming out. Don't do anything stupid."

"Like what? You locked the door."

"Just . . . don't do anything."

"Stop stalling, pantywaist, it's just a rat."

He glowered at her, slipped open the bathroom door, and shut himself inside. "I don't see it," he called out.

"It likes to hide," said Susan. She stood up, walked to the door, and held the bottle of lotion over the doorknob. She squeezed it tightly, pouring out a massive blob of thick, creamy ooze. She smeared it around, making sure it was thick and visible.

"There's nothing in here. There's not even a hole where a rat could get in."

"Maybe it came in through the drain."

"They can't come in through the drain."

"Not with that attitude they can't." She used her clean hand to squeeze even more lotion onto her fingers. "Poor dumb thug. You'll be a dumb thug all your life."

"Listen, bitch, if this is just some kind of game to piss me off and waste my time—" He opened the door and stopped, staring at her. "What are you doing?"

"Do you know how fast this ReBirth stuff is supposed to work?" She held up her hand, dripping white slime like a movie monster.

"That's . . ." He shook his head. "That's not ReBirth."

Of course it wasn't, but she was betting he'd be too cautious to test it. "They gave it to me last night," said Susan, looking at it idly. "Something about the plan going into motion, I don't know. They don't tell me anything."

He took a half step forward, but no farther. "Get out of the way."

"You've done it before, right? Used the lotion, I mean? That's how you lost your neck and turned into Larry number four." She stepped forward and he stepped back. She couldn't help but smile. "What's the matter, you don't want any?"

"Get out of the way," he said again.

"It doesn't matter where I go," she said, "it's all over the doorknob, too." She held out the bottle, aiming it at him like a weapon. "And I can squeeze this hard enough to hit you all the way across the room—I've been practicing. But really, it wouldn't be that bad to be me, right? You'd have great hair, if nothing else." She paused, widening her eyes in mock surprise. "Oh yeah, but then you'd, uh . . . lose a few things, too." She stepped forward again, gesturing at his crotch. "I hear they just . . . fall right off. Not to mention you'd start having periods, and I guarantee those are even more unpleasant than you've heard."

"Stay away from me."

"Give me the keys."

"I'll scream for help."

"Give it a few weeks and you'll be screaming in a much higher pitch." She thrust out the bottle and he flinched backward.

He shook his head. "They've got plenty of lotion. They'll change me back."

"Sure they will," said Susan. "They'll be falling over themselves to rebuild their perfect enforcer, who couldn't even stop a nineteen-year-old girl from escaping. If all those muscles aren't helping you do your job, what makes you think they're going to give them back?" She pointed the lotion bottle straight at his face, staring into his eyes as coldly as she could. "Give me the keys."

His hand hovered over the gun on his belt. "I'll kill you."

"You wouldn't dare."

"You hit me with that stuff and I won't have anything left to lose; I'll jump right over this chair and beat you to death with your own legs."

"Then give me the keys, and it will never come to that."

He looked at her, waiting, thinking, then unclipped the key ring and tossed it; Susan caught it with her gooey, lotioned hand, almost dropping them as they slid through the ooze.

"Stay there," she said.

He didn't move. She backed up to the door, jangling the keys until she found the right one. "Stay there," she said again.

He stayed, eyes seething with rage. Susan reached to the side, glancing at the door for just half a second, just barely long enough to aim the key, then shoved it in and turned it. The lock clicked open.

"Stay," she said one more time. She opened the door, slipped into the hall, and pulled it closed behind her. He wouldn't dare touch the knob, but she locked it anyway, leaving a smear of lotion on the handle.

"One of the girls is escaping!" the thug shouted, his voice a guttural roar. He banged on the wall, and Susan flinched. "Third floor! The blond girl! Somebody stop her!"

"Didn't think he'd stay quiet," Susan muttered, and looked around quickly. She didn't know exactly where the front door was from here—she'd only been out of her room once—but she could hear movement to the right, so she jogged left. There was nothing around the corner but another short row of locked doors.

"She's down there," said a voice. She heard footsteps running toward her, raised her lotion bottle to the height of Larry's face, and squeezed a huge glob of it right as the man rounded the corner. He stumbled back with a scream, clawing at the chemical sting in his eyes, and she jumped past him as he tripped and fell. Another Larry stood at the end of the hall, gun drawn, and Susan stopped short.

"Get down on the ground," the Larry said.

The thug behind her groaned on the ground, wiping at his face. "She got it right in my eyes! I'm going blind!"

"He's not just going blind," said Susan, aiming the bottle. "I've left two genetic mutants in my wake so far this morning—you want to be the third?"

"That's not ReBirth."

"You want to take that chance? Do they tell you anything about us?" asked Susan, inching forward. "I'm one of the scientists who invented this stuff—I've seen firsthand what it can do. But look who I'm talking to—you guys have seen it, too. You've even used it, and you've seen it used on us. How many men did you start with, and how many of them have been turned into women?"

She could see his eyes flickering over her, glancing at the lotion on one hand and the bottle in the other.

"Arrrgh," said the man on the floor, crouching on his hands and knees in obvious pain. "Somebody just kill her!"

"You can shoot me, or rush me, or whatever you want to do," said Susan, "but sooner or later you're going to have to touch me, and I am *covered* with this stuff." She squeezed another blob onto her hand and smeared it across her face and arms. "I'm willing to do whatever it takes to get out of here—are you willing to do the same to stop me?"

The Larry hesitated, gritting his teeth as he considered the possibilities. He swore and shook his head. "What do you want?"

"Are you crazy?" shouted Locked-Up Larry; he was just behind the door. "Don't let her go!"

"You already let her go!" Hallway Larry shouted back. "And for the same reason!"

"I'm not going to hurt anyone I don't have to," said Susan, "but if I *do* have to, I'll make you wish you'd never heard of ReBirth."

Larry jerked his chin toward the lotion bottle in her hand. "Who is it?"

"Does it matter?"

He watched her, then shook his head and shrugged. "What do you want?"

"Just let me out." She pointed at the locked door to her old cell. "I've got Locked-Up Larry's keys, and I assume there's a car out there to go with them. I leave alive, you keep your DNA, everyone's happy."

"And you go straight to the police."

Susan shrugged. "Probably. You'll still have plenty of time to leave before any of them get here."

He stared for another moment, then took a step backward. "Get out of here."

The man on the floor screamed in anger. "You're not going to let her get away!"

"You've already been hit with it," said Larry, "I haven't. You'd do exactly the same thing in my place." He shook his head. "We're not getting paid enough for this." He backed away, through the hall and down the stairs, and Susan followed him carefully. He led her to the front door, opened it for her, and stepped back well out of reach as she went through it. She reached for the knob to close it behind her, but he stopped her with a motion of his hand. "Don't touch anything." He opened the door, let her out, and closed it behind her.

Susan jogged down the wide, ornate driveway toward the row of parked cars, fumbling with the key ring as she looked for a car remote. People were shouting in the house behind her, but she didn't dare look back. Her fingers were too slick from lotion, and she dropped the keys; instantly she sank to her knees, discarded the lotion bottle, and used both hands to find the car remote and click the unlock button. A car chirped, but a loud crash from the house nearly drowned it out. *Hurry!* she shouted at herself, not daring to imagine the fight that must have started inside. She clicked the button again, and again and again and again, following the chirp to a sleek red sports car. She climbed inside, shrieking as a gunshot rang out behind her. She shoved the keys in the ignition, the car roared to life, and she tore out of the driveway like the fires of hell were behind her.

25

"Better lighting on the runway!" Kerry shouted. "We need to see skin, not washed-out blobs." He'd already tired of the underwear model and chosen a new body, though he was only halfway through the transformation, and his face had an exotic look somewhere between a Mediterranean surfer and a Polynesian samurai. Decker/Lyle had to admit it looked pretty cool. "Come on, guys," Kerry continued, "you've done fashion shows before, haven't you? Let's get it right this time!"

Decker/Lyle rubbed his eyes tiredly, sitting next to Sunny in the semidarkened event center. "The police called me again last night," he said.

Sunny laughed. "The honorable officers Luckesen and Woolf? Still chasing down their burglary suspect?"

"And their bank robbery suspect," said Decker/Lyle. "And their manslaughter suspect. He killed a bank teller, you know."

"Accidentally," said Sunny, "or so he swore to us when we finally tracked him down. But we did, and he's in São Tomé now, so relax—you're the only Lyle left."

Decker/Lyle shook his head.

"More red," Kerry shouted, standing in a pool of light and examining his hands. He looked up at a man on a scissor-lift, hanging heavy black lights from an elaborate metal scaffolding. "The skin tones are too pale! We need—" He stopped. "We need one of the Vickies out here, they're the ones I'm worried about."

"We can't change the whole lighting scheme for one girl," the man on the lift called down. "You've got fifty girls in this show."

"And half of them are Vicky!" Kerry shouted back. He turned and shouted off stage. "Hannah? Where's Hannah?" He cupped his hands around his mouth. "Dammit, Hannah, you're the stage manager, why aren't you on the stage?"

The sound system squealed, and a woman's voice boomed over the speakers. "I'm in the booth, Mr. White, what do you need?"

"I need Vicky."

"Which one?"

"Why would I care which one? They're identical—that's the point."

"I think they're in the dressing room."

"Well, get them out here! We're doing a lighting test!"

There was a pause, then the speakers boomed again. "You need more red."

"I know I need more red!" Kerry stormed off the stage. "Vicky!"

Sunny frowned. "I always hate these shows. We've been working on this for months, and we're still not ready."

"You don't have to go onstage," said Decker/Lyle. "I'm the one giving the science speech."

Sunny raised an eyebrow. "You mean there's still science in that speech? I thought Cynthia cut out everything more complex than 'it makes you pretty.'"

"That's it in a nutshell," said Decker/Lyle. "I kept what I could, but you know her."

"What I wish we'd gotten was 'Mr. DNA,'" said Sunny. "You know, the little cartoon guy from Jurassic Park? He could explain this whole thing."

Decker/Lyle laughed drily. "And then a swarm of Vickies would charge off the stage and eat the audience."

Sunny's phone rang, and he looked at the screen. "It's Cynthia. Hang on." He tapped the screen and held it up to his ear. "What do you need?" Pause. "You're kidding. Hang on, we'll find a

TV." He stood up quickly, dropping his phone back into his pocket. "Come on, we're on TV."

Decker/Lyle stood and followed him. "We've been on TV all summer."

"Not the ads," said Sunny, weaving a path through chairs and electrical equipment toward a side door. "This building—this event. There are protesters outside."

Decker/Lyle followed him through the twisting side halls to the sound booth, where Hannah, the event center's stage manager, was reviewing a list of sound cues with a room full of technicians. Sunny walked to an angled screen and tapped on it. "Is this connected to the satellite?"

Hannah swung around on her chair and clicked a switch. "Should be, what do you want to see?" The screen flickered to life.

"Local news," said Sunny.

Hannah clicked a few buttons, flipping rapidly through channel after channel, stopping on a scene of the Manhattan Center. The street outside was filled with protesters, many of them carrying signs. A young, black reporter named Amber Sykes was speaking in the foreground.

". . . suspected to be members of the same religious watch group that picketed the Yemaya Foundation headquarters earlier this evening."

Amber walked to the side, and as the camera followed her a man came into frame: older, maybe early fifties, with a salt-and-pepper blend of close-cropped hair. "This is the Reverend Joseph Wade," said Amber, "leader of the protesters. Reverend Wade, can you tell us what, exactly, you're protesting here?"

"I represent a multidenominational Christian society called the Holy Vessel," said the man, "formed last month when the so-called Guru Kuvam, really just a failed surgeon named Brett Halley, began spreading his dangerous philosophy of 'secular salvation.'"

"And you're here at the Manhattan Center . . . ?" Amber prompted.

"What he's really promoting," said the reverend, ignoring her and speaking straight to the camera, "is the use of unregulated drugs, and an attitude of outright blasphemy against the sacred nature of our God-given bodies."

"That's . . ." Amber paused, seeming unsure of what to say.

"They've linked us," whispered Sunny. "They're protesting Kuvam at our event; they know it's the same lotion."

"They don't even know that it's lotion," said Decker/Lyle.

"But they know it's the same substance," said Sunny. "Kuvam's been too aggressive with his New Age angle; people have been connecting our hospital stunt to his for weeks, but now this group is connecting us to *him*, personally, and that's bad. The red states are gonna hate us." He leaned forward and pressed the button for the PA. "Kerry, come to the sound booth right now. Drop whatever you're doing."

The reporter was still trying to get a straight answer from the reverend. "So you are, in fact, the same group that protested the Yemaya Foundation earlier today?"

"We are," said the man. "His actions, and the actions of NewYew, cannot be tolerated."

"So you believe there's some kind of connection between Guru Kuvam and tomorrow's announcement from NewYew?"

Lyle is the one who went to Kuvam, thought Decker/Lyle. *New-Yew suspected it, but Ibis figured it out for certain. What was he trying to accomplish?*

The reverend straightened up, looking directly into the camera. "The evidence is all too clear: the Pickett family in Jersey, and the Shaw twins from here in New York, are all part of the same thing. They're cloning human beings, and it's an affront to God."

Sunny's cell phone buzzed, and he fished it back out of his pocket. He sneered and showed the screen to Decker/Lyle.

"Cynthia again." He held it up to his ear. "Yeah." Pause. "Yes, of course I heard it. What do you expect me to do? It's not like I can walk out and tell her to stop." Pause. "No, he's still backstage somewhere—oh, here he is."

Kerry rushed into the room. "What's so urgent? We have a huge problem with the Vicky costumes, and the whole sequence at 15:30 is going to be ruined if we can't fix it."

Hannah and her technicians shuffled through their papers, looking for 15:30.

Decker/Lyle pointed at the screen, drawing Kerry's attention. "This is worse."

Kerry looked at the screen; the reverend was still talking. "I'm not saying they killed the little girl," said the man, "heaven knows I hope they didn't. But the one they have now isn't the one they started with: she's an exact copy of her sister, grown in a lab somewhere. It's the same with the cancer lady: she's an exact copy of her daughter. These aren't people, they're clones— they're artificial constructs, designed to look like us and act like us and, ultimately, to replace us. It's not a salvation, it's an abomination."

Kerry watched the screen intently. "Protesters?"

"Obviously," said Decker/Lyle.

"At least they've got it wrong," said Kerry. "If they're protesting something we're not actually doing, what do we care? It's free advertising, and this time tomorrow they'll look like idiots."

"Yes," said Sunny in the background, still talking on the phone, "Kerry just said the same thing."

"She's asking all the wrong questions," Kerry muttered. "Come on, lady, talk more about the girls! We saved that baby's life!"

The reverend was still talking. "Of course the clones don't have souls. This guy Kuvam—I refuse to call him a 'guru'—is preaching a specifically antireligious message. This is the Tower of Babel all over again: they've decided they can get to heaven without God, without doing anything He says, so they're building

an empire of something—of drugs, or some other substance—
so they can circumvent the commandments and ignore all the
rules and build salvation all on their own."

"I know he sounds crazy," said Sunny, hissing into his phone.
"It's still going to hurt us."

Decker/Lyle looked at Kerry. "I thought you said this kind
of coverage was good?"

"The cloning stuff was good," said Kerry. "This religious stuff
is poison: the only good press we had that Kuvam didn't was the
conservative angle. Churches still liked us, because we were saving babies without any crazy talk about New Age cults. Now this
guy's telling the world we're part of Kuvam's cult, and that's bad."

"Press is press," Sunny insisted to his phone. "And any press
is good press, right? We don't care what Ma and Pa Kettle think,
tonight or tomorrow. All we have to do is play this down and
sell to the trendsetters, and a few weeks from now the yokels
will fall right into line."

"This sucks, but it'll pass," said Kerry. "We've got to get back
to the show."

"Wait," said Hannah. She looked at her assistants, then back
at the three executives. "Okay, I'm just going to come right out
and ask it: we all thought the cloning stuff in your show notes
was a joke, but now this guy on the news is saying the same
thing." She narrowed her eyes. "Is it real?"

Sunny looked back at her. "Does it matter?"

She shrugged. "For what you guys are paying, I'd manage a
show for Captain Baby Killer and His Puppy-Stomping Pirates."

Sunny smiled. "It's all real. And if it stays real, and stays good,
we'll double your fee."

Hannah saluted. "Arrr, Cap'n."

164 DAYS TO THE END OF THE WORLD

The lights went down, and the crowd fell silent. Backlit screens around the edges of the theater began to glow, and a low bass rumble shook the floor; Decker/Lyle could feel it in his shoes and up his legs, humming at the base of his spine.

"Everyone wants to be something."

The voice poured out from the speakers, rich and deep and dripping with effortless authority. They'd paid good money for that voice—not just in hiring him, but searching for months in advance to find the perfect combination of warmth, trust-worthiness, and hipness. They needed this event to say "Our product is revolutionary and edgy and exactly what you've always wanted," and this guy's voice said it right from the first syllable.

The screen on the stage exploded with light, shapes, and colors whirling over and around and through each other in a frenzied dance, resolving at precisely the right moment into a close-up shot of a model's face—one of the Vickies, eyes sultry, hair swept dramatically across her cheek. The screens on the walls pulsed with life, and abruptly all the lights cut out and the room fell dark again.

"Good job," said Hannah's voice, tinny and distant in Decker/Lyle's headset. "Prep the shatter, cue voice-over in three, two, one, go!"

"Everyone wants to be young."

"Screen two!" shouted Hannah, and once again the stage

erupted in light and sound as the shapes reappeared, whirling around each other in a subtle double helix before resolving again into a quick succession of images: a man on the beach, shirt unbuttoned and chest shaved; a girl in tight jeans with one leg propped up on a motorcycle; another close-up of Vicky, eyes eager, lips parted.

"Shatter!" shouted Hannah, and the image broke apart with a bright audio hit of tinkling glass, plunging the theater into darkness a third time.

Decker/Lyle could feel the energy in the audience—not much, but it was growing. They were willing to be impressed, but they'd seen this kind of thing before.

You haven't seen anything yet.

"Ready video on screen one, slide reel on my mark, cue voiceover in three, two, one, go!"

"Everybody wants to be thinner. Taller. Shorter. Happier." Images surrounded the audience, not just on the main screen but on every side, on the backlit screens and on the walls and in subtle projections on the floor, subconscious bursts of light and collective memory defining HEALTH and YOUTH and BEAUTY and HAPPINESS in their most iconic incarnations. "We want better curves, softer lips, harder abs, smoother hair. We spend billions of dollars every year to become exactly who we want to be." The flashing images shifted, becoming charts and graphs and product shots: Dove and L'Oréal and Axe and Botox, arms and thighs and breasts sectioned off with the black dotted lines of a surgeon— interspersed, almost subliminally, with a diagram of butcher cuts on a cow. "We spend our lives in the pursuit of a body our body was never meant to be, filling our homes with tubes and bottles and treadmills that give us the illusion of perfection without producing any real change. It's time to stop."

One of the side screens froze on an image of ReBirth.

"It's time to escape the tyranny of our DNA."

Another screen froze on ReBirth, and then another.

"It's time for a whole new you."

More screens stopped, one after another, the high-speed chaos of images locking one by one into the single image of their bottle and logo.

"It's time . . . for ReBirth."

"Hit it!" shouted Hannah. The giant screen at the front, the last one still flickering, stopped abruptly, showing the ReBirth bottle towering over the audience, then slowly dissolved into a video of a heavy American housewife. Small white titles in the corner of the screen identified her as BETTY YORK.

"I've always tried to be thinner," said Betty in voice-over. On the video she was moving through her kitchen, preparing a meal for her family.

"Nice job, everyone," said Hannah. "Let's bring down the side screens." The backlit screens faded slowly to black, and the theater fell silent as the video kept talking.

"I want to be healthier. I want to be happier." The video showed the whole family—pure American heartland, with two handsome boys and a blond-headed girl—eating some kind of hearty casserole, while Betty picked at a salad. "I want to look good for my husband." The video showed the couple together, smiling happily but carefully framed to emphasize the woman's weight. "I tried diets and exercise and everything I could think of, but it's this body." The video showed her walking up the stairs, each step waddling and laborious. "I'm not lazy," said Betty. "I've done everything I can, with diets and exercise and every product out there. Isn't there anything that can help?"

Betty stopped on the stairs, defeated, and the image dissolved to another woman—thin this time, but with a short, dark face and an overprominent nose. She spoke directly to the camera. The titles in the corner read KATHERINE BAIRD.

"I know I'm not attractive," said Katherine. "It's okay, I can admit it: five decades of feminism have hammered home that I don't have to be beautiful to be valuable, and I believe that. That still doesn't change what I see every day. That doesn't change the way others see me. You know what else I learned from feminism? That I could be anything I wanted. Well, I want to be pretty, dammit." She looked away, eyes distant. "I want to be pretty."

There were more women in the video, one after another, each an average American woman with average American problems: they were too heavy, or too short, or flat chested, or hairy, and on and on. The last woman—number ten, Pamela Dillon—was five foot two and stocky, her ankles thick as moon boots and her waistline straight and masculine. "I used to be a model," she said, "back when I was a kid in college, but twenty-five years and three kids later I just . . . that's life, I guess. I just wish it didn't have to be." She wiped a tear from her eye. "I just wish there was some way I could get that back. I wish there was some way to look like a model again."

Decker/Lyle leaned forward, peering around the curtain. If this next part worked, it would blow their socks off.

"House lights up a bit," said Hannah. "Cue the spot on dream girl."

A woman walked onto the stage: tall and striking, with long legs, a rich mane of honey-colored hair, and a body that looked like it had been poured into her tight red dress. She smiled and waved at the audience, and Decker/Lyle heard a murmur of recognition; this was Victoria Carver, the model from the still photos at the beginning of the presentation. She was stunningly gorgeous, but more than that the buildup had conditioned the audience to *see* her as gorgeous—it had defined her as the ideal to which the other women aspired. Her red dress sparkled subtly in the spotlight. She took the center of the stage and called out energetically.

"How about those women, huh! Aren't they beautiful!"

The audience cheered, eating out of her hand. She smiled devilishly, clapping with them until the applause died down.

"Those women are America," said Vicky. "In an industry defined by fashion models and skinny actresses and rugged, hard-bodied men"—her eyes twinkled—"those ten women are the real customers. They are the ones who buy our makeup, they are the ones who buy our clothes, and they are the ones we think about when we design our products. How can we help them? What can we do to meet their needs?" She took a few steps, engaging the audience casually as she spoke. "Did you know I had the chance, thanks to NewYew, to meet each and every one of those women, and do you know how much they spend on health and beauty products in a single year? You have hand lotion, eye cream, shampoo, conditioner, body wash, facial cleanser, foundation, lipstick, eye shadow, eyeliner, blush, lip gloss, a hundred other makeups and colors and haircuts and lip waxes and *other* waxes, and that's not even mentioning the exercise bikes and the treadmills and the gym memberships and the tucks and the nose jobs and—I'm running out of breath." The audience laughed, and she milked it with an expert pause.

How much did we pay for this girl? Decker/Lyle wondered. *I haven't seen a model this charismatic in . . . ever. She's almost as good as the woman Ibis hired last year for the trade show, and she was the . . . wait.* He closed his eyes and listened to her speak.

"So what's the point, you're saying, get to the point. We've already seen the women and we've already seen the products in the little light show, and we've been here for how long now and still no one's just come out and told us what this ReBirth thing is."

Decker/Lyle's jaw dropped. *That is the woman from the trade show. It's the way she talks—the voice is new, but the cadence and phrasing are all the same.* He opened his eyes and peered at her. *She's a Vicky now?*

The woman continued. "So what is ReBirth? I'll tell you: ReBirth is the future. ReBirth is the answer to each and every one of those women's problems. I went and talked to them, like I said, and do you know what I told them? I told them that with one single application of ReBirth, they could look like me. Hair, body, lips, everything. And I think I look pretty good, don't you?" She held out her arms and turned around, giving everyone a perfect view of her legs, back, chest, and butt. The audience clapped appreciatively.

"Ready on kabuki," said Hannah. "Light presets for 15:30 on my mark."

"Just one product," said the Vicky. "Throw away all those other things and replace them with one simple product. Do you think it could work?" There was a scattering of hesitant applause, and Vicky smiled broadly. "Not sure? 'Who is this crazy woman on-stage?' You've seen enough of me—I think it's time we bring them out. Ladies?"

"Go!" shouted Hannah, and abruptly the massive theater screen dropped, a vast white wall disappearing to the floor in the blink of an eye, and the lights came up on ten more Vickies, each with identical wavy hair and identical long legs and identical red dresses. The sound system roared to life, blasting Aerosmith's "Sweet Emotion" as the women stepped out, perfect in their practiced synchronization. Even in the theater, live, just a few feet from the audience, they looked like a special effect. And then the guitars crashed loudly into the song's main verse and the syn-chronized line broke step, exploding into a flurry of action— each woman alternately waving at the audience, or posing for the cameras, or dancing to the music. Eleven gorgeous women, all perfectly the same, each completely different.

This is it, thought Decker/Lyle. *This is where they stare in silent shock, or charge the stage in revolt, or maybe, if we're lucky, clap their hands a little.*

What's it going to be? Outrage or joy?

The audience cheered like mad.

27

Lyle checked his water filter carefully—that was the key. It was natural to assume that the ReBirth batches had been failing due to contamination, and even more natural to insist on filtering his own water. They hadn't suspected a thing. He'd rigged a series of pool filters, aquarium filters, and other purifiers, and the water dripping out at the end was the cleanest he'd ever seen. Of course, the water didn't matter; all he really needed was the filters.

Different water filters were made of different things, but one of his special requests—not his only request, but buried inconspicuously in the list—was a CrystalBlue pool filter. He knew the brand from his days in college chemistry, and he breathed a sigh of relief when the Ibis thugs had dropped a box of them on his desk. He'd been terrified the company didn't even make them anymore. One of the CrystalBlues had been duly inserted into his filter contraption, but the others had all been disassembled, dissected, and collected in a pile of his last great hope: potassium permanganate. He was being watched by closed-circuit cameras, of course, but they didn't know what he was doing. He'd even added some of the chemical to a batch of ReBirth, just for appearances, being careful to keep any glycerine out of that one.

Glycerine was a common enough ingredient in skin products, thanks to its texture, but potassium permanganate and glycerine together were so flammable they didn't even need heat—they'd just burst into flames, all on their own, and water would only accelerate the reaction. With as much of the stuff as he'd managed to collect, he could start a fire they'd have to evacuate the whole building to put out.

At 11:34 a.m., on the third of July, he stacked all his books and papers and magazines on a single table. It was the day of the ReBirth product launch, and he knew he'd already missed the beginning; it was certainly too late to stop it. But this was as quickly as he'd been able to prepare everything: the potassium permanganate, the glycerine, and a box full of real, authentic, functional ReBirth. They'd stolen it from NewYew and given it to Lyle so he could study it in action. He had to get it out of here, and in just a few seconds—

Suddenly his door opened, and Ibis's two massive enforcers rushed toward his pile of books and papers, and Lyle knew that they'd realized something was going on. He dumped the bulk of his potassium on the books, being careful not to get any on himself, and flung the last bit in the faces of the thugs, blinding them for a few precious seconds. His glycerine was stored in a glass jar, and he shattered it on the desk with a crash, heaving great gobs of it onto the books with his hands. The pile darkened, smoldered, and burst into flame, a bright chemical fire that raced across the rest of the pile, lapping it up hungrily. The thugs lunged for Lyle and he swung a wild fist; they dodged him easily, but small globs of glycerine flew from his fingers, pelting them in the face, and when the great blaze behind him triggered the fire-suppression sprinklers in the ceiling, the water splashed down on the enforcers and mingled with the glycerine and the potassium and their faces lit up like dry kindling, burning and blistering and crackling like mad demons. The men fell back, clawing at their faces, and Lyle stared in shock, losing two, three, four precious seconds before regaining his senses and grabbing the box of ReBirth. Tiny glass vials rattled inside as he ran out the open door, through the sprinkler-drenched halls, mingling

with the chaos of men and women dashing back and forth
through their cubicles, some trying vainly to cover their desks
and papers and computers, others simply running for the exits
with coats above their heads, impossibly trapped in a summer
rainstorm right in the middle of their office building. The fire
roared behind them, spreading eagerly through the laboratory
and out into the hall, up through the ceiling, down through the
floor, and here and there Lyle saw himself in the crowd—in a
black suit, in a blue one, in a soaked white shirt sticking slickly
to his own foreign chest. Nobody knew who anyone was, and
as the fire crackled voraciously behind them and the two burning thugs ran wildly through the crowd nobody cared who he
was. He swallowed hard, never stopping, and ran to the stairs
and down.

28

"Let's get down to brass tacks," said Decker/Lyle, staring calmly into the spotlight. "The history of science has been focused on one thing, and one thing only: the ability of the human race to overcome its weaknesses. In the earliest days, at the dawn of time, humans realized they didn't have fur like the animals, so they created clothes to keep themselves warm and protected. Tigers used their claws to kill their food, but humans didn't have claws so they invented knives. Cheetahs used speed to catch their food, but humans couldn't run that fast so they invented spears and bows to close the distance quickly. As time went on we started curing the inequalities within our own species: one man couldn't work as fast as another, so we invented tools; a woman couldn't see as well as another, so we invented eyeglasses. Today we can correct even more staggering inequalities, using cutting-edge technology to fix a faulty heart, or help a lame man walk, or bring a stroke victim back from the brink of death. We can do all of these things, and we do them every day, and we do them because we've told ourselves—or someone has told us—that we can. That we *should*. But how many of those solutions are temporary?"

Decker/Lyle reached into his jacket pocket and pulled out a pair of glasses, holding them up for everyone to see. "Now everyone take a good look at these, because they're the future. Can you see them? They're my old glasses, with a pretty heavy prescription; when I was going through college I used these day in and day out—I used them so much they wore two grooves in my head, right over my ears. Who in the audience has something like that?" He heard a murmur of response, and smiled. It was a true story, not about Lyle but about Decker. None of the other executives had noticed, or at least they hadn't cared. "So what about these old, ugly, uncomfortable things makes them the future? The answer's simple: they're obsolete. A few years ago I got sick of these things so I went in for laser surgery; I got rid of an awkward, external aid to my vision and just fixed my vision. That, friends, is the future. Forget high heels, and makeup, and hair dye, and all the other things you do to *pretend* to change your body. The new way, the future, is to go right to the source and actually make yourself better."

He reached into his other jacket pocket and pulled out a vial of ReBirth—empty, of course—and held it up. "ReBirth changes your body, the same way laser surgery changes your eyes, or Botox changes your skin. In fact, ReBirth is far more effective than any other method of physical change because it goes right to the core, right down to the DNA. Say you want better skin; you could use makeup to cover up the wrinkles, or an antiaging lotion to reduce the wrinkles, or you could go for Botox or a face-lift and actually stretch that skin out to get rid of the wrinkles altogether. Or, with one application of ReBirth, you could actually change the way your skin works. It gets right down inside your skin, right into your cells, and talks to your DNA. 'Hey, DNA, why are you making such ugly, dry skin?' 'Because that's how I am,' says the DNA, 'it's all I know how to do.' 'Well,' says ReBirth, 'let me show you how to do it right,' and then it tweaks a DNA strand here and another strand there and suddenly your cells aren't making dry skin anymore, they're making perfect skin—they're making Vicky Carver skin. And Vicky Carver legs, and Vicky Carver eyes, and a Vicky Carver heart. Did you know Victoria Carver has one of the healthiest hearts I've ever seen? We actually took her into a doctor, just to make sure, and he said she was innately resistant to heart disease, heart attacks, heart murmurs . . . plus her good heart makes her circulation stronger, so she's less likely to have problems with spider veins and varicose veins and muscle tremors and strokes. All just because she was born that way, because of her DNA. If you tried to correct every inequality between your body and Victoria Carver's you'd need makeup, lotion, hair dye, a personal trainer, a tailored wardrobe, extensive cosmetic surgery, and a heart transplant—and even that would leave scars, so you still wouldn't be able to match her exactly. Or. You could take thirty seconds, rub on some ReBirth, and have that same stunning body in about a month. Take a look at this."

Decker/Lyle turned around and swept his arm across the screen behind him—a new one, to replace the dropped kabuki— where suddenly there appeared a massive chart of women's faces, row after row and column after column. "This is the ReBirth family, and it's growing all the time; if you go on our website you can find this exact chart, live as of thirty seconds ago. Using this chart you can find precisely the right body for you: do you want to be short? Tall? Thin or muscular? Blond, redhead, brunette? It's all here. Every face on this chart represents a vial of ReBirth, each designed for what we call an imprint: a specific set of genetic traits that the lotion will write into your DNA. Let's start with the basics, what we call the NewYew Guarantee." A small paragraph in the corner of the chart zoomed out to fill the screen, and Decker/Lyle read it aloud. " 'Every imprint in the ReBirth family holds to the highest standards of health and beauty: good skin, good bones, a perfect heart, and O negative blood.' Why O negative blood? Because that's a universal donor, making it safe for everyone." He turned back to the audience. "What this means is that no matter which imprint you pick, you'll always be getting the healthiest body possible, with no congenital defects, no diseases, no major allergies, and no inherent weaknesses of any kind. You'll have perfect proportions, perfect vision, perfect skin, and great hair. But that's just the baseline. Now we get to have some fun."

Decker/Lyle turned and pointed at the screen again; the NewYew Guarantee shrunk back down to the corner, revealing once more the chart behind it. "What do you want? Let's say you want to be around five feet six inches, with high cheekbones, green, wide-set eyes, a slim, Roman nose, nice dark hair, and you want to fit into, say, a size two. Can ReBirth help you?" One of the faces on the chart lit up and expanded, filling the screen. "This is Monica; she fits every one of those criteria. Now, let's say you want the exact same thing, but with blue eyes." Monica's face shrunk back down and the face next to it expanded. "This is Laura. Let's say you want the same thing, but with a C-cup." Laura's face shrunk, and another expanded. "This is Kristen. You see what I mean? Any body you want, ReBirth has an imprint for you. But this is only a tiny portion of the chart—let's look at the whole thing again."

Kristen's face shrunk back down, and the full chart once again filled the screen. "This is my favorite part," said Decker/Lyle. "We have a full spectrum of skin tones, so you can find exactly the product you need no matter what ethnicity you come from— or what ethnicity you want. We have everything from pale Celtic to bronze Mexico to jet-black Africa, and every color in between, each and every one of them absolutely gorgeous. Imagine that for a minute—imagine a world where you can change your skin color like you change your hair. That's a world without racism. That's a world where no one will ever feel the sting of discrimination, because the entire concept will be meaningless. When NewYew sets out to change the world, we don't do half measures."

The audience cheered, and Decker/Lyle clapped with them. *They're eating it up,* he thought. *It's working perfectly.* After a moment he quieted them down. "I'm very glad to see that you're as excited as we are by the possibilities ReBirth gives us, not only as individuals but as a society. This chart represents more than seventy different imprints, and get ready for this." He pointed at the screen and the entire image changed, showing a vast chart not of women but of men. "We've got the same incredible selection for men, as well. You want to be taller? Broader? You want a stronger chin, or just straight-up stronger muscles? More than seventy choices await you, to give you exactly the body you want—but that's still not all."

The screen changed again, showing a different chart, smaller this time, with larger images. "Let's take a look at the ReBirth specialty lines, which I'm really proud of. There are a lot of body types that might not have the same wide appeal, but still have a lot of the value to the right customer. How about a body built for speed, imprinted with DNA from world-class sprinters? Or a body built for strength or endurance, or a body gifted with the ideal shape and muscle distribution for swimming? The highest levels of athletic achievement are governed not by effort but by genetics; some of us are simply too short for basketball, or too big for gymnastics, or maybe we're disabled and can't compete at all. Thanks to ReBirth, there's nothing holding you back but your own drive and dedication."

Decker/Lyle glanced around at the audience. "Let's do another demonstration. Ms. Carver, can you come out here, please?" One of the Vickies walked out onto the stage, and the audience applauded again. She waved and smiled. "Thank you, Victoria. Now, earlier—"

"Wait," she said, smiling, "I'm not Victoria."

"You're not?" It was all rehearsed, of course, but Decker/Lyle tried to make it sound sincere. "But . . . are you sure?"

The woman laughed. "Pretty sure. I'm Betty York."

Decker/Lyle widened his eyes. "You're Betty York? The . . . big . . . woman . . . from the video?"

"It's okay, you can say it," said Betty. "I was fat."

"Well, you look fantastic," said Decker/Lyle. He looked at the audience. "Doesn't she look fantastic?"

The crowd cheered, and Betty wiggled her hips just a bit, showing off her new body.

"Wow," said Decker/Lyle. "Just wow. Well, Betty, maybe you

can help me with this. Earlier in my presentation I talked
about all the things someone would have to use in order to get a
body like that. I understand you used a lot of those things, is
that correct?"

"I used every product I could find," said Betty. She smiled
again. "In fact, I brought them all with me."

"You brought them all with you," said Decker/Lyle. "What
a"—he looked at the audience and furrowed his brow—"startling
coincidence." The crowd laughed, and he turned back to Betty.
"Why don't you bring them all out here, and we'll count them
off as we go."

"All right," said Betty. "Let's start with skin creams and lotions and body washes—all the basics that help get your body
ready for everything else." As she spoke another Vicky wheeled
out a large table covered with tubes and tubs and vials of lotion.

"That's a lot," said Decker/Lyle.

"That's just the skin," said Betty. "Don't forget shampoo, conditioner, and maybe a little hair dye." Another Vicky brought out
an armload of bottles and set them carefully on the table. "Now,"
said Betty, "throw in all the makeup: foundation, concealer, eyeliner, eye shadow, mascara, blush, lipstick, lip gloss, some tooth
whitener, some glimmer for your cheeks—and naturally you need
it in multiple color combinations, so you're ready for different occasions." While she spoke the Vickies went in and out, filling the
table with more and more products.

Decker/Lyle looked at the audience. "This is a lot of stuff."

"I'm not through yet!" said Betty. "I have a bunch of appli-
ances, too, like hair dryers and curling irons and a scale for the
bathroom, and that's just the stuff I have at home—for the really
big stuff I have to go to a salon. I did manicures, I did pedicures,
I had haircuts and highlights and waxing, I went tanning, I even
did microdermabrasion." The Vickies were now bringing out
enormous things, each propped up on wheels: pedicure chairs,
tanning beds, even a hairdresser and a manicurist.

Decker/Lyle grinned broadly. "And you brought all this stuff from home?"

The audience laughed, and Betty continued at full speed. "There's more. I exercised. I had a gym membership and a personal trainer. I bought a treadmill for my house. I bought those expensive diet drinks, and meal-replacement shakes, and calorie counters." The Vickies kept up their procession, stacking first the table and eventually the entire stage with more things and bits and people. "I tried everything," Betty said, "and when that didn't give me the results I wanted, I tried Botox and cosmetic surgery. I had my stomach stapled. I had my cellulite lasered off. I . . ." She paused, staring at the massive pile that now completely filled the stage. "Wow, I didn't realize how much stuff there was until now that I can see it all in one place."

Decker/Lyle nodded, looking at the vast collection, giving it time to sink in for the audience. "Betty," he said at last, "can you tell me how much money you spent on all this stuff?"

"Oh, it scares me just to think about it," said Betty.

"But do you know the number?"

"I do," she said, grimacing. "It's really embarrassing." She looked at the audience, grinning sheepishly. "Last year alone it was . . . about thirteen thousand dollars?"

The audience gasped, and Betty turned red. *That's great,* thought Decker/Lyle, *you can't fake that.* He heard a loud intake of air as the audience gasped and whispered among themselves.

Decker/Lyle put a consoling hand on Betty's back. "Would you believe," he said, "that that's actually . . . the low end of the national average?"

"Really?" asked Betty. More whispers from the audience.

Decker/Lyle looked at the audience. "The average American woman spends between twelve and fifteen thousand dollars a year on health and beauty products. It's a shock to see it all in one place like this, but this is completely typical. Fifteen thousand dollars a year, just so one woman can look like another. Now."

He held up the vial of ReBirth, then turned back to Betty. "Betty, you've used ReBirth; you've seen what it can do. Was it easy?"

"It was the easiest thing I've ever done."

"Did it take up a lot of space?"

"It's just a tiny vial," she said, "it's smaller than a tube of lip gloss."

"Not bad compared to all that," said Decker/Lyle, pointing at the pile on the stage. "Right?"

"Not bad at all."

Decker/Lyle looked back at the audience. "One single vial of ReBirth can do everything that pile can do—can replace it altogether—saving you time, and space, and money. Betty, we gave you the ReBirth sample for free, but do you have any idea how much it costs for a retail consumer?"

"To replace all of that?" asked Betty. "Fifteen thousand dollars?" Decker/Lyle shook his head. "Ten thousand?" Decker/Lyle shook his head again, and Betty shrugged, flustered.

Decker/Lyle held up his hand, the fingers splayed. "Five thousand dollars," he said. "Less than a third of what you might pay for all of this"—he gestured at the pile behind him—"for the easiest, simplest, most effective beauty product in the entire world." He handed Betty the vial of ReBirth. "There you go, Betty, that's all you need." He smiled; this would be fun. "What are you going to do with the other ten thousand dollars you just saved?"

Betty's eyes went wide. "I—" Her shock was genuine; this wasn't part of the rehearsal. "Ten thousand dollars? I'm going to Paris! I'm going to the Caribbean!" She stood up straight and beamed with an indescribable joy. "I'm going to hit the classiest beach in the world and show this body off!"

For the umpteenth time that day, the audience erupted in frantic applause.

29

Amber Sykes smiled at the camera. "That's the latest report, live from the launch of NewYew's astonishing new product. Don't forget to come down and see us in person, in just ten minutes, when NewYew will give away a bottle of ReBirth to one lucky person on this very street." The massive crowd roared behind her, and she couldn't resist a tiny wink at the camera. "This is Amber Sykes with New York One. Back to you, Alan!"

"And . . . we're out," said Sam, her producer. "We're on air again in seventy-two seconds. This is nuts."

The cameraman rolled his shoulder. "This is killing me."

"You're doing great, Monty," said Amber. "Who's the next interview?"

"Reverend Wade," said Sam. "Same kooky religious dude from yesterday. The network wants a follow-up."

"Being religious doesn't make him kooky," said Amber. "Be nice."

"I don't like him," said Sam, but his face brightened as the reverend approached. "Welcome back, Reverend Wade! Right over here, please."

Monty pushed through the crowd to find another good spot, right by the curb with a good mix of rally-goers and protesters behind them. Amber looked in her compact one more time, then snapped it shut and dropped it in her pocket. Sam counted down the last few seconds and pointed at Amber.

"Thank you, Alan, we're back once again at the NewYew launch with a man we interviewed last night, the Reverend Joseph Wade. Tell me, Reverend, you told us last night that NewYew was abducting people and replacing them with lab-grown duplicates. Now that the truth is out, what do you think of today's announcements?"

"I had the details a little wrong," the reverend admitted, nodding, "but I was right about the most important thing: cloning is an abomination before God. It is a sin, and a mockery of His image. Mankind was created in His image, and it's the height of arrogance for us to screw around with it like this."

"I'm religious myself," said Amber, "but let me ask you: if 'God's image' is a wide enough category to include both you and me—different people, different races, and even different genders—then how does changing your look from one human face to another qualify as a mockery of that image?"

"It's not about how we look," the reverend said, "it's about *why* we look that way. God gave you your body for a reason, and He gave me mine for a reason, and it's not our place to turn up our noses at a gift from God."

"So changing your appearance is wrong?" Amber asked. "I put on makeup just a minute ago—does that make me a sinner?"

"Of course not," said the reverend, "but that's entirely different—"

"What about plastic surgery?" asked Amber, pressing the attack. "Have you been protesting that, as well?"

"Would you use it?" asked the reverend suddenly.

Amber stopped, remembering just a second too late to close her mouth.

The reverend stared at her, probing. "You're obviously a huge fan of the stuff, and we've got a sample coming out here in just a few minutes. I'm sure they'd give you a drop or two for an on-air demonstration. Will you use it?"

Amber pursed her lips, thinking. "My . . . face is my livelihood," she said. "A reporter is a public figure; I need to look like me or I wouldn't even have a job anymore."

"But a new face could get you a new job," the man countered, "and probably a better one. When you were fresh out of college, trying to break into reporting, how many times were you rejected for being too young, or too short, or not pretty enough?"

Amber swallowed. "That is uncalled for."

"But that is exactly what we're talking about," he said fiercely. "We are quantifying beauty; we are telling people that they aren't good enough as they are. You've been pushing this stuff all morning, so tell me: will you use it or not?"

In the corner of her eye Amber could see Sam waving his hand across his neck: *Cut the segment, end it now, and get out of here.*

"I . . . I'm proud of who I am. . . ."

"You're the fluff reporter in a dead-end network," said the reverend. "This can't be why you got into reporting—you must have been aiming higher. How much higher do you think you could go if you looked like Victoria Carver?"

"I—"

"How much further could you go if you were white?"

"That's it," said Sam, barging past Monty and planting himself between Amber and the reverend. "This is over—there's no more interview, and you should be ashamed of yourself, sir, completely ashamed—"

"Wait!" called a voice, and Amber looked up to see a blond girl shoving her way through the press of people. "Wait," said the girl again, panting and out of breath. "I have to say something. Is that still recording?"

"Not for long," snarled Sam, pointing at the camera. "Monty, turn it off!"

"I'm serious," said the girl, "this is the scoop of the day." Amber guessed she was just out of high school, maybe nineteen years old. Slim and blond. "I have information about NewYew that the world has to know." She looked behind herself and shifted a few feet to the left. "Make sure you get the door in the back of the shot, 'cause in about thirty seconds we're going to get swarmed with NewYew security."

"We're still live," said Sam, astonished, putting a finger to his earpiece. "They've kept us running through the whole thing—they say they want more of the mob."

"Then we'll give them some." The girl looked at the camera. "You ready?"

"Rolling."

The girl composed herself and looked straight into the camera. "My name is Susan Howell," she said. "I worked at NewYew helping to test ReBirth in its early stages, and I became accidentally infected with a sample of lotion that touched my boss, Lyle Fontanelle. When I started turning into him they—"

"Wait," said Amber, stepping into the picture. She glanced at the camera, smoothed her hair, and continued. "You said that ReBirth turned you into a man?"

"Yes," said Susan. "It put me in the hospital, until they used some more lotion and turned me back into myself."

The crowd began murmuring loudly; none of them had heard that the lotion could change your gender. Amber hadn't even heard it. *It makes sense, but . . .*

"For the last four weeks I've been a prisoner in a house on Long Island," Susan continued, "number 35480 Red Hosta Lane—I escaped, but there are still more than twelve other prisoners who need to be found and rescued, and the executive board needs to be arrested immediately."

The crowd was yelling now, an angry, braying roar full of loud, contradictory voices. Some were yelling about the kidnapping, others about the lotion, and a large contingent was yelling directly at Susan, calling her a liar and a swarm of other epithets. Amber struggled to stay on camera, but the crowd was pressing in, and the reverend was riling up the crowd with a growing chant of "God made man and woman!"

"NewYew is conducting illegal experiments," Susan shouted, "they are kidnapping and torturing innocent people, they are vile and evil and they need to be stopped, and—"

The doors to the convention center slammed open behind them with a bang, and a team of black-suited security officers boiled out into the crowd. Susan swore and dropped the mic, ducking past Monty and fleeing into the mob. The security team shoved desperately through the people, to catch her, but somebody shouted, "They're giving away free samples!" and Susan disappeared as the crowd surged forward like a tide.

30

It's okay, Lyle thought. *Nobody knows what I look like.*

At least not yet.

He clutched the box tightly to his chest, glancing nervously at the other people on the street. The burning building was blocks behind him now, distant sirens screaming at the crowd to stand back. The people he passed on the street were talking either about the fire or ReBirth—it seemed the entire city knew about it, both because of the miraculous stories they told of its effects, and because some kind of mob riot that had started outside. Lyle ignored them; he'd get the details later, now he had more pressing business. He had an armload of the most valuable, most dangerous substance in the world, and he was alone in the bustling heart of New York City.

New York is nicer than people think, he told himself. *No one's going to steal it. I did this once before, even later than this, and I was fine; nobody killed me or mugged me or even looked at me sideways. I'm fine.* He moved gingerly through the crowd, trying not to touch anybody. *Nice or not, they could bump me or knock me or even brush past me, and who knows what could happen. This is nearly twelve ounces of the stuff, sixteen half-ounce vials and one large four-ounce bottle. One accidental spill and Manhattan would get a lot less diverse.*

All around him he heard whispers of ReBirth: Did you hear? Have you seen it? Did you know what it can do?

Just four more blocks. Lyle paused at the corner, waiting for the light. In the limited access he'd had to the Internet—read-only, with no chance to send a message—he'd researched other potential cases he thought ReBirth could help. A school crossing guard in the Bronx who'd lost his leg in a car accident—could ReBirth regrow a leg? It regrew a woman's breasts, so it could probably do a leg. It turned your body into an ideal template of itself, no matter what it was like before. How did it do that? The more he studied it, the more he realized just how aggressive it really was. It was terrifying, in a way, to think of what would happen if—

Somebody bumped his elbow, and the box fell. Lyle's heart stopped.

The cardboard burst when it hit the ground, flapping open and scattering vials of lotion across the sidewalk: a dozen or so half-ounce vials, and one four-ounce bottle. Lyle watched, frozen in horror, then fell to his knees and began quickly gathering them up. *It's okay,* he thought anxiously, *no one's going to steal them. New York is nicer than people think—*

"Let me help you with those," said a friendly voice, and Lyle turned to see a woman crouching down to reach for a vial. He lunged toward her, grabbing it first, nearly stepping on the four-ounce bottle in the process. It skittered into the road and Lyle suppressed a curse.

"No," he said, "it's nothing, I can get them all, please don't help."

"Oh, it's no trouble," the woman said, reaching for another, "if I dropped something I know I'd be grateful for someone to stop and help me."

"No, really," said Lyle, and then another person crouched down to help. The man picked up a vial of lotion, dropped it in the cardboard box, and smiled at Lyle.

"You okay, sir?"

"Yes," Lyle hissed through his teeth, scrambling now on his knees to collect the lotion before anyone noticed what it was. "I'm fine, thank you, please just go on"—he waved them off—"do whatever you were doing, I can manage it."

"Wait a minute," said the woman, staring at the vial in her hand. "Is this the . . . is this the stuff from TV? The stuff from the riot?"

"The cloning lotion?" asked the man. He stood up, holding a vial up to the glow of the sun. "It is. ReBirth." He looked at Lyle, frowning. "Where did you get this? You've got," he looked down, "sixty, maybe eighty thousand dollars' worth of the stuff here."

Lyle closed his eyes. *Now I'm screwed.* Almost immediately the crowd around them stopped.

"Eighty thousand dollars?"

"Is that the stuff from the news?"

"How much money did you say?"

Eighty thousand dollars retail, thought Lyle, bracing himself for the rush, *who knows how much on the black market.* He eyed the group tensely, his hand opening to reach for another vial—

In a flash the crowd descended like an avalanche of hands and feet, reaching and grasping and stepping on each other's fingers and wrestling for control of the tiny vials. Lyle abandoned the last few loose ones and dove for the cardboard box, ready to cut his losses and run, but another man reached it just as he did. Lyle pulled on it vainly, trying to curl himself around it, all the while shouting "Everybody get back! You don't understand!" but no one seemed to listen. The man yanked the box from Lyle's hands and stepped back triumphantly, only to be mauled by a pair of women—one of them, Lyle noted, the same woman who'd first stopped to help him. Another man rushed into the fray and Lyle backed up, stunned by the frenzy, and then the traffic light changed again.

The flow of traffic shifted, cars surged forward past the melee, and too late Lyle remembered the four-ounce bottle of lotion lying in the street—not labeled for sale, and thus ignored by the crowd who hadn't recognized it for what it was. He took a step toward it, saw a truck come barreling down the street, and dove behind a signboard just in time. The truck hit the bottle with all its weight, Lyle heard a pop, and suddenly the whole crowd was hit with an explosion of white lotion—it landed on hands, faces, and hair; it misted into the center of the crowd; it smeared from one to another as they fought. By the time the first person screamed it was too late.

"It's all over me!"

"Where did it come from?"

"I don't want to turn into you!"

As fast as it gathered the crowd dispersed in a thunderstorm of terrified screams. Lyle saw a lotion-smeared woman racing toward him and jumped into the street to avoid her, barely missing another oncoming car. The fear swept through the streets in a widening circle, lotioned victims shouting and sobbing as they ran or stumbled or pleaded with others for help. Some ran from them, others stopped to help, not knowing what had happened, and touched the lotion themselves. Still others dashed back into the center to grab the unbroken vials still littering the ground, and the fight started over. Nobody knew what was going on, or how the lotion worked, or what they could possibly do to stop it.

Lyle knew exactly what to do. He ran.

31

Wednesday, July 4
Everywhere

163 DAYS TO THE END OF THE WORLD

NEWSCASTER: Good evening, I'm Lisa Maxwell, and this is *Channel 6 News* in Milwaukee. In our top story tonight, Brett Osborne, the newly hired manager of the local ReBirth clinic, was arrested this evening after a domestic dispute with his wife, Diane. Osborne received a shipment of the so-called cloning lotion in his store, opened it early, and applied it to his wife without her consent. The police were called when the neighbors heard shouting and several loud crashes. Channel 6 reporter Carlos Lancaster is live on the scene—Carlos, can you tell us any more about what happened?

CARLOS: Yes, Lisa, I'm here at the Osborne home and as you can see, the police are still here, more than an hour after the call; the issue is turning out to be much murkier than anyone expected. We have two men here who've offered to talk to us: Officer Schwartz is in charge of the scene and Aaron Greer is a state attorney—they've actually brought an attorney to consult with the police, because this entire episode is so bizarre. Can you tell me, Officer Schwartz: this seems like a simple domestic call, so why all the confusion?

OFFICER: When we initially arrived, the first officers on the scene heard shouts and name-calling, things like that; they knocked on the door and saw the home in disarray. Several objects had been broken but no one seemed to be hurt. Our problem here is that the only crime that seems to have been committed is the original application of the lotion.

CARLOS: And putting lotion on someone would not normally be considered a crime.

OFFICER: Not normally, no, but because of the nature of this particular lotion . . . it *feels* like something illegal happened, we just don't know what it is.

CARLOS: And you, Mr. Greer, what is your take on the situation?

LAWYER: For one thing, we don't even know if this works. The ReBirth lotion sounds completely ridiculous, literally almost impossible to believe, and yet NewYew has obviously spent millions, maybe billions of dollars on creating and distributing it, and I can't think of why they'd do something like that if it were all a hoax.

CARLOS: So if the lotion doesn't actually alter Mrs. Osborne's DNA, this is all moot?

LAWYER: It's still a domestic disturbance, and they'll probably be fined for bothering the neighbors, but you're right—if the lotion doesn't actually do anything, the fine is the worst that will happen.

CARLOS: And if it does work?

LAWYER: If does work, then. . . . Then we've got an entirely new area of law that no one has ever dealt with before. We simply don't have the legal infrastructure to deal with this kind of crime: we could charge him with reckless endangerment, maybe, but unlawfully turning one person into another person? It's simply unheard of. There's nothing about this in any law book outside of . . . the starship *Enterprise*.

CARLOS: Unbelievable. This has got to be one of the craziest domestic calls you guys have ever had to make. At least for now. [Turns to camera.] Lisa, we'll keep you updated as the story progresses, but both Officer Schwartz and Mr. Greer wanted me to stress just how dangerous this lotion can be, especially if used incorrectly or without consent. It goes on sale tomorrow, so please, everyone, be careful or you might see these guys knocking on your door.

MEG CARSON: Welcome back to the *Morning Show*, coming to you live from Times Square. I'm Meg Carson, and outside the window you can see the crowd is super excited about our next guest, one of the most controversial figures in America: the man known as Guru Kuvam. Joining him in our studio are Donna and Melissa Pickett, who claim that Kuvam healed Donna of cancer. Mr. Kuvam—

KUVAM: Please, call me Guru.

CARSON: Um, okay. Guru Kuvam. When this story broke just over a month ago everyone could see that Donna looked like the new twin sister of her daughter Melissa, and seeing them together here in our studio I have to say that the similarities are impossible to ignore.

[Donna and Melissa smile; they are nearly identical.]

CARSON: When your news first broke, nobody knew what to make of it, but given the events of the last few days, naturally we're all wondering if your so-called naturopathic treatment was in fact simply a dose of ReBirth.

KUVAM: That is correct, Megan, but it is incorrect to dismiss ReBirth's naturopathic origins. Naturopathy as a medical discipline heals the whole body, bringing out the best in that body and allowing it to heal itself. Donna's previous cancer treatments ignored this and focused on small parts of her body, in an attempt to kill the cancer by brute force, but I have treated her whole body by changing it; by cleansing it. She has used that power to heal herself.

CARSON: But doesn't that seem kind of invasive to you? I mean . . . it's not really her body anymore, is it? It's Melissa's.

KUVAM: It's Melissa's genetic code, but Donna's body. They're no more the same person than a pair of identical twins is the same person—let us say instead that they are two different people sharing a common point of origin, as indeed we all do.

CARSON: Perhaps you can answer this, then: Where did you get a sample of ReBirth more than a month early? Did they give it to you? Is this part of a NewYew publicity stunt?

KUVAM: They did not give it to me, and I did not steal it. Let us say instead that the universe itself brought ReBirth into my hands. The world, the media, the corporations that control these substances—all they care about are the superficial trappings. They want money, or beauty, or power, and they can have them; the vibrant force of human nature doesn't care about these things. NewYew has given us a commercial product, but the universe, through NewYew, has given us life. They have given us immortality. Do you see the potential, Megan? Do you see the hands of the universe reaching out to embrace you? There should be nothing that troubles us anymore: no worries of disease, because ReBirth has cured all our disease; no worries of hate because ReBirth has removed all our differences. We are one people now, united and eternal, and nothing can take that—

[Guru Kuvam's head jerks back with a loud crack, bright red blossoming from his forehead. Behind him the glass window shatters, and the studio is abruptly filled with sounds of cars and people and screaming. The women duck behind couches, cameramen and stagehands scurry for cover, and a second barrage of bullets tears through the studio. A man charges in front of the camera, waving an assault rifle wildly in his hand.]

GUNMAN: The heretic has fallen, and with him his abominations! [A third round of gunfire erupts from off screen, and the gunman falls as police and security guards rush toward him. The gunman gasps his final words.]

GUNMAN: I give my life gladly. My resurrection will be a true one.

———

NEWSCASTER: We are coming to you live from the midnight launch event for the ReBirth clinic in Santa Monica, where twenty-four-year-old singer and movie star Cristina Francis has been attacked. Sources close to Francis tell me she was here for the event, just like hundreds of other curious onlookers, when out of the crowd one of the first ReBirth customers emerged from the clinic with a sample of blank lotion and lunged at Francis, smearing her with it in an attempt to imprint it with her DNA. I'm standing here with Ben Thompson, one of many eyewitnesses. Ben, can you tell us in your own words what happened next?

THOMPSON: We tried to catch him, right? Like, the whole crowd—we were gonna tackle him, but he had the lotion just out there, in his hands and stuff, and there was no way to grab him without getting it on us, you know? And Cristina Francis is great and everything but I don't want to *be* her, like, maybe my girlfriend could be her, but not me, especially because then people might be attacking *me* all the time for *my* DNA. And I told my girlfriend to grab him, but she was all scared and no one else would touch him, either, so he got away.

NEWSCASTER: Thank you. Many bloggers and analysts have been predicting exactly this kind of attack ever since ReBirth was announced yesterday: the rise of the so-called gene-arazzi, who will ambush celebrities not to take their pictures, but to take their DNA. Nobody expected it would happen this quickly, however, which seems like an ominous sign for the future. Back to you.

32

"The noose is tightening," said Sunny. "My guy in the FDA says they're working with the FBI and the military, and planning something big—raiding our manufacturing plant, seizing our records, everything. We have until Friday at the latest. I think it's time to go now."

Decker/Lyle looked around the boardroom, a flutter of nerves in his stomach. This was it: he'd stayed with them, he'd helped make the product launch a huge success, and even when Susan turned up outside he'd ignored her, staying true to his NewYew cronies. They trusted him implicitly now. It was time to see what the next phase was.

At the same time, he felt a stab of guilt. The NewYew executives had treated him, in a way, even better than the Ibis ones had. He was making more money now than he ever had before, and had forged what he felt was a real friendship with Sunny. His life here, as Lyle Fontanelle, was working great—what was to stop him from just . . . slipping into it? Saying goodbye to Ibis and Abraham Decker and everything else, and staying as Lyle forever? It was tempting. Decker/Lyle was torn.

It had become a very familiar feeling.

"They're never going to let us out of the country," said Jeffrey.

"That's why we're going in my private yacht," said Cynthia. "Assuming you don't mind a few weeks at sea, we can be in São

Tomé without ever having to cross a border, reveal a face, or show a passport."

Decker/Lyle smiled. "You guys really did think of everything." *Screw Ibis,* he thought. *This is what I want—good friends and no worries on a tropical island, with more money than I could possibly know what to do with. Ibis would kill for this information, but . . . what do I care?* He laughed. *Live it up.*

The executives stood, rolling their chairs in toward the conference table for the last time. Sunny held the door as they walked to the elevator, and Kerry punched the down button.

"I'm kind of jealous," he said. Kerry was staying behind—the company needed somebody stateside, and Kerry had changed his face so many times he was unrecognizable. He could run things in secret, and the feds would be none the wiser.

Decker/Lyle smiled. "We'll try not to have too much fun."

"Oh, I'm going to have fun," Kerry laughed. "I'm a newly minted billionaire in the greatest city in the world—don't worry about me. But I won't have a beach like you guys."

"You can't have everything," said Sunny.

"I'm sure as hell going to try," said Jeffrey.

The elevator dinged, opened, and they stepped in. Jeffrey pushed the button for the parking garage, and a moment later Kerry punched the button for the thirty-fourth floor. "I almost forgot the cash," he said. "We made a lump withdrawal for you to take on the boat; three briefcases."

"You need a hand?" asked Sunny.

"Like, a third one?" asked Jeffrey. "Can ReBirth do that?"

"Shut up, Jeffrey," said Cynthia. "And no, Sunny, I need you to sign some papers on the way out." The doors opened on the thirty-fourth floor. "Lyle can help him."

"Sure thing," said Lyle. On the thirty-fourth floor he and Kerry stepped out, collected the briefcases, and waited for the next elevator. When they reached the parking garage the others were already in the limo idling softly by the doors. Kerry passed his two cases in, and held the door as Decker/Lyle climbed in after.

"Have fun," said Kerry, and closed the door.

The limo pulled away, and Jeffrey started tearing the foil from a bottle of champagne. "It's finally here!" he shouted. "Let's celebrate!" He popped the cork, and the other executives cheered as they shifted and squirmed out of the way of the spurting foam. Jeffrey poured glasses, nearly spilling one as the limo tipped up, driving out of the garage and into the street.

Cynthia looked at Decker/Lyle. "So where's this boat?"

Decker/Lyle smiled, confused. "Isn't it yours?"

"I—yes. Of course. I just wondered if you'd moved it." She smiled back, a strange mixture of embarrassment and . . . *Is that guilt?* Lyle looked at the others, catching the tail end of a disapproving glance from . . . Jeffrey? *Since when does Jeffrey dare to look at Cynthia that way?*

"Why would I move your boat?" he asked.

"It was just a slipup," said Sunny. "Give her a break, it won't happen again."

Decker/Lyle looked up sharply. "Wait, what?" *Why were they acting so weird?*

"I'm just saying," said Sunny, "we're all new to this. I mean, sure, we've been practicing these characters for weeks, but—"

Lyle's head seemed to fill with alarms: *They're not acting like themselves because they're* not *themselves.* "You're duplicates."

The other executives looked at each other with confused half smiles, as if he'd just accused the sky of being blue. "Well . . . yeah," said Cynthia. "Aren't you?"

Decker/Lyle didn't answer, his mind racing with the implications. These were all duplicates. What did that mean?

The fake Jeffrey's eyes went wide: "He's real. They stuck us in a car with the real Lyle."

"Why would they give us the real Lyle?" asked the fake Sunny, stammering. "They . . . we're . . . supposed to go to the Bahamas now, right?"

The fake Cynthia went pale. "They told me Buenos Aires."

The fake Sunny lunged for the door, but the handle wouldn't open.

Decker/Lyle looked over his shoulder, scanning the crowded Manhattan street behind them. *Is that another limo going the other way?* He couldn't tell. He turned back around, frantic. *What's going on?*

The money, he thought, *they wouldn't give us money if they were—* He pulled the nearest briefcase onto his lap and snapped it open. It was full of newspaper.

"Oh, shi—"

The limousine exploded.

33

Lyle was dead, which the real Lyle took as a welcome relief. He'd spent the last week and a half terrified that someone would find him—Ibis or NewYew or the press or the cops. It seemed like everyone was hunting him. But then the entire executive staff of NewYew had died in a car bomb, and suddenly Lyle was free.

Until a few hours later, when another Lyle was found floating in the East River. And if there were two Lyles, the press said, why not more? Surely the father of human cloning had more than one copy of himself. And so he was a fugitive again.

Dead or not, Lyle was too afraid to go outside, and so he hid in his grandmother's house, watching the TV or the computer or his phone, or more often, all three at once. He watched the news scroll by with story after story about ReBirth: it was the best-selling product in its market. It was the primary topic of every talk show, late night and daytime. Police were cautioning against its use. Religious groups were decrying it as a sin, or a salvation, depending on which group you were talking to. People were using it wrong, or too much, or in ways Lyle had never dreamed: there was a thriving black market for celebrity DNA, and everyone from movie stars to political leaders was afraid to go outside.

I guess I can't blame them, thought Lyle. *I haven't left the house in more than a week.*

Lyle's grandmother was a rugged old woman now nearly a hundred years old, who slept almost twenty hours a day and spent the other four nearly oblivious to Lyle's presence. She never talked to anyone but the maid and the neighbor boy who delivered her groceries, and when either of them came Lyle hid in the back-yard, crouched in a small wooden toolshed, praying his grand-mother wouldn't choose that moment to remember he existed and say something to her visitors.

Now it was night, and he didn't dare to turn on the TV, wor-ried that anyone who might be watching the house would see the light and know he was there. Assuming anyone was watch-ing the house at all. He'd never seen anyone, but if the govern-ment was smart enough to be checking his relatives' homes he had to assume they were also smart enough to be discreet about it. He padded into the kitchen, opened the cupboard, and closed it again; there was nothing there. It was time to leave another note asking the neighbor boy to make a run to the store.

There was a noise by the back door, and Lyle froze. *It's a bur-glar. Or it's one of the Ibis Lyles. Or maybe it's just the wind tapping the tree against my window.* He heard it again, a loud click or a knock, not like a friendly knock on the door but a determined, mechani-cal thunk; someone was definitely there. He scrounged on the counter for a weapon, finding a knife handle in the darkness and holding it determinedly in front of him. *It's a killer,* he thought. *It's an assassin, from Ibis or the government or even from NewYew—I wouldn't put it past them. Maybe that Christian group linked me to Ku-vam and decided to take me down, too. Too many people want me dead.*

He took a cautious step toward the back door, holding his knife in front of him, watching the doorknob slowly turn of its own accord. He raised the knife, hands trembling, and the lock opened with a click. The door swung open slowly, and Cynthia stepped in. She was dressed in loose black pants and a black turtle-neck, a pair of small metal lock picks glinting faintly in the star-light.

Lyle stared at her, confused. *Cynthia knows how to pick locks?*

Cynthia scanned the room and recoiled with a start when she saw him, staggering backward. "Geez, there's a dude with a . . . spoon?" She paused, regaining her composure, and a large man, also dressed in black, swung into the doorway with a pistol aimed straight at Lyle's chest. Lyle yelped and dropped his knife, which clattered away from him on the tiled floor. He peered at it in the light from the doorway. It *was* a spoon.

"This the guy?" asked the big man, and Cynthia nodded, whispering, "Yeah, I've seen that face a hundred times. I took better care of it, though—geez, man, the least you could do is take a shower every now and then."

"Cynthia?" asked Lyle.

The large man stepped in carefully, pushing past Lyle and sighting down each hall and doorway with his gun. "Is there anyone else in here?"

"No," said Lyle. "What are . . . who are you? And Cynthia, why are you dressed like a burglar?"

"Because he is a burglar," said another woman. Susan stepped into the doorway with a wry smile. "This is Tony Hicks, he was in our product test. Sorry about the break-in, we didn't know if you were awake. Or alive."

"I . . . ," Lyle stammered. "What?"

Susan came in, patted him on the shoulder with a smile, and pushed past him. Cynthia—*or Tony*, thought Lyle—came in behind her, glancing back outside suspiciously before closing the door.

"Doesn't look like anyone followed us," he/she said, then turned to Lyle. "You got anything to eat?"

"We're good," said the large man, returning from the front room and sliding his pistol back into a holster on his belt. "Nobody else in the house, but a hundred-year-old lady, and she's not waking up anytime soon. It's possible they've got him bugged more subtly, but I doubt it—if they'd heard us come in, they'd have done something by now."

"All right, stop," said Lyle, "everybody stop right now and tell me exactly what's going on. Susan I know, and if that's actually Tony, then I . . . still don't have any idea what's going on." He looked at the large man. "Who are you? And then who are you really?"

"His name is Larry," said Susan, pulling out one of the kitchen chairs and sitting down. Tony/Cynthia was still rooting through the fridge, one hand keeping the light switch off and the other holding a small flashlight. "Larry was one of our guards at the NewYew prison estate in the Hamptons. Well, I suppose technically he was most of our guards, but this one is the original."

Larry tipped an imaginary hat. "Nice to meet you."

"You're talking about the house from your thing on the news?" Lyle asked. "The police checked that out—there was nothing there."

"We scattered right after Susan escaped," said Larry, leaning against the wall.

Lyle's eyes went wide. "So that was real? I knew NewYew had probably done something to you, but I thought you were in São Tomé with the others—"

"No one was in São Tomé," said Tony/Cynthia, giving up on the fridge and starting in on the cupboards. "Except maybe Carl; we never saw him with us. They took everyone who'd been compromised by the lotion—all the test subjects, all the factory workers, everyone—and kept us in Cynthia Mummer's house in the Hamptons. Or my house, I guess, technically, if I wanted to share it with six other Cynthias. Don't you have any food?"

"There's probably some cans of something in the side pantry," said Lyle, pointing at a tall cupboard in the corner, "but . . . how are you Cynthia? It doesn't make any sense—you should be me."

Tony/Cynthia turned on him suddenly, blinding him with the penlight. "What do you mean 'should be'? You made me into you *on purpose?*"

"No!" said Lyle, squeezing his eyes shut and holding up his hands defensively. "No, of course it wasn't on purpose—we didn't even know what the lotion did until it did it to you. But everything we've learned about it since says you should have turned into me, not Cynthia."

"Back off, Tony," said Susan, then turned to Lyle. "It did turn him into you, but when NewYew caught up with him they turned him into Cynthia, and they turned some of the others into Jeffrey Montgomery and . . . the Asian guy, the lawyer."

"Sunny?"

"Yeah. They had about four or five of each, plus me, and they offered us a million dollars each to help keep them out of jail."

"How?"

Susan shrugged. "We still don't know, but that car bomb was probably part of it. Whatever it is, it's probably still happening—I think Tony here's the only other one who ran."

Lyle looked at the woman prowling restlessly through his kitchen, holding a can of SpaghettiOs and slamming drawer after drawer.

"Where's your damn can opener?"

"Why'd you leave?" asked Lyle.

Tony/Cynthia frowned. "What do you mean?"

"She offered you a million dollars; anyone would have taken that. Why'd you leave?"

"I was *going* to take it," he/she said, "but then I went into menopause." He opened another drawer and peered in. "I figured that hag deserves whatever I can do to her."

Susan nodded, all business. "When the house evacuated, Larry and Tony ended up in a car together, driving to the new safe house, and started talking."

"Turned out neither of us was real happy with NewYew," said Larry, "so we took a wrong turn and disappeared. We did a few drive-bys of the corporate office, kind of staking the place out, making some plans, and we ran into Susan doing the same thing. We started talking, and she insisted that you were the key to bringing them down."

"We've tried every address where I thought you might be hiding," said Susan. "I'm glad we found you."

Lyle was still staring at Larry. "So you worked for them?"

"I was part of what we'll call a 'private security company,'"

said Larry. "We did odd jobs for Cynthia Mummer all the time—
anything she couldn't do above the table. They cloned me because,
well, look at me." He spread his arms and stood up straight; he
was well over six feet tall and built like a bear. "I was always the
guy nobody wanted to mess with; now nobody wants to mess
with any of them."

Lyle nodded, admitting the point, then waved toward the
counter. "Can opener's in the drawer under the microwave."

Tony/Cynthia wiggled the can and smiled. "Thanks, man."

Susan leaned forward. "Larry's been invaluable, and Tony's
got a pretty wide range of skills. I didn't think anyone could
find a way through the web of security out there, but he's got
chops."

"So they're really watching me?" asked Lyle. "I wasn't sure."

"They're everywhere," said Larry.

"Your block's got an old irrigation canal running between the
backyards," said Tony, demonstrating the narrow width with his
hands. "It's a foot and a half, maybe two feet wide, full of weeds
and junk. A lot of these old neighborhoods have them, from like
a hundred years ago, but those geniuses staking out the house
didn't seem to have any idea."

Susan put her hand on the table, pulling Lyle's attention back
to herself. "We make a good team," she said, "but you, Lyle;
you're the key. You've got to help us bring them down."

"Bring NewYew down?" asked Lyle. "Like, the whole
company?"

"The executives are already in hiding," said Susan. "But the
company, and ReBirth itself, is still active. Everyone else in that
car was a duplicate, but they never made a duplicate of you. They
thought they were killing the real Lyle, because they know that
you're the only one who can bring them down. You have all the
knowledge, all the personal testimony, all the keys to the closets
full of skeletons. You can destroy NewYew, you can destroy
ReBirth, you can—"

"No," said Lyle, "I don't want to destroy ReBirth."

"What?" asked Susan. Her mouth hung open in disbelief. "Are you serious? After everything they've done to us? To you?"

"The company, sure," said Lyle, "the company's evil incarnate, but the lotion itself is good. I mean, in theory. It can be used for good things."

"I'm a *woman*," said Tony/Cynthia. "I don't even know how to wipe myself when I pee. What the hell kind of 'good' are you talking about?"

"Not you, obviously," said Lyle, "but other people—the twin girls, or the cancer patient, or that boy in Hoboken with cystic fibrosis—we made him a twin of his brother. Three more weeks and his body will be totally healthy."

"That was Guru Kuvam's project," said Susan, frowning. "Were you mixed up with him?"

"I'm the one who gave him the lotion."

Susan threw up her hands. "Come on, Lyle, how many different ways are you trying to end the world, here? Have you done anything worthwhile at any step of this process?"

"We're giving people life, Susan, we can't just stop."

"We can," said Susan firmly. "This stuff is evil—you don't know what's it like to have it used on you."

"Yes I do," said Lyle. "Didn't you know? It's gotten me, too."

Susan narrowed her eyes. "You?"

"I'm a clone of myself." He stared at her a moment, then stood up suddenly and pulled up his T-shirt. "See my stomach? I had my appendix and gallbladder removed a few years ago—I had five little scars from the endoscopic surgery: here, here, here, here, and here. Do you see anything?"

"I see some belly button lint," said Tony/Cynthia.

Susan scowled. "The scars are gone." She looked Lyle hard in the eyes. "My elbow scar is gone, too, from when I had my tennis injury. What does it mean?"

"It means that ReBirth is rebuilding us," said Lyle, "not just once but constantly. You're probably thirsty all the time, right? And starving?"

Tony/Cynthia looked down at his can of pasta, and tucked it quietly behind him on the counter.

"Your body is being aggressively rewritten," said Lyle, "over and over and over again, getting rid of everything that doesn't match the template."

"Is it supposed to do that?" asked Larry.

"It's not supposed to do anything!" Lyle said. "It's a moisturizer, for goodness sake, it's a *hand lotion*. Nothing it does makes sense. Do you know why nobody's knocked it off yet?"

"There's a black market," said Susan.

"That's just somebody repackaging NewYew's lotion," said Lyle. "I'm talking about actual knockoffs, where someone else has found the formula or reverse-engineered it or whatever, and started making their own. That's the first thing everyone does when any new product hits the market, but no has done it with ReBirth because it's impossible: it won't work when anyone else makes it. It doesn't work for anyone but us."

"This guy's crazy," said Tony/Cynthia softly.

"There hasn't been time for knockoffs yet," said Susan, staring angrily at Lyle. "It's only been out a few days."

"It was stolen months ago," said Lyle. "Ibis even kidnapped me, and *I* spent weeks trying to do it, and I still couldn't. I told them the same thing I'm telling you: it doesn't follow any rules that make any kind of sense. And it's far, far more aggressive than we thought."

Susan stood, walking to the wall. "It doesn't matter how it works—all we need to do is destroy it."

"And what?" asked Lyle. "Destroy every bottle in existence? Kill everyone who's already been infected?"

"We're not going to kill anybody," said Susan fiercely. "All you have to do is testify, bring down the company, and—"

"Now you're the crazy one," said Lyle. "You can never get rid of this. It's out there, and it's everywhere, and it will never go away."

"So what do you want us to do? Hide in a hole and pretend it isn't happening?"

Lyle gestured around at his darkened house. "Yeah, I think that's pretty obviously exactly what I decided to do."

Tony/Cynthia planted herself in front of him, hands on her hips, and shot Lyle a look that was almost, but not quite, the same fearsome look Cynthia made when she was mad. "Listen, buddy. We came here because NewYew is doing something wrong, and we want to stop them. Your testimony can do that, and we're not going to let you just sit here doing nothing."

"You might be able to cut a deal," said Larry. "Give them the other executives and you walk free."

"The point is this," said Susan. "Are you going to turn yourself in willingly, or are we doing it for you?"

Lyle narrowed his eyes, feeling suddenly cold. "What do you mean," he asked, " 'willingly'?"

Larry's bulk filled his left-side peripheral vision. "I think you know exactly what we mean."

Lyle swallowed. "Fine. Let me get dressed, then." Susan nodded, and Lyle padded down the hall to his room. *Is this it? Turn myself in to the police or they'll do it for me? I don't want to go to jail— if I even end up in jail. ReBirth is too powerful, and the government's just going to do the same thing Ibis did: put me in a room somewhere, and force me to make more. But who knows what they'll use it for?*

He turned on the shower, and looked through his grandpa's old clothes. The only things he had to wear.

But. . . .

But Susan came to me. She had a problem, she needed help, and she came to me. Even though . . . He knew that there was no chance between them, there never had been, and yet . . . *She came to me. And she had a very impersonal reason, but . . . Was she changing?*

Did people ever really change?

Lyle looked out the back window, trying to see the little irrigation path Tony/Cynthia had mentioned. He'd never known it was back there, but now that he was looking for it there was an obvious space between his grandma's fence and the neighbor's. What else had he been looking at for years, and never really seen?

Jail, he thought. *Federal custody. What good would it even do, striking back at NewYew now that ReBirth was already out? If the damage was already done, what good would it do to punish them, and who was he to do it?*

He looked at the shower, listened to the water hiss down, a curtain of white noise drowning everything out. He couldn't even hear the three intruders anymore, and for a moment he closed his eyes and imagined they were gone, and everyone was gone, and everything, and he was free. He didn't have to turn himself in or go to jail or anything. He couldn't hear a sound.

And they couldn't hear him.

He looked at the shower again, then the window. *What do I want? Not jail, and not to help the government make ReBirth for who knows what new power scheme.* He knew what he didn't want, but what *did* he want? He wanted to people to listen—to finally stop thinking about themselves and listen to him, to all the ways he knew ReBirth could be good and helpful. All the ways it could save the world. Maybe he'd get a chance to do that in prison, but he'd have better luck out here. Kuvam was dead— why couldn't Lyle step up and start helping people in the same way Kuvam had?

Lyle made up his mind in a flash, and dressed quickly in his grandfather's old clothes. He pulled on his grandpa's shoes and eased the window open, jumping out and catching on the roses as he tumbled past them. He ran to the back fence, glancing back at the dark house, searching in the dark until he found the irrigation channel—a narrow, bricked ditch behind the bushes that hadn't seen real irrigation water in years. He glanced again at the house, then pushed his way into the ditch and disappeared into the darkness.

34

Thursday, July 12
9:22 A.M.
Pressroom, the Capitol, Washington, D.C.

155 DAYS TO THE END OF THE WORLD

"Thank you for coming," said the speaker. "I'm Senator Eric Moore, special liaison to the Department of Homeland Security. It is with a heavy heart that I approach you today with a very grave announcement. This is not something we do lightly, but under the circumstances we have no choice. Please allow me to set the stage with a couple of news stories."

He opened a slim leather binder and began reading. "On Thursday, July eleventh, reformed rapist Clay Burgener returned home from work, reached for his doorknob, and found it smeared with something white and viscous. Forensic tests show that the substance was an imprinted sample of ReBirth hand lotion. One of Burgener's victims was found by police just two blocks away, and confessed to planting the lotion in the hope that Burgener, transformed into an attractive woman, would be raped, as well, and thus experience the same hell he'd forced so many women to endure. The woman is awaiting trial; Burgener is under close hospital supervision, and has already shown signs of increased estrogen production."

The crowd said nothing, tense and nervous. They'd heard this before—they were waiting for the announcement at the end. Moore surveyed them carefully, then turned the page.

"On July seventh, at approximately eight thirty in the morning, Brian Yancy arrived at his high school in Casper, Wyoming, dressed in a black trench coat and heavily armed: not with guns, but with ReBirth. Over the course of the next half hour he sprayed and infected nearly thirty-seven students with lotion that had been imprinted with his own DNA. When police, wearing hazmat suits, finally subdued the teen, he told them he was sick of not fitting in at school, and wanted to let the rest of the students know what it was like to be him."

The crowd sat in uncomfortable silence. Moore turned the page. "One more. That same night, late in the evening, the Codwell family of Bamberg, South Carolina, was attacked by men in traditional Ku Klux Klan attire; Tyler Codwell, his wife, Marylou, and their two children were all dragged out on the lawn, tied down with baling twine, and sprayed liberally with ReBirth. An anonymous letter to the local newspaper stated, and I quote, 'God has given us the means to cleanse His earth.' Similar incidents were recorded on July ninth and tenth throughout the country, targeting Mexicans, Arabs, and in one case, whites."

Moore closed the binder, stared at it a moment, then looked up. "ReBirth was introduced with a lofty potential, but day by day, story by story, the dregs of our society are proving its true use. As of this morning, the FDA has reclassified ReBirth from an herbal lotion to a biological weapon." A buzz of urgent whispers rose up from the crowd, and Moore raised his voice. "Effective immediately, anyone possessing or using ReBirth, in any capacity, will be considered a terrorist and a threat to national security. All stock owned by stores or suppliers will be confiscated; all manufacturing facilities will be shut down and their assets held indefinitely. The originators of the product, the cosmetic company NewYew, will be closed down immediately, its remaining executives arrested, and its records seized for federal trial. The U.S. government will not see its citizens sprayed, tortured, and remade by this or any other harmful biological agent. That is all."

The pressroom exploded in noise, journalists leaping to their feet, hands raised, shouting for attention. Moore held up his hand for silence, but a man in the back stepped into the aisle.

"How can you even think about doing this?" asked the man.

"ReBirth may have some bad uses, but it is still the greatest medical breakthrough in the history of our species. We can cure cancer with this—we can live forever. You are shutting the door on our very future."

Moore eyed the man carefully. *There's something wrong with him,* he thought. *That's not a journalist's question.* He wore a brown hat and had long hair that obscured his face. Moore glanced to the side of the stage, locked eyes with one of the security team, and nodded almost imperceptibly toward the suspicious man. The guard faded back into the rear halls immediately, speaking into his wrist. Moore looked back at the man in the audience.

"We are restricting ReBirth the same way we would choose to restrict any technology of similar power," said Moore. "X-rays are an invaluable tool for doctors and dentists, but that doesn't mean we let just anyone play around with them. We have to have rules, or the world falls into chaos."

"And is it not chaos that you threaten with this announcement?" asked the man. He stepped forward, walking slowly toward the stage. Moore's mental alarms clanged wildly, and out of nowhere a swarm of black-suited security guards surrounded the man on all sides. Their weapons weren't drawn; they were waiting for the man to make a move. He stopped and smiled benignly.

"You think I'm here to harm you," he said, and shook his head. He pulled off his hat, and with it a wig, exposing softer, browner hair underneath.

I know him, thought Moore, *I just can't put a name to it . . .*

"I am not here to bring death," said the man, "but life, for I am life—the energy of the universe made form and flesh." He took off his glasses; his name was on the tip of Moore's tongue. "It is ReBirth that has saved me," said the man, "and so it will save us all." The shock of recognition hit Moore like a speeding truck.

"Kuvam," he whispered.

The guru dropped his costume and raised his arms, turning slowly so the full crowd—and every camera—could see him plainly.

"Behold!" he shouted. "I am Lazarus, risen from the dead. I am Siddhartha, Elijah, and the phoenix in his ashes. I am the sun that sets and the sun that rises again.

"I am the new day."

35

"They're taking it all for themselves," said Susan, seething with rage. "Did you hear what he said on TV? Not 'destroy your lotion' but 'give your lotion to us.' They're stockpiling it!"

"At least they're getting it off the streets," said Larry. "That's good, right?"

"That's terrible," said Tony/Cynthia. "I still need to get out of this body."

"Getting it off the streets doesn't count if all they do is put it somewhere else," said Susan. "It needs to be destroyed, and that's never going to happen if the most powerful government in the world holds a massive depot of it! Can you even imagine what the CIA could do with that stuff? The NSA? It's not a beauty product or a biological weapon, it's the greatest tool of espionage the world has ever seen. They could replace anyone who speaks out against them—they could replace foreign leaders." She kicked the tray table her breakfast was sitting on, scattering it across the room. "What's going on? This makes me so angry!"

"Getting angry doesn't solve problems," said Larry. "*Acting* on anger solves problems."

"You're right," said Susan. "We need to act. We need to protest. NewYew has bigger problems now than trying to kill us, so let's go public—let's picket the steps of City Hall—"

"That's not what I mean," said Larry. "There are activists all over the place already, and nobody is listening, and three more voices isn't going to make any difference. It's time we stop shouting and really get their attention."

"Okay," said Susan. "I'm listening. What do you have in mind?"

"They're dismantling the bottling plants tomorrow," said Larry, "but you know where those plants are. Is there one we can hit?"

"Hit?" asked Susan.

"Hit," said Larry. "Shoot at. Blow up. Is there a ReBirth plant we can get to before the government does, and destroy all the lotion before they take it?"

"Whoa," said Tony/Cynthia. "That's a big step up from a picket line."

"Yep." Susan nodded, trying to convince herself that this was a good idea. She knew something needed to be done, but to actually blow something up? "It's just like . . . spiking a tree," she said.

"Exactly," said Larry.

"We're not actually hurting anyone," she said. "We're just . . . creating a situation in which, if they do something wrong—like try to take a bunch of lotion—they'll hurt themselves."

"Exactly," said Larry. "I know some guys who work with explosives—"

"What guys?" asked Susan. "Like, terrorists or something? I don't want to work with terrorists."

"Susan," said Larry, "we're going to blow up a building."

Susan nodded again, then looked at Tony/Cynthia.

"Well," said Tony/Cynthia. "Are we serious, or are we serious?"

"Okay," said Susan. "Call your guys. Let's do this."

36

The NewYew manufacturing plant was in a low valley in Upstate New York, surrounded by trees and little else. Susan adjusted her grip on the binoculars, watching the men in the factory yard as they loaded barrel after barrel of ReBirth onto a fleet of trucks. American soldiers, armed and alert. She thumbed the button on her walkie-talkie. "I don't feel good about this."

Larry's voice came back, tinny and faint through the scrambled signal. "What do you feel worse about: attacking soldiers, or giving the government several thousand gallons of blank ReBirth?"

Susan grimaced, and thumbed the radio again. "This is treason."

"What do you feel worse about?" Larry repeated. "Treason, or giving the government several thousand gallons of blank ReBirth?"

"Fine," said Susan. "But we can do this without hurting anyone, right?"

"Not hurting anyone would have been a lot easier if we'd gotten here last night," said Tony/Cynthia, speaking through a third radio. He and Larry were on the far side of the factory complex, hidden behind a low rise with five of Larry's "contacts." "We could have blown the whole factory before the soldiers even showed up."

"Oh, I'm sorry," said Larry, "maybe we should have let *you* mobilize and arm a makeshift terrorist cell in eight hours."

"It's been twenty-four hours," said Tony/Cynthia.

"Yeah, I needed some extra time to find, purchase, and assemble two exceptionally illegal explosive devices," said Larry. "I apologize that 'accomplishing important objectives' is a real-world activity that takes actual time to perform."

"Stop arguing," said Susan. "How soon are we ready?"

"Three minutes," said Larry. "You've got the phone to trigger bomb one?"

"Right here." Susan held it up with her free hand: a little prepaid flip phone that couldn't be traced to any of their names. "What's this one going to blow up?"

"The generator by the back fence," said Larry. "One of my guys just placed it."

Susan picked up her binoculars again and looked for the generator—it was a hundred yards away from the trucks. She thumbed the walkie-talkie again. "How big is this explosion going to be? That won't hit any of the lotion from there."

"That one's not supposed to hit the lotion," said Larry, "that's our distraction: you blow the generator, the soldiers all look at it, and we pop up behind them. Then we lovingly yet firmly convince them to lay down their weapons, and we blow up the trucks with bomb two."

"Does 'lovingly yet firmly' involve shooting them?" asked Susan. "I really don't want to hurt anyone."

"That's why you're blowing up the generator," said Tony/Cynthia. "There's nobody anywhere near it."

"But what about you guys?" asked Susan. "And that *America's Most Wanted* greatest hits compilation you've got with you?"

"If you're not ready for this, tell us now," said Larry. "We're about to do something that we can't do halfway: either this is important enough to warrant attacking our own government, in which case some soldiers are bound to get in the way sooner or later, or else this *isn't* important enough and we walk away now. There's no middle ground."

Susan shook her head, watching the soldiers through her bino-culars. Was she ready for this? Those men had families. They had names.

And if they took this ReBirth, innocent people might lose their names and their faces and everything else.

Susan opened the flip phone, and held her finger over the but-ton. "I'm in. Just . . . don't hurt anyone unless you have to."

"Bomb two is ready," said Larry. "Everyone check in."

"Ready," said Tony/Cynthia.

"Ready," said Susan.

"My men are ready, too," said Larry. "Give us a countdown and blow the generators."

"All right, then," said Susan. "Let's betray our country. Three, two, one." She pressed the button, and listened as the phone beeped softly.

Nothing exploded.

"You're supposed to push the button at the end of the count-down," said Larry.

"I did!"

"They're closing the trucks," said Tony/Cynthia. "We've got to do something."

"Call the bomb again," said Larry. "Maybe it just hasn't gone through yet."

"I've called it twice," said Susan, her fingers stabbing madly at the flip phone's keypad. "It won't connect—what kind of use-less cell plan did you buy that doesn't have service in the only place we actually need the phone to work!"

"Stop shouting!" said Larry. "They're going to hear us!"

"They started one of the trucks," said Tony/Cynthia. "They're getting away!"

"Do something," said Susan.

"Do what?" demanded Larry.

"I don't know!" said Susan. "Just . . . something!"

She heard a shot, and looked up in shock.

Seconds later it seemed like the entire factory yard was filled with gunfire. Susan dropped her radio and flip phone and grabbed her binoculars. Her heart was beating so fast her hands felt numb. She scanned the yard from her position in the trees, seeing Larry and his men locked in a firefight with the soldiers. Some of the soldiers were already lifeless on the ground, their friends dragging them to cover.

One of the trucks started moving, and then another. *They're getting away,* thought Susan. Larry's team was pinned down by the soldiers, and the army was sure to get at least three trucks onto the road, if not all four. *I have to do something.* Susan grimaced, screaming silently in her head, and then got up and ran.

The factory yard was a mess of cars and bodies and rubble. Susan hadn't been counting how many soldiers were dead, but she knew it couldn't be many—most of them would still be up and shooting. Someone fired a burst into the windshield of one of the trucks, and it swerved wildly; the attack was slowing them down, certainly, but it wasn't going to stop them. Susan patted the cell phone in her pocket and ran the other way, toward the generator and the useless bomb. It wasn't big, but it was the only weapon she had.

She found the brick of C-4 tucked into the space between two fuel tanks for the big gas generator. She didn't know much about bombs, but she probed the connections with her finger, and everything seemed secure. The pins were pressed snugly into the C-4, the detonator was plugged in, the cell phone was attached to the detonator . . . and turned off. She snarled a curse at whatever idiot had placed the bomb, and reached for the button to turn it on—and stopped. The call hadn't gone through, but the phone would register a missed call as soon as it powered up, and even that small signal would trigger the explosion. She stared at the phone, her finger hovering over the power button. There was no way to trigger it remotely anymore.

We've already started this, she thought. *We can't stop now.* She stood up, gripped the bomb in one hand, and ran.

The firefight was forty yards away, the soldiers surrounded by a ring of black SUVs. Some of the trucks were still working their way toward the main road, but the main group of soldiers was crouched in the middle of the ring, covering the trucks as they made their escape. *As long as they don't turn around and see me—*

—a shot went past Susan's ear, and she lowered her head and kept running. *They saw me.* Thirty yards. Another shot, and then another. She took a risk and pressed the power button on the phone, holding it tightly while the phone came slowly to life. Two more shots. Twenty yards. Another shot. The phone lit up, power coursing through its circuits, and Susan clenched her teeth, praying that she had just a few more seconds before it booted up enough to received any kind of a signal. Two more shots, and a sharp sting in her leg. She staggered, lost her footing, and as she fell she hurled the bomb forward over the top of a black SUV. Halfway through its flight the phone chirped loudly, singing a jaunty marimba as it arced down into the center of the enemy, and exploded.

Susan hit the ground hard and covered her head, deafened by the roar of the fireball and seared by the sudden heat. The SUV took most of the force of the blast and she gasped for air, reeling even from the cushioned shock. Her ears rang, the world eerily silent, and her eyes were too blurry to see. She forced herself to stand up, to keep going; the enemy would be shocked, like she was, but they might not be dead yet. She stumbled over a fallen soldier and picked up his weapon, limping around the shattered SUV, seeing a soldier reach out toward his rifle. She fired as she walked, blasting anything that moved and pumping to reload— *boom, ke-chak, boom, ke-chak, boom.* Three trucks pulled toward the gate, slowly gaining speed, but thanks to her bomb the tattered remains of Larry's team were now free to move, and they charged out from their gully, pelting the trucks with bullets. The first truck veered sharply to the right, nearly colliding with the other, but the second truck sped up and pulled ahead just in

time. Larry jumped in front of the third truck, killing the engine
block with a burst from his rifle, and the fourth truck slammed
into it, jackknifing itself and slowly tipping as its own momen-
tum pulled it in the wrong direction. The second truck roared
through the hail of gunfire and burst through the gate, escaping
onto the main road just as the fourth truck finally passed its balance point and tipped over. The barrels crashed down, a tidal
wave of ReBirth exploding out as they hit the ground and burst
open. Susan fired at the escaping truck, but it was too far away;
it turned a corner and disappeared.

Susan blew out a slow breath and walked toward the final up-
right truck, skirting the pool of lotion on the ground. Larry and
his men were rounding up the survivors, and she approached one
who seemed to be the leader, kneeling on the ground with his
thumbs zip-tied behind his head. He looked at her venomously.

"You'll never be able to sell this stuff," he said, "it's garbage.
All the good stuff was already gone."

"We've got two trucks of ReBirth here," said Susan. "Three
if the stuff on the ground is salvageable. Is any of it blank?"

The man laughed, shaking his head. "You don't even know
what batch this is? It's not blank, it's not a supermodel, it's not
an athlete, it's not even a celebrity." He laughed again, wild and
desperate. "It's the first batch—the accident."

"He's lying," said Larry.

"Of course he is!" Susan shouted. She took another step toward
him. "You wouldn't have fought so hard to keep it if it was
useless."

"We were trying to destroy it," said the agent. "Do you know
what will . . . ?" He went quiet. Closing his mouth tightly.

"What will what?" asked Susan. "Do I know what will what?"

"I'm not telling you anything."

Ke-chak. Susan held the shotgun just a few feet from his face.

"You're a lot more hardcore than I realized," said Tony/
Cynthia.

"Listen," said Susan, stepping closer to the agent. "I'm in this all the way now. I've killed so many American soldiers today I've lost track—one more or less isn't going to change anything if they catch me. So you tell me why you risked your lives to destroy four truckloads of useless lotion, or I'll move my magic finger and make your head disappear."

The agent stared back, eyes cold as iron. "You just fought and died and murdered for four truckloads of Lyle Fontanelle."

Susan frowned. "It's all Lyle?"

"This is the accident batch. He imprinted it before they knew how it worked."

"Hooray!" said Tony, running to the pool and thrusting in his hand. "I'm a llama again!"

"You want to be Lyle?" asked Larry. "He's a wanted criminal."

"I don't care who I am," said Tony, grabbing his crotch, "as long I get little Tony back."

"If that lotion gets out . . . ," said Susan. He paused. "Tony might be the only person in the world who's happy to be Lyle." She paused, her mind racing. "The black market for ReBirth is already growing, government crackdown or not. But if that market were suddenly flooded with lotion that nobody wanted, and no one could tell the difference—"

"Then no one would trust the lotion anymore," said Larry. "They'd stop using it completely, because the only alternative is to turn into Lyle."

"Lesson learned," said Susan. "Problem solved. We'll have a few extra Lyles running around, but no one will ever use ReBirth again. People will destroy every bottle of it they can find."

"You're insane," said the agent, "you can't do—"

Boom.

Ke-chak.

PART THREE
THE COMMON MAN

37

Friday, August 17
11:22 P.M.
Somewhere in Atlantic City

119 DAYS TO THE END OF THE WORLD

"Looking for a date?"

Lyle walked on, keeping his head down. The girl called after him, but not eagerly, and moved on to the next guy after Lyle continued to ignore her. He passed an alley, heard vague scuffling and the thud of a muted punch. He pulled his hood down farther over his eyes and kept walking.

Every dollar he owned was shoved in his shoes and underwear, with just a small roll of bills in his pocket—something to give the muggers to avoid a beating. It was just a couple of bucks, and he looked poor enough. If they ever guessed he had nearly five thousand dollars hidden somewhere on his body he'd be dead.

Of course, if anyone figured out who he really was he'd be as good as dead anyway. NewYew had been tried, convicted, and dissolved, its component parts—those legitimate enough to continue in operation—spread to the four winds and gobbled up by eager cosmetic competition. Every employee the courts could find had been duly punished for their connection to ReBirth, the world's most popular biological weapon, but the government was hungry for more. They wanted him to make more, but he refused to be a part of it. He wanted to help people who needed it. He'd already given away the last remnants of the lotion he'd taken from Ibis, curing a handful of cancer patients in back-alley deals, and now he needed more. That meant going to the places were ReBirth was still being sold: to parking lots and overpasses

and back-alley beauty clinics, asking questions and trying to figure out where the dealers got their lotion from. If he could find
more blank ReBirth, he could do more good in the world. . . .

A car drove by, slowly, and Lyle turned away, pretending to
talk on a phone, keeping his back to the street until the car was
gone. Hiding from the police had put him in some very dark
places, with some very dangerous people.

"You want a date?"

Another girl, barely half a block from the first. Lyle glanced
at her, mumbling his refusal, but stopped short when he saw her
face. The girl laughed.

"That's right," she said, spreading her arms. "Victoria Carver.
You ever do a movie star, baby?"

"Where'd you get that?"

"God and my mama."

Lyle stepped closer. "This is ReBirth," he whispered. "Where
did you get this dose? Where'd you get the DNA?"

"You're ruining my image, buddy," the hooker hissed. "Guys
like to pretend I'm the real thing, get it?"

"Fine," said Lyle, "you're Vicky Carver, just . . ." Lyle grunted
in defeat. What good would it do to track down some random
arm of the black market? "Never mind." He fished in his jeans
for his wad of bills and pressed it into her hand. "Sorry."

She stared at the money in shock, but swore at his back a
moment later as he walked away. "Five bucks, huh? What am
I, homeless?" Lyle adjusted his hoodie and kept walking.

"Looking for some ReBirth?" The voice was deep, and when
Lyle glanced to the side he saw that the speaker was tall and
narrow, nearly seven feet, with shadowed features that looked
hawklike in the streetlights. "Heard you talking to the lady."

"Maybe," said Lyle. He swallowed, wondering if this dealer
might finally be the one to give him the info he needed. Belat-
edly he glanced up the street, as if expecting a cop car to leap
out from behind a bush. He looked back at the man. "What do
you have?"

"Not saying I have anything," said the man. His bass voice rumbled. "ReBirth's illegal, you know that as well as I do."

"Then why'd you bring it up?"

"Because I might know a guy," said the man. "Depending on what you're looking for, anyway."

Lyle bit his lip. "Originals," he said. "Not the celebrity stuff like her, the real NewYew stuff. Does your guy have any of that?"

"Probably," said the man. His voice was conversational, but always with a hint of professionalism. "How much you looking to spend?"

Lyle spoke carefully, hoping that any thieves listening in would be fooled by a simple misdirection. "I don't have it on me, but say . . . a thousand."

The man laughed. "What the hell kind of ReBirth you think you're gonna buy with one thousand dollars?"

"That's not enough?" Prices had gone up.

"If you ever find a place where that is enough you let me know, and I'll shop there, too."

"Who carries around more than a thousand dollars?" asked Lyle. "Especially on a street like this?"

"Smart people," said the man, his deep voice rich with authority. "People who care about the product they're buying. You want to go cheap on something that alters your DNA, you be my guest; you go across the street there and that kid in the red hat'll sell you a drop of ReBirth for a hundred bucks—but you get what you pay for. You're playing Russian roulette with him and everyone like him: might end up with any kind of face, any kind of body, maybe a woman, maybe nothing at all. A hundred bucks for a drop of L'Oréal. Or like as not these days, you'll end up as Joe."

"Who's Joe?"

"Joe Average; some no-name that's been cropping up all over these days. Don't know why they'd make a lotion of him, but there's an awful lot of him on the market."

Lyle frowned, concerned. He didn't remember anyone in their

list of imprints who could be considered average. He'd have to follow up on it later; for now, he steeled his courage and looked the salesman in the face. "I can go as high as five, but for that I want the real stuff—the blank stuff."

The man shook his head. "Five won't get you blanks, but it'll get you a pretty face. Something Latino maybe, or Asian. Good bone structure."

"Latino?"

"You wanna retain the benefits of racial privilege you gotta pay a little more. Eight at least for a white guy, seven if you're buying for a lady friend, or if you swing that way yourself. I don't judge."

Lyle glanced up the street again, then back at the man. "Where do they get it?"

"You are like a stupid question machine."

"ReBirth was seized by the government," said Lyle. "They have all of it, or they're supposed to, so where does your 'friend' get the stuff he's selling?"

"I don't have time to sit and chat about stuff I don't know anything about."

"But of course you know," said Lyle, dropping his voice and leaning in closer, "we're just both pretending you don't, so please . . . stop pretending and tell me."

"This conversation is over," said the man, and he rose to full height, towering over Lyle, and turned and walked away without another word. Lyle cursed himself for pushing too hard. *I need to know where they get it,* he thought, *especially the new stuff, this "Joe Average."* The more he thought about it, the more he wondered if maybe he knew exactly who this Joe Average really was. *What if that's me? What if the Lyle lotion got out, somehow, and more Lyles will be cropping up left and right?* He looked back down the street, saw Victoria Carver again, and wondered how she could possibly afford that kind of black market DNA. He made a quick decision and started back toward her. She was standing in a pool of lamplight, dressed in a too-short skirt and a jacket that would have looked expensive if he wasn't comparing it to the cost of her face. She saw him coming and looked away, trying to catch the eye of a car passing by on the street.

"I changed my mind," he said.

"Too late."

"I don't want . . ." He fumbled for words, having no idea how to pick up a hooker. "I just want information, but I'll pay for your time." She stepped away. "I'll pay double," he said. She stopped and turned back slowly.

"What kind of information?"

"Do you have somewhere private we can go?"

She thought a moment, then nodded. "I got a place." She turned and started walking, without waiting to see if he followed. He hurried to catch up, terrified that someone would see him, wondering at which point, exactly, what he was doing became illegal. Surely walking down the street with a prostitute wasn't illegal all by itself? He wanted to ask about her rates, realizing that he had no idea how much money he'd just promised to double, but was too scared to do it in public. The woman led him to a cheap motel, not far from the cheap motel he was staying in himself, and stopped at the front desk. The man there was drab and sagging; he looked at her, glanced disinterestedly at Lyle, and handed the woman a key. Lyle looked away, cursing himself for letting the man see his face, and followed the fake movie star to a first-floor room in a dark back corner of the parking lot.

Lyle spoke the instant the door closed: "How much, exactly, are your rates? I need to get the money."

The woman rolled her eyes. "You don't have it on you?"

"I do," said Lyle, "I just . . ." He didn't want to show her where he was hiding it, or inadvertently let her see how much he had. "Give me a minute, I need to use the bathroom first, just tell me how much."

She stared at him flatly. "Four hundred bucks."

"Four hundred dollars?"

"You said double," said the woman, gesturing at her body, "and this doesn't come cheap."

"Fine," said Lyle, "just . . . I'll be right back." He slipped into the dingy motel bathroom, locking the door behind him, and carefully pulled off his right shoe. Inside his shoe, under the orthopedic insert, was a slim stack of hundreds, and he counted out four of them. *This is too much,* he thought suddenly, *I could live for weeks on this, and she won't know anything anyway, but I . . .* He remembered her scorn from before, and imagined her rage if she found out he'd just wasted more of her time. She probably had to pay for the room, and the man at the front desk didn't look like the kind to be happy with a cut of zero dollars. *I've already got her here,* he thought, *I may as well ask her.* He replaced the insert, tied the shoe tightly back on, and flushed the toilet, just for appearances. He unlocked the door and stepped back out to find the girl still standing by the door, her jacket still on.

"You didn't wash your hands."

"I . . . didn't actually do anything, I was just getting money."

"You flushed."

"Look, here it is, four hundred dollars." He walked across the room and handed her bills; she looked at him just a moment before taking the bills, counting them, and tucking them into her purse.

"I could just leave now," she said, gesturing at the door. "Nobody pays up front."

"Call it a professional courtesy," said Lyle, too tired to keep arguing. "Now, I won't pretend that neither of us knows the realities of prostitution, so I'll just say it: you have a . . . pimp, a business manager, who paid for that DNA. Is it the guy at the front desk?"

"A business manager?"

"How much did it cost?" he asked. "Normal ReBirth, the models and such that NewYew packaged before the crackdown, goes for five to eight thousand dollars on the street. How much did you, or your business manager, pay for Victoria Carver?"

"Are you for real?"

"Please just answer my question."

The woman sighed and sat down. "We could have done this in a restaurant, you know, where I could get something to eat."

"I don't want to discuss this in public."

She shrugged. "My 'business manager,' who is not the guy at the front desk, paid twenty thousand dollars for this body. That's cheaper than most because Victoria's pretty common, but most of them are on the West Coast and I'm one of the only Victorias back here in the East, so . . ." She gestured vaguely, as if that explained itself.

Lyle furrowed his brow, shocked at the price. "There's no way you're making that back at two hundred dollars an hour."

"Most of my appointments are prearranged," she said, "high-priced call-girl stuff, fancy hotels and everything. This with you is after-hours work, something for my own pocket instead of his debt." She pulled out a pack of cigarettes.

"That's bad for your health," said Lyle, feeling immediately stupid about it. Smoking was probably the least dangerous part of her lifestyle.

"Shows what you know," said the woman, and lit one up. "ReBirth heals my lungs faster than I can screw them up, and since you're not letting me eat . . ." She took another puff.

"You're right," said Lyle, nodding. He hadn't thought of that, and decided that his own dose would protect him from the secondhand smoke just as easily. He ignored the wisps of blue smoke and got back to business. "So. Victoria Carver's DNA comes at twenty thousand dollars a pop. Are there others, other women, that have more expensive DNA?"

"It's not the DNA, honey, it's what you do with it."

"But there are others?"

She nodded. "My 'business manager' has other girls, yeah.

Cristina Francis and Hermione Granger and like that—big with the nerds. Says if he could get a Princess Leia he'd be a millionaire, but that ship has sailed, hasn't it?" She took another long draw on the cigarette, and blew out a cloud of smoke.

Lyle nodded. "Do you know how much those other girls cost?"

"Hourly or for the night?"

"I mean their DNA."

She tapped the cigarette into the motel ashtray—which hadn't been cleaned since the previous occupants, Lyle noticed. Maybe even before them. "Why are you so interested in all this, huh? Sick of being Joe, want to make the switch to something new?"

Lyle looked at her closely. "Joe?"

"Joe Average," said the woman. "You thought I wouldn't recognize you? I had a client three days ago with the same exact face, same wonky color in his eye, so either you have amnesia or a twin or you got some bad lotion that made you who you are. Maybe that's it, then: you got some bad ReBirth and want revenge on the sellers?"

Lyle put his hand up, half reaching for his eye with the heterochromia, and stopped halfway. "How many of these 'Joe Averages' have you seen?"

"Only the two," said the woman, "but I've heard the stories. Bad lotion on the market, people thinking they'll turn into Enrique the shirtless fireman, and getting Joe instead."

"And you put it together that I was one of them."

She held up the cigarette with a smile. "You understood what I meant about my body rebuilding itself faster than the smoke could hurt it. And you didn't say anything about the secondhand smoke." She took another puff, and blew the smoke out softly. "That doesn't make a lot of sense for an anti–tobacco crusader, but it makes all kinds of sense for another ReBirth clone."

Lyle nodded. "You're good at this."

"I've been in this business a long time."

But you're barely in your twenties, thought Lyle, looking at the girl, then realizing that while the body was mid-twenties, the woman inside could be almost any age at all. "How long?" he asked.

Her eyes narrowed, her mouth curving up in a smirk. "You really want to know?"

"It's okay, I'm a doctor."

"I've heard that one before."

Lyle's face reddened.

The girl leaned back in her chair, draping her arms across the armrests like a woman totally in charge of her situation. "Let's just say I was in this business long enough to get out of it, and then to get back in again when someone offered me a brand-new, twenty-five-year-old body."

Lyle stared, then laughed drily. "I can't say that I blame you."

"It'll be fun while it lasts," she said, nudging her curves here and there, straightening her clothes. "I've been twenty-five before." She looked up. "Nothing lasts forever."

"This will," said Lyle softly. "Same as the lungs, same as everything; it rebuilds itself back from any damage it takes, including age. You'll be twenty-five forever."

She raised her eyebrow. "You serious?"

Lyle nodded.

She gazed at him oddly, studying him as if for the first time. "How do you know that?"

"I told you, I'm a doctor. Sort of."

"Who are you?"

He thought about it, wondering again, as he had for months, who he really was. "I'm nobody," he said. "Just a face in the crowd." He paused, just a moment, then looked at her squarely. "Do you know where I can find the dealer your business manager buys from?"

"Yeah," said the girl, tapping the ashes from her cigarette. "Yeah, I think I can help you out."

38

"Hi, everyone!"

The audience cheered, and Amber Sykes waved back enthusiastically.

"Welcome to the show!" said Amber. The audience continued cheering, egged on by large signs just off camera, and slowly quieted as the signs dimmed. "We've got another great lineup for you today, starting with the guest that *everybody's* been wanting to hear from, possibly the most controversial figure in America—maybe the world—please welcome Guru Kuvam."

The crowd cheered: not everyone could book a guest like Kuvam, but Amber wasn't just anyone. She'd gone from fluff reporter to talk show host in record time, thanks mostly to her ReBirth launch coverage, and eventually Kuvam had actually approached her about being a guest. Amber walked to the side of the stage and shook the Guru's hand as he entered—a tall man, lanky but powerful, clad as always in distinctly nonstandard clothing. Today it was a Peruvian serape, thick and wooly and brightly colored. His shirt and pants were loose beneath it, simple and unadorned. His feet were sandaled. He embraced Amber, kissing her on the forehead, and the young host was quick enough to milk her momentary shock into a laugh from the audience. She led the man to the couches in the middle of the stage, and when he sat he crossed his legs, yoga-style, on the center cushion. Amber sat on the other couch.

"Welcome to the show." She gestured at his crossed legs. "Make yourself comfortable."

"The lotus pose helps energy flow unimpeded through my central core."

"That's . . . exactly what my yoga instructor keeps telling me," said Amber. "Now. Can I start with the big thing first?"

He smiled knowingly. "Everybody does."

"You're dead."

The audience laughed at that one. They'd heard the explanations before—it had been weeks, after all—but Amber wasn't a news anchor, and this was not an in-depth interview. Her frankness, that vague sense that she was somehow out of her depth, was what made her show unique. She was playing it well, and her producers loved every minute.

"There is no death," said Kuvam. "I was shot, I left, and I returned."

"So there is death," said Amber, "it's just that yours didn't last very long."

"Is death not defined by its permanence?" asked Kuvam. "It is an ending—of consciousness, of thought, of metabolic function. But no longer. Now endings, too, have ended, and there is nothing left but everything. Life and light."

Amber hesitated just a moment in her answer, shooting a sidelong glance at the audience. "But I guess—and this is probably the second-most obvious question—but I guess that this is probably just ReBirth, right?"

"That's what I said."

"I'm talking about the lotion," said Amber, "not the . . . metaphysical principle. You're not the real Kuvam, you're a friend or a follower or something, who took his DNA and made yourself into a copy of him. Right?"

"Again," Kuvam intoned, "that's what I said. You speak of ReBirth, the trademark, as if it were different from the spiritual rebirth of a human spirit. The life that flows through us, as a species, is connected. I am Kuvam; I was Kuvam; I have always been Kuvam. The body I inhabit is but a single facet of who I am and who, by extension, we all are. A single organism, not just human but encompassing all life. Eternal life."

"But it's eternal life as someone else," said Amber. "Whoever you were before you were Kuvam, that's not who you are anymore. Right? Not everybody wants that."

"Do you want to die?"

The Internet picked up that sound bite almost immediately; before the next commercial break it had already become a meme: "Kuvam Threatens X," insert your favorite movie/celebrity/politician/animal here. Amber, for her part, stumbled only a moment before responding.

"Not . . . anytime soon."

"But eventually, then, you want to die? You choose death?"

"My lawyers are going to run us both ragged with this," said Amber, visibly shaken, "so let's just clear the air right now and say, for the record, that you're not actually threatening my life?"

"There is no threat but impermanence," said Kuvam, "and your own desperate need to cling to an identity you can't maintain. Humans age. Skin sags. Muscles and brains atrophy. You will never again be the person you are right now, in this moment, and yet you boldly choose to die rather than give it up."

"That's . . ." Amber stumbled over her words, overbalanced by the Guru's sudden swerve. Her producers shook their heads, screaming counterattacks and advice into her earpiece, which only confused her further.

"Who are we?" asked Kuvam, looking now not at Amber but at her audience, at the camera that broadcast his face to millions of homes and computers and phones across the world. "Do you know who you are? Do you know what makes you you? We are the ships of Theseus, broken and repaired in an endless cycle. Does your body persist? Every molecule in it, every cell, is different from the molecules and cells that constructed it at your birth. Are you still the same person? 'Through my mind,' you say, but does your mind persist? Your memories ebb and flow like the tide—you have lost more of your mind than you can ever regain. Are you still the same person? 'Through my soul,' then, that ethereal anchor that never changes and never dies: God's serial number to mark you at the gates of heaven. Is that truly all you are? If you are less, then what does it matter? If you are more, then what more? You are not your clothes, your car, your bank account, your youth. Your body will age, your face will fade, your friends will leave; there is nothing of you that remains but the memories of others and even those, too, will disappear like mist in flame. What are you clinging to? Why do you resist the inevitable? The earth has offered you no choice but oblivion, and we as a species have filled that void with hollow dreams, but ReBirth has changed everything. True immortality—not spiritual immortality, not post-mortal immortality, but the literal continuance of your physical, tangible life. It is the great revolution of the soul, our chance to throw off our chains, to break out from the chrysalis of earthbound dust and become more than we ever dreamed—"

"It's time to break for a commercial," said Amber, jumping in as the stage manager cut Kuvam's microphone feed. Her voice wavered. "But stay tuned because my next guess is going to blow your socks off: a female lawyer who used ReBirth to turn herself into a man, applied for a new job at the same company, and is now earning twice what she made before." She smiled hollowly at the camera. "Coming up next on *Amber Sykes*."

39

Lyle counted the money in his pocket: $2.84. All that remained of his weekly food budget—which still had to cover tomorrow. Sundays were easier, though, with churches opening one-day soup kitchens. Lyle had given up on permanent soup kitchens about a week ago, when a server looked at him a little too closely. Had the server recognized him? Had she reported him to the police? Or was it all completely innocent, and Lyle was jumping at shadows? It didn't matter, in the end; Lyle couldn't afford not to be paranoid. He was the most wanted man in America.

But he hadn't eaten all day, trying to trace a web of lotion pushers, and now it was late, and he was starving. He found a burger joint—not a chain, just a mom-and-pop dive—and went in.

The restaurant was long and narrow; the door led to a skinny walkway past the counter, with a handful of well-worn tables in the back. The walls were plastered with stickers and flyers for local bands and clubs and churches. The register was helmed by a sturdy woman with jet-black hair pulled up under a hairnet, her arms red from the heat and scarred from a lifetime of slinging greasy burgers over a hot griddle. This comforted Lyle—to see someone scarred was to know they were real, an authentic original. ReBirth erased scars just like it erased everything else.

There were two other people in the restaurant, each sitting by himself in the back, quietly eating. Lyle stayed against the wall, as far from the counter as he could get without looking suspicious, and examined the menu. Burgers and fries and Greek food. He could afford almost none of it.

"Take your time, honey, I'm not going anywhere." She looked to be somewhere in her forties, but her voice was older, more rugged.

He found a grilled cheese sandwich for two bucks; adding ham would bring it to three, which was out of his range, so he stepped to the counter and asked for the plain cheese version.

"That all you want?"

"That's it."

"No ham?"

"No."

"Fries and a Coke?"

"No, thank you."

She looked him up and down, probably deducing all too easily that he couldn't afford it. She lingered on his face, and Lyle turned to the wall to examine the various posters, feigning intense interest in the announcement of an exciting new sales opportunity.

Next to the sales flyer was a poster for the Yemaya Foundation, giving the same address Lyle had used on his first meeting with Kuvam. It seemed years ago now, but it was only a few months. *So much has changed.* The poster seemed to be advertising not Kuvam's medical clinic, or whatever multicultural work the Yemaya Foundation had been involved in, but some kind of meeting. Lyle frowned and leaned in closer.

Learn salvation at the feet of the Guru Kuvam.
Put an end to death and suffering by embracing
the light of the universe. All is as one.
Every night at 6.

"Grilled cheese."

Lyle turned around, fishing his money from his pocket. "Two dollars?"

"Two ten with tax." She placed the plate on the counter, a greasy stack of blackened toast oozing cheese from the middle like a bleeding wound. She took the money and rang it up. "Don't I know you?"

Lyle froze. *My beard's coming in, my hair's growing out. There's no way she could recognize me.* "I don't think so, I'm just passing through town." *My beard's never been thick enough, that's got to be it. I was stupid to come in here.*

"Yeah," she said, "you're that guy from the news." Lyle turned to bolt out the door, but in that moment the door opened and a large man pushed through, filling the narrow pathway with his body. The cook seemed to recognize the new man, and spoke to him eagerly. "Doug, look at this guy, this is exactly what I was telling you about."

The big man looked at her a moment, as if trying to remember the context of her comments, then turned to Lyle in a rush, eyes wide. "Holy crap, Ted, is that you?"

Lyle opened his mouth, having no idea who Ted was but wondering, just for a moment, if it would be safer to claim his identity instead of his own. The cook answered first.

"That's not Ted," she said, "but that's exactly what he looks like—it's the guy from the news, right? The lotion guy." She looked at Lyle as if for confirmation.

"I'm not the lotion guy," said Lyle quickly.

"Who were you going for?" the cook asked him. "Ted—that's my husband, Ted—he was trying to get one of those Brazilian kids, Ronaldo I think the name was." She shot a salacious look at the big man in the doorway. "Twenty years old if he was a day. Body like that guy in the movies, the superhero movies, you know the ones. Delicious." She turned back to Lyle. "But the kid's got a good heart, right? That's the important thing. Better than Ted's, anyway, and we can't afford another heart attack— we had to mortgage the house just to pay the doctor bills on the first one. Is that you, too? Heart attack?"

Lyle, only half sure he was following her, shook his head. "No."

"You're lucky," said the cook, "they're the worst. Ted nearly dies, we mortgage the house, and then the doctor says he's probably going to have another one, and what else are we going to mortgage? So we look at the one hand and we look at the other, and five thousand dollars for Ronaldo is a whole lot cheaper than fifty thousand dollars for another heart attack—fifty thousand if we're lucky—so we sell the car and find a dealer and the next thing you know Ted's this guy, this guy from the news."

"You used ReBirth," said Lyle quickly, finally getting a handle on the situation. The cook gave him a dark look and he clamped his mouth shut again.

"Nobody's using ReBirth," she said loudly, "it's illegal," but she leaned in close to Lyle and the big man in the doorway. "He didn't use ReBirth just like you didn't use ReBirth—but here you are, and there he is, out on the street because he can't hold a job with a criminal's face. This lotion guy, Mr. Fontanelle or whatever—you know how many laws he's broken? Public enemy number one, and there's my Ted with his face." Her eyes softened, and she pushed the grilled cheese sandwich closer toward him. "I accidentally put ham on this even though you didn't ask for it. If you're Jewish or anything I can make you another one."

Lyle stared at the sandwich, both touched and terrified by the woman's story, and by her sudden kindness at the end of it. His mumbled thanks as he took the sandwich was drowned out by the big man's booming voice.

"Let me see you," said the big man; the cook had addressed him as Doug. He grabbed Lyle by the shoulders and turned him, studying him with a careful eye. "Yeah, I've seen this one around. Ted got the same one?"

"The very same one," said the cook.

"How many have you seen?" asked Lyle. The cook's kindness had made him bolder.

"Five, maybe six," said Doug. "They're hiring them at the docks, if you're looking for work. It's not your fault you got a criminal's face."

Lyle said nothing, and took a bite of sandwich.

Where were all the Lyles coming from? None of the NewYew lotion had been imprinted on his DNA—they'd made sure of that—and as far as he knew no one else had stolen any. Certainly he'd never been ambushed in the street like so many celebrities had. So who had gotten it, and how?

And why?

He turned to the cook. "I'm trying to track down the people who did this," he said, "to me and to Ted and to everyone else. I know you didn't buy any ReBirth," he said, phrasing his sentence as carefully as possible, "but if you happened to know of a place where I could find some, maybe someone Ted's talked to recently . . . ?" He trailed off, not sure exactly how to finish the request without coming right out and saying it. The cook stared at him a long time, then pointed at the wall behind him.

"Hand me one of those papers."

Lyle pulled the Yemaya Foundation advertisement off the wall and handed it to her; she scribbled something on the back and folded it in half, handing it back. "Don't do anything stupid."

"I won't," said Lyle. He shoved the paper in his pocket, clutched his grilled cheese sandwich, and walked outside.

40

The diner cook's contact led Lyle to a dealer, who led him to another dealer, who didn't like Lyle's questions and pulled a gun. Lyle ran, the dealer chased him, and around the first corner shot and killed the wrong man. Lyle hid, terrified, but realized that the newly dead body on the sidewalk had his face: it was another Lyle, and the dealer thought he'd killed the right one. The dealer left, and Lyle struggled to calm his terror, and the next night he went back to spy on the dealer in secret, watching to see who brought him his stash. That led Lyle to spy on another minor supplier, who led him to a major supplier, who led him to a man named Stephen Nelson.

Stephen Nelson walked through Central Park almost every day, sometimes buying a hot dog, sometimes chatting and laughing with other men in suits. Street hot dogs seemed like a strange choice for an obviously wealthy executive, especially considering that most of his other lunches were buried in private rooms at high-end Asian fusion restaurants, but after a few days Lyle noticed a pattern: on the days when he ate hot dogs, Nelson carried a briefcase. No briefcase, no hot dog. Another few days of observation revealed the final piece of the puzzle: every time Nelson bought a hot dog, the same stranger was buying one at the same time, carrying an identical briefcase. Nelson would walk up, set his case on the ground, buy a hot dog . . .

. . . and leave with the other man's case.

Lyle wanted a closer look at the man, and rattled his pocket for change. He found just enough to buy a hot dog of his own—his entire remaining food budget for the week—and approached the cart, holding up a single finger to the proprietor. While the vendor prepared the dog Lyle stole a closer look at the man with the briefcase, and felt a surge of fear and excitement when he realized he couldn't determine the man's race. That probably wouldn't mean anything to anyone else, but Lyle had made a career of identifying race—in designing his cosmetics and calibrating the various colors, he had become an expert in skin tone, in eye shape, in facial proportion. It was his job, and he was very good at it. This man had dark skin, somewhere in the middle of the African spectrum, but with vaguely Middle Eastern features and a markedly Persian nose. His hair, in its color and appearance and spacing, was Asian, and his bright blue eyes were shockingly atypical compared to the rest of him. He was handsome, but completely unidentifiable.

To be presented with a racial background that Lyle couldn't determine was a big deal, and meant one of two things: One, the man came from a long line of racially adventurous ancestors. Two, and more likely, the man had multiple genomes warring for attention. Before Lyle could even finish wondering which of NewYew's various connections would experiment so liberally with overlapping ReBirth treatments, he knew the answer.

"Kerry."

The man looked up sharply, his mouth half full of hot dog.

"Kerry White," said Lyle. He hadn't been planning to say anything to the man, but it was too much of a shock, and he couldn't help himself. "It's you, isn't it?"

The man tensed, as if ready to run, but as he peered more closely at Lyle a light of recognition dawned in his eyes. "Lyle? Like, the real Lyle? Is that really you?"

"What are you doing here?"

"This isn't a good place to talk," said Kerry, reaching into his pocket. He pulled out a folded wad of bills—Lyle couldn't tell how many, but saw that the outside layer, at least, was a hundred—and handed it to the hot dog vendor. "You tell anyone what you've seen or heard just now, you'd better be the world champion at hide-and-seek." He smiled brightly and slapped Lyle on the back. "Walk with me." He picked up the briefcase, and walked through the park. "Obviously we have to start with proof of identity: who first came up with the idea of using ReBirth commercially?"

Lyle nodded—it was the perfect question, because nobody outside the executive board could possibly know the answer. It was too embarrassing, and they'd never discussed it with anyone. "Jeffrey."

Kerry smiled and slapped him on the back again. "Good to see you, man, where've you been?"

"What are you doing here?" Lyle asked again. "That was a handoff, right? Stephen Nelson is selling ReBirth, and when you switched briefcases just now that was you giving him more lotion and him giving you money."

"Looks like we'll have to change some procedures," said Kerry, "or cut out the weak link of whatever chain led you here."

"I've been investigating the black market sellers," said Lyle. "It wasn't easy."

"But it worked," said Kerry. "Somebody named names."

"Two somebodies," said Lyle, "but they did try to kill me afterward. So that's something."

"They tried and failed? How hard can it possibly be to kill you, you're like a . . . homeless Pillsbury Doughboy. No offense."

Lyle glowered. "None taken. In their defense they did kill *a* Lyle, just not the right one."

"That," said Kerry, "is becoming a bigger problem every day." He climbed the path to the western edge of the park, stepping out onto the street, and Lyle followed him north.

"Do you know where the Lyle lotion is coming from?"

Kerry shook his head. "I probably know less than you do, if you're investigating the black market. Somehow, about a month ago, it just started cropping up everywhere. I promise we're not the ones selling it, but a lot of our sellers have picked it up on the side."

Lyle studied him. "You don't seem very concerned."

"I'm concerned about the future," said Kerry, "when and if it becomes a problem for us. As of now, it isn't significantly cutting into our profits, and we're hoping that it actually drives people toward our product instead of away. We're trying to start a 'verified seller' program, so you can be sure of what you're getting, but controlling street dealers is like herding cats."

"You'll never pull it off," said Lyle. "Do you know the kind of margins the street sellers are getting for my DNA? It blows your business model out of the water—a street-level pusher makes more on a single sale of unmarked Lyle Fontanelle than in four sales of branded ReBirth. Whoever supplies them is practically giving it away, and the dealers are hawking it for the same sky-high prices they get for your stuff. If they didn't have to sell the real stuff to keep the prices high, they'd drop you altogether."

"That's because people like money, Lyle. That's what you never seem to understand."

"The dealers, yes," said Lyle, "but what about the supplier? Someone out there is working night and day to distribute Lyle lotion, without making any money at all. In a world that claims to be driven by money, that's terrifying."

Kerry stopped on the sidewalk, thinking. He chewed his lip. "You're right," he said at last. "That's very strange."

Lyle shook his head. "'Strange' doesn't begin to cover it."

Kerry started walking again. "No matter. We'll find a way to deal with it."

"You're not taking me seriously," said Lyle. "You never do. Let me talk to Sunny."

"I'm the only one left," said Kerry.

Lyle's eyes widened. "So that car bomb—that actually got them? Sunny and Cynthia and everyone?"

"What? No, of course not. They're in São Tomé, just like we planned."

"Not me, though," said Lyle, and a hint of bitterness crept into his voice. "Was saving me ever part of the plan, or was I car bomb fodder from the beginning?"

Kerry put a hand on his shoulder, guiding him into the apartment building; the doorman frowned at Lyle's filthy clothes and patchy beard, but Kerry waved him away. "Of course we were planning to save you, Lyle. You thought that we thought that the Lyle we killed was you? Of course we knew he was a fake, but he was just so eager to please us we kept him around until the big day. And he did a bang-up job on that launch presentation." They stepped into an elevator and Kerry punched the top button—the suites. Lyle could only imagine how much a suite in this location must be costing him. The doors closed, and Kerry turned to face him directly. "So: no free lotion, even for a former shareholder, but what else can I give you? You need money? You look like you could use it—though I guess that's understandable, since you're a wanted criminal."

"So are you."

"Kerry White is a wanted criminal," said Kerry slyly. "My name is Armando del Castillo, and Armando's not wanted for anything but his gorgeous body."

"I don't want your money," said Lyle, feeling angrier than he'd expected at the suggestion. "You're a drug dealer, Kerry, I can't support that."

"And you're the greatest drug designer who ever lived," said Kerry. "At least take some credit for it—let me give you, what, a hundred thousand?"

The elevator stopped on the top floor, opening into a small but luxurious lobby. Instead of a hall leading to myriad small apartments, there were two ornate doors, each leading to its own private penthouse. Lyle whistled at the obvious wealth. "Nice place."

Kerry shrugged. "It'll be a lot nicer once I buy the other unit.

Rock-star neighbors are just as noisy as the stereotype suggests."
He opened the door, revealing a giant penthouse that seemed to
ooze money. The main room was dominated by a massive wall
of windows looking out over Central Park. Lyle walked to the
windows and stood in awe. "How much are they charging you
for this place?"

"A lot less than that view makes it worth," said Kerry. "Wait
'til tonight, when the city lights up and this room just overflows
with more barely legal tennis players than you've ever seen in one
place at a time. It's heaven."

"You throw parties?"

"Why on earth would I have a place like this and not throw
parties in it?"

Lyle turned back to him, confused. "What about Carrie?"

"I told you, I'm Armando now."

"No, I mean your wife, Carrie."

"Oh." Kerry frowned, scrunching his forehead in thought.
"She might show up. You interested?"

"Are you serious?" asked Lyle. "Saving her was the thing that
started this whole stupid product in the first place, and now you
don't even know where she is?"

"Things change . . . ," said Kerry weakly, but he was cut off
when the front door opened again and Cynthia walked in, deep
in conversation with a Bluetooth headset.

". . . the deposits have all been made, and Kerry's back so we
probably have the new payments. I'll—" She stopped short, staring
at Lyle. "He has a Lyle with him."

"Not just *a* Lyle," said Kerry, pouring himself a drink from a
glass decanter by the wall. "*The* Lyle."

"*The* Lyle?" asked Cynthia. She paused a moment, listening
to her headset. "That's what I thought, too," she said. "Looks
like we blew up the wrong one."

Kerry rolled his eyes.

Two thoughts flashed through Lyle's mind in a single instant:

first, that Cynthia was supposed to be in São Tomé. Kerry had told him she was there, and if he'd lied about that, what else had he lied about? Lyle was too trusting—practically conditioned, he thought, to going along with whatever the other NewYew executives told him. Even months away from them hadn't dulled their power, or his own naïve gullibility. He mentally kicked himself, wondering what he'd gotten himself into.

The second thought followed quickly on the first, a fierce reminder that he knew exactly what he'd gotten himself into, and that getting back out of it was going to be absolute hell: Cynthia said that she'd thought they'd blown him up. Kerry had lied about knowingly killing the impostor. They'd been trying to kill the real Lyle all along.

And now he was alone with two of them, thirty floors from escape, with who knew how many Larries waiting in the back rooms of the house.

Kerry was already moving, his taut model's body charging toward Lyle, head down, arms pumping. The room was wide, but Kerry would be on him in seconds. Lyle stumbled backward, bumping into a designer couch, nearly slipping on the polished floor, scrabbling in his jacket pocket, Kerry barely two yards away, and then Lyle found his gun and pulled it out and fired, and Kerry dropped to the floor with a strangled cry.

"Now he's shot Kerry," said Cynthia to her earpiece. "I'm going to have to call you back."

Lyle looked up, wide-eyed, but Cynthia slipped back out the door and into the lobby, closing the door behind her. Kerry swore on the floor, clutching his shoulder. "You shot me!"

"You were attacking me!"

"Not with a gun! Where the hell did you get a gun anyway?"

"All the homeless Pillsbury Doughboys have them," Lyle growled, and shoved the gun back into his jacket pocket. He grabbed a small blanket off the back of a couch—more of a shawl, really, once he had it in his hands—and wrapped it around the flailing man's shoulder. "If you're moving that much I didn't hit anything important. Stick it out and the ReBirth will heal you in a couple of weeks."

"That's," Kerry grunted, his teeth clenched in pain, "a four-thousand-dollar throw."

"Then stop bleeding on it," said Lyle. He pulled the knot tighter, eliciting another string of painful curses from Kerry, and stood up. "Is there any other way out of here?"

"The window," Kerry snarled.

"Wonderful," said Lyle, jogging to the kitchen, "you're very helpful." He made a quick circuit of the house—gun back out and ready, in case there was anyone else lurking in a back corner—but the apartment was empty, and there were no other exits. He ran through again, looking for a stash of ReBirth, but found nothing.

"We don't keep the lotion here," shouted Kerry. "Do you think we're idiots?"

Lyle went back to the living room, looked around again, and saw the briefcase from the park handoff. Maybe there was something in there? He pulled it up onto the back of a couch and tried to open it, but it was locked.

"I thought you didn't want our dirty money," said Kerry. He had barely moved from his spot on the floor, and Lyle could just see him through the gap between a sofa and a chair.

"I didn't want you to *give* me money," said Lyle. He held up the briefcase, and walked toward the door. "This is me robbing you, that's different."

"How is stealing money better than earning it from ReBirth?"

"Just . . . shut up," said Lyle. He reached the door, only to realize he had no free hands to open it. Which did he dare to set down, the money or the gun? How many Larries were waiting on the other side of the door, or at the bottom of the elevator, or in the lobby? He stared a moment longer, then turned and walked to the window. The fire escape wasn't the best option, but it was the best one he had left.

"Lyle?" said Kerry. His voice was weak.

"Yeah?"

"Thanks for not shooting my house. This stuff's really hard to replace."

"No problem," said Lyle. "Say hi to Carrie for me." He pushed open the window, stepped out onto the metal walkway, and started climbing down.

41

Friday, September 14
9:10 A.M.
The Pentagon, Washington, D.C.

91 DAYS TO THE END OF THE WORLD

Ira Brady, one-time CEO of Ibis Cosmetics, sat in the back of a conference room, watching it slowly fill with generals and analysts and politicians—everyone important enough to be invited to the briefing. One of the men paused to shake his hand, and he stood with a smile.

"General Blauwitz," said Ira, "so good to see you again."

"And you, as well, Senator Moore." Blauwitz clapped him on the back, as familiar as if Ira were actually the real Senator Moore. Which, as far as anyone in this room knew, he was. He'd been Moore for almost four weeks now.

The room quieted, and Blauwitz got straight into his presentation, switching the lights off and a projector on. "Thank you for coming," he said. "This briefing has been called to discuss the situation in São Tomé, and our options for appropriating the NewYew facility there."

"'Appropriating,'" said a woman in a military uniform. Ira recognized her as General Clark. "That's an awfully diplomatic synonym for 'conquering.'"

"The facility in São Tomé is the only such facility in the world still capable of producing ReBirth," said Blauwitz. "Call it what you want, but we need that facility under our control as soon as possible. ReBirth is the most single powerful tool of espionage ever created."

Ira/Moore smiled at the irony.

General Blauwitz cycled to the first slide in his presentation. "This is the first obstacle in our way; we don't know his name, but this is his face." The slide showed a tall African man, his features twisted in an angry scowl. He was wearing a green military uniform with a red beret, clutching a well-used AK-47. Similar men milled around in the background of the photo, and the audience of officers and politicians leaned forward, probably trying to determine if the other soldiers were copies of the first, or if their inability to tell them apart was some kind of latent racism they hadn't realized they held. Blauwitz let them off the hook with an explanation: "For now we'll call him Lagbaja, which is generic enough. NewYew has begun manufacturing Lagbaja in their compound on São Tomé—"

"Excuse me," said Alexis Miller, one of the mid-ranking officers. "What do you mean, NewYew is 'manufacturing' a man? ReBirth can't build new people, can it?"

"A better word would be 'mass-producing,'" said Blauwitz. "NewYew has adopted the worst excesses of the child army and actually found a way to make them worse. They're recruiting children, but instead of just arming them they're treating them with NewYew and turning them into Lagbaja—six foot five, and two hundred pounds on average. Through satellite reconnaissance and our agents on the ground, we place the count somewhere around five thousand copies."

"That's abominable," said Miller.

"The morality of it is beside the point," said Blauwitz. "The more pressing matter is that five thousand Lagbajas make it very hard to mount any kind of successful invasion. NewYew essentially owns the island now."

"I don't like any of this," said Miller.

"You're not here to like or dislike it," said General Clark. "You're here to tell us what to do about it."

"We're running out of ReBirth," said Blauwitz, and the room grew quiet. "The lotion we seized from NewYew's manufacturing facilities will last us for years," he continued, "assuming we

want to turn people into attractive models with good circulation. If we want to do anything more interesting—if we want
to use blank lotion, for example, which is the technology's primary political application—we have very little to work with and
no way to make more. All of our attempts to re-create their
formula have failed."

"So you need more than the facility," said Miller, "you need
the people who run it."

"We need Igdrocil," said Blauwitz. "It's the only ingredient
we haven't been able to identify."

"Because it's not in the formula," said Ira/Moore. He'd tried
everything he could think of to reproduce the lotion, and now
he was just going to use the U.S. government to go in and take
it for him. "Igdrocil shows up in the ingredients list, but not in
the recipe. Many of our analysts suspect that it's an artifact of the
manufacturing process, rather than a literal substance."

"Senator Moore," said General Clark. "You told me you had
a plan to present to us."

"I do," said Ira/Moore, and stood up. "If you'll permit me,
General?"

"By all means," said Blauwitz.

Ira/Moore walked to the projector, unplugged Blauwitz's
laptop, and plugged in his own. "Let me introduce you first to
Jessica." He clicked the trackpad on his laptop, and the first slide
popped up: a cheerleader, maybe nineteen years old, grinning
energetically as she posed with her pom-poms. Her face was
framed by bright blond pigtails. "Jessica is the youngest of New-
Yew's ReBirth models, marketed with a slim, muscular build for
customers interested in gymnastics and similar sports. She's five
feet even, ninety pounds soaking wet, and—more germane to
our discussion—we have approximately eight hundred ounces
of her DNA. If we weaponized that DNA, we could turn New-
Yew's army of Lagbajas into an army of Jessicas. I think you'll all
agree that our invasion would be much simpler under those circumstances."

"How do you intend to weaponize it?" asked Blauwitz.

"By dumping it in the water supply," said Ira/Moore. "Testing shows no loss in effectiveness, even when the lotion is severely diluted."

"I'm concerned about the wide-scale use of a biological weapon," said Clark. "What if it hits civilians?"

"Then São Tomé gets a really big cheerleading squad," said Ira/Moore. "It's not the best human rights situation in the world, but we're talking about invading a neutral foreign power. We're not the good guys here."

"Are we at all concerned about the racial issue?" asked Miller. "Most of the population, and obviously all of the Lagbajas, are black, and you want to turn them white?"

"NewYew was nothing if not thorough," said Ira Moore, clicking to the next slide. It showed a woman of almost exactly the same build, but African instead of Caucasian. "This is Sally."

"The color is not the issue," said General Clark. "The Lagbajas are trained soldiers, and turning them into Sallies or Jessicas isn't going to change that. The ReBirth models are fit and healthy, genetically predisposed to a level of physical prowess that their army regimen is only going to enhance. My daughter was a cheerleader; I'm pretty sure these girls can still shoot a gun."

General Blauwitz raised his eyebrow. "Have you ever seen a ninety-pound girl fire an assault rifle?"

"You're right," said Ira/Moore. "We need something debilitating—something that brings them down so powerfully that by the time they realize what's happening they won't be able to do anything about it." He looked around the room and saw them nodding, waiting expectantly. If he'd proposed this final plan first they would never have accepted it, but now, intrigued by the possibilities of genetic warfare, they were ready. Now that Ira/Moore had planted the idea, they wanted to see what ReBirth could really do.

He clicked the trackpad. "Allow me to introduce Toby, the soldier of the future. Toby is six years old, congenitally blind, and suffers from late-stage leukemia. Because it is a disease of the chromosomes, this leukemia would be transmitted through the ReBirth and forcibly propagated onto every target in the invasion zone—and because his body is so small, the early stages of transformation would require a significant loss of mass, exacerbating the flulike symptoms that have become associated with ReBirth. Our simulations predict that a dose in their water supply would incapacitate the general population in approximately ten days. We walk in, take the island, and then turn them back into whomever they want once the population is subdued. It's the easiest invasion in history."

"That's what I'm talking about!" said Blauwitz eagerly.

"You can't be serious," said Miller. "Biological weapons are prohibited for a reason—they're unethical, they're inhumane, and this one in particular is both degrading and offensive on top of that, to about twenty different minority groups. We'd be the mustache-twirling pariahs of the entire world community."

"Biological weapons aren't reversible," said Ira/Moore. "ReBirth is. A week or so of lying on the ground, blind and too weak to move, and then they're back to normal, in whatever body they choose."

"Some of them would die," Miller insisted.

"It's a war," said Ira/Moore. "Some of them will die no matter how we choose to invade. This way it'll be relatively few of them, and they won't die violently, and everyone who doesn't die can be a hundred percent better four weeks later with no lasting effects."

"You don't call rewriting your DNA a lasting effect?"

"They've already rewritten their own DNA by becoming Lagbaja," said Blauwitz. "Hell, we could turn them back into Lagbaja if they really want to; by then it won't matter."

"How are we going to know which ones to prosecute?" asked Clark. "By the time we start making arrests nobody in that complex will even have an identity anymore. Are we just going to pick up the best-dressed Tobies and hope they're the executives?"

"Arrests are a secondary concern," said Ira/Moore. "We want ReBirth, and the means to make more of it."

"I like the plan in theory," said General Clark, "but without any blank lotion it's impossible to carry out."

"There's plenty of blank lotion on the black market," said Ira/Moore. "Surely there's enough room in our budget for that? It's cheaper than sending soldiers."

"But then why invade at all?" asked Miller. "If we can get blank lotion on the black market we can ignore this whole offensive debacle completely."

"We're invading because having ReBirth is only half of our goal," said General Clark. "The other half is making sure nobody else has it. Everything Senator Moore has suggested we do to São Tomé is something that an enemy nation could do to us, and that makes ReBirth the most powerful weapon since the atomic bomb. Even more powerful, because it can be used to destroy a people while leaving their infrastructure intact. Imagine a Russia, or a China, or an Iran, with the ability to turn the entire American population into Toby the cancer patient. We're planning to save the people of São Tomé afterward, but no invading power would give us the same courtesy. Two weeks and we're too sick to move, four weeks and we're dead, and every last bit of land, technology, money, and natural resources we've ever had are just lying on the ground for a conquering force to march in and take. They could live in our houses and drive our cars. If you question the need for the American government to be the sole owner of this technology you are a brainless jackass unfit for your job." The general's voice was like ice, and her eyes seemed to scorch the room like lasers. She stared for a few more moments, then turned to Blauwitz. "Put this into motion. I want Toby's DNA in every human cell on that island within four days, and I want us in undisputed possession of São Tomé one week later. This meeting is adjourned."

42

Saturday, September 15
7:30 P.M.
Yemaya Foundation, Hell's Kitchen, Manhattan

90 DAYS TO THE END OF THE WORLD

Lyle squeezed into the back of the room, shoulder to shoulder with several dozen copies of himself, and realized that he'd never been more uncomfortable in his life. The room was filled with Lyles, his own face and hair and size and weight repeated on nearly two hundred people, differentiated only by their clothes. Their features, of course, were subtly different—ReBirth didn't make exact duplicates, just identical twins based on the same DNA—but that only added to the creepy vibe that hung over the room, making Lyle sick to his stomach. When everyone looked so similar, tiny variations became prominent, and as Lyle scanned the room he saw some with a slightly sharper nose, or a narrower mouth, and he couldn't help but study the way that their different clothes and haircuts changed the overall look of his face. He studied each face in turn, over and over, until it became too much. Looking at Guru Kuvam was a welcome respite from the sickening sameness.

"You are not criminals," Kuvam was saying. "You have a criminal's blood, and a criminal's bones, but so does every child of a wayward father, and we do not blame a child for his father's actions."

Great, thought Lyle, *another speech about how we're all innocent because we're not the real Lyle. Fat lot of good that does me.*

Kuvam held meetings almost every night now, whenever he wasn't on TV, or out preaching in hospitals and prisons the new path he called the Light of Life. Lyle had been talking to every pseudo-Lyle he could find, trying to figure out who had sold them their faulty lotion, trying to trace it all back to the source, and more and more they mentioned these meetings, a kind of self-help group for Lyles with Kuvam as their therapist.

"What the world does not realize," said Kuvam, "is that we are all connected—all living things are tied together in an unbreakable web of power, and not just living things but rocks and trees. Nature, and the vast reaches of space beyond. What are human beings but chemicals? Water and salt and carbon, iron in our blood, energy from the sun filtered through the chlorophyll of plants and into our bodies as food. And this energy is not the only part of us that comes from the stars—every mineral in our cells comes from the depths of the earth, and the earth was formed by particles of matter thrown out by distant stars and supernovas uncountable millennia ago. We are ancient beings, composed of the very stuff of the stars, the shining children of the universe."

The guru paced the small stage as he spoke—a nervous habit Lyle hadn't seen in him during their first meeting, and he wondered who this man had been before he had rewritten himself with Kuvam's face and body.

"And if everyone is connected in a web of light and stars and blood and life," the guru continued, "then we are all the same. I am the same as you, and you are the same as me, and we're both the same as the richest man in the world and the poorest child in the gutter. We are different faces on the same all-encompassing being, different manifestations of the core, primal force of light and life. And if we're all the same, what does it matter if you're you or me or Lyle or anybody else?" There was a murmur of agreement from the crowd, and Lyle was surprised to realize that not everyone in the room was ignoring Kuvam's New Age nonsense. "You've always been you, and you'll always be you," Kuvam continued, "but you've always been Lyle, too. It doesn't matter what you look like, because that doesn't change who you are, because you still are, and always will be, *us*." Another murmur of approval. "You are no less than you were before, you're greater. You've gained knowledge, which is light, which is life. And if everything is light and life, then you have gained everything."

The crowd was excited now, calling out affirmations of the guru's words, and Lyle realized that this wasn't a self-help group, it was a religion. He frowned, wondering how so many people could fall for the same ridiculous story, wondering if maybe the nature of Lyle conversion—of unwitting nobodies duped into buying the wrong thing—self-selected for a group of gullible people with malleable minds.

But the more he looked at the roomful of doppelgängers— the more he saw his own face lit up with two different shades of desperate hope—the more he realized that they weren't dupes, and they weren't nobodies. They were people whose lives had been ripped away, whose face and identity and entire sense of self had been destroyed. They were nodding and smiling and shouting approvals because Guru Kuvam was the first person, and maybe the only person, to tell them they were okay, that they weren't freaks and criminals. The world hated Lyles, but here they were kings.

"I have a special guest today," said Kuvam, and Lyle was immediately embarrassed by the thrill of hope that shot through his chest: Is it me? But he gestured to a man offstage who stepped in front of the crowd with a friendly smile. "This is Tracy Erickson," said Kuvam, "a representative from the ACLU."

There was a smattering of applause, and Tracy began to speak with a firm, impassioned voice. "Thank you, Guru, for this opportunity. My name is Tracy, like he said, and I'm an assistant legal council for the American Civil Liberties Union. You know us, we're the weirdos always suing somebody or other for oppressing cannibals or neo-Nazis or something like that." There were a few laughs, but most of the crowd seemed confused at the sudden change in tone, and Lyle assumed that many of them, like him, didn't know where this was going. "We handle thousands of cases a year," said Tracy, "protecting civil rights for everyone in the country, but naturally it's only the controversial cases that make the news. And we take the controversial cases because somebody has to. Because everybody, no matter who they are, no matter what they've done, deserves to be treated like a human being. You've probably experienced this yourself in the last few weeks, haven't you? You got some bad ReBirth, turned into Lyle, and now all of a sudden you lose your job, you lose your health insurance, maybe you lose your family or your bank account or your car. Everywhere you used to go, everything you used to do, you can't, because you have the wrong man's face, and you can't go anywhere to complain about it because the substance that gave you this face is a biological weapon and you could be branded a terrorist just for possessing it. Many Lyles have, in fact, been arrested, but frankly there's too many of you now for the cops to bother with. Thousands of Lyles around the country, maybe tens of thousands, and hundreds more every day."

The mood in the room turned angry, not at Tracy but at the realities he was bringing back to the front of their minds. Kuvam had made them feel better for a moment, but at the end of the meeting they would still have to go back into a world that hated them. Many of them, like Lyle, might not even have homes to go to.

"That's where we come in," said Tracy. "You can't fight for yourselves, and no one will fight for you, but we will. The ACLU has opened a case to fight for Lyle rights—not just a case, but a campaign. Today we began raising funds, and first thing Monday morning we'll hit Washington with lobbyists and interest groups, with private meetings with some of our oldest friends in the government, and with public meetings all over the country to raise awareness and sympathy for your cause. Within the next few weeks we'll roll out a series of nationwide advertisements, including TV and web, to call attention to the injustices happening to Lyles every day." He grinned, and Lyle could tell he'd arrived at the crux of his speech. "And this is the best part. Cases like this tend to have a lot of negative inertia, just by nature. People don't really 'see' civil rights violations until they've been personally hurt, and the criminal angle is another hurdle on top of that. But you have one thing going for you that will make this case completely unlike any other—volume. There are so many of you, and the number is growing every day; it's going to be on everyone's mind, on everyone's lips, and it's going to gain us a lot of traction. Tens of thousands of people being discriminated against because of their DNA. You realize what you are? You're a racial minority. People deny you jobs and loans and even service in stores and restaurants, not because of what you do but because of what you look like. That is blatant racism, and that's something that will get the world on your side.

"Starting Monday, we propose legislation to have Lyle Fontanelle recognized as an official minority group, with all the rights that come with it."

43

Larry, Susan, and Tony/Lyle sat around a small motel table, dressed in yellow hazmat suits and measuring bits of Lyle lotion into small, clear gelcaps. On the dresser nearby a small TV filled the room with faint blue light that made their suits a sickly green.

"This is Giancarlo Finotto with BBC World, on site at one of the most daring robberies in European history, and an aftermath so shocking it has shaken the Christian world to its core."

"Turn this up," said Susan, "I want to hear it." Larry reached over to poke the TV with a thick, rubber glove, then went back to his work as the report continued.

"Early this morning, at approximately 4:24 a.m., a group of what appear to be black-clad commandos broke into the Cathedral of St. John the Baptist and stole the Shroud of Turin, allegedly the burial shroud of Jesus Christ and said by many to depict the image of his face. Barely an hour later, someone posted this video on YouTube claiming credit for the theft."

An Internet video filled the screen, with a play button and a progress bar floating near the bottom. In the center of the video was a man in stark silhouette, his face invisible, standing in what appeared to be a white, plaster room. He spoke in English but his accent was South American.

"I am a representative of a multidenominational Christian organization called the Holy Vessel, and I speak on their behalf when I apologize for this crime we have committed. The Lord has told us thou shalt not steal, and yet we have, and for that we will beg His forgiveness when He returns in His glory." He held up the Shroud in front of him, in a small spotlight that showed only his fingertips in blue rubber gloves. "The Shroud of Turin bears small drops of blood, left on the fabric from the death of our Lord Jesus Christ. Even now our scientists are analyzing samples of this blood, reconstructing a full DNA sequence, and when they are done we will apply that DNA to a sample of blank ReBirth."

Susan gasped. "Holy sh—"

"Do not blaspheme," said Tony/Lyle.

"Quiet," said Larry. His earlier disinterest was gone, and he stared intently at the TV.

The silhouette set down the Shroud, picked up a Bible, and read a passage. "The Scriptures tell us: 'For I know that my re-deemer liveth, and that He shall stand at the latter day upon the Earth,' and we have spent centuries preparing for His return. But the Scriptures also tell us: 'Prepare ye the way of the Lord, make His paths straight.' Can the Lord return without our help? The Lord can do anything. But the path He follows is winding and long, and each new turn delays His coming. It falls on us to make that path straight, to prepare His way and hasten His road, and then 'the Son of man will come in the glory of His Father with His angels; and then He shall reward every man according to His works.'" He set down the Bible. "Do not be found wanting when your God walks again upon the Earth, for He shall come with fire and with brimstone to slay the unrighteous. Amen.'"

The video ended, and the camera cut back to the reporter. "The authenticity of the Shroud of Turin has been hotly debated ever since its discovery," the man said, "and there is no guaran-tee that the Holy Vessel will be able to produce a man geneti-cally similar to Jesus Christ. It is also possible, though, that this may be a moot point: Christian theology has one of the most destructive apocalypse scenarios in the world, and if this or any group determines to play that scenario out, there's no telling what might happen. Giancarlo Finotto, BBC World."

"Why are people so stupid?" asked Susan. She stared at the TV a moment longer, then threw her lotion syringe at the screen. "Why doesn't anybody get it?!"

"What I want to know," said Tony/Lyle, "is who beats us?"

Larry cocked his eyebrow. "Who beats who?"

"Christians," said Tony/Lyle. "I'm Irish Catholic, born and raised, proud child of all the hellfire and damnation you could ever want, but this guy says we're just 'one of the most destructive' apocalypses. Everything I sat through in Sunday school, and we're still only 'one of the most destructive'? Who beats us?"

"Probably the Norse," said Larry. "In the Christian apocalypse all the bad guys burn but all the good guys get saved, plus God's still alive at the end of it. In Ragnarök everybody kills everybody—humans, trolls, giants, dragons, everybody, all up close and personal." He mimed a close-range stabbing. "Even the gods get shivved in the ribs. There's only two people left, and they start a new world."

Susan seemed to be ignoring them, still watching the TV.

"Wait," said Tony/Lyle, "that's their end of the world—the Garden of Eden? That's, like, the worst science fiction cliché ever."

"Well, it wasn't exactly a cliché when the ancient Norse based their civilization around it."

"They based their civilization on drinking and beating people up," said Tony/Lyle.

"Makes you wonder why it's not a more popular religion," said Larry. "And it's not exactly the Garden of Eden, by the way—the two people are there, but they don't necessarily live, they just . . . start a new world."

"They're dead?"

"It's Ragnarök, haven't you been listening?"

"How do they start a new world if they're dead?"

"I don't know."

"They're going to cause a holy war," said Susan. She paused the TV, eyes unfocused. "We've tried to dissuade them from using the lotion, and all they're doing is using it more." She'd picked up her syringe from the floor, only to stare at it, think for a moment, and then thrown it violently across the room. A moment later she threw the gelcap she'd been filling, and a moment after that she swept her arm violently across the table, smashing bottles and vials and knocking it all to the floor.

"Whoa!" shouted Tony/Lyle, stumbling back as the pile of materials crashed straight into his lap.

"Watch out!" Larry cried at the same moment, dropping his tools as he leaped to his feet. He hesitated a moment, then grabbed Susan's shoulders and pulled her back from the table, keeping a tight grip as she struggled to escape.

"Let me go!"

"Calm down," said Larry. "Just take it easy, we're all friends here."

"We're wasting our time!" she shouted. "All these stupid syringes and gelcaps and none of it is working!"

"Tens of thousands of Lyles," said Larry, "and you say it isn't working?"

"Oh, we're making plenty of Lyles," said Susan, "but we're not destabilizing the market. We're trying to convince people ReBirth is too dangerous to use, but all we're doing is driving up the price. It's time for a new plan."

"I agree," said Tony/Lyle, "even without knowing what it is." He took off his hazmat hood. "Anything that gets us out of these damn suits."

"Careful," said Larry, "you're covered with lotion."

"And?" asked Tony/Lyle. "I'm already Lyle, what's the worst it can do to me?"

Larry shrugged, and Susan started gathering up the fallen lotion. "It's not about quantity," she said, "it's about precision. We don't turn everyone into Lyle, we turn key people into . . . someone. I don't know who yet, but if it's the right people and the right DNA, we can get our message out there."

"The world's already full of genetic terrorists," said Larry. "Every politician in the country wears a hazmat suit, everywhere they go. Who can we hit?"

"I'm working on it," said Susan. "For now, we recruit. I have friends from some of the protests I did in college—activists, rebels, that kind of stuff. They'll help us."

"And what about all this stuff?" asked Tony/Lyle. "We still have gallons of Lyle lotion that we could get arrested just for looking at. I don't want to haul it around, or leave it somewhere as evidence against us."

"So we flush it," said Susan. "We smash the bottles, burn the rug, and dump the lotion down the drain." Her voice was quiet but fierce. "And then we change the world."

44

Wednesday, September 26
6:27 A.M.
Ayra de Menezes Hospital, São Tomé

79 DAYS TO THE END OF THE WORLD

Carl Montgomery had the plague. It had swept the entire island in just a few days, rendering everyone—even the natives, who should have been immune—practically too weak to move. It hit adults the worst, causing them to void their bowels and bladders in an almost constant stream. Several had already died of dehydration, but only the servants; Carl and his son were receiving the best care money could buy. Even with that, though, they were immensely ill. Even the doctors were sick.

"We need to go to a real hospital," said Jeffrey. His voice was weak, barely audible from the far side of the room. "We need to go to Lisbon."

Carl summoned all his strength to tell him off. "I didn't build a palace on an island with no extradition just so I could extradite myself."

"We're going to die," whispered Jeffrey.

"I don't die," Carl snarled, and forced himself to sit up. His hands gripped the bed railings fiercely, and he smiled viciously. *You can't take my strength,* he told the plague. *Kill everyone on this island, and I'll still be here.*

"Is that the nurse?" asked Jeffrey.

"It's me, idiot," said Carl. He had remade himself as a copy of his son, young and healthy, but now that the plague had come he was back in his wheelchair again. No matter: he'd been weak before, and he'd still built a company that practically ruled the world. He could get through this, too. He found the control stick on his wheelchair and drove it out the door and into the hallway. He bumped against something too low for him to see, an obstacle in the middle of the hall, and when it moaned he realized it was another patient, or maybe a nurse or doctor, too sick to move. "Get out of my way," he rumbled, "some of us have things to do."

His eyes were failing, too, but he could see that the hallway was littered with bodies. Pale bodies, when they should have been brown. He rolled back toward the nearest one, peering closer, and recognized his private nurse. Well, almost: his body was shriveling, and his skin was discolored. Splotchy, and almost pink in places. What plague was this?

And then it hit him, and he roared in debilitated rage. This was no plague.

This was ReBirth.

Someone had infected the entire island—Carl's island—with ReBirth, turning everyone on it into somebody so small and weak they couldn't resist. And whoever it was would be invading soon, it couldn't possibly mean anything else. Carl would find who'd done this, and he'd make them pay.

Who was he turning into? Somebody small, he knew, because the adults were shrinking. Somebody weak, by the same reasoning, and judging by his failing vision it was somebody blind, as well. But there was something else in the DNA, hidden under the rest. Not just size and age, but a sickness—something devastating deep in the genes. Worming itself into him cell by cell. He had to reach the factory in time; he had to get new DNA before it all came crashing down.

He waited in front of the elevator, his crumpled reflection staring back from the shiny metal doors. He'd seen that face somewhere . . . was he turning into someone he knew? The doors opened, and the image disappeared. Carl drove in, gasping for breath, shoving a fallen body out of his way with the rubberized bumper of his wheelchair. The interior of the elevator was mirrored, and as the door closed he saw his image again, surrounding him on every side, repeated a thousand thousand times into the endless distance of the parallel mirrors.

Wisps of old man's hair clinging to the top of a round, sickly head. Sunken eyes. Oxygen tubes curving around his ears and into his nose. He'd seen that face, or a hundred like it, every day in his NewYew office for years. A little bald child.

"I have cancer," he said.

The doors opened, and he tried to back up, but the way was blocked by something the electric motor wasn't strong enough to push. More bodies, filling the hallway, stacked two deep by the elevator as if they'd been crawling toward it for help. He pushed the control stick as far as he could, but the chair wouldn't move. He stared at the mirrored walls of the elevator, and the little boy with cancer stared back. Carl screamed in rage, a hoarse, impotent whisper, and on every side of him an endless line of dying reflections screamed in silent unison.

He pulled himself forward, lowering himself out of his seat, determined to crawl to the NewYew compound if that's what it took. The IV tube pulled loose with a painful pinch, and when he flopped to the floor the oxygen tube ripped free from its tank. He gasped on the floor, his vision dimming, the cancer eating him alive. His arms seemed hollow as he reached forward, trying to crawl over the legs of a little fallen replica of himself. The world swam in his view; his ears roared like seashells. He dragged himself forward an inch. His sphincter fell apart, liquid excrement dribbling down his legs and soaking his hospital gown. He dragged himself another inch.

He choked, gasping for air, and reached toward the door.

45

Friday, September 28
3:45 P.M.
The Pentagon, Washington, D.C.

77 DAYS TO THE END OF THE WORLD

"They don't have it," said General Blauwitz. A still photo of his face filled the screen on the wall, and his voice echoed tinnily through the room. "They have manufacturing facilities, they have other kinds of lotion, but they don't have blanks."

General Clark frowned. "Have you looked everywhere?"

"Don't patronize me."

"This doesn't make any sense," said Ira/Moore. "Why would they not be manufacturing blanks? For storage, if nothing else?"

"Obviously there might be samples somewhere," said Blauwitz, "and we're still searching, but I'm telling you: they were not manufacturing blank ReBirth anywhere on this island. I don't think they even knew how. Where we expected to find blanks we've found vast stores of inert ReBirth, chemically identical to the stuff we've tried and failed to make on our own."

"Still no Igdrocil," muttered Ira/Moore. He pounded the table in fury. "If they don't have it, who does!"

"I can't guarantee anyone on this island is still alive," said Blauwitz. "That Toby lotion really did a number on their communal digestive system—it looks like this snowballed into flu, dehydration, and then a malaria outbreak before they even had time to get leukemia. I don't know if I can overstate this: this island looks like the world ended."

"For them it did," said Miller.

"I'll save who I can," said Blauwitz, "but it'll be all I can do

just to clean it up before anybody else sees it. We can't let anyone know what happened here. I'll call you later." He severed
the connection.

General Clark stared at the room. "Congratulations, we've
made a bad situation worse."

"Did the lotion work faster than normal?" asked Miller.
"What happened?"

"We were too concerned about the lotion's direct effects and
didn't consider the side effects," said Ira/Moore. "There wasn't
enough food and water on the island to keep up with the demands of a mass increase in metabolism."

"That still sounds like we're putting it lightly," said Clark.

"Now we know what happens when ReBirth gets used on a
large scale," said Miller. "Our espionage gadget just became a
weapon of mass destruction."

"We need Lyle," said General Clark. "Not a knockoff, the real
thing. He's the only one who knows how to make ReBirth."

"If he's even alive," said Miller.

"He's definitely alive," said Ira/Moore. "But he doesn't understand ReBirth or Igdrocil any better than the rest of them."

"You're sure of this?" asked Clark.

He never made it for us, thought Ira/Moore, *but that might have
all been a deception. Just biding his time until he could burn our building
down.* He sighed and threw up his hands. "No, I'm not sure.
But how do we find him? He has the best disguise in the world.
Current estimates suggest we have more than seven thousand
Lyles on the East Coast alone, and more than twenty thousand
total in the country. There's at least three thousand in Arizona—
we think Mexicans have been using the lotion to jump the border.
And because we can't tell them apart, if we start grabbing Lyles
and interrogating them we're literally never going to stop. We'd
interrogate the same guy a dozen times."

"We could . . . tag them?" said Clark.

"They're not bears," said Miller. "Besides, the ACLU's starting to make waves over these Lyles, and anything we do to them will fall under even closer scrutiny than before."

"Seriously, though," said Ira/Moore, a slow grin spreading across his face. "Why not tag them?"

"I was joking," said Clark.

"The Lyles are criminals, right?" asked Ira/Moore. He leaned forward, excited by his new idea. "By the definition we created, anyone who uses ReBirth without government sanction is a terrorist; that's why I'm in this meeting, representing Homeland Security. The ACLU can go and screw itself once Homeland Security gets involved. We've never prosecuted more than a handful of ReBirth biological weapons cases, and then only for dealers, but we have the *power* to prosecute anyone. I say we don't just talk to the Lyles, we round them up: every single one of them has broken the law, so why not arrest them?"

"Because you just told us there's more than twenty thousand of them," said Miller. "We don't have anywhere to put that many people, certainly not in any of the prisons this administration keeps underfunding."

"Then we form camps," said Ira/Moore. "I know this sounds extreme, but we can do this—we have the legal power, and we have the legal precedent. Every single Lyle out there has been trafficking and using a biological weapon. It is, effectively, illegal to be Lyle Fontanelle. All we have to do is start punishing people in violation of that policy. And in the process, we question each one until we find the original."

"I don't like this," said General Clark.

"Everything that happened on São Tomé could happen here," said Ira/Moore. "As soon as Al Qaeda or North Korea or who knows who else gets hold of some ReBirth, suddenly we're a nation of blind cancer patients dead of dehydration and plague, torn apart by dogs in the streets. Are you willing to do what it takes to stop that?"

The room was silent. Finally General Clark nodded. "Get the

camps organized before you make an announcement—and be diplomatic when you do it. If we tell them it's a prison camp we'll start a civil war. Call it . . . amnesty. A chance for non-terrorist ReBirth users to come clean, and get help."

"Get help?" asked Miller.

"Under ideal circumstances, yes," said Clark. "As long as we've got them all in one place we may as well do something to help them regain their old identities. If possible. But finding the real Dr. Fontanelle is our number-one priority." She sighed and shook her head, seeming to deflate in her chair. "This is going to be hell."

One of the Lyles at the train station had Down syndrome.

Lyle couldn't help but stare. He had seen his own face in subtle variations a thousand times now, maybe ten thousand times, and while none of them were perfect replicas they were incredibly, uncannily similar. Ten thousand identical twins, however different they might be in the details, were still more or less identical. To see an outlier so wildly different was almost as big of a shock, at this point, as the first Lyle clone had been so many months ago. The Down syndrome clone was standing with a woman, and it was all Lyle could do not to walk straight to him and pepper them both with questions.

Fascinated or not, though, Lyle was still intensely paranoid, and he scanned the train platform carefully for anyone who might be watching. The government was actively searching for Lyles now, rounding them up into "Amnesty Centers," and Lyle had started disguising himself to stay free: dyed hair, a fake mustache, a hat and gloves, even a makeshift fat suit with extra bulk around his midsection. Anything to break up his profile and distinguish him from the thousands of other Lyles that seemed to be coming out of the woodwork. There were at least five Lyles on the platform now, probably headed into Manhattan to turn themselves in. *What will happen to them?* he wondered. *Should I just go with them, and stop running? What will they do when they find out I'm the real Lyle? Kill me, or imprison me, or force me to make more ReBirth?*

Maybe they won't even care. That thought scared Lyle more than any of the others.

When Lyle had first gone into hiding, it was just to get away from Ibis, and from the police, and from everyone else who wanted to capture him. Then he'd stayed in hiding as some kind of self-styled Robin Hood, bringing ReBirth to the terminally ill, but that was more of an illusion that anything else; he'd helped, what, five people? Six? He had no resources, and all his efforts to find more had led to dead ends. Now he was hiding simply to hide. Because continuing on one path was easier than finding a new one.

But now . . .

Now, a Lyle with Down syndrome changed everything. For months he'd been trying to figure out how ReBirth did what it did, and here was the best lead he'd ever had: an anomaly. A corner case in which the process didn't work the same way it had in every other. Figuring out why ReBirth didn't work right with this man might help him to figure out what "working right" meant.

Lyle finished his study of the platform, then studied it again, just in case. There didn't seem to be anybody waiting to jump out and grab him. He leaned away from his pillar and walked toward the couple. *Down syndrome is a genetic disorder,* he thought, growing more scientifically excited as he approached them. *Maybe ReBirth reacts differently to that? But it's cured all the congenital disorders they've tried it on before—why not this one?*

He stopped in front of the couple. "Excuse me, sir."

The Lyle stared at him a moment, then smiled broadly and held out his hand. Lyle shook it.

"Can I help you?" the woman asked. Her attitude was clipped and cold, her voice strained and her eyes bloodshot. Lyle imagined she'd spent a lot of time recently worried and crying, which seemed appropriate. He kept his own voice as soft and nonconfrontational as possible.

"I'm sorry to bother you," said Lyle, "but I'm a doctor, and I couldn't help but notice this man's condition. Please, may I ask you: did he have Down syndrome before he used ReBirth?"

"I really don't want to talk about this," said the woman.

"I didn't," said the man. He had a slight lisp. "It started five weeks ago. A bad dose."

"A bad dose," Lyle mused, looking at the other Lyle's face: his own face, but with the classic characteristics of Down syndrome. Almond-shaped eyes, a slightly flat nose, smaller ears than normal. The eyes, interestingly, showed the typical Lyle heterochromia, a patch of light in a darker iris, but here it was multiplied into a dozen or more small spots. Lyle didn't know what would cause something like that. He searched his memory for what little he knew about the causes of Down syndrome, but it was far from his area of expertise.

"We're going to the Amnesty Center," said the woman. "Do you think they can change him back?"

"Have you tried a dose of other lotion?" asked Lyle. "From a different source?"

"Of course," said the woman, "we've tried everything, but it never goes away."

Lyle frowned. "That doesn't make sense. How many doses has he used?"

"Before or after the Down syndrome?"

Lyle froze for half a second. "He used other doses of ReBirth before the bad one?"

"I was an actor," said the man.

The woman nodded. "He kept changing for different roles. The fourth dose turned out to be Lyle Fontanelle, so we tried a fifth, hoping it could reverse it, but this time it was a Lyle with Down syndrome. I didn't think that was possible." Her eyes were wide and pleading. "Please say you can help him."

Lyle's mind reeled: five doses of ReBirth in three months, and who knows how many since then. There wouldn't even be time for one to finish before the next started in. Kerry had done something similar, but . . .

"Do you think it's because we stacked Lyle on Lyle?" she asked.

"I don't think that's it," said Lyle. He'd been overwritten with his own DNA at least once, and it hadn't done anything. The wheels were turning, though, and he had his own theory about what had happened. It wasn't going to make her feel any better. "I don't think it was a bad dose, either."

The woman grew tenser, her mouth pinched in worry. "What happened?"

Down syndrome is a chromosomal disorder, he thought. *A human being is supposed to have forty-six chromosomes in twenty-three pairs, but a person with Down syndrome has an extra in pair twenty-one. Three chromosomes instead of two.* If this man had six different genomes all warring for control of his body, sooner or later something was bound to go wrong. The signals got crossed, or confused; maybe the lotions even attacked each other. The plasmids in the lotion were designed to unroll and mimic DNA long enough to write portions of themselves onto the host DNA—if one bit of ReBirth got to another bit of ReBirth halfway through this process, rewriting not just the host's genetic code but the competing rewriter itself. . . . He swallowed. *There's no telling what could happen if they started doing that.*

"What happened?" she asked again.

Lyle looked at her, speechless. There were dozens of chromosomal disorders, and so many ways for the chromosomes to become disordered: inversions, insertions, translocations. The list went on and on. *If ReBirth can do this, and if ReBirth is even half as aggressive as it seems to be, this could mean the end of . . .*

. . . of human genetics.

"Please, sir," the woman sobbed, "tell me what I can do for him!"

Lyle looked up sharply, shocked back into the real world. "Don't take him to the Amnesty Center."

"But they can help him—"

"They can't help anyone," said Lyle. "It's a scam." He pulled on his fake mustache, tearing it off in one long, painful tug. "I'm just like you, okay? And I'm trying to help you. Take your husband to the Amnesty Center and he will spend months or years in what is essentially an underfunded prison camp; in his condition he'll probably die in there." Lyle dug in his pocket for cash, some of the hundred thousand he'd stolen from Kerry, and handed her a wad of thousands. "You want my advice, go to the other side of this platform, take the first outbound train that comes along, and get as far away from civilization as you can. Rent a room on a fishing island or something; get away, stay hidden, and wait it out."

The woman stared at the money.

"Wait what out?"

If this means what I think it means . . . Lyle shook his head. "The end of the world."

47

Lyle returned to his grandmother's place only to find himself already there, dressed in a pink floral nightgown and dead in his grandmother's bed.

"Grandma?"

The dead Lyle's hair still held the chemicals from the old woman's last perm—faint wisps of curly, snow-white hair with over nearly half a centimeter of strong brown growth at the scalp. The room smelled of death and excrement. The intense nutrient needs of the transformation had apparently been too much for her ancient body to handle.

Lyle covered her with another sheet from the closet, and retreated to the living room to try to figure out his next move. He could place an anonymous call, but to who? The country's infrastructure was falling apart; electricity was still turned on, and water and gas were still flowing through the pipes, but the society that used those staples was crumbling. There were millions of ReBirth cases in the country; a massive percentage of them, especially in New York, were Lyles, and the military was scouring the streets for every Lyle they could find. More Down syndrome cases had cropped up, and leukemia and other cancers, all generated spontaneously by the lotion. Almost no one dared to use the lotion, and yet more clones—almost all of them Lyles—were surfacing every day. Nobody knew where they were coming from.

The political situation was no better. Half the world's nations had closed themselves off, terrified that another nation would try to replace their leaders, or threaten their religion, or make a desperate, São Tomé–style attack in a mad grab for resources. Private citizens were doing the same thing on a small scale, encasing themselves in hazmat suits or a homemade equivalent, buying up piles of food storage and guns. Lyle could call a mortuary about his grandmother, but who would answer the phone? Who would care? It was the end of days.

Lyle searched the house for food, but there was little to be had. His dying grandmother had eaten almost everything she owned during the transformation, up to and including a can of water chestnuts he knew for a fact that she hated. Lyle took a long drink from the sink, washing the dishes carefully when he was done—because his grandma would want them that way—and then scrounged through the shed for a shovel. Even if there was no one else around to bury her, the least he could do was bury her himself.

It took him an hour to make a hole big enough, and two more hours after that to make it deep. It was almost midnight when he carried her body—his own body, filthy and brittle and hollow as old bones—to the small backyard of the home she had lived in all her life. He laid her gently in the dirt, said a silent prayer, and covered her with moist shovelfuls of earth. He'd never buried anyone before, let alone himself, and he felt a morbid shiver race through him as he covered her legs, her chest, and finally her face. *His* face, gaunt and skeletal at the bottom of a grave. He filled the hole and patted it down, ringing it with rocks from the garden. He had no headstone, but found a picture of her and his grandpa on the mantelpiece, and placed that on the mound instead.

Lyle showered and changed his clothes. It was one in the morning. He'd realized weeks ago that if the government was determined to imprison all Lyles, then the simplest answer was to not be a Lyle. Even knowing that, though, he'd hung on doggedly, refusing to give up the last remnants of his identity. It wasn't sentimental reasons—it wasn't that he loved being himself, because over the last few months he'd grown to hate being himself. Over the last few years, maybe, if he was being honest. It was more than the ubiquity—the news stories, the wanted posters, the people on the street. It was the knowledge that he, somehow, was the cause of it all. He'd thought at the time that he was trying to stop it, but looking back he realized that all he'd really done was whine and pity himself. And that's all he'd been doing for years. So no, he wasn't maintaining his DNA because he liked being himself.

In some ways, he realized, he'd clung to his identity because it was the only thing he had left. He had thrown out his driver's license and other ID cards to protect himself from the law, destroying every evidence that he was the "real" Lyle Fontanelle, and all he had left was a face shared by a hundred thousand others. It wasn't much of an identity, but it was his. In a world where so many people had lost themselves, he'd kept himself— as damaged and criminalized as he was—and he'd drawn some kind of strength from that.

But it was a meaningless gesture, and an increasingly dangerous one. Millions of people around the world had taken the plunge and changed themselves, so why not him? His resolve had weakened, and tonight, burying his own body in a shallow grave, his resolve had snapped in half. It was time to start a new life.

He hadn't been following the black market for weeks, but he knew where the old dealers had hung out, the old hot spots where a paying customer could score some ReBirth. Lyle counted his money—still most of Kerry's hundred thousand—and hid the majority of it in an ankle brace he'd started using for just this purpose. With his pants worn long, no one could even tell it was there. He hid the rest of it in various pockets and waistbands and shoes, separated so that a single mugger wouldn't take a dangerous amount, and then raided his grandma's dressers and nightstands for jewelry. If he was going to get some ReBirth, he needed to be ready to pay for it.

He walked through the dark streets, keeping his ears open for cars—especially the army's Lyle wagons—and his eyes always scanning for dealers. He approached one likely dealer and recognized the same seven-foot giant he'd met before, though of course he had no way of knowing if it was the same man. He approached the man casually—noting, with practiced eyes, the three thugs waiting in the background.

"You're out late," said the man. His voice was deep and sonorous.

"I'm looking for something," said Lyle, beginning the verbal dance of codes and implications that passed for a drug negotiation. "I was wondering if you might give me directions."

"I know where a lot of things are," said the man. "And I'm not doing anything else, so why not?"

"A friend of mine's an athlete," said Lyle. "Nice guy, good bone structure. Maybe you know where he lives?"

"Maybe," said the man. "Maybe the guy I know isn't the guy you know. How much does he earn in a year?"

Lyle did his best to stay calm and professional. "A hundred thousand."

The man smiled. "I'm pretty sure I know that guy. It's dangerous on the streets this time of night, though—you want a ride?"

Lyle nodded. He'd seen this before. Once the dealer knew you were serious, they moved the deal to a car; it kept the negotiations private and, if things went bad, mobile. "Sure."

The man stood up, and a moment later a black car with dark, tinted windows slid up to the curb, beams from the streetlights rippling across it like water. The tall man got in, and Lyle helped himself in to the other side. When the doors were closed the car began driving slowly through the neighborhood, and the tall man spoke to him directly.

"You have a specific model in mind, or just whatever I got in stock?"

"Anything that's not Lyle," said Lyle.

"If all you want is non-Lyle, I've got plenty of celebrities—"

"No celebrities," Lyle said quickly. "Nothing identifiable. I just want to be . . . different. I want to be background noise."

"You and every other Lyle in America," said the dealer. "Celebrities used to be the expensive stuff, now it's cheap."

"Then what can I get for a hundred thousand?"

"The cheap stuff."

Lyle's jaw dropped. "You've got to be kidding."

"How desperate are you to not be Lyle anymore?" While Lyle struggled to find an answer that didn't destroy his negotiating power, the dealer pointed at him with a long, slim finger. "Exactly. Now consider that there's more than a hundred thousand of you, and they're all just as desperate. I can name my price for what I have left, and I can turn you away and still find another buyer before morning."

Lyle grimaced. "What celebrities do you have?"

"Does gender matter?"

That stopped Lyle short, staring at the man as he searched himself for the answer. After a moment he nodded. "Yes."

"Not so desperate after all, then. The price list is upside down, now that anonymity's such a priority. I could put you in a Tom Cruise for fifty, but for the full hundred thousand we could go all the way up to C-List: daytime soaps, and a couple of people from *Dancing with the Stars*."

Lyle nodded. "How much for a guy that did, I don't know, a few pilots? Maybe died on *CSI*?"

The dealer snorted. "You don't have that kind of money."

"Make a recommendation, then," said Lyle. "You know your stock better than I do."

The dealer pulled a small notebook from the seat-back pocket, and consulted it quickly in the dim light from a passing streetlamp.

"How about a former model, couple of series, and a stunning performance as 'Security Guard' in an episode of *90210*."

"What's his name?"

"Dan Wells."

"Never heard of him."

"Most people haven't."

Lyle frowned. "He did a few series, though? I mean, he's famous?"

"Famous enough, but the average American isn't going to know him in a crowd. Especially if you put on some weight and get a different haircut." The dealer leaned forward. "Look, man, I can't offer you a complete unknown. That's not what the lotion was designed for—if he wasn't famous enough for people to want to be him, I wouldn't have his DNA in the first place. Now, if you have twice the money you claim to have, and you're just holding out on me for some reason, then we can talk about 'Cheering Man Number Three' in a crowd scene from a Lifetime movie. Otherwise, Dan Wells is the best I can do."

Lyle pondered the question. A former model would be in better shape, probably more tan, certainly better groomed—if Lyle took his DNA and then completely let himself go, he'd be almost unrecognizable. He hoped. But there were more concerns than just the fame. "How do I know it's not Lyle?"

The dealer's eyes widened, as if Lyle had just offended him. "I couldn't stay in business if I sold Lyle."

"Everyone sells Lyle," said Lyle. "Even people who think they don't usually have some in their stock. Do you test for it? Do you have any kind of quality assurance system?"

"My word as a businessman."

"We couldn't even discuss this sale on an empty street," said Lyle. "You'll forgive me for not taking a drug dealer at his word."

"Then let's be honest," said the dealer. "I'm a criminal, selling a biological weapon to other criminals. If you're not satisfied with your product, be a man and just shoot me."

Lyle stared at him. "I have to admit that's a compelling argument."

"Then do we have a deal?"

Lyle hesitated only a moment. "We do."

The car rolled to an elegant stop at the next dark corner, and the dealer pulled a briefcase from under the seat in front of him. "You have the hundred?"

Lyle reached into his ankle brace and pulled it out, a thick stack of sweaty bills. "Sorry about the . . . dampness."

"Money is money," said the dealer. He opened the briefcase and pulled out a plastic baggie with a single gelcap pill inside, the pill containing a single drop of white lotion. The baggie was labeled with a sticker that read DAN WELLS. Lyle handed him the money, the dealer handed Lyle the baggie, and a moment later he was standing alone on the street corner, staring at his prize. His money drove away and turned at the light, disappearing forever. Lyle looked back at the baggie.

"It's now or never."

He opened the baggie and took out the pill, discarding the empty plastic bag in the gutter. The gelcap was warm in his hand, and slightly tacky as the moisture from his hands slowly started breaking down the gel. All he had to do was crush the pill, or squeeze it, or even swallow it, and he'd never be Lyle again. That tiny drop was all it took.

He'd never used ReBirth on purpose—he'd sent it out into the world, and he'd used it on Susan, but never on himself. Was he really ready for this? He thought again about the Lyle with Down syndrome, his chromosomes destroyed by competing ReBirth samples. Would the same thing happen to him? Something worse? Surely public execution would be better than congenital cancer.

He wanted it all to be over. To stop running, to stop being afraid. To stop being Lyle Fontanelle. He crushed the capsule in his fingers, and smeared the lotion between his forefinger and thumb.

48

Three weeks later, Lyle was still himself; the lotion had either been Lyle DNA or plain old lotion. He couldn't escape himself, it seemed, plus now he was broke.

The Lyle Camps were becoming infamous: the squalid conditions, the humiliations, the hunger and thirst. The secondary camps had it the worst—after they figured out who you were they shipped you off into hard labor and the brink of starvation. The former was intended to solve the latter, but they couldn't feed them fast enough. There were too few resources left in the country these days, and too many Lyles.

Lyle had heard the latest numbers on TV earlier in the evening, catching the tail end of a news story as he waited for night to fall so he could try to find some food. "Nine hundred thousand Lyles in the U.S. alone," it said. "There are now more Lyles in America than Pacific Islanders, including persons of partial Hawaiian descent. There are more Lyles than Navajo, and experts predict that if the number of Lyles continues to rise at the current rate it will reach one million by late next week, two million the week after, and three million by Thanksgiving. That will be more than all Native Americans combined."

Lyle heard a lull in traffic and peeked out. He had a few seconds to dart across the street, and he jumped up to take it. Flatbed "Lyle wagons" cruised the streets in this area, rounding up Lyles and hauling them off to the camps, and it was all but impossible to keep clear of them. He'd stretched his meager food out as long as he could, laying low in an old drug den— now more of a flophouse for refugee Lyles—and ventured out tonight under cover of Halloween. He had a small rubber mask, an old Ronald Reagan costume, and hoped that he could at least make it to the store and back without getting caught. The mask was good cover, but it narrowed his vision and made it hard to run. He scanned the street up and down before dashing across to the other side. There was a cigarette shop there run by an old Ethiopian man who didn't ask questions, and Lyle figured he could spend the last of his money and stock up on whatever the old man had—you could never tell from one day to the next what any store would manage to find and sell. Lyle could make it a few more days, at least, and then . . . He didn't know.

He thought about robbing the store, but it felt cruel and wrong. *That's not who I am,* he thought. *I haven't fallen that far yet.*

A light and a siren flared up behind him, and without even thinking Lyle ran.

"Please no," he muttered, "don't take me now." He ducked down an alley and leaped over a body—unconscious or dead he couldn't tell—and bolted for the far end, hoping to make it over the fence before the police could follow him. He'd never been especially fit, but months of living on the street had made him lean and wiry, and this was not the first fence he'd climbed. The cops were close behind him, but he cleared the fence and leaped down, pelting down the alley and into the street—

—right into the side of an armed soldier.

"Stand down!" the soldier shouted, and Lyle barely had time to orient himself before five soldiers surrounded him in a semicircle, their rifles raised and trained on his chest. "Remove the mask, sir!"

"I'm sorry," Lyle stammered, taking a step back, "I wasn't attacking or anything, I was just running—"

"Remove the mask, sir, or we will remove it for you."

"President Reagan," said a voice behind Lyle's back, and a

moment later the two cops who'd been chasing him puffed into view. They looked familiar, but Lyle couldn't place them.

"Please stand down, Officers," said the leader of the soldiers, "we have this one."

"We had him first."

"Sure you did."

"We're all on the same team, guys," said one of the cops. Lyle saw the man's nametag—Luckesen—and the odd surname sparked a memory. Luckesen and Woolf, the same two policemen who'd arrested him for a house robbery in . . . *It seems like years ago, but it was only, what, March? April?* Lyle dropped his head, terrified that they would recognize him, but almost immediately he laughed at the idiocy of the idea. He was crying, too, and blinked the moisture away. *They see a dozen or more Lyles every day,* he thought. *They won't know me from any of them—and they have no way of knowing I'm the real one.*

Both the cops and the soldiers were dressed in what had become the standard urban "armor": long pants tucked into boots, long sleeves snapped into long gloves, and a helmet with a face shield. No exposed skin. The soldiers were further dressed in thick, armored vests and groin pads, and Lyle remembered just a few months ago seeing that same costume in news footage of soldiers in Africa and Afghanistan. An occupying army, now called home to occupy New York. It was too much, and Lyle felt the tears come harder and hotter.

"He might not even be a Lyle," said a soldier. "For all you know he hasn't even done anything."

"Of course he's done something," said Officer Woolf, "he was running. But on the off chance he's not actually Ronald Reagan, how about we take that mask off. If he's a Lyle, he's all yours. Otherwise we take him into the station and figure out what else he's guilty of."

"And then we buy him a drink," said Officer Luckesen, "and congratulate him for somehow avoiding Lylehood."

"Take it off," said a soldier. Lyle was still crying, hearing the words without understanding them, and didn't move. "I said take it off!"

Lyle pulled off the mask, squinting at the sudden influx of light in his peripheral vision.

"No surprise there," said Woolf. "Have fun with him."

"Get in the truck," said a soldier, and gestured with his rifle for Lyle to start walking. The truck was a standard military flatbed, covered with an ad hoc cage of wood and metal and chicken wire. Lyle paused at the back of it, looking up at five other Lyles with sad, desperate faces, crouched in the corners with their arms wrapped around themselves for warmth. *I could tell them who I am,* he thought. *I could tell them I'm the real one, I could prove it to them, and then I'd go to a real prison instead of this hellhole.* Almost as soon as he thought of it he discarded the idea. Lyle Fontanelle, the real one, was the cause of all this—the mad scientist who'd destroyed the world. He had to convince them he was somebody else.

"Do you require assistance into the truck, sir?" The soldier's question was polite and formal, but his voice was a businesslike growl. He was only asking because he had to, and his assistance was not likely to be comfortable.

"I'm fine," said Lyle, hoisting himself up. "I can do it." He wandered to the back of the cage and sat down by the others. "So," he said, trying to think of Lyle-based small talk. "How long have you all been Lyles?"

"Five weeks," said one. The other four chimed in with time frames of their own, ranging everywhere from ten weeks down to two. The first one looked back at him. "How about you?"

"Way too long," said Lyle. He took a breath, playing with the mask in his hands. He needed to convince the camp he was one of these men, an innocent bystander accidentally cursed with the face of a war criminal. That would take details, and those details had to sound authentic. He nodded. "Five weeks for me, too," he said, trying out the story to see how well it fit. He looked up. "How did it happen?"

They told their stories one by one, Lyle listening intently for any information he could use to blend into the crowd. One of them had bought black market ReBirth to try to impress his girlfriend; another one had bought some for his girlfriend, and accidentally gotten it on both of them. "I thought we could be, like, lesbians together, but then we turned into men and I broke up with her." Two of the Lyles in the truck had originally been women; one had used the lotion to hide from an abusive husband, figuring life as a Lyle was still better than life as a victim. The other just wanted to be taller.

"I never used it at all," said the last Lyle. He was the one who claimed to have only been a Lyle for two weeks, still halfway through the transformation. He must have been fairly Lyle-ish before—same height, same race, same gender—because the transformation was advanced enough to be easily identifiable. *Or maybe we're all just getting really good at seeing Lyles,* thought Lyle.

"Is that really your story?" asked the Lyle One. "You never used it, so you're not a criminal and they have to let you go? You know that doesn't work."

"I never used it," Lyle Five insisted, shrugging helplessly. "It's illegal—no offense to any of you—so I never touched the stuff. I was never even tempted. And then one day I just . . . started changing."

"That's not how it works," said Lyle Two. The one with the Lyle-ized girlfriend. "You probably got it on you and just didn't notice, like I did."

"Or somebody put it in the water," said Lyle Three. "You heard what happened in São Tomé."

"Those pictures were fakes."

"That's just what the liberal media wants you to think."

"Oh, here we go, a nutjob."

"Wait," said Real Lyle. "Maybe it really is in the water. The number of Lyles has ballooned in the last month, exponentially, but the black market availability has dropped off, so where are they getting it? And almost all of the new Lyles have been right here in New York City, so it's obviously something local. Why not the water?"

"Who would put Lyle lotion into the water?" asked Lyle Five.

"White supremacists," Lyle Three spat. "Turn everyone in New York City into a white guy, and you've just wiped out a massive chunk of blacks, Asians, Latinos, Indians, you name it. They're whitewashing the whole city."

"Maybe they did it as some kind of power grab," said Lyle One. "I mean, like, it's illegal to be Lyle, right? So if they make everyone Lyle, we're all criminals and they can throw us all in jail, just like this. Pretty soon the whole country will be a jail, and they'll control everything."

"Maybe it was Lyle activists," said Lyle Four softly, "trying to make Lyles so prevalent no one bothers to hurt them anymore."

"That's stupid," said Lyle Three.

"What if it was an accident?" asked Real Lyle.

The others frowned at him. "What?"

"What if somebody stole a whole ton of Lyle lotion," said Real Lyle, "like the stuff that disappeared from the NewYew plant when the government tried to seize it. They tried selling it on the black market, but they didn't realize it was all Lyle, and when they did they stopped and they dumped it all—flushed it down the toilet, dropped it in a reservoir, whatever. What if somebody thought they were getting rid of it, and poisoned our water supply by accident?"

The group was silent, thinking. After a long moment Lyle Four whispered: "That's the scariest theory yet."

"I know," said Lyle, wrapping his arms tightly around himself for warmth. "I know."

49

Thursday, November 1
1:15 A.M.
New York

43 DAYS TO THE END OF THE WORLD

The truck eventually dropped them off at a local holding cell, and Lyle spent the night in the gym at a Brooklyn rec center, lying on a cot in a grid of nearly three dozen Lyles. They gave them jumpsuits to replace their old clothes, and almost immediately Lyle lost track of which Lyles were which—they all looked the same, even to him—and decided to just keep to himself instead. Most of the Lyles had apparently decided the same thing. The next morning they joined another group, probably a hundred Lyles in total, and together they were herded into the backs of the flatbed cage trucks for the drive upstate. It was colder on the highway than it had been in the city, and the soldiers issued them blankets to keep warm, though not enough for the group. Lyle didn't put up a fight and thus never got one; he huddled in the center of the crowd, out of the wind, and tried to stay warm.

Their destination, Lyle noted with surprise, was the old NewYew plant, converted to a Lyle Camp, and he chuckled humorlessly at the irony. The guards were cold and stoic, nearly faceless behind their plastic riot masks, and they backed the trucks up to the front gate one at a time, unloading their cargo of Lyles into the vast open grounds of the camp. Lyle was in the second truck, and waited patiently for his turn, breathing slowly and trying to stay calm. The crowd in the truck thinned, and Lyle practiced the lies he'd concocted. He shuffled to the back of the truck and looked out over the crowd.

Ten thousand Lyles looked back.

"Keep moving," said a guard, and Lyle jumped down, shocked into silence by the sheer quantity of Lyles. The new Lyles fresh off the truck were herded into a long line, and Lyle fell into place, shuffling forward as each new person was registered. He'd seen enough movies about prison to expect a lot of hooting at the new guys, but the mood instead was somber and clinical. Bored. The ten thousand Lyles in the camp saw the same faces every day, everywhere they looked, and a hundred new iterations didn't add anything interesting to their world.

The line split, feeding into five smaller lines each with their own clerk, and Lyle soon found himself standing before a large woman with a laptop and an assortment of boxes. "Name?"

"William Shears," said Lyle quickly.

"Address?"

"Homeless."

The woman looked up, her expression only barely concealing her disdain for anyone without an answer to such a basic question. "You need an address. Finding out who you really are is the whole purpose of the Amnesty Camp program. Give me the last address you had, and when your number comes up they'll try to connect you to your old life."

So they are *trying to catalog us,* thought Lyle. *What will they do when they find out who I am?*

"Sir?" the woman pressed.

"It's 4770 Ring Street, Star City, Iowa." They'd know it was a false address when they tried to process him, but at least it gave him time to think of some other way to hide.

"Thank you," said the woman. "You will be processed and interviewed in the order you arrived." She hit a button on her laptop, and a small printer spat out a plastic label with the number 11874. She stuck it firmly to a bracelet and snapped it around his arm. "Do not lose this."

"Is this an identifying code or a like a 'take a number' number?"

"Both."

"Wow." Lyle looked at the number again. "What number are you on now?"

"We're on 463."

"Wow," Lyle said again. *It's going to be easier to lose myself in here than I thought.* He looked at the squalid camp again. "How does the food work?"

"Army MREs, once a day. Make it last." She looked at him pointedly. "And get in line early."

"Gotcha."

The woman turned to look over his shoulder. "Next!"

"That's it?" asked Lyle.

The woman glared at him. "What else do you want?"

Lyle stared at the camp, too lost to even answer the question. "I don't know. How . . . do they tell each other apart?"

"Hell if I know. Next!"

Lyle stepped away from the table, and the guards ushered him through the gate. He stared at the vast sea of Lyles, trying to comprehend it but it was too big.

Or, he told himself, exactly the right size. He looked at his bracelet number again: 11874. If he played it right, he might never get processed at all. He walked to a Lyle who was leaning against the wall of the factory, and leaned up next to him.

"There were a hundred of us on that truck," he said, "give or take. How often do the trucks come in?"

"Every day."

"The same size?"

The man nodded. "Give or take."

Lyle nodded, watching the crowd. "And how many do they interview?"

"On a good day? Fifty. Most days we're lucky to do half that."

Lyle nodded, and tugged on his bracelet. "Do these come off?"

The Lyle by the wall shook his head. "You don't want to lose that—it's your only ticket out of here. And anyone farther down the line than you are is going to be awfully interested in taking it away from you."

"Or they might be willing to trade for it," said Lyle. "A little bit of their MRE, for jumping a hundred people forward in the line? That's an easy trade to make."

The Lyle by the wall raised his eyebrow. "Are you crazy? You'll never get out of here."

"That," said Lyle, "is exactly the point."

50

"Congratulations," said Larry. "You've raised the most pathetic army the world has ever seen." Their entire band of revolutionaries had gathered together for an announcement—tie-dyed potheads, wrinkled hippies, tattooed vegan goths with more piercings than skin. Seventy-four forgotten, angry people who only fit in with each other.

Larry hated them.

"Try to get over it," said Susan, leaning against their van. "This movement is bigger than the people in it."

"For the record," said Larry, "I also hate calling it a movement. It's like we're pooping out justice."

"Wait," said Tony/Fabio. "Isn't that *why* we call it a movement? Now I'm disappointed."

"We need revolutionaries," said Larry, "not . . . hippies."

"These are both," said Susan. "Everyone we recruited knows this is a war, and they're ready to fight."

"They're tree huggers," said Tony/Fabio.

Susan shook her head. "They're more likely to spike a tree than hug it."

"Fine," said Larry, "we have our revolution, and then we're done with them. Only a raging idiot would want to let that pack of Communist baristas rebuild anything resembling a government."

"The new world's going to have Communist baristas in it, too," said Susan. "You may as well just get used to it."

"As long as they stay baristas and not politicians."

"You're not a politician, either," said Tony/Fabio, "you're a hired gun. Who says you get to make all the important decisions?"

"I'm not saying I do," said Larry, "I'm just saying that they're idiots. And they're Socialists, which is redundant."

"We never used to fight," said Tony/Fabio with mock sadness. "I think you liked me better as a woman."

"I think I liked you better as a prisoner," said Larry.

"Let's get this meeting started," said Susan. She walked to the front of the group and shouted for their attention. "All right!" she said. "Eyes up here." The room quieted. "It's time for the next phase—we've built our revolution, we've laid all the groundwork, and now it's time to make it happen. We want change!"

The group shouted back in agreement.

Susan ticked off each point on her fingers. "We want the government to change. We want their policies to change. We want their vision to change. We want their attitude to change. But more than anything, more than anything in the whole world, we want ReBirth to change. We want it to disappear. We want every last drop of it destroyed."

The crowd murmured their approval, and Susan paced back and forth, stoking their anger. "Kuvam calls this a world without fear, but I'm still afraid. He calls this a world without death, but people are dying every day. You know what I call this? A world without meaning. A world without logic. There are five million Lyles is this world now, and nobody knows where they're coming from. There are nearly thirty million other victims, in thousands of makes and models. Nobody knows if they're going to wake up one morning as somebody else—as Lyle, or as Victoria Carver, or as some half-dead cancer boy in a corrupt government takeover."

The crowd cheered even louder at this—if there was one thing

Larry and the hippies shared, it was a passionate distrust of the government.

"Today," said Susan, "I'm going to introduce you to the next phase of our plan. We tried to scare them, to show them how terrifying a world with ReBirth can truly be, but they're not scared. They think they can't be scared—that their ReBirth factories and their hazmat suits and their ivory towers can keep them safe, but we're going to show them. Bring him out."

Larry and Tony/Fabio opened the van, opened the crate in the back of it, and led their guest toward the dais.

"You've been collecting blank lotion," said Susan to the revolutionaries. "You've been stealing it on the streets and taking it from the government and scrounging it in every corner of the country. Now we have enough, and we're going to teach the world to be afraid again. We're going to cross the bridge to Manhattan, break into the UN, and turn every world leader in there into this guy."

Larry brought their guest up onstage, and he spread his lips in a wide, leering grin and hooted madly.

"This is Mr. Bubbles," said Susan. "He's a chimpanzee."

51

Lyle had managed to lay low for three and a half weeks now, and was confident he could do it indefinitely if it came to that. He knew the facility already, of course, and could navigate it more easily than the other Lyles, but that wasn't the main thing. He could stay hidden simply because he was the only Lyle in the complex who wanted to. The others were clamoring to get out, buying and selling their slots in the interview queue, desperate for any chance to convince the guards that they didn't belong here, that they needed to be somewhere else, that they had a real life and a real identity, and could you please help me get back to it? In a crowd like that, Lyle could hide forever. He sold his queue slot day after day, digging himself deeper and deeper into the interminable wait in exchange for a piece of bread or a packet of beans. He wanted nothing, and the camp asked nothing of him.

On some level, this bothered him.

It wasn't that he wanted to get out; the Lyle Camp wasn't wonderful, but for a man facing death row it was a welcome alternative. What bothered him was his own lack of ambition. Just months ago he had been important—he had been the chief scientist of one of the largest health and beauty companies in the world. He had made things. He had accomplished things. He had created and dreamed and lived. And now he was just sitting in a derelict factory, biding his time, waiting for . . . for what? For the prison guards to get bored and give up? For the government to change its policies? For the world to fall apart in some kind of nuclear apocalypse? How did he think this was going to end?

"Maybe it never will," he mused, but that was the whole problem. The idea that endless sameness could appease him. When had he become this man, so willing to sit and wait while the world moved around him? Or maybe he'd always been like this. He tried to think back to the things he'd done before, to what a "normal" life had been for him. Wake up in the morning; take the train to work; talk to Susan; endure a meeting with Cynthia; take the train home; watch *Star Trek*; eat a low-salt meal, maybe a piece of chicken and a plate of brussels sprouts.

Brussels sprouts. The Ibis Lyles had said they'd inherited his taste for them, as if the genetic code for the layout of his tongue had somehow predisposed them to love the flavor. Lyle sat on a catwalk above the factory floor and watched the Lyles mill around below him, hundreds in here and thousands more outside. New ones every day, each a tiny variation of the unique individual Lyle used to think he was. Did they all like brussels sprouts? Did they all watch *Star Trek*? Did they all lead quiet, unassuming lives, never making waves, the same routine for years on end? Lyle had never had ambition, he realized. He'd become a scientist because he was good at it, because it came naturally to him. He'd gone into cosmetics because the opportunity was there, fresh out of college, and after he'd paid his dues and gotten his job experience he'd never bothered moving on. He didn't speak up. He didn't change.

"How many of you actually lived your lives," he called down. Nine hundred identical faces looked up, some finding him immediately, some searching in confusion for the source of the voice. "How many of you actually have something to go back to, something real, something that isn't just this, in a different building, in a different face: just milling around and pretending that it all means something?"

Some of the faces found him; some of them spotted some other Lyle on the same catwalk and looked at him instead. Lyle stood up, abruptly furious at the relentless nothingness that had defined his entire life. "How many of you have never made any real decisions? You sit there, at your desk in your cubicle, at your desk in your dorm room, at your stupid counter in your dead-end job slapping cheese onto somebody else's sandwiches. This isn't the life you wanted? Well, that one wasn't, either. The only difference now is that the blinders are gone, and the truth is right in front of you, and you can't pretend you're unique anymore just because you don't look like every other face in the world. Because now you do. Now it's obvious. Now you're just me, and I'm you, and we're all him, and him, and him, and none of it means anything. You all want your lives back? How many of you actually used them for anything?"

Some of the Lyles yelled back angrily; some talked to each other; some dropped their heads or slinked into corners. Lyle yelled again: "How many? How many?" Suddenly a hundred identical fingers pointed up, not at Lyle but off to his left, and he looked up just in time to watch himself climb onto the railing of the catwalk and step off, arms pinwheeling as he fell a hundred feet to the floor. A hundred Lyles shouted in one voice, scrambling out of the way.

It wasn't even the first suicide they'd seen that day.

"Attention," said the PA system, and the room fell quiet. "I have been instructed to announce that the terrorist Susan Howell has been caught and found guilty of treason. She will be publicly executed in one hour, outside the south fence. That is all."

Lyle looked south, as if he could peer straight through the wall and into the field beyond, and past that to the fence and the execution and Susan. *Susan.* Why were they killing her here? Why now? There was no reason for it.

Unless it was a ploy to reveal him.

Lyle looked down at the floor to see some of the other Lyles trying, without any tools, to clean up the mess of the jumper. The soldiers never came inside anymore, for fear of riots. Lyle crossed the catwalk to the stairs, and followed the slow trickle of other Lyles headed south to see the execution. Trick or not, Lyle wanted to be as close to the front as he could. It would be the only way to tell.

The army had set up a platform just beyond the south fence, and the yard outside was already crowded with hundreds of curious Lyles. Lyle managed to work his way to the front, wondering if each Lyle he brushed past was someone he'd talked to before, someone with whom he'd shared a meal or traded his queue number. Maybe he knew them on the outside—his neighbors from Queens, or fellow commuters from the train, or a worker in his own office.

Did they have the real Susan, or a ReBirth clone? They had her DNA. And she was, by all accounts, a real terrorist, but executing her here only made sense if they were trying to flush Lyle out of hiding. Except they didn't know which camp the real Lyle was in. They had camps all over the country. Did they make a fake Susan to kill at every single one?

Next to the platform was a truck, surrounded by armed soldiers. Who would come out of it?

The canvas flap on the back of the truck was thrown open from the inside, and an officer stepped out, followed by . . . Lyle craned his neck to see. A girl. Blond. Susan's height, Susan's build. His breath caught in his throat. The girl stepped down and lifted her hands to brush her hair from her face—both hands, because they were cuffed together. She looked up, and Lyle saw again how beautiful she was, how young she was, how sad and tired and weathered she was. The crowd behind him was restless, shifting and craning their necks and shouting: there were catcalls, and demands to release her, and demands to kill her, and a hundred other things lost in a jumbled roar.

The officer—a general, Lyle saw, though he couldn't read the nametag—followed Susan onto the platform. She wasn't fighting. *The real Susan would be fighting,* Lyle thought, but even that he couldn't be sure of. They were about to kill her, for goodness sake—what if her spirit was finally broken? He walked her to the end of the platform. He didn't offer a blindfold. The general walked back to the other end and a half dozen soldiers formed a line in front him, weapons at their sides.

"Ready!"

The soldiers brought their rifles up. Lyle looked in desperation at Susan, wondering what he should do. *If I say anything. I'm next.*

"Aim!"

The rifles tipped forward, six black lances pointed straight at her heart. Susan faltered, her brave mask crumbling into fear, and Lyle screamed.

"It's me!" he screamed. It was the one thing that none of the other Lyles could possibly think to say, because they didn't know who Susan was. They didn't know the connection, and they didn't know this was a trap. And they didn't know that springing that trap was the only way to save her. Lyle clung to the fence and howled as loudly as he could. "I'm the real Lyle Fontanelle!"

Almost immediately a soldier was there, grabbing his arm through the fence, and dozens of others leaped immediately into action, pointing their weapons and shouting for the crowd to move back. When the army had cleared a path along the fence to the gate, more soldiers entered and surrounded him. The general approached him, his face grim and uncertain. His nametag said Blauwitz.

"Who first came up with the idea of using ReBirth commercially?" asked General Blauwitz.

The same question Kerry used to identify him in the park. It was something only the NewYew executives would know—a perfect way to assure that he was the real Lyle, but also a clear sign that somehow, impossibly, NewYew was behind this. Lyle glanced at the truck, then at Susan, still standing on the platform with five black rifles pointed at her heart. Lyle looked back at the general.

"Jeffrey," he said.

Blauwitz slapped a pair of handcuffs on Lyle's wrist, and the other on his own. There was no way to lose him in the crowd now. "We got him!" the general shouted. "Pack this up."

The general pulled him toward the gate, surrounded by their armed escort. Beyond the fence the soldiers lowered their weapons, and Susan breathed a sigh of relief. One of the soldiers unlocked her handcuffs, and she smiled.

"Was she real?" Lyle asked.

"The real Susan Howell?" asked Blauwitz. "Don't I wish."

They led him to a black SUV, locking the gate behind them as ten thousand screaming Lyles begged to come, too. Blauwitz unlocked the cuffs and opened the door, and Lyle climbed in awkwardly.

"You're with them now?" asked Lyle. The door shut behind him, and they were alone.

Cynthia's eye's glittered. "They wanted to find you, and I knew how. I traded you for a position on their committee."

"The Execute Lyle Committee?"

"Execute you?" asked Cynthia. "Lyle, you're the most valuable person on the planet right now. You're going to save the world." She grimaced and pressed herself closer to the door. "But first you're going to shower. You smell like somebody murdered a wrestler in an outhouse."

General Blauwitz opened the front door and climbed in. "Everybody ready? Time to visit the UN."

PART FOUR
REBIRTH

52

Lyle knew how the lotion worked.

The Lyle with Down syndrome had been his first big clue, but the final piece that did it was right there in the papers Cynthia had given him: box after box of newspapers, net news printouts, recorded news videos, and even private government reports. The key had been in NewYew's procedural accounts of how they manufactured the lotion. The only batches that worked, that had active cloning capabilities, were the ones that had blank ReBirth mixed into them at the factory. Just like that very first batch, way back when they'd started, where Jerry had mixed in Lyle's sample to help match the consistency. Everything had propagated from that one tiny bottle he had mixed together in his lab. It was a random mutation in the RNA.

He knew how it worked, but it didn't matter. The world was falling apart, and knowing why wasn't going to save it.

The lotion itself was no more widespread than any typical drug problem—more noticeable, perhaps, because of its visual nature, but not really any more prevalent than cocaine or marijuana or meth. The massive surge of Lyles in the New York area was an admitted exception, and the government had apparently come to the same conclusion Lyle had: ReBirth was in the water supply. Anyone who could had been urged to evacuate.

Much more dangerous than the lotion's civilian usage, the news outlets all agreed, was the lotion's appeal to governments themselves. The various religious side effects had been bad enough, most notably the Holy Vessel's divine cloning experiment and the resulting New Crusade. Latin America was still burning, from Argentina to the Southwestern U.S. The various countries of the Middle East had either descended into chaos or been locked down under fascist control. Even China, ostensibly nonreligious, had seen its share of denominational uprisings.

Potentially much worse, however, was the fallout from São Tomé. Before the invasion the world's governments had wanted ReBirth as a weapon; after it, they feared it like a plague. The only way to avoid São Tomé's fate was to destroy ReBirth or to be the sole owner, and the possibility that someone might achieve the second option made everyone too jealous to consider the first. Governments themselves, as entities, had become as addicted to ReBirth as any crackhead. They had to have it, or they would be destroyed by those who did.

At 6:13 in the morning, Lyle and Cynthia and their military escorts loaded themselves into Humvees and trekked across the city. Lyle was shocked to see how much of a wasteland it had become. Makeshift fences had been erected around "clean" zones; groups of homeless huddled around trash can fires; shanty towns and lean-tos had sprouted up in every alley and park, ominous not so much for their existence as for the fact that the police hadn't knocked them down. Law was disappearing, and Lyle knew that civilization itself was not far behind.

The UN building was ringed with guards and barbed wire, protecting the last vestiges of a fading world government. Their small procession stopped at the gate, showed copious IDs, and traded a long series of complicated pass codes before the barricades were finally moved aside. They drove down into a subterranean parking garage only to be greeted by more guards, who walked them through the same tense rituals. Eventually satisfied, if not actually trusting, the guards opened the elevator and Lyle followed his escorts with mounting trepidation. He still had a box full of unread reports clutched awkwardly under his arm.

"This is where we'll be living for the next several days," said Cynthia. "We've requested an airlift to D.C., where it's more secure, but for now this is as secure as we can get."

"The sooner you can solve this, the better," said Blauwitz.

"I don't know what you're expecting me to do," said Lyle.

"Do you know how the lotion works?" asked Cynthia.

"I think so," said Lyle. "I haven't done the tests, but I think I've finally worked out the theory of it. But that doesn't mean I can do anything about it—you need a team of scientists in here, real genetic scientists, I'm just a . . ." He threw up his free hand and turned to General Blauwitz. "I make lipsticks for a living, General. If you want someone to color match your eyes and your eye shadow I'm your man, but saving the world? Please tell me you have a backup plan."

Blauwitz looked grim. "You are the backup plan."

"I've heard that before," said Lyle. "You're not the first people to kidnap me and hope for the best."

The elevator door opened, and a tall, older man greeted them with a smile. "Dr. Fontanelle, it's good to see you again. I'm Eric Moore, Senate liaison to the Department of Homeland Security."

"Another member of our 'Save the World' Committee," said Cynthia.

Lyle fumbled with his heavy box of papers in an effort to take the man's outstretched hand. "I'm sorry, sir, I don't remember meeting you before."

"I looked different," said Moore, and he smiled almost wickedly. "It was back in my prime."

Lyle stared at the man, the word "prime" sparking some half-forgotten memory. He couldn't quite place it.

"When Ibis abducted you, you said you couldn't help them," said Moore. "They held you for weeks, and all you did was run up their expenses and set their lab on fire. Our theory is that you were refusing to help them, spending all your time on a carefully calculated plan of escape instead. Can you confirm this?"

Lyle stammered. "How did you know I was abducted by—
Holy hell. Prime?"

"What?" asked Cynthia.

"Nothing," said Ira/Moore. "It's shocking, I fear, how completely our best laid plans have all come crashing down. But you,
Lyle: we need to believe that you know more than you let on.
We've pinned an awful lot of hope on you. An entire world of
hope."

Lyle felt sick and confused—did the others know that Moore
was a ReBirth clone? Would they even care? He wondered if he
should expose him, and realized he had no way to prove it, and
realized further that here, at the end of the world, it might not
even matter. He shrugged helplessly and sighed. "I'll tell you
what I know, but I don't know how much it will help."

"Nonsense," said Cynthia. "He's a genius. The only scientist
in the building who's been on the cover of *Scientific American*."

Lyle looked at her oddly. "Do you mean there are other
scientists?"

"I mean we have a cover model," said Cynthia.

"I'll tell everyone you're here," said Senator Moore. "We'll
call for you when we're ready."

Cynthia led Lyle down another hall, and he followed awkwardly with his box. "He should never have questioned your
abilities," she snapped. Now that the two of them were alone
she seemed much more furious than an insult to Lyle should
reasonably have made her. She was taking this personally, and
Lyle wondered how much of her current power, including her
freedom from prison, was based on his own performance in the
upcoming meetings. If he screwed it up, would she take revenge?
The thought made him queasy, and he hurried to catch up.

"Are they expecting some kind of presentation?" Lyle asked.
"I don't have anything prepared—"

"You just got out of prison," said Cynthia. "No one's expecting PowerPoints and handouts. My guess is they'll want to hear
as much as you can tell them about the lotion itself, followed

by a Q and A, which will inevitably turn to the topic of solutions. Sound smart and confident the entire time—a stretch for you, but do your best—and we'll get out of this fine."

"Be honest," said Lyle softly, hoping no one was close enough to overhear. "You know as well as I do that there's no cure for this, no magic reversal. When ReBirth changes your DNA, nothing can change it back but more ReBirth, and we're already seeing where that road takes us. What are you expecting us to accomplish in there? What can we even do?"

"Think of it like a hostile corporate takeover," said Cynthia. "The human race is a company, and ReBirth's going to buy us out, gut the executive board, and rebrand us into an extension of itself."

"So how do we survive a biological merger?" asked Lyle. "Try to convince a hand lotion we're too valuable to fire?"

"We accrue so much stock that the buyout makes us rich," said Cynthia. "And here we are, me out of hiding and you out of a prison camp, with the hopes of the whole world pinned on us. I'd say we're doing pretty well."

Lyle frowned. "How do you intend to cash in your stock in this metaphor?"

Cynthia raised her eyebrow. "If I tell you everything, what's left for me?" She stopped at a door and opened it, revealing a sleepy but well-groomed receptionist yawning at a desk. "Lyle, meet Lilly. I'm sick of your names already."

The woman stood up, and Lyle found himself reflexively analyzing her appearance: African American, attractive; good hair that she hadn't been keeping great care of lately; good skin, especially around the corners of the mouth and eyes, which was important for a makeup model; passable hands, though nothing they'd use in a nail polish ad; a slim body, though not an especially curvy one. Her strongest feature was her young, open face with striking eyes and a bright smile, which managed to stay bright even when it was wrapped around a stifled yawn.

He looked at Cynthia in surprise. "I thought you were joking about the cover model."

Lilly rolled her eyes. "I don't even have makeup on."

"Lyle hired half our models at NewYew," said Cynthia. "Give him a minute, he'll figure it out."

Lyle frowned and looked at Lilly again, wondering what he'd missed. She pulled on a coil of her hair. "I wore it straight back then."

"Natural Blue Black," said Lyle, snapping his fingers and almost dropping his box. "Number 328B."

"I'm impressed," said Lilly. "I don't even remember the color, let alone the part number."

"Lyle's full of stupid little facts like that," said Cynthia, brushing past her to the larger office beyond. "Did you send my message to Ambassador Larracilla?"

"You already asked me that," said Lilly, glancing at Lyle with a smirk, "and I already told you that I did. He hasn't sent a response." Lyle was shocked at her combative attitude—Cynthia wasn't the kind of person you got snarky with.

"Counting just now I've asked you *three* times," Cynthia called out from the other room, and her voice held exactly the level of distaste Lyle expected. "I'm trying to stress to you that this message is important."

"And counting just now I've answered you *four* times," said Lilly, "so maybe I'm taking this more seriously than you are."

Lyle's jaw nearly dropped.

Cynthia stepped back into the room, her expression icy. "Are you saying I should have woken you up in the middle of the night to remind you?"

"You did wake me up in the middle of the night to remind me."

Cynthia glared a moment longer, then walked back into her office. "Since you obviously have so much time on your hands, take the same message to Ambassador Hitudeki—and make sure you change all the country references. I don't think Japan will be persuaded by our offers to Mexico." Cynthia closed the door, and Lilly sat back down at her desk with a laugh.

"I can't believe you said that," said Lyle.

"Which part?"

"Any part." He set his box of papers in one of the chairs by the wall, and sat down in the chair next to it, just across from Lilly. "Nobody talks like that to Cynthia—it's like walking into a buzz saw."

"She's all bark," said Lilly, tapping away on her keyboard. "Maybe before, but in here I'm one of the only allies she has. If you've ever thought of the United Nations as some kind of paragon of peace and cooperation, you are in for a big surprise. It's like Carrie White's locker room in here. And the worse it gets outside, and the closer they come together inside, they still exclude her because it's a big stupid boys' club. I'm practically her only friend."

Lyle raised his eyebrow. "That's how you treat your friends?"

Lilly smirked. "'Friend' was a strong word. She's still a gorgon, she's just . . . a gorgon who's not allowed to eat me."

"Gorgons don't eat people," said Lyle. "But don't worry, I see your point." He looked at his box of papers with a sad, internal sigh, then dropped it unceremoniously on the floor. "Screw it," he said. "I could read a thousand news reports and still not know how to change anything." He looked at Lilly. "Cynthia's position here is much more interesting. Were you here when they brought her in?"

"Actually she's the one who brought me in," said Lilly.

Lyle leaned forward. "You, specifically?"

"I don't know why." Lilly looked up at him, her face clear and guileless. "Most of the nonmodel, nonwaitress credits on my résumé are office assistant kind of stuff, receptionist and that kind of thing. Maybe she just . . . had an old file and looked through it for candidates? I don't know."

Lyle shook his head. "Every file NewYew had was entered into state's evidence when the company dissolved, so there's no way Cynthia could just accidentally have one. Even if she'd stored encrypted copies online somewhere, why go to all the trouble of accessing them just to hire a secretary? No offense."

"Why would that offend me?"

"I don't know," said Lyle. "Just being polite." He steepled his fingers, trying to think. "If she accessed the NewYew files it must have been for something more, something to do with ReBirth, but what would she be doing in the part of the files that had old models' names in it? There's nothing important in there. Again, no offense."

"Who do you normally talk to, that you have to say 'no offense' after every sentence?"

"Cynthia."

Lilly laughed. "That explains it. That one *was* slightly offensive, though, even though I know what you're saying."

Lyle stared at her, wondering if he'd seen her somewhere else than on the box photo. "What's your last name?"

"Washington," she said. "Why?"

"Lilly Washington," said Lyle, staring blankly as he listened to the name. He'd heard it somewhere, or seen it. "How many times have you left this building since you were hired?"

"Why does any of this matter?"

"Because I think I saw you in our list of prospective ReBirth models," said Lyle. "And I think you were rejected. Have they let you leave?"

"Well, I'm not a prisoner here—"

"Have you ever left?"

Lilly paused, then shook her head. "Not since the day after I was hired. Most of the ambassadors are living here these days, and their staffs."

"Have you tried to leave?"

Lilly paused again, and her face fell. "No. They bring in everything we need, though, and it's dangerous out there. It almost doesn't matter what this job pays, this building has running hot water. Sometimes they forget to bring the right food—"

"Lillian Washington," said Lyle, snapping his fingers. "Grandmother with breast cancer, tonsils removed in the fifth grade, and still signed up on your parents' insurance. You have celiac sprue."

Lilly's eyes narrowed suspiciously. "Are you stalking me?"

Lyle laughed nervously. "I get that a lot, actually. But no, no stalking, I just have a very good memory. Just now you said that sometimes they forget to bring in the right food, and by that you mean gluten-free. You were rejected from the ReBirth program because you have a genetic disorder called celiac disease: you can't digest wheat gluten properly."

"Any gluten, actually, but wheat's the usual culprit."

"That's probably why you had your tonsils taken out, back before you were diagnosed, and they didn't know why you got sick all the time."

"How do you know all of this?"

Lyle laughed tiredly. "I've recently become an expert in genetic illness. Don't worry, all I know is your medical history."

"That's still a lot."

"Here's my theory," said Lyle, leaning forward. "Cynthia wasn't just looking for an assistant, she was looking for one she could trust—one she could be as certain as possible was exactly who she said she was, and not a spy from . . . I don't know, anywhere. Even within this building you say nobody trusts each other. So she went through our list of rejected models and found someone with a genetic disorder debilitating enough that no one would ever want to copy it, yet light enough that it wouldn't interfere with your work. Then she cross-referenced that with the old résumés on file to see which ones had secretarial experience. Filter for all those crazy requirements, and the only one left is Lilly Washington: make sure she's still herself, untainted by the lotion, and boom, she's hired."

Lilly stared at him, mouth hanging slightly open. "I . . ." She shook her head. "Here I thought I was hired for typing sixty words a minute."

"Sorry."

"What does it mean, though?" she asked. "Say it's true: what does it tell us? That Cynthia's paranoid?"

"No one's ever argued with that," said Lyle, "but no one's ever said she's stupid, either. Even the people who hate her. If she's protecting herself this closely, it means her position here, and mine, and yours for that matter, are a lot more tenuous than we thought."

Lilly laughed, but the sound was completely devoid of humor. "Welcome to the end of the world. Find me someone whose position isn't tenuous and I'll buy you a pony."

Lyle laughed back, and in that moment he seemed to see her in a new light. He returned the gentle tease. "Can you afford a pony on what she's paying you?"

"A cigar, then."

"I don't smoke."

Lilly smiled. "I'll dip into my savings, and buy a pony to smoke it for you."

Lyle smiled, too.

The outer door opened, and Ira/Moore stood imperiously in the doorway. "Come with me, Doctor. Time to meet the General Assembly."

53

"This session of the United Nations General Assembly will now reconvene."

Lyle sat nervously in his seat between Cynthia and Ira/Moore, overawed by the size and scope of the room. It was a wide auditorium with rounded walls, filled from front to back with more counters and tables and chairs than he could count. Most of them were empty. The walls were lined with four rows of windows, one on top of the other, which during a normal session were presumably filled with translators or other observers but today were mostly dark and empty. The walls leaned in, and Lyle felt like they were looming over him dangerously. At the front of the room sat a podium, and behind it a broad desk on a dais; behind that a golden wall rose up like a monolith. Even with the room mostly empty, Lyle felt compressed by the sheer weight of the room's legacy.

"The nation of Japan would like to point out that we barely have twenty members left in attendance," said the Japanese ambassador. "No resolutions we vote on here can possibly be passed."

"The United Republic of Tanzania is tired of listening to Japan whine about this."

"It's a serious concern," said Japan.

"Here we go again," said Estonia.

"Every member nation was invited," said the man at the

podium, "and their failure to attend must be taken as a voting abstention, the same as every other attendance issue." He had an American accent, and Lyle thought he recognized him from the news, but couldn't put a name on him. He leaned over to Cynthia and whispered softly.

"Who's that?"

"Chad."

"He doesn't look African."

"He's from the U.S. State Department. His name is Chad."

"Oh." Lyle sunk back into his chair.

"Japan is right," said Libya. "One or two attendance abstentions is quite a different thing from a hundred and seventy-three of them."

"Then what do you propose instead?" demanded Mexico. "Should we just sit back and do nothing while the world falls apart around us? We've invited them and they're not here—let's try to get something done anyway."

"The nation of Estonia," said Estonia, "has heard enough of this assembly's arguing to last a lifetime. The scientist has arrived, and I say we listen to him. If he has anything valuable to say it will be more than this room's heard in weeks."

"The nation of Samoa agrees," said Samoa, "but does so in a slightly more polite manner."

"Fine," said Chad. "The General Assembly officially recognizes Dr. Lyle Fontanelle, and invites him to take the podium." He stepped aside, and Ira/Moore nudged Lyle to stand up. Lyle walked slowly to the front of the room, his footsteps echoing as he went. He hadn't exactly been expecting applause, but even so, the silence felt crushing. His mouth was completely dry when he reached the front of the room.

The spotlights made it difficult to see everyone, scattered as they were across such a wide room. "Good morning," he said. "Ladies and gentlemen of the . . . United Nations—or the General Assembly? Is that how I address you?" He heard a murmur from the Estonian section, and wondered what they were saying about him, and in that moment he felt something inside of him snap. He was sick of being scared, sick of being dragged around, sick of being mocked by the people who'd brought him here to help. Twelve hours ago he'd been dying by inches in a prison camp, and now he was standing at the podium of the United Nations. His stock, as Cynthia had put it, was on the rise. If he had power now, even for a minute, he was going to use it.

Lyle looked back up at the auditorium, peering into the unlit depths. "I'm sorry, can everybody come up here to the front? All close in where I can see you? I feel like I'm talking to an empty hall."

"You *are* talking to an empty hall," said Estonia.

"You, too," said Lyle, pointing back at the Estonia delegate. "Everybody, right up front. Get friendly. If this is the last group of sane . . . anyone in the world, let's at least act like it."

"That's not the way we do things," said Japan. "There are rules of order we can't expect you to understand—"

"I don't want to understand them," said Lyle. "You've been following your rules throughout this whole process and look where it's got you." He gestured at the vast, empty room. "I think your rules are stupid." He stole a glance at Cynthia and saw her red-faced and fuming, but still keeping silent. *You don't have the power here,* he thought at her. *If not even your secretary's afraid of you, I won't be, either.*

The delegates still hadn't moved, and Lyle spoke again. "Come on, guys, you can do it. Right up here. Bring your little name-tag plaques if you feel weird without them." The Mexican delegate stood up and came forward, grinning wickedly at Lyle's breach of form. "Good," said Lyle, "there's one. Mexico wins the prize; somebody get him a candy bar. Who's next? Here, you know what I'm going to do? I'm going to unplug the microphone and just start talking about ReBirth. Mexico's the only one who's going to hear any of it." He unplugged the mic and more people came forward. Soon most of the remaining assembly members were clustered in the first few rows, twenty delegates and nearly twice that many staff members. Cynthia, Lyle noticed, was no longer fuming, and wore her standard face of arch calculation. He'd impressed her. Lyle looked away from her and scanned the group with a surge of his earlier fear.

"Wow," said Lyle. "All in one place there's kind of a lot of you."

"We've moved our seats," said Bangladesh. "Now stop wasting our time and talk."

"Right," said Lyle. "What do you want to know?"

Kenya raised his eyebrows. "You don't have a presentation?"

"This time yesterday I was trading cigarettes for prison food," said Lyle. "I know more about ReBirth than apparently anyone else in the world, but no, I don't have a presentation. Ask me questions."

"Why did you create it?" asked Germany.

"By accident," said Lyle. Some of the delegates seemed shocked, but Lyle was past caring. "A lot of preliminary studies have been done using gene therapy to heal burns, and I was trying to use the same technology in an antiaging cream. It was a wrinkle remover."

Kenya scowled. "You destroyed the world with a wrinkle remover?"

"Not personally, no."

"But how does it work?" asked Tanzania. "How did it turn from a wrinkle remover to . . . whatever it is now?"

"It was the retrovirus," said Lyle, and shot a quick glance at Cynthia. "That's what I thought at first, and I was right, but it took me months to figure out exactly what was going on. See, the technology uses a plasmid to express a heat-shock protein—" He stopped with a sudden frown. "How many of you are scientists?" The delegate from Libya raised his hand, but he was the only one. "Okay," said Lyle. "Let me see if I can translate this into normal human-ese. You all know what DNA is?" They all nodded their heads. "Do you know how DNA works?" This question met with far less confidence, and Lyle glanced around for something he could use to explain it. He spotted one of the Filipina staff members wearing a zippered sweater, and smiled at her kindly. "Excuse me, ma'am, can I borrow your sweater? Thank you. I'll give it right back." He walked back to the center of the group, standing in front of the podium, and zipped the sweater closed.

"A strand of DNA is like a zipper," he said, "and all of the little teeth inside of it, all the little metal nubbins, are the blueprints it uses to build more cells. Imagine that each little nubbin is a different command: this one tells your body to make skin, this one tells it what color of skin to make, this one tells it what kind of skin to make, and so on. That's grossly oversimplified, but you get what I mean. Now, in its normal state a strand of DNA is all zipped closed, like this sweater, so when your body wants to read those blueprints and get its new instructions, it has to zip it open." He zipped the sweater halfway open. "When it's open like this, another very similar strand called RNA comes in, kind of zips itself onto a little piece of the DNA, and copies it; then it can take what it's learned and go tell the cells what to do. It's a very stable process because the DNA and RNA both use a careful proofreading process to make sure the instructions don't get screwed up partway through. The lotion I created uses a little chunk of self-contained DNA called a plasmid, which has just enough instructions to say 'Hey, skin cells, produce more collagen.' Your RNA would read it, think it was the real deal, and produce more collagen. That's how it fought burns, and that's how it removed wrinkles.

"Now: that entire plasmid process is overseen by a retrovirus to make sure it doesn't get out of hand. A retrovirus is kind of like RNA, but it works backward—instead of zipping up, it zips down. That's important for later, so remember it. When it's working correctly the retrovirus chaperones the whole transfer of information and makes sure the plasmid doesn't do anything stupid like injure the cells, or start replicating new garbage cells without stopping, which is another way of saying 'cancer.' The retrovirus should be our best friend in this scenario, but that's the great irony of it. Because it zips backward instead of forward, it bypasses all the proofreading that RNA normally goes through. This makes it extremely vulnerable to mutation, and that's exactly what happened to ReBirth."

Libya spoke up. "It can't just mutate to start cloning people."

"No it can't," said Lyle. "That's what confused us for so long. What it can do, and what it did do, is mutate in such a way that it started working in the wrong direction. Instead of writing the plasmid instructions onto the human host, it started writing the human host onto the plasmid. Worse than that, it was somehow compressing the human instructions in such a way that they could be stored, in full, on a plasmid."

"That's two very specific mutations in a single retrovirus," said Libya. "The odds of that are . . . I can't even calculate them. They're astronomical."

"They are," said Lyle, "but it only took the one. One mutant retrovirus copying DNA wouldn't have done anything, we wouldn't even have noticed it was there, but one mutant retrovirus aggressively rewriting every other genetic communicator it came into contact with created a cascade effect that altered the entire batch of lotion, and that batch altered every other batch it touched. Think of it like a zombie apocalypse on a molecular scale: the first retrovirus found another and said 'you should be doing *this* instead,' and then those two found two more, and then those four found four more, and every time we mixed a new batch we added more retroviruses and they got rewritten, too. That's why no one has been able to reproduce the lotion outside of our original factory, because they were starting with fresh ingredients instead of the mutation. In our factory we started each new batch with a sample of the old, mostly as a shortcut to match the texture and consistency, so it had a chance to infect all the new lotion."

"So if we had a sample of blank ReBirth," said France, "we could make new lotion."

"You could," said Lyle. He paused, watching the delegates, surprised when they didn't leap out of their chairs. "What, isn't this the part where you all race back home and build up your stockpiles and glare at each other from bunkers?"

"The twenty nations still active in this assembly are beyond that," said Zambia. "We recognize that the world has hit a tipping point, and working together is the only way we can expect to accomplish anything."

"Which is not to say," said Israel, "that we won't be making new lotion. We'll just be making it together."

"What possible use could you have for new lotion?" asked Lyle. "I know none of you have left the building in a while, but have you at least looked out the windows? The world is ending out there—Manhattan is practically a shantytown, and the rest of the world is arguably worse. Do you know how I finally cracked the code on this retrovirus thing? I found a ReBirth user with Down syndrome—a dose of ReBirth rewrote his genes wrong, giving him one more chromosome than he was supposed to have." He held up the sweater. "Imagine that the DNA is unzipped, and a retrovirus is zipped onto it happily rebuilding the whole thing, and while that's happening another retrovirus shows up and starts rebuilding them both. That's how that happened, and that's how aggressive this retrovirus is. Virtually all of the DNA transcription in the entire body of an infected person is being performed by ReBirth instead of by the natural processes, and that means the proofreading system is gone. Our biological process is completely unregulated. The occurrences of Down syndrome and Turner syndrome and Klinefelter syndrome are up worldwide; the cancer rate is through the roof; I talked to a doctor a month ago who said he had two new cases of Wolf-Hirschhorn microcephaly spontaneously generating in adults. Name a chromosomal disorder and I'll bet you a hundred bucks someone within a mile of this building has it."

"But we have to face the realities of the situation," said China, and Lyle cut him off before he could go any further.

"That's exactly what I'm telling you," said Lyle. "You have to face reality. This meeting can't be about consolidating power or whatever you're trying to do here."

"We have to face the realities of the situation," China repeated calmly. "The world isn't just ending; in many places it has already ended. The cascading effect you saw in the retroviruses has been repeated in human society, and the effects of ReBirth are being seen in new places every day. The hundred and seventy-three nations not represented in today's meeting have given themselves up to an arms race more frantic than the Cold War, and for which not even the strongest of us are prepared. I received word only two hours ago that Russia has declared war on my country, striking across the border to seize our mines and oil basins. It is only a matter of time before they do the same in Alaska and Canada. Any sense of global stability we once had is crumbling faster than we can even catalog it. Do you think we are here because we have something to contribute? That we have some kind of miraculous solution to put our planet back in order? We are here because we have nowhere else to go, and no hope that anything else will make a difference."

There was a moment of shocked silence, broken only by a soft voice in the back: "Samoa agrees, but does so in a slightly more upbeat manner."

"So why are we even here?" asked Lyle. "If nothing matters, and we can't help anything, why have a meeting? Why bring me in to explain all this? Do you think there's a 'cure' for ReBirth? There's not. That's not how it works—nothing can reverse it but more ReBirth, and I've already explained what a bad idea that would be. What's left? What are you going to do? Why do you want ReBirth?"

"We could hit Russia with it," said Nepal. "When they're done with China they'll get around to my country sooner or later."

"If we ReBirth Russia they'll ReBirth us back," said Mexico. "Some of us were paying attention during the Cold War."

"As the only nation ever actually attacked with nuclear weapons," said Japan, "I want to remind everyone how poorly that strategy works."

"But stockpiling ReBirth has a regenerative effect, as well," said Zambia. "If an aggressor attacks with ReBirth, we can use our own and heal our populace before anything bad happens. Nuclear weapons never had that capability."

"That won't work in practice," said Germany. "A strike that hits as quickly as São Tomé's did wouldn't leave any time or infrastructure to deploy the lotion defensively. And don't forget what prompted the São Tomé attack in the first place: they had a bunch of ReBirth, and an enemy nation wanted it. Hell, a *friendly* nation wanted it, and became an enemy overnight. No offense, Chad."

"Shut up."

"We can't just ignore a good weapon because using it could make people mad," said Bangladesh.

"That's exactly what we should do," said Mexico. "Seriously, was I the only one paying attention during the Cold War?"

"America ignoring nuclear weapons wouldn't have stopped the Cold War," said Chad. "It would have gotten us destroyed by Russia."

"By the Soviet Union," Russia corrected. "But yes, it would have."

"This argument could go on for hours," said the Philippines. "Most of us haven't even had breakfast. I say we break for an hour, come up with some good ideas, and start again."

54

Three days later, they still didn't have any good ideas.

Lyle had gotten into the habit of eating an early breakfast with Cynthia, mostly just because Lilly was there, but in the process he had started to see Cynthia outside the bounds of her calculated public persona. It had humanized her, in a way, but at the same time it left Lyle feeling profoundly uncomfortable. Without makeup, without her hair carefully arranged, without her business skirts and fitted jackets and pens and papers and computers and phones—without the accoutrements that made her "her"—she was as disturbingly unreal, in her own way, as the subtle variations he had seen on the thousands of not-quite-Lyles and other ReBirth clones. His opportunity to get to know her better was, in the end, just one more piece of reality twisted and bent.

She sat this morning in sweatpants, barely awake. "The coffee in here is terrible," she growled.

"If it's so bad don't drink it," said Lilly, sipping from her own foam cup—not coffee, but grapefruit juice. She abhorred coffee, even aside from the celiac issues; she'd never tasted it, but hated the smell. Lyle quite liked both the smell and the flavor, but avoided it here out of deference to her.

He was beginning to realize he had a tendency to do that.

"Don't talk to me," Cynthia growled. "I can't retaliate properly until I've had at least one cup." She took another sip and grimaced. "It's like drinking thin mud."

Lilly laughed. "Would it be better if it was thick mud?"

"It would be better if you were dying in a gutter," said Cynthia.

Lilly looked at Lyle with wide eyes. "That's a new one."

"She's almost done with her cup," said Lyle, "she can retaliate properly now."

"Her thin mud has necromantic properties," said Lilly.

"Her thin mud," said Cynthia, "has granted her enough lucidity to know that the General Assembly is getting nowhere. The mobs stormed the gates yesterday, and inside we're still just arguing in circles. They'll be arguing until the building burns down around them."

"Then what's your next move?" asked Lyle. "I assume you have one."

"I have several," said Cynthia. "Choosing between them will take at least one more cup of coffee."

"You realize that coffee's not actually a stimulant," said Lilly.

Cynthia grunted. "Spoken by someone who's never actually tried it."

"That's exactly my point," said Lilly. "The boost you get from coffee is just an addiction response called 'withdrawal reversal.' Your body needs it, so you feel down, and then you drink it and you go back up, but the net energy gain is zero. All the caffeine does is restore you to where you would have been in the first place if you weren't a caffeine drinker."

"That's idiotic," said Cynthia.

"When a sandwich can put you in the hospital, you start paying a lot of attention to food," said Lilly, and turned to Lyle with an arched eyebrow. "You're a scientist, Lyle, tell her."

Lyle chose his words carefully. "It's definitely addictive, and a lot of what you're feeling right now is, as you say, withdrawal reversal."

Lilly pointed at Cynthia triumphantly. "Hah!"

"'A lot,' but not all," said Cynthia, with a look in her eye that showed she was far more alert than Lyle had given her credit for.

"It's definitely also a stimulant," he said. He shot the girl an apologetic glance. "It's the most well-known, widely used stimulant in the entire world. Sorry."

"But that's just what Big Pharma tries to tell you!" Lilly protested.

Lyle frowned. "Big Pharma?"

"Big Business, then," said Lilly. "Big Everything. Caffeine is valuable to you as a stimulant, fake or not, but it's valuable to them as an uncontrolled addictive substance. Get a kid hooked on energy drinks, make him think he can't function without them, and boom—you've got a customer for life."

"Make sure to ask for tinfoil on the next supply shipment," said Cynthia. "I don't think we have enough on hand to make you a hat."

"Mock me if you want," said Lilly, "but let's remember who's lucid and who's not, and which one of us relies on a chemical to become so."

"That doesn't imply causation," said Lyle, before he could stop himself. He hadn't intended to contradict her any further, but he hadn't expected a shaky science discussion, either. Lilly shot him a probing glance, and he reluctantly finished his thought. "You're saying that you wake up quickly because you don't use caffeine, but it could just as easily be that you don't use caffeine because you're naturally inclined to wake up quickly."

"That," said Cynthia, "was amazing." She looked at Lyle with something almost like respect. "Watching him stand up to the General Assembly was one thing, but telling a woman he likes that she's wrong about something? I'm impressed, Fontanelle."

Lilly raised her eyebrow. "A woman he likes?"

Lyle did like her, though not in the way he'd liked Susan. *Maybe that's a good thing,* he thought. Susan was young and beautiful, but she was also . . . well, he didn't know what else she was. A political activist, and a college student, and an intern. He'd been infatuated with the idea of her, but knew almost nothing about the woman herself.

Lilly, though, had become a friend.

"What can I say?" said Lyle, trying to brush it off. "I spend all day with two women, and one of them is . . ." He almost said "Cynthia," but it felt too cruel. Especially since she'd just complimented him. "A model," he said instead, though he cringed the instant he said it. Lilly was beautiful, yes, but he liked her for so many more important reasons.

"Well," said Lilly. Her attitude was stiffer than a moment ago. "There you go."

Lyle felt like he'd punched her in the stomach, and didn't know how to take it back.

"We can't get out by land," said Cynthia, changing the subject. "I've got a yacht in the Chelsea docks, but I don't know if I can make it through the city. We have to rely on Washington to come and get us, but they're taking so long."

"This is the United Nations," said Lilly. "They won't just forget us."

"We can hope," said Cynthia, still hunched over her coffee, her eyes distant and lost in thought. "If and when they do arrive, I definitely wouldn't count on them taking a junior receptionist when they go. It'll be vital personnel only."

"Then we need to make sure we're vital," said Lyle, and stood up with a stretch. "I'm going to take a shower, and then I'm going to observe the General Assembly for a few more years."

"Good luck," said Lilly. "I hope the shower line's not too long."

"And wash your backbone while you're in there," said Cynthia. "You've never had one before, and I expect it to be a little confusing at first."

Lyle walked away, thinking. He'd never thought of himself as being spineless, but the last few months had changed his perspective and he couldn't deny that he had been. He'd run from confrontation, he'd said yes to ideas he'd hated just to avoid an argument, he'd gone along with their horrible scheme to sell ReBirth just because . . . *Because it was the path of least resistance,* he thought. But he was different now, and it had taken Cynthia to make him see it.

Sure, he thought. *Perfect timing. I grow a backbone just a couple of months before it doesn't matter anymore.*

The thought made him frown—not the thought, but the wording. *A couple of months? Can I really quantify it like that?*

If the world really ends—if all our worst fears come true—how will we know? Is it a nuclear bomb? A public announcement? Gods and angels and fire and brimstone, and the Earth rolled up like a scroll? Or will we just wake up and it will be over?

When the world ends, what's going to take its place?

55

"The thing we've failed to consider is that none of these solutions might work at all," said Mexico. "ReBirth is out there, and it's going to stay out there, and there's no avoiding it. Every plan we've come up with either ignores it, or tries to defend against it. Maybe it's time to embrace it."

Lyle tried not to roll his eyes. He'd been in the UN building for nearly a week now, shot down a hundred flawed theories, listened to a thousand broken plans that nobody could agree on. A mob had rushed the fence again on Sunday, and this time someone actually made it over the top before getting shot through the head by a guard. The mob had shot back, and the guards had been forced to retreat; only tear gas and snipers had dispersed them in the end.

Lyle was fed up with the assembly's indecision, but on the other hand . . . what were they supposed to decide? How were they supposed to find a solution to an unsolvable situation? And worse yet, how were they supposed to stop trying? The Chinese-Russian war raged on, Southeast Asia was on the brink of at least five wars of its own, and South America formed new nations and alliances so fast the U.S. State Department had stopped trying to keep up. The world was a mess, and if there was any way out of it these twenty men were the most likely to find it. They couldn't give up, and yet they couldn't win. Lyle was trapped in a hell of political boulder-rolling.

"We've already talked about embracing the lotion," said Tanzania. "We spent two entire days last week embracing the lotion, and every scenario was another disaster. Are we talking in circles now?"

"We've been talking in circles the entire time," said Estonia.

"We've only talked about embracing the lotion as a weapon," said Mexico. "I'm talking about accepting and accounting for the realities that ReBirth has thrust upon us. Everyone in this building drinks bottled water, because the water system outside has been contaminated with ReBirth. People all over Manhattan and Upstate New York are turning into Dr. Fontanelle, or into other people, whether they've ever used the lotion or not. We've had similar reports from Tibet, Russia, Brazil, India, Australia, and today from Mexico City."

"And that explains his sudden interest," said Bangladesh. "Some of us have been trying to talk about this for days."

"Then let's talk about it," said France. "There's ReBirth in the water—that's a reality. What do we do about it? Can it be filtered out?"

Twenty heads all turned to Lyle, and he shook his head helplessly. "You think you're the first people to think of that? Unless these lotion dumps were deliberate contaminations, which I doubt, they almost certainly happened through normal sinks and drains and toilets that lead straight back to the standard reclamation plants—which, obviously, did nothing. We could try to augment the filtration process with heat or chemicals or other things, but honestly most of these plants already do pretty much everything they can do without harming the human population, so no, I doubt there's any way we could get this out of the water supply."

"If we can't filter it out of the water system," said the Philippines, "maybe we can kill it in the body. It's a virus, right? So can't we use some kind of antibiotic?"

"Antibiotics are for bacteria," said Lyle.

The Philippines glared. "Obviously I mean whatever the viral equivalent of an antibiotic is."

"That's called 'plenty of rest and chicken soup,'" said Lyle. "There *is* no viral equivalent of an antibiotic—a vaccine, maybe, but that could take years to develop, and there's no guarantee it would even be possible. The way this retrovirus turns everything into itself, a vaccine might strengthen it instead of kill it."

"But it might work," said Germany. "We don't know until we try."

"If it could be cleaned from water, it would have been," said China. "If it could be attacked in the body, somebody's immune system would have stopped them from cloning. None of these things have happened. We need something concrete, and we need it now."

"We haven't talked about the future yet," said India.

"That's because we're still trying to make sure we have one," said Israel.

"Dr. Fontanelle," said India, standing to address him formally. It was the first time someone had done so, and it got everyone's attention. "The rumors have dogged us for months, and I must know for certain. Does ReBirth make you immortal?"

The room was quiet. Lyle swallowed, suddenly nervous.

"Only if you use multiple doses," said Bangladesh. "Each dose sets you to a certain age, and then you age, and then a second dose would reset you back to the same age again."

"That kind of power could be abused," said Zambia.

"What do you think everyone's fighting about?" asked Japan.

"I'm afraid that's not entirely accurate," said Lyle. He sucked in a breath through gritted teeth. "The first dose you take is technically the only one you ever need. Biological age, as we understand it, is an expression of your DNA at varying stages of its existence. Your genes as an infant were building your body in a very different way than your genes as a teenager, and so on. With ReBirth constantly resetting your genes to a target state, you will effectively never age. That's not immunity from violent death or anything, but yes, people who have used it even once, even by accident, will never get older, and they will never die from natural causes."

The delegate from India sat down, his face somber.

"I had hoped this aspect was just a rumor," said Japan.

"The best we can hope for is 'flawed extrapolation,'" said Lyle. "I suppose time will tell. But if everything works the way we think it works—and so far it has, flawlessly—then we're looking at a sizable portion of the world population that is effectively immortal."

"That," said Mexico, "changes things."

"Technically it is the opposite of change," said Tanzania, "but I know what you mean."

"Carry this through to its logical conclusion," said Germany. "What are the estimates these days, fifty million ReBirth users worldwide? Sixty?"

"Counting accidental and unwilling cases," said Kenya, "we're probably closer to a hundred."

"That's not too bad," said Nepal. "I mean, in comparison to the entire world population? We're over seven billion now; that's less than a tenth of a percent."

"At least twenty million of those cases are me," Lyle added, "just in case anyone wants to put a human face on the numbers."

"Ha ha," said Estonia drily.

"A tenth of a percent makes a hundred million people sound small," said Mexico, "but consider that ReBirth is still around, and still infecting people, and unlikely to go anywhere. We've accrued a hundred million immortals in only five months—that's higher than the world birth rate, and it ignores the death rate. If we do the same every five months—if we do even half of that every five months—we're looking at an overpopulation problem we've never even imagined. Inside of, what, thirty-five years, it will have infected the entire world population, and the birth rate will keep adding people to the pool, and ReBirth will ensure that none of them ever leave."

"So what are our options of curbing this?" asked Japan. "We've already talked about getting the ReBirth out of the water, and that won't work. Maybe we could take the people away from the water—evacuate every contaminated area."

"And try to fit a world's worth of people in only half the world's space," said India, "resulting in the same overpopulation problem from a different angle."

"But it wouldn't fill up as quickly," said Israel.

"We could reduce the birth rate," said Zambia, "though I can think of very few humane ways to accomplish that."

"So let's talk about the inhumane ways," said Estonia. "We could kill the immortals."

"China will not be a party to institutionalized murder," said China.

"That didn't bother you fifty years ago," said Germany.

"Look who's talking," said Israel.

"Nobody's killing anybody," said Tanzania. "We won't even consider it."

"Don't be so naïve," said Mexico. "Most of you aren't part of the New Crusades—Latin America has already been at war for weeks, and most of the world is following."

"Are you suggesting that the numbers will balance out?" asked Kenya. "Because I don't want to pin our world's future on the hope that we'll all kill each other faster than we can make more people."

"Will ReBirth really get to everybody?" asked France. "It's in the water systems of some major cities, but that's not going to affect the entire world. We'll still have plenty of normal, mortal humans."

"So we can solve our population problem by denying people immortality?" asked Samoa. "We're not fools—we know that this would become a class issue. The rich would buy themselves eternal life, and the poor would die to keep the world from overflowing. None of us should be comfortable with that."

"So now we're obligated to give immortality to everyone?" asked Mexico. "I don't like the idea of a caste system any more than you do, but a world where nobody dies is a world that will run out of space and resources. We'll be packed so tightly we'll have nothing to eat but each other—and eating the poor, in my mind, is far worse than oppressing them."

"This is ridiculous," said Chad. "We're supposed to be talking about solutions, not . . . immortal cannibals."

"We are talking about realities," said France. "They're not pleasant, but they're not ridiculous, either. Given the nature of ReBirth, this is what will happen. This is where our world is headed. And because the problem is extreme, our solutions will have to be extreme, as well. We may have reached a point where oppression or even execution—as much as I despise them both—may be the only moral choices we can make."

"So we embrace the lotion," said Estonia. "Zambia asked for a humane way to reduce the birth rate, and we have one: ReBirth."

"ReBirth doesn't alter reproductive function," said Lyle.

"Not by itself," said Estonia, "but what happens if we turn everyone into a single gender?"

The room went deathly quiet.

"That's preposterous," said Germany.

"Is it?" asked Estonia.

"Yes," said Tanzania. "You're talking about ending the human race."

"What end?" asked Zambia. "The human race is immortal now—that's the whole problem. Making us all immortal men, some kind of idealized ubermensch, would assure that we have the benefits of immortality without the crippling overpopulation."

"It's really kind of a utopian ideal," said Bangladesh. "An eternity of idealized supermen, with the time to really dig into our problems and solve them, without having to relearn history's lessons with every new generation—"

"I don't think it's a utopia at all," said India.

Nepal frowned. "Why not?"

"Because I'm not gay," said India. "And if I'm going to live for a million years, at some point I'm going to want to have sex again."

Estonia threw up his hands in disgust. "Seriously? That's your issue here? We're talking about the end of the human race—of changing that end into a utopian ideal—and all you can think about is sex?"

"It's not all I think about," said India, "but I assume I'm not the only one in the room who thinks about it occasionally. We're all adults here. The people you want to save are human beings, and humans have sex. And in the world you're proposing, all of that sex would be gay. Everywhere you turn, men and men and men."

"There's nothing wrong with being gay," said Chad.

"Nothing wrong for other people?" asked France. "Or nothing wrong for you? Because he's right, and that's exactly what we're discussing here: turning you, and me, and everyone else in the entire world into a gay man. Personally, I wouldn't want to be a part of it."

"Then the solution seems obvious," said China.

"Come up with a different plan?" asked Lyle.

"Turn everyone into women," said China.

And everyone fell silent again.

"An entire world of lesbians," said Mexico.

"Immortal lesbians," said Japan.

"However we do it," said the Philippines, "the benefits are clear. We eliminate all prejudice, because everyone's the same. There's no racism, no class system, no oppression of any kind, because everyone is *the same.*"

Turning everyone the same reminded Lyle of the prison camp and its ten thousand Lyles. It didn't fill him with confidence.

"Latinas have won more Miss Universe titles than any other group," said Mexico. "Obviously the choice should come from us."

"That's not how we should choose this," said Lyle.

"Latinas only win because the judges are biased," said India.

"Our models and actresses are more famous in more countries than anyone else's."

"They're not more famous than ours," said Chad.

"Too pale," said Tanzania. "The most beautiful women are African."

"Or African American," said Chad. "America's got everything."

"The most beautiful women are Asian," said Japan.

"America . . . concedes that point," said Chad. "Let's get one of those Korean girl groups, the pop stars."

"Will you listen to yourselves?" Lyle shouted. "The world is ending, literally, right outside your doors, and you're arguing over supermodels? A thousand different plans to save the world, and the only one you agree on is the one full of lesbian sex?"

"We are stopping a crippling overpopulation problem and ushering in a golden age," said France. "Immortal supermodel lesbians are a necessary side effect, and wow, that sounds horrible when I try to explain it like that."

"You're disgusting," said Lyle.

"We're realists," said Tanzania. "You've been in these meetings—you know what's going on, and how impossible it is to solve. The world is determined to tear itself apart, and we don't have the power or the influence or the resources to stop it. This plan doesn't fix our present because nothing can fix our present, but it can fix our future."

"How are you even going to carry this out?" asked Lyle. "Just . . . grab some poor girl's DNA and flood the world with it? Turn everyone in Russia into Victoria Carver and Russia will still get conquered by Victoria. People will still be killed and oppressed by Victoria Carver, and the fact that they're also Victoria Carver when it happens won't make it a utopia."

"Not immediately," said Estonia, "but you have to give it time. The apocalypse will be terrible, but it will end. The differences that caused it will be forgotten because everyone who survives will be equal. The world will stabilize."

"It's not an ideal solution," said Japan, "but we don't have any ideal solutions left."

"So you're giving up," said Lyle. "I can't believe it."

"Sometimes the paramedics can't save everyone," said Mexico. "It's not giving up to call a dead body dead."

"We're not dead!" shouted Lyle.

"What do you want us to do!" cried Tanzania. "We're not gods. You want us to stop the war? With what political leverage? You want us to win it? With what armies? The only weapon we have left is the one you created, Dr. Fontanelle, and we are trying to use it to build instead of destroy."

Lyle fumed. "You're using it to play out an adolescent fantasy with the lives of seven billion people!"

"Then give us a better idea!" yelled Samoa, rising to his full height, and the fury in his face made Lyle press back into his chair. "Everyone in this room has suggested solutions, even my staff has suggested solutions, but all you've done is shoot them down. You're waiting for a good idea but there are none—nothing we come up with will make everyone happy, or solve every problem, or fill every need. Nothing *good* is left. We are choosing the lesser from an army of evils, and if our choice shocks you it is because even a lesser evil is monstrous. Forget the girls, forget the details, forget everything else: this monster is all we have. Give us a better one or leave us alone."

Lyle looked at him, feeling his hands tremble, his palms sweaty. He looked at the others, at the room, at the high ceilings and the dark corners and the rows of empty tables stretching back into oblivion.

"I thought the world would end in months," said Lyle softly. "Maybe I was optimistic."

He stood, turned, and walked out of the room.

56

Somebody screamed.

Alan Byrne woke frantically, eyes wide, chest heaving. A dark wind moaned outside his windows, creeping ice-cold tendrils through the gaps along the sill. Shadows shook and trembled on his wall—a pale moon shining feebly through a wind-tossed tree. He looked at his wife, but she was lying still; he put a hand on her shoulder, not shaking but simply feeling. She was warm. He leaned close and heard the low hiss of her breath. She was fine. The scream hadn't come from her.

The wind moaned again, and Alan looked up at the window, pulling the blanket tighter around his shoulders. *It must have been the wind,* he thought, *just a howling gust of wind,* but then he heard it again: a high-pitched scream, short and desperate. It was a scream of pain and terror. And it was unmistakably human.

Alan pulled back the covers and sat on the edge of his bed, shivering as he pulled on a pair of thick woolen pants. They were as cold as the room, and he hoped they would warm quickly. He added a heavy flannel shirt and his thickest winter coat, and when he heard the scream again he cursed and ran, shoving his feet inside his boots and racing outside without waiting to tie them. The wind bit his cheeks and whipped his short hair. His lead farmhand, Brendan, was standing in the yard already, scowling at the darkness.

"You heard it, too," said Alan.

"It's a banshee," Brendan spat. "Death is here for someone."
Alan shook his head. "You know that's just old stories."

"And you know they're true."

Alan didn't answer. Brendan had always been superstitious, leaving shamrocks on the door frames and leaves of ivy soaked in water. Alan didn't have time for it, with the farm failing and the family nearly bankrupt. He peered into the night. "Did you hear where it came from?"

"North," said Brendan, pointing, "by the barns."

"Someone's rustling the animals."

"Or being trampled by them." Brendan started walking, not north but northeast, and Alan hurried to catch up.

"Where are you going?"

"The barns."

Alan scowled. "The barn is that way. You're headed straight for the irrigation ditch."

"Aye. And there'll be water in it," said Brendan. "Crossing running water wards off evil spirits."

"You're a damn fool," said Alan, but the scream sounded again, long and wailing this time, and Alan shivered despite his heavy coat. He could hear it better now, and it was different than he'd thought it was; stranger and darker. It wasn't the cry of someone hurt or dying, and the silence between each scream meant it wasn't desperation. Someone was screaming, a woman, he thought, loud and terrible and for no reason he could think of. Sadness, maybe, or fear. A loss of hope, or a lament for death.

Maybe it was a banshee.

"Across the canal, then," said Alan, turning on his flashlight, "but hurry. I don't want Cassie to hear it." If you didn't hear the banshee, then it wasn't your death that made her cry.

They crossed the yard and passed through the gate, latching it tight behind them, then trudged through the mud and snow across the field to the ditch. A pair of footprints had already come and gone this way, bouncing in and out of the beam of Alan's flashlight.

"These are yours?" asked Alan.

"Aye," said Brendan, "when I opened the gates for the water."

That eased Alan's mind, but only some. The darkness screamed again when Alan was halfway across the walk that spanned the ditch, and he gripped the rails for support. The flashlight slipped from his hand and disappeared into water with a gulp; the light diffused through the liquid like a ghost, then guttered and died.

"The second barn," said Brendan. "By the pigs."

"We should never have crossed the ditch," said Alan. "It doesn't do any good to keep the spirits from following, if we're walking right toward one."

"Maybe there were more," said Brendan.

"And maybe we've wasted time and lost a light just to approach the barns from the back side."

They crept forward, ears pricked up for any sound in the darkness. The pigs were squealing now, riled by something, and Alan heard the creaks and thuds as they butted against the boards of their enclosure.

"They'll be trampling each other soon," said Brendan.

"Then we hurry," said Alan, and walked more quickly around the side of the barn. Someone in the barn screamed, unformed and inarticulate, and pigs squealed and stamped and bit, and Alan ran the last few steps to the door and flung it open. The pigpen roiled in the darkness, fat shadows running and tumbling and fleeing madly from everything and nothing. Alan clicked the light switch, and the bulbs above exploded with a blinding flash and ear-bursting pop. Sparks showered down, and Alan's eyes were seared with a single frame of vision: hairy pink shapes and blood-streaked snouts and wide white eyes.

"The light!" Alan cried. "There's someone in there, find the light!" Brendan pushed past him through the door and fumbled on the workbench for another flashlight. He found it, and swept the light across the pen: pig after pig, snouts and hooves and tails. The scream came again, mingling with the squeals and filling the barn like a wraith. Alan ran to the edge of the fence but he didn't climb in, didn't dare wade through that field of gnashing, trampling flesh. The battered planks shook beneath his hands. The screams came faster now, formless and terrified and horribly, painfully human amid the bawling of the pigs, and all Alan could think was *It knows we're here,* and it was all he could do not to turn around and run. The narrow light darted back and forth, across the chaos, searching for the screamer, and when it passed across a human face Alan cried aloud and staggered back. It shone in his mind like the afterimage of a flash, bright white in the light beam, eyes wide with terror, mouth open and screaming, nose flat and thick and brutish. A snout.

Brendan swore and crossed himself, and brought the light back slowly, almost unwillingly, to shine again on the screaming face. It was a human, yet not a human; it was a pig, yet not completely. Wide and misshapen, sitting up on haunches a pig would never have, wires of black hair bristling up above a face both human and pig and profoundly neither. One pig ear flopped on the left, while a curled human ear pressed against the other side like a squashed pink cabbage. Its mouth held human teeth and porcine tusks; its snout dripped strings of mucus; blue eyes peered out in abject terror. It raised its foreleg, two jointed, human fingers probing helplessly beside a deformed hoof. The pigs around it swirled in a frenzy, goaded to madness by the beast's endless, awful screaming.

The screaming of a human throat inside a monster's body.

57

Lyle stood by the window and watched the mob outside. Soldiers lined up along the perimeter, well back from the fence in case the crowd had weapons. General Blauwitz shouted over a megaphone, telling the crowd to disperse, but they chanted back and drowned him out, demanding food and water and justice.

"That one has both genders," said Lyle, pointing to a screaming, naked body at the front of the crowd. It was furiously cold, but the person screamed and chanted along with the others, waving his/her body like a piece of damning evidence. Inside the building, lined up next to Lyle, a dozen other people turned their heads to see where he was pointing.

"I didn't realize you made transsexual formulas," said Lilly.

"We didn't," said Cynthia. "That's someone halfway through transition."

"Or permanently stuck in transition," said Lyle. "Conflicting genomes constantly overwriting each other. The secondary sexual characteristics might even come and go over time."

"Some of them look like zombies," said Ira/Moore. "It can't raise the dead . . . right?"

"They're probably just sick," said Lyle. "If there's really not enough food in the city, their bodies can't provide enough materials to feed the changes. They'll end up with stunted growth, deformations—all the problems we associate with a lifetime of malnutrition, but condensed into four weeks." He winced involuntarily, watching the gaunt, misshapen bodies stagger almost blindly in the background. Some of them were probably literally blind. It wasn't this bad in the rest of the country, they knew that from the news, but it was still bad. Even with the military helping, there weren't enough relief workers to get supplies where they needed to go. And there weren't enough supplies anyway.

Chad walked into the room, pressing himself against the window for a long look outside before finally speaking. "Blauwitz and his men have barricaded the bottom floors. All the stairs are sealed at the third floor, and the elevators are locked. They're blocking all the ground-floor windows, as well, but that's just a stalling tactic. We can't actually keep them out of the building."

"And how soon do we leave?" demanded Cynthia.

"Choppers should be here within the hour," said Chad. "Delegates in the first wave, then any other politicians, then women, then men. They can't land anything big up there, so it'll take at least four waves, maybe five, and you can't take anything with you."

"I don't have anything anyway," said Lilly.

"Where are they taking us?" asked Lyle, trying to keep a cheerful outlook. By the priority Chad had outlined, Lyle would be in the last chopper out—not a death sentence, by any means, but raising his chances significantly that something could go wrong.

"Virginia," said Chad. "It's the only seaport we still have significant control over, and the airport's still ours, as well. We can get the delegates home—those that still have homes—and the rest of us will just . . . hunker down." He paused. "We'll wait."

"Virginia is the safest place for it," said Ira/Moore. "The military will be everywhere."

"That's where the president is?" asked Lilly, but Chad laughed drily.

"We haven't had a president in weeks. There is substantial information that he'd been replaced." Chad winced at a sudden realization. "Obviously that's classified."

"How about whoever turned up the evidence of his replacement?" asked Ira/Moore. "Is there any evidence that *he'd* been
replaced?"

"That's a long, dark spiral of second guesses you're getting
into," said Chad. "The short answer is 'we're doing our best.'"

"The short answer does not inspire me with trust," said Cynthia. She turned to Chad. "I want out in the first wave."

"You're in the third."

"Then make me a delegate," said Cynthia. "Lyle and I both—
you can't afford to lose us."

"What do you have?" asked Chad. "You gave your information,
and it was worthless. We're no closer to a solution than we were
before you came."

"But we taught you how to make more," said Cynthia. "We
opened entire new avenues of possibility!"

"*He* did," said Chad. "All you did was help us find him. Lyle
will go in the first wave," said Chad, "and you will follow—in
the third wave." He looked outside again. "The mob'll be over the
fence before the choppers even get here. This is going to get
tense." He turned and walked out the room, calling a final in-
struction over his shoulder. "Everyone's gathering on the top
floor. Show up late, and we leave without you."

Cynthia glowered after him, with a look that could melt steel.
"I'll have his head," she snarled. "The third wave—why doesn't
he just throw me to the wolves himself?"

"I'm in the third wave, too," said Lilly.

"There's not going to be a third wave," said Cynthia. "They'll
evacuate the delegates, they'll come back for the senator and the
State Department, and they'll leave the rest of us to rot."

Lilly looked out the window; the mob was throwing rocks
now. "Really?"

"We're all getting out," said Ira/Moore.

Cynthia sneered. "That's easy for you to say."

"We should give them our food," said Lyle.

"What?" Everyone in the room looked confused, and Lyle wasn't sure which one had asked it.

"The mob," said Lyle, "we should give them everything we have. We're leaving in an hour anyway, right?"

"Were you not listening just now?" asked Cynthia.

"They'll come back for everyone," said Lyle. "They'll take all of us, and we'll be fine, and we won't need our food. And since we can't take it with us anyway, let's give it away. It'll buy us some good will, at the very least."

"And who's going to give it to them," asked Ira/Moore. "You? Do you really want to walk out to that fence and hope they don't stone you to death?"

"Half of them are Lyles," said Lyle. "I'm practically one of them."

"Unless they put it together that the Lyle on the inside of the fence might be the real one who got us all into this mess in the first place," said Ira/Moore. "They'd tear the bars apart with their teeth just to get to you."

"It's too late anyway," said Lilly, and they all looked to the window. Three rioters had already climbed the fence, only to be shot down by the soldiers inside, but more were coming, scaling the bars, swarming over the top, and shooting them would mean shooting into the backdrop of thousands of civilians. The soldiers hesitated, and it was all the time the rioters needed. The locks were snapped open, the chains broken, the gates opened, and the mob flooded in.

"Get upstairs," said Ira/Moore. "Everybody go, now!" He didn't wait to see if they followed him, but bolted out into the hallway. Cynthia grabbed Lyle firmly by the arm and dragged him out with her, Lilly running close behind.

Lyle shook Cynthia's hand away as they reached the elevator. Ira/Moore was frantically pressing the button.

"They said they locked the elevators," said Lilly.

"I can hear the motors running," said Ira/Moore.

"I think they only locked the bottom floors," said Lyle.

"I can hear the motors running," Ira/Moore repeated. "The elevator cars are moving, just be patient."

"We should take the stairs," said Lilly.

"It's thirty-nine floors," said Cynthia, "and we're on the fifth. We'll never make it in time."

"Have you ever actually taken stairs?" asked Lilly. "It doesn't take two minutes per floor."

"The elevator's going to come," said Ira/Moore, but the longer they waited, the more nervous Lyle got. He shifted on his feet, looking at the door to the stairway, listening for the sounds of the mob. The building was almost eerily quiet.

Cynthia folded and unfolded her arms, pausing every few seconds to push the up button again. Ira/Moore pressed his head against the metal doors. Lilly played with the cuff of her sleeve until she'd twisted it so tight Lyle thought her hand would turn blue.

Lyle opened the door to the staircase.

"It's going to come," Ira/Moore insisted.

"Quiet," said Lyle, "I'm listening," and stuck his head into the stairwell, holding his breath, listening for voices. For footsteps. *There they are.* "There's someone in the stairwell."

Lilly paled. "Chad said they locked the bottom floors!"

"Locks are easy to break," said Lyle.

"It's probably just people on other floors," said Cynthia, "giving up on the elevators and running."

"Probably," said Lyle. "That doesn't mean they're on our side."

The four of them looked at each other. Lilly slipped off her heels. "Let's go."

They ran through the door, bounding up the stairs, clutching the railing as they rounded each corner. Other voices and footsteps echoed around them, but they couldn't tell if they were coming from above them or below them. The tenth floor, the fifteenth floor, the eighteenth floor. They were slowing down. Lilly paused and Lyle pushed her forward, gasping for breath.

Ira/Moore ran ahead without waiting, up and up and up. Cynthia clung to Lyle's side like a remora.

"I need a rest," said Lyle.

"You can rest at the top," Cynthia hissed.

The twentieth floor. The twenty-fifth. The thirtieth. Now even Lilly, in better shape then either of them, seemed winded and faltering. She paused again, panting, and this time Lyle stopped with her. Cynthia wheezed in behind them, her teeth gritted.

"Eight steps per flight," Lyle wheezed. "Two flights per floor. A hundred and forty-four steps to go."

"A hundred and sixty," said Lilly. "We have to reach the roof, not the top floor."

"Whatever we're hearing is definitely below us," said Cynthia. "It's getting closer."

Lyle could hear it now, as well, closer now, almost on top of them. He looked around for a weapon, but there was nothing. They dragged themselves up another sixteen steps. Another thirty-two. Another 112. When they reached the top floor they were greeted with a wall of rifle barrels aimed straight at Lyle's face, but the soldiers lowered their weapons when they recognized the women with him.

"I told you they were coming," said Ira/Moore. The soldiers hustled them out onto the roof, where a cold wind stung them. Nearly a hundred people were huddled together for warmth, delegates and staff and service workers, all waiting for the helicopters. None of them had a coat.

"We can't raise anyone on the radio," said Chad. "It should only be another twenty minutes."

"Have you heard from General Blauwitz?" asked Cynthia.

"Not since we lost the fence," said Tanzania. "He's either captured or too busy to talk."

"Or dead," said Estonia.

The roof was narrow and cramped, even without the people—most of it was taken up with satellite dishes, radio antennas, and other bits of scaffolding. The entire perimeter was ringed with a screen, like a fake wall, and Lyle was glad there was essentially no chance of falling off the edge. The helicopters, he assumed, would try to land on the roof of the elevator housing, which rose above the rest of the rooftop like a miniature warehouse in the middle. He didn't know how sturdy it was, but it was the only place wide enough and flat enough to work.

"This just keeps getting better," said Cynthia. "Can we see anything?"

"Nothing in the air," said Chad. "The UN grounds are swarming with rioters, and most of the streets outside."

"Send the women back inside," said Mexico. "The soldiers can hold at one floor down, and keep at least some of us warm." They repositioned the guards, and urged the women back into the stairwell, packed tightly in the limited space. Lilly cast a last glance at Lyle before she disappeared.

Lyle almost offered her his spot on the first helicopter.

Almost.

Cynthia kept an iron grip on Lyle's arm, returning every suggestion to wait inside with a glare icier than the air. They left her alone, and watched the skies for helicopters.

The hour mark came and went.

"Give it time," said Chad. "Getting them here at all was a logistical miracle; getting them on time is asking a little much."

Another twenty minutes passed. Ira/Moore kept everyone back from the edge of the building, hoping no one on the ground would see them and try to come up. "Maybe they don't know where we are," he offered.

"Maybe the doors are holding," said Tanzania. "Or the general is."

Another twenty minutes. Another hour.

"It's going to be dark soon," said Libya. "We can't survive the night out here."

"This is the most defensible location," Japan protested, but he shivered as he said it.

"Tell the guards to clear the top floor," said Chad. "We'll seal the entrances as well as we can, and keep a watch up here for the choppers."

"Bet you're glad now they didn't give all the food away," said Cynthia.

Lyle shrugged. "We don't have it up here anyway."

"We'll still need it," she said, "this time tomorrow when nobody's come for us, we'll have to go down and get it."

"They'll come for us," said Lyle, though he didn't feel remotely sure of it.

"This is our last stand," said Cynthia. "We need to get out, anyway we can, with enough of these bigwigs in tow to give us some leverage if we make it to Virginia."

"Are you trying to save them, or use them as hostages?"

"Call it what you like," said Cynthia, pointing down at the East River. "There's a whole harbor full of boats down there, and this building is right on the edge of it. If we slip out the back and keep to the water we can go anywhere, free of rioters and ReBirth and everything else."

A sudden burst of gunfire echoed dully through the roof below them, and the women who'd been huddled in the stairway now stumbled out in a terrified mob. Several of them were covered with gobs of thick, white hand lotion.

58

The crowd on the roof screamed and ran, a deadly stampede in the narrow, crowded space, and Lyle saw at least one man go down as the terrified people swarmed over him. There was really only one place to go—behind the elevator housing—and Lyle was carried along with the crowd, struggling to keep his feet and desperate to catch a glimpse of Lilly. Was she hurt? Was she hit with whatever lotion the unseen attackers were throwing? Was it ReBirth, or just a generic lotion being used to scare them? A stray bullet punched straight through the floor in front of him, clipping the shin of a man in a suit. Lyle stopped in his tracks, was bowled over from behind, and went down.

A foot planted itself on Lyle's back, then another on his outstretched arm. He curled into a ball, feeling two more errant stomps on his midsection, trying desperately to shield his head with his arms. He screamed in pain when a high-heeled shoe planted itself solidly on his calf muscle. The woman tripped and went down. A burst of gunfire roared through the air, no longer muffled by the building, and Lyle knew the fight had reached the roof. He rolled to the side and fell from a ledge, his heart in his throat as he imagined all thirty-nine floors flying past him in a rush, but it was barely a foot down. He'd fallen into a low gutter that ran around the edge of the roof, and cowered there in the darkness, hoping the attackers wouldn't see him.

"Get them up here," said a voice, and Lyle couldn't help himself: he uncovered his head and looked up.

It was Susan, in a black combat vest, armed with holstered guns and a squeeze bottle of lotion in each hand. A group of similarly dressed people behind her—not just an angry mob but a well-armed paramilitary force—hustled two bound captives out of the stairway. Lyle couldn't see their faces, but they wore standard police uniforms; they hadn't come from the UN compound, but outside somewhere. *Why would they bring them up here?* he wondered.

And whose DNA is in those bottles?

One of the rebels saw him and squirted a long blast of ReBirth toward his face. Lyle twisted away and scrambled to his feet, shedding his contaminated suit coat behind him as he ran; he didn't think the lotion had touched his skin. The far end of the building was a chaos of screaming and shoving, too many people crammed violently into a space too small to hold them. The crowd had wrapped around the back side of the elevator housing and started to flow back toward the first side of the building again, but a group of rioters with guns and lotion blocked them off. Lyle felt a hand grip his arm like a vise, fingernails biting deep into his flesh, and turned to see not Cynthia but Lilly, her eyes wide with fear.

"We're gonna die," she said.

"I think it might be something worse," said Lyle.

The revolutionaries clambered up a ladder to the top of the elevator housing, and Susan appeared above them on the rim of the roof. She sprayed her bottle of lotion onto the crowd, packed too tightly to move or dodge. Lyle cringed, ducking low with Lilly to avoid the spray of ReBirth. Ira/Moore caught a thick bead of it on his ear and screamed like a child, trying desperately to get it off. With so much lotion in the crowd they were contaminating each other now, squealing like pigs in a slaughterhouse.

"You're the only leaders the world has left," said Susan. "If anyone can get the word out, it's you."

"Our own countries have forgotten us!" shouted Tanzania, and got a face full of ReBirth for his trouble.

"The countries of the world are convinced that ReBirth can solve their problems," said Susan. "You need to take this message back to them, and you have four weeks to do it. ReBirth is not the answer, it is the problem."

"You think we don't know that?"

Another squirt of lotion.

"Even here," said Susan, "at the end of everything, you've been talking about using the lotion again. Using it more. Trying to save a world that will only be saved when you. Stop. Screwing. It. Up." Every word brought another spray of white lotion. She spoke to her followers. "Bring them up."

The revolutionaries muscled the bound prisoners onto the makeshift stage of the elevator housing, and Lyle got his first good look at them. It was the same two cops he'd seen before, officers Woolf and Luckesen, still in their uniforms and looking like they hadn't changed in weeks. ReBirth had apparently been working on them the entire time, for their faces were darker, their foreheads more sloped, and their brows more prominent. Their posture was wrong, almost simian, and hair had begun to grow on almost every inch of exposed skin. Lyle realized too late what they were turning into, and the realization took all the strength from his limbs; he clung to Lilly's shoulder like a child on the edge of a fathomless pool.

"Monkeys," he said out loud. He looked up. "You're turning us into monkeys."

Susan extended her lotion bottle, ready to squeeze a blast of chimpanzee DNA in his face like she'd done with the others, but stopped at the last minute. "How long have you been a Lyle?"

"Forty-two years," he said softly. "It's me, Susan."

Her face was twisted halfway between happiness and anger. "You did this."

"You and I both did it," he said. "You know we didn't mean to."

The sound of gunfire echoed over the roof, and the noise seemed to snap her back out of whatever brief reverie had caused her to pause. Susan's face resolved into a hard, cruel expression Lyle had never seen before. "Don't blame me."

"Don't blame yourself," said Lyle.

She raised the lotion bottle again, but her chest blossomed in a spray of red blood and she collapsed to the roof, tumbling off the edge of the elevator housing onto the frightened crowd below. Her plastic bottle burst at the impact, spraying out lotion like a ReBirth grenade.

Someone was shooting, dozens of someones, and the roof erupted in screaming again, people pushing and shoving and trying to get away, trying to find shelter from the lotion, trying to wipe it off on the only thing they had, which was each other. Lyle and Lilly pressed themselves to the farthest fringes of the group, doing everything they could to avoid the lotion.

The revolutionaries were shooting at the other end of the roof, and Lyle could see that more UN soldiers had appeared there, fighting their way up from below and taking the rioters from behind. He thought he caught a glimpse of General Blauwitz, but he was too busy ducking the violent mob to see clearly.

"This way," said Lilly, and pulled him toward the west side of the elevator housing, and the narrow walkway that ran between it and the edge of the roof. Susan's body, and the circle of ReBirth around it, had created a small clearing at the wall, and Cynthia was already crouching there, pulling something from her purse. Two revolutionaries stood at the corner, firing down the walkway to the soldiers on the far side and ignoring the frothing mob behind them.

Lyle stared at Susan's body, too shocked to know how he felt.

"There's an access hatch to the elevator shaft," said Lilly. "I saw it when we ran through here before."

"And a shootout between it and us," said Lyle, trying to force himself out of shock. "No good."

"So we get rid of them," said Cynthia. She pulled a small handgun from her purse, clicked off the safety, and shot the two revolutionaries in the head. "There."

Lyle gripped the wall for support. "I'm going to go back into shock now."

"You carry a gun?" asked Lilly.

"You don't?" asked Cynthia.

"If we're going to go, let's go," said Lyle, and dove around the corner heedless of the gunfire. He found the access hatch and kicked it open; the door tumbled down into a bottomless black shaft.

"We need some delegates or it's no good going anywhere," said Cynthia, scanning the crowd for anyone important enough to save. "They're our ticket to safety in Virginia." A group of staff advisers and secretaries were crowding toward them, eager to escape through the hatch, but she held them off with her pistol. Lyle looked to the other end of the roof and saw soldiers and revolutionaries and men in suits all locked in battle. A new wave of revolutionaries boiling up from the staircase pushed the soldiers back, and Lyle found himself face-to-face with General Blauwitz and the delegate from Mexico, both armed with assault rifles.

"This building's lost," shouted Blauwitz. He saw the access hatch. "Get as many delegates as you can and make for the basement. There are tunnels into the city."

"Already on it," said Lyle, and nodded toward Cynthia, who had filtered the most important people out of the group trying to enter the walkway. She'd managed to collect Samoa, China, and India. Lyle crouched at the access hatch, wincing as a stray bullet clanged against the wall above his head, and offered the opening to Lilly. "Ladies first."

"You're damn right," said Cynthia, pushing past Lilly and climbing into the hole. "If any of you bastards stepped in Re-Birth I don't want to get it on my hands." She started down, and without her to hold them off the crowd surged into the narrow space, clamoring to escape through the hatch. Many of them were covered with lotion. Lyle helped Lilly in next, then followed after, easing in backward to the cold metal rungs of the maintenance ladder. He clung to the bars, not looking down, moving one rung at a time and trying not to think of the thirty-nine-story drop below him.

China came in above him, and after him another, but in the darkness Lyle couldn't see who it was. He hoped it was another of the delegates. He continued down, one rung after another, remembering how hard it was to climb all these floors in the first place and wishing that they could have had this showdown on a lower floor. He looked up, nearly three floors now, and saw a long line of people on the ladder with a pale square of moonlight at the top. There were shouts, and a scream, and a body came tumbling past him. He couldn't see if it was a man or a woman. It thumped loudly on something close below him, and he heard another shout of surprise from Lilly. He ventured a look down, praying she hadn't been knocked from the ladder, and saw instead that she and Cynthia were standing on the roof of an elevator. The body had landed on the ceiling hatch they'd been trying to open.

Lyle hurried down the last few rungs and helped move the body aside, touching it gingerly in case it was contaminated with the chimpanzee lotion. It was a man in a suit, and when they managed to open the ceiling hatch light flooded out to reveal him as the corpse of Estonia.

"Ambassador Rebane," said Cynthia. "You're in the way." There was a gap in the iron framework that led to the neighboring shaft, and she shoved him through it. He disappeared almost instantly into the darkness. The Chinese delegate had reached them by now, and India close behind. "This should be the thirty-fifth floor," said Cynthia. "Let's go." Lyle and China each grabbed one of her arms and helped lower her into the elevator car, and as she ran to the control panel they lowered Lilly in after her. The delegate from Mexico joined them next, and as Lyle and Russia helped India through the opening Samoa reached the bottom of the ladder behind them.

"Who's next?" asked Lyle.

"The general is after me," said Samoa. "And after that I don't know. One of the delegate's assistants, but I don't recognize the language."

"Tell the general to jump," shouted Cynthia. "I'm pretty sure this thing works."

"She can't be serious," said Mexico, grabbing a cable.

"General, jump!" Lyle shouted quickly. "She's always serious!" A chorus of pleading screams answered back, and two black forms detached from the ladder and fell through the air. The general fell only a few feet; the man above him fell much farther, and broke his ankle with an audible snap as he landed. The third person up on the ladder jumped, as well, but a moment too late, for Cynthia hit the button and the elevator launched itself down as the latecomer was still falling. He fell faster than the elevator, but only just, and caught up with them five stories later with a sickening crunch that broke the roof of the car. Lyle and Samoa both slipped through the sudden gaps in the structure, trapping their feet and legs in the twisted metal.

The elevator stopped and the doors slid open, only to be immediately strafed with gunfire. Lyle was still wedged in place, trying to extricate his foot without slicing it open on the metal edges, and couldn't see a thing. He heard a few quick shots that could have been Cynthia's gun, and General Blauwitz and the Mexican delegate used the moment to drop through the hatch and return fire with their heavier rifles. Lyle strained against the metal, feeling it tear through his pants and lacerate his skin. The Chinese delegate helped him, then did the same for Samoa. The man with the broken ankle lay beside them, moaning softly in a language none of them could understand. Lyle looked through the open hatch and saw splashes of blood all over the elevator car, but he couldn't tell who they belonged to. The gunfire moved farther away, retreating down a hall, and Cynthia called up for Lyle to hurry. Lyle lowered himself into the car, finding the Indian delegate's body slumped and bloody in the corner.

"They got him as soon as the doors opened," said Cynthia. Lyle looked around wildly, and saw Lilly in the hallway beyond, holding a looted submachine gun with wide, terrified eyes. He walked toward her, but Cynthia shouted behind him. "Who the hell is that?" Lyle looked back to see the Samoan delegate lowering the broken assistant through the hatch.

"I don't know who he is," said Samoa. "Just grab him."

"Leave him," said Cynthia. "He's not important enough to slow us down."

"I'm not leaving him," said Samoa. "And I *am* important enough to slow you down, so grab him." Cynthia didn't move, so Lyle caught the dangling man and held him while Samoa dropped down after. Samoa slung the now-unconscious man over his shoulder in a fireman's carry and they moved out into the hall. Lilly looked at Lyle with wide eyes; she didn't seem capable of firing her gun effectively, but didn't seem interested in giving it up, either. They were in some kind of service tunnel beneath the complex, and met up with Blauwitz and Mexico around the next corner.

The general made a quick count of their group. "This is all we have?"

"India didn't make it," said Lyle. "There might be more on the ladder, but I guess we left them behind."

"All the other delegates got hit by the monkey lotion," said Cynthia. "There was no point waiting." She gave Samoa a pointed glance. "Nobody else was worth saving."

"None of you were hit?" asked the general.

Lyle shook his head. "I don't think so." They checked each other quickly, and found nothing.

"There are tunnels into the city," said Blauwitz. "We'll have to go up to the surface streets eventually, but we can at least bypass this particular mob."

"And run straight into another one," said Cynthia. "We need to go out the back and into the river—we can find a boat and get out of here."

" 'Out back' is FDR Drive," said Russia. "There are boats across the river, but nothing on this side for blocks in either direction."

"I don't think we could swim the river in this weather," said Samoa.

"Definitely not with that dead weight on your shoulder," Cynthia snapped.

"Boats are a good idea," said China, "but not in the East River. The closest dock is the UN school, fourteen blocks at least, and if there's nothing there we'll have to go all the way down to the Brooklyn Bridge."

"If we're going that far we'd be better off crossing the island," said Mexico. "The Hudson's got boats all over the place."

"The Chelsea Piers," said Lyle quickly. "Cynthia's got a boat there." He was pleased with himself for remembering it, but the predatory triumph on her face made him feel like she'd somehow manipulated him into announcing her own plan for her.

"It's called *Mummer's Hoard*," she said proudly. "Big enough for all of us; gassed up and ready to go."

"The tunnels, then," said Blauwitz, and they followed him through a maze of hallways. The UN complex was far bigger than Lyle had guessed—far bigger, he suspected, than the delegates had guessed, as well. Every now and then they heard distant shouts or screams or gunshots, but the farther they walked the more the sounds faded away, and after a series of locked metal doors they disappeared completely. At last Blauwitz led them up a long staircase and through another locked door. The building they'd entered let them out onto Forty-Second Street, almost to Second Avenue. Lyle looked back toward the river to see that the UN building had caught on fire.

"Keep a low profile," said the general. "We don't want to attract any attention."

"Then we should drop the half-dead body," said Cynthia.

"Maybe people will think it's an all-dead body and get scared away," said Lilly. Her voice was shaky, Lyle noticed, but her eyes were grim and determined.

They walked quickly, trying to look purposeful rather than scared. It was nearly seven now—not late, but it was December and the sky was already pitch black. With power out in so much of the city the buildings had become tall, dark monoliths that blocked out the stars. Lyle felt like a rat in the bottom of a deep black maze, scurrying through the narrow tunnels and hoping none of the bigger rats tried to eat him.

Blauwitz led them over a block to Third, to put some distance between them and the mob, and then cut south down the long avenue. A hospital on Thirty-Second was still running on on-site power, and looked to have crowd outside, so they turned on Thirty-Third to avoid it. Here and there they passed other shapes in the darkness, running and hiding as furtively as they were. They traveled south again on Fourth, and the general quickened their pace.

"The Armory's just down here," he said, peering ahead. "We might be able to get some help there; a vehicle if we're lucky, reinforcements at the very least."

"There's not enough room on the yacht for that many," said Cynthia. "We have to get the delegates off, and we can't risk a mutiny of desperate soldiers."

"American soldiers don't mutiny," said the general, but as they neared the Armory they found it dark and abandoned, the doors chained and the windows barred. "I don't understand," he said, rattling the front door. "They should be here."

"Let's at least rest," said Lilly. "We've come almost twenty blocks, and some of us don't have shoes."

"Then loot something," said Cynthia. "I'm not dying for your feet."

"Listen," said Mexico, holding a finger in the air. They paused, holding their breath, and Lyle could hear it, too—another giant crowd, somewhere nearby, *chanting* something.

"Just a couple of blocks away," said the general.

"Madison Square Park," said China. He shrugged. "Maybe they're in line at the Shake Shack."

"Or murdering the Sixty-Ninth Regiment," said the general. He started jogging west. "Let's go."

"Are you crazy?" asked Cynthia. "We're not going toward it."

"There might be someone in danger," said the general.

"That's exactly my point."

"This mob's not looking for us, so we can at least take a peek," Blauwitz called back over his shoulder. "I'm not letting them hurt any more soldiers."

They hurried to catch up, Lilly hanging back farther and farther as her bare feet grew more sore. They could see the lights now, giant bonfires in the park that cast massive, dancing shadows on the buildings around them. The chanting grew louder, though they couldn't tell what the crowd was saying. A single voice with a megaphone was shouting something wild and incendiary in the middle of it all, but Lyle couldn't understand him, either. "Can anyone hear what they're saying?"

"It sounds like 'the bomb,'" said Samoa.

"They're saying 'Kuvam,'" said Lilly. "It's a cult meeting."

The general paused, halfway to Madison Avenue, listening carefully. After a moment he turned and led them back to Fifth. "We'll skirt the edges," he said. "If it's Kuvam's people they're probably not violent, but we don't want to push it." They went south again, two more streets to Twenty-Fifth, and saw for the first time the sheer size of the crowd. Lyle gasped. Ahead of them was Madison Square, at one of those massive New York intersections between two normal streets and the sharp diagonal of Broadway, and the cultists had converted the entire thing to an open-air temple. Bonfires covered the ground, lanterns and banners waved from the nearby buildings, and in the midst of it all were Lyles—hundreds of Lyles, thousands of Lyles, standing and bowing and perching on fences and clinging to windowsills and chanting, all of them chanting, the same words over and over:

"Kuvam," and "ReBirth," and "All is light." The buildings glowed orange in the flames, and Kuvam himself—reborn like the Phoenix—stood on a bus and preached the gospel of eternal life.

"We're going around," said Cynthia stiffly.

"There's no soldiers in there," said Blauwitz. "Not in the center or on the perimeter or anywhere. Not in uniform, anyway."

"I never knew there were so many," said Samoa. "I mean, I knew, but I . . . I had no idea."

"We go around," said Cynthia again. Her voice was equal parts steel and terror. "Four more streets, eight more streets, however many it takes to never see them again. Down and around and across to the river." She moved away, and the others followed, but Lyle stayed rooted in place, staring at the chanting Lyles. It was . . . he didn't know. He felt a hand on his arm, and turned to see Lilly's wide eyes staring into his.

Her voice was soft. "What is it?"

"I'm thinking about . . ." He trailed off, and turned back to face them. Thousands, maybe tens of thousands, moving and chanting in unison. "They're happy. They love what they're doing. They've found something they love, and they're ready to give their lives for it."

"Do you want to join them?"

He turned again to look at her, shaking his head. "No, I don't. That's the weird thing. They're all me, and they're all happy, but I . . . I don't want to be a part of it. I wish I did—I wish I had anything in my life that I loved that much. But I don't. And if they're me, then . . ." He gave up talking, and simply watched them.

"Come on." She turned and walked away, pulling him gently with her hand, and he followed her into the darkness.

59

The *Mummer's Hoard* bobbed gently in the water, far from either shore, while the refugees wrapped themselves in blankets and stared at the fallen city, trying to decide where to go next. Pitch-black buildings surrounded them, illuminated here and there by headlights and private generators and dull orange fires. The sky was gray with stars.

"We can't go to Virginia," said Mexico. "Or I suppose we could, but we're not going to find anything there."

"Just because they didn't come for us doesn't mean they're gone," said Russia. "Maybe they couldn't send the helicopters—or maybe they sent them, but they arrived too late. We don't know."

"We should go to Washington," said Lilly. "We can get there by boat, right? The big . . . Potomac River and everything."

"It's too long and too dangerous," said Blauwitz. "There's a thousand wrong turns once we start up the Chesapeake Bay, and if they're as dark as this we'd never find the right one—and the wrong one could just take us to another mob. Better to try for Norfolk: it's a straight shot down the coast, and if there's any significant base of military power it will be there."

"Then why didn't they come for us?" demanded China. "Military power that abandons its politicians is not the kind of power we want to run to."

"If it's a choice between military and mob I choose the military," said Samoa.

"And if you had a third choice?" asked Lilly.

"I'd leave everything," said Samoa. "Down the coast to Florida, and then out to the Bahamas, the Caicos, the West Indies. Find a place untouched by the troubles and wait there for as long as it takes."

"Those islands will have their own mobs," said China, "just like everywhere else."

Mexico looked at China sternly. "If you don't like the islands and you don't like Virginia, where do you want to go?"

China shrugged helplessly. "I don't know. Home. It won't be any better there, I know, but . . . it's home."

"The power we need to be running to isn't military or political," said Lyle, "it's scientific. What we need right now is clean water and uncontaminated food, and ideally an ongoing source of both." He shivered in the night air. "And shelter."

"That's easy enough to say," said Blauwitz, "but where are we going to find it? The best place to be right now is some wing nut survivalist's bomb shelter in the Arizona desert, but we can't exactly get there in a yacht."

Lyle smiled, suddenly and eagerly, and pointed an excited finger at Blauwitz. "A bomb shelter! That's exactly where we need to go, and I know just the one."

"You have a lot of wing nut survivalist friends on the Jersey Shore?" asked Cynthia.

"The Plum Island Animal Disease Center," said Lyle. "It's like a mini-CDC off the eastern tip of Long Island. Government run, fiercely paranoid, and completely sealed and self-sustaining. They even have a recirculated water system."

Mexico shook his head. "You told us the retrovirus couldn't be filtered out by purifiers."

"It can't," said Lyle, "but this is better than a purifier—it's a closed system. Water on the island gets used, cleaned, and used again. Outside water never even enters the cycle, so unless we do something stupid to contaminate it, it will never be touched."

"That's ideal," said Samoa.

"It's closed to outsiders, obviously," said Lyle, "but I'm sure the general could get us in."

"That takes us farther from Virginia," said Cynthia.

"Not by much, though," said Mexico, "relatively speaking."

"They'll have gas so we can refuel," said Lyle, "and if there's any way of getting a message to whatever world leaders are left, they'll have the facilities to do it."

"I like it," said Samoa, and smiled slyly. "Not a tropical island, but I'll take what I can get."

"I suppose it's as good as anywhere else," said China.

"Our best bet is to go south around Manhattan and then up the East River to Long Island Sound," said Blauwitz. "That's close, but still a few hours, and it's already after midnight. I can steer us well enough through the little channels while the rest of you sleep, but when we hit open water we'll need Cynthia to take over."

Cynthia smirked. "People who own yachts own people to sail them. I don't know how to do it."

"I don't think 'own' is the word you were looking for," said Lyle.

"I can sail," said Lilly. The others looked at her in surprise, and she shrugged. "I did a Henri Lloyd shoot, and the guy who owned the boat wanted to show off."

Cynthia stood up and turned to the cabin stairs. "I'm going to sleep. Wake me when we get there, or when we're boarded by mutant pirates. Whichever comes first." She disappeared below-decks, and the others looked at each other.

"I'm not going anywhere," said Mexico, nodding toward his rifle. "If we get boarded by mutants I want to see them coming."

"We'll be fine," said Blauwitz. "Everyone else in a boat is doing the same thing we are: running as far as they can. Let's just hope we're all running in different directions."

Lyle followed Lilly to the helm, where she poked around the controls a bit to familiarize herself. The yacht had a sail, currently stowed, plus an onboard prop and a GPS. She fired up the motor and Lyle looked outside nervously, scanning the darkness for any trouble the sudden noise might have attracted, but there was nobody around them in any direction.

"We won't need the sails," said Lilly. "It's easier this way." Outside, the delegates huddled together for warmth, watching for trouble, and when the general came in to take the first turn at the helm Lyle and Lilly did the same, wrapping their blanket around both their shoulders to maximize their body heat. Lyle smiled apologetically.

"This isn't normally how I treat the company secretaries."

"Shut up and put your arm around me," said Lilly, pressing closer. "I'd rather be warm than politically correct."

Lyle pulled her tightly against his side, and they watched the dying city slide by through the windows. "This isn't how I thought it would end."

"Who said it's over?"

"Observational evidence," said Lyle, but paused and shook his head. "Sorry. I shouldn't be such a pessimist. The world isn't over 'til we give up on it."

"Just so you know," said Lilly, "you're not the kind of world-destroying mad scientist I was expecting when they told me you were coming to the UN."

"It's never the ones you expect," said Lyle. "Scientists are like serial killers that way." He pursed his lips. "Sorry, that was a really bad joke."

Lilly watched the city quietly for a moment, then spoke again. "Do you feel responsible?"

Lyle frowned. "Of course I feel bad—"

"I didn't ask if you felt bad, I asked if you felt responsible."

"That's a very tricky question."

"That's the best kind."

Lyle tried to answer, but couldn't think of anything to say.

The boat moved south past Jersey City, curved around the Battery, then trekked up past Brooklyn, past the bridges, past the burning remains of the United Nations. Lilly fell asleep on his shoulder, and Lyle watched quietly as his life slid away in the darkness: Roosevelt Island, Rikers Island, his home in Flushing, all the landmarks of who he was and where he came from and what he thought he meant. All the *things* that had stood in place of *meaning*. The boat left the river and turned north into the wider bays, passed the parks and promontories that loomed up on either side before fading away into nothing. The next time he looked up he found the general under his arm and Lilly steering the ship. It took him a few minutes to shake off the impression that each one had transformed into the other.

The boat was slowing, bobbing more noticeably in the water, which is probably what woke him up. "How long was I asleep?"

"Just a few hours," said Lilly, and pointed ahead. "I think this is it."

"Is this where the GPS said to go?"

"Yes," said Lilly, "but it just went crazy."

"Then this is it," said Lyle. "The government doesn't like satellites looking at its secret labs." He shook the general awake, and together they walked to the window to look out at the complex before them. Plum Island had a small dock, with prominent signs and buoys restricting public access. As they drew closer a voice on a megaphone told them sternly to clear the area, and General Blauwitz argued for nearly ten minutes in his attempt to pull rank. Even then, the argument only ended with Blauwitz calling their bluff and steering the boat toward the dock. The guard didn't shoot, but he greeted them with a loaded rifle.

"You shouldn't be here."

"There's a lot of things that shouldn't be," said Blauwitz. "We have a wounded man and three UN delegates; I outrank everybody on this island and I'm commandeering it as a safe haven."

"This is a research lab specializing in contagious plagues," the soldier insisted. "You are bringing contaminants into a clean facility, and you risk taking even worse ones with you."

"Then tell us what we can't touch," said the general, "and we won't."

"The entire island."

"Redefine your bubble of personal space," said Blauwitz, stepping out onto the dock. "We're staying, and you're under my command now. Dr. Fontanelle, tie up the boat while the sergeant here shows us to our rooms."

The soldier continued to protest, but Blauwitz could not be swayed, and Cynthia, once she entered the argument, was a force of terrifying will the guard was completely unprepared to deal with. The group of refugees followed him into one of the buildings, Samoa carrying the assistant with the broken ankle, and they huddled around the space heater while the soldier called his superiors.

"You have a working phone line?" asked Cynthia. "Call Washington immediately."

"I'm calling the other side of the island," said the soldier. "We haven't been able to reach anybody outside in hours." Whomever he was calling must have picked up, for he turned his attention abruptly back to the phone and spent the next several minutes nodding and saying "I told them that" over and over. Finally Blauwitz wrenched the phone from his hand, yelled into it for a minute, and hung up.

"They're coming to pick us up. This is just the dock; the main facility's a few minutes away. You're going to get in trouble," said the guard. "*I'm* going to get in trouble."

"If there's anyone left to get us in trouble it will be the best news we've had in days," said Lyle.

A pair of headlights flashed in the window, followed almost immediately by a second pair. The first driver stayed in his truck, the motor running to keep warm, but the second, a woman with a heavy parka and a thick wool hat, ran through the cold to the guardhouse.

"You're the ones, huh?" She looked at the sick assistant, wrapped in a blanket but obviously suffering. "He needs a doctor."

General Blauwitz stood and shook her hand. "I assume you have doctors?"

"Plenty," she said, "but no physicians, and no real medical treatment facilities."

"I'm afraid you're still our best option," said Blauwitz.

"That's the impression I'm getting," said the woman. Her voice lowered, and she looked at the haggard group with obvious worry. "Is it really as bad as we think it is?"

"It's worse," said Cynthia. "New York City is gone, we can't contact anyone else, and whatever government is left is either unwilling or unable to do anything about it. We're here because your lab might be the only local source of uncontaminated water."

The woman frowned. "Uncontaminated by what?"

"By me," said Lyle. He stood and shook her hand. "I'm Lyle Fontanelle."

"The original?"

"I'm afraid so."

"I'm Dr. Kendra Shorey," said the woman, "lead researcher for the ADC. Let's go, then." They loaded everyone into the two trucks, and Lyle found himself crammed in the front seat between Cynthia and Dr. Shorey. The engines had been left running, and the cabs were almost hot after the cold run across the yard. Shorey threw it into gear and rumbled down the unlit road.

Lyle pointed to a bright glow just visible over the tree line to the north. "Is that the lab?"

"Yes it is," said Shorey, "but you're not getting anywhere close to that. Living quarters are all farther west on another beach."

"Are there other refugees?" asked Cynthia.

Shorey shook her head. "Most people in the middle of a worldwide plague run away from contagious disease centers."

"It was his idea," said Cynthia.

"And it was a good one," said Shorey. "We're not exactly

happy to have you, but I can't deny that this is probably the safest place on the East Coast right now."

Lyle felt a warm glow of contentment, and watched the trees flash by in the beams of the headlights. They reached a wide clearing, and the small lights at the far end of it slowly resolved into buildings—a handful of single dwellings, followed by a cluster of larger, barracks-style structures.

"This used to be an army outpost," Shorey explained. "It can hold a lot more people than the skeleton crew we've got running it today." She parked in front of one of the U-shaped barracks buildings, and the second truck pulled in behind her. "I'll unlock it for you and then see if I can get the heat turned on. I'm pretty sure this building's still connected. . . ."

She led them in and then wandered off through the halls, her voice echoing faintly through the empty building as she talked herself through her search. Lyle breathed out, watching the moisture form a visible cloud in the cold front room, and followed Lilly into the room beyond. Someone had apparently declared the empty barracks to be a storage facility, for the walls were stacked high with crates of canned food, bottles of water and soda, old computer equipment, and rows of dusty filing cabinets. The other refugees wandered in after them, then continued on through the rest of the building, searching for beds and blankets and other stores of food.

When they were alone again, Lyle looked at Lilly and was struck by a sudden urge to be close to her. He picked up a bottle of Coke—unfrozen, which spoke well of the building's insulation—and stepped closer. "Lillian Washington, would you care to join me for a drink?"

He couldn't distinguish her features in the darkness, but she took a step closer to him. "I'd like that very much."

"Might I offer you . . ." He peered at the label. "Whatever I just picked up? Diet Coke."

She cocked her head to the side, and he saw the faint outline of a wince on her features. "Do they have anything else?"

Lyle's smile fell. "Oh, the caffeine thing." He turned back to the stacks of supplies. "They might have something caffeine-free, but I can barely read the labels in here."

"My concern is the food dye," said Lilly. "A lot of places make caramel coloring with cereal proteins, so even if the bottle says it's gluten-free, it's safer to just say no to any kind of cola." She smiled sadly. "Sorry to ruin the moment."

"It's okay. I never realized how hard it was for you to eat something that won't kill you."

"Food labeling is only accurate to a point," said Lilly. "A lot of things don't even show up on an ingredients list. When was the last time you saw fluoride on a bottle of Coke?"

"Why would there be fluoride in a bottle of Coke?"

"Because we fluoridate our water," she said, "and then we use water in everything. Even the regions that don't fluoridate still get it through soda and juice and hot dogs and whatever else gets shipped all over the—"

Lyle ran from the room in a panic, shouting for the others as he careened through the dark house. "Don't drink anything! Where are you? Don't eat or drink anything!" He heard voices and a handful of answering shouts, and caught up to the rest of the group at the top of some basement stairs. Dr. Shorey was just getting ready to go down when Lyle ran up to them, still panting from his sprint through the halls. "Don't drink anything."

"What are you talking about?" asked Cynthia. "You're the one who said this place was safe!"

"We have a closed water purification system," said Shorey, "both here and at the lab. Everything else is canned—nothing's contaminated."

"The canned stuff is the problem," said Lyle. "Any food made in a contaminated area could have the ReBirth retrovirus. We can't eat anything packaged in the last five months."

60

1 DAY TO THE END OF THE WORLD

"I think I've got somebody!" said Blauwitz.

Lyle looked up, and the delegates and scientists with him, a row of heads popping up like gophers. The entire group had been on laptops and cell phones and radios for two straight days, trying desperately to get a signal in or out. In the corner, the man with a broken ankle slept fitfully, doped on painkillers and antibiotics. The group dropped their own equipment and ran to the general, clustering around him eagerly.

"Who is it?" asked Dr. Shorcy.

"Let me talk to them!" Cynthia demanded.

"Be quiet," Blauwitz hissed, "I can't hear." He pressed the phone close to his ear, covering his other ear with his hand. They held their breath and listened to him listen. "Hello?" he probed. "Hello, can you hear me? I can hear you, can you hear me?" He sighed in relief. "Oh, thank God."

The crowd of hungry refugees clasped each other's arms and shoulders excitedly, biting their tongues to keep from cheering.

"My name is Glenn Blauwitz, I'm a general with the United States Army, who is this?" Pause. "Hello? Are you still there? Hello?" He snarled and slammed the phone on the table. "I had him! He said he could hear me!"

The group deflated, many of them already wandering back to their own fruitless searches. The general rubbed his eyes with the palms of his hands, and Lyle shook his head. That was the closest one they'd had—their first two-way communication. Lyle's stomach rumbled, and he thought of the giant pile of food they'd locked in the back room, too suspicious to ever eat it. There was no real danger with anything packaged before July, but the lotion had technically existed since March, and their fear of misprinted packaging dates had caused them to eventually rule out anything from the past full year. They had water, constantly recirculated and repurified, but their food supplies were critically low.

"It was just a kid," said Blauwitz. "Probably didn't even know how to use his cell phone."

"How many kids do you actually know?" asked Lilly.

"You should have let me talk," said Cynthia. "You came on too strong—'I'm a general with the United States Army.' What was he supposed to think, that you needed his help? He thought you were going to arrest him and he hung up."

"I don't think you talking to him would have made him any less scared," said Lyle. "We need Lilly to talk to people—she's sweet and innocent; people will be falling over themselves to help her."

"That's not a bad idea," said the general. He raised his voice so the whole room could hear him. "The next person who gets a connection, let Lilly talk."

"What is she going to say?" asked Mexico. Lyle still had trouble remembering the man's real name.

"I'll ask them for help," said Lilly. "Tell them where we are, that we have no food—"

"You can't tell them where we are," said Cynthia, "what if they come for us?"

"We want them to come for us," said Lyle.

"We don't know anything about them," said Cynthia. "They could be bandits coming to steal our supplies."

Lilly frowned. "Who would answer a distress call by stealing all their stuff?"

"I would," said Cynthia.

"If we're not asking for help why are we even doing this?" asked Dr. Shorey. "Are you just lonely?"

"We don't need to be afraid," said the general. "If anyone tries to attack us we've got five armed soldiers on the island, not to mention Ambassador Larracilla's better with an assault rifle than any of us."

"We're doing this because we need to see what's out there," said Cynthia. "We've got the manpower, like he said, and we've got enough boats to stay mobile—we need to learn who's out there, learn where they are, and strike."

"I'll make sure to leave that part of the plan out when I finally talk to someone," said Lilly.

"We're not pirates," said Lyle.

"He's right," said China, "we don't need to raid other refugees. We can probably get all the supplies we need just crossing to Long Island and raiding empty houses."

"That's not what I meant," said Lyle.

"We have at least a week of food," said the general, "more if we ration it carefully. If we haven't made contact with anyone in a week, *then* we can start thinking about supply runs."

"The earlier the better," said Samoa. "No sense waiting for the last minute."

"There is if we're trying to avoid breaking the law," said Dr. Shorey.

"You think there are still laws?" asked Cynthia. "You're adorable."

"We're talking about days, but we might be here for weeks," said China. "For all we know it could be months. We need to plan for the worst-case scenario."

"The worst-case scenario is that the world has too many Lyles in it," said Shorey. "Some temporary instability followed by some very specific clothing ads. Give the riots time to die down and the government will restore order."

"The Russian government, by then," said Cynthia. "I don't think you're grasping the full weight of our situation."

"I don't think any of you are," said Lyle. "The Plum Island scientists haven't seen what it's like out there, but the rest of you have. ReBirth is in the water, it's in the food, and it's warping the human genome in unexpected, horrifying ways. People have extra chromosomes, they have not enough chromosomes, they have two genders, they have monkey DNA, for crying out loud. We didn't even know it worked on nonhuman DNA, but guess what? It works on everything. It goes everywhere. For all we know it's in the water table now, systemic to the entire biosphere—do you have even an inkling of what that means? It's going to change the entire biological population of this planet, and it's reached a point where almost every single one of those changes is a degradation of function." He pointed at the Chinese ambassador. "He said our worst-case scenario was spending a few months here, but that is hopelessly, stupidly optimistic. We're going to be here for years, and that's a best-case scenario. Cancer is somewhere in the middle. The worst case is that you get so much competing DNA in your cells that you spend eternity as an androgynous chimpanzee squirrel with a cognitive disorder." He gestured at the building. "We have a self-sustaining clean water system here, and that makes us potentially the safest people on the planet, but it also means we can't go anywhere." He shook his head. "Maybe ever."

"You said the retrovirus was prone to mutation," said Mexico. "Eventually it's going to stop working."

"Each one that mutates will be rebuilt by the billions of others," said Lyle. "It's never going away."

Dr. Shorey looked at Cynthia. "Is he right about all that?"

"He's being typically histrionic about it," said Cynthia, staring at him coldly, "but yes, he's probably right. He usually is."

Lilly frowned. "Then why are you so mad at him?"

"She's not mad, she's planning something," said Lyle, looking back at Cynthia. "That's a lot more terrifying than anything I just said."

"You're not talking about a riot," said Samoa. "You're talking about . . . Armageddon."

"And that means we're not waiting out a riot," China continued. "We're founding a civilization."

"That's a little extreme," said Mexico, but China cut him off.

"Is it?" he demanded. "Years, he said, the last uncontaminated humans on the planet. We shouldn't be focusing on scavenging food, we should be bringing in more people. We're supposed to repopulate the planet with what, three women?" He looked around at their group. "How many are on this island?"

"I'm not comfortable with the direction this conversation has taken," said Lilly.

"We'd have to get them soon," said General Blauwitz, "before they become contaminated—and we'd have to make sure they were clean."

"The Connecticut coast would be better than Long Island," said Cynthia. "You'll get working-class people with a wider skill set than just 'gestation.'"

Dr. Shorey's jaw dropped. "Are you encouraging them to raid the coastline for women? Are we Vikings now?"

"I'm not a brood mare," said Cynthia with disdain. "If we're going to do this we're going to do it right."

"We're not going to do it!" said Shorey.

"Let's all calm down and think about this," said Lyle. "I'm sorry I scared you, I'm . . . pretty scared myself, and I'm sorry. The general's plan is still the best—for now. Wait here, try to contact anyone we can, and hope there's still a government left when the dust settles. We might need food, but we do not and will not need women." He grimaced, and shot a sidelong glance at Lilly. "Beyond the obvious equality-based reasons for which a society will always need women. You know what I meant. The future's going to suck, maybe not as bad as I said, but we can deal with that when the time comes. For now we've got a food shortage, a potential power shortage if or when the gas lines shut down, and what I'm fairly certain is a Libyan diplomatic adviser with a broken leg and a raging infection. Let's solve these problems first."

"Those are all important goals," said the general, "but we can't stop trying to make contact. A lucky break there could solve all our other problems for us."

"We split into teams," said Mexico. "Lilly and the general stay on the phones, the rest of us on the other problems; we can break into smaller teams when we come up with solutions."

"The dying man is our first priority," said Lyle. "Dr. Shorey's medicines have been helping, but they're not enough. We need a real doctor, or a paramedic, or . . . I don't know." He rolled his eyes. "What we really need, and I can't believe I'm saying this, is blank ReBirth to turn him into a clone of himself. That would fix the ankle for us and solve most of his problems right there."

"We have some," said Shorey. The entire room gasped, frozen in place, staring at her. She looked back with wide eyes. "We're Homeland Security's private pandemic lab, you didn't think they'd send us a sample?"

"We need to destroy it," said Lilly, but almost everyone in the room shouted "no" in unison.

"We might need it," said Blauwitz.

"We could use it," said Cynthia.

"We can save our sick guy," said Lyle. "The only possible good use for that lotion is medical; that's what I told NewYew, and that's what I'm telling you. With the limited facilities we have, turning him into a clone of himself is the only realistic way to save his life."

"How much do you have?" asked China. "We could turn all of us into clones of ourselves." He looked around the group, hoping for support. "It's the best preventative measure we can take to keep everyone healthy—unless you like the idea that a broken ankle might kill you, too."

"Our food is low as it is," said Lyle. "Give everyone the elevated nutrient needs ReBirth requires and we'd never be able to feed everyone."

"You're already a ReBirth clone," said Dr. Shorey. "Does that mean you get more food than we do?"

"It also means he lives forever," said Cynthia, "while the rest of us age and die."

Lyle shook his head. "You say that like it's part of an evil plan."

"Isn't it?"

"I don't have evil plans," said Lyle, "I . . . barely have plans. I'm just telling you that a bunch of clones will eat more food than we, at this point, can reasonably produce."

"If we have to start farming this island we'd be prone to a lot more injuries," said Mexico. "Continually regenerating bodies would be a big help."

Lyle almost laughed. "Now you're using subsistence farming as an argument *in favor* of accelerating your subsistence needs?"

"Do we even have enough for everybody to use?" asked Samoa. "How many people are on the island?"

"We can manufacture more," said Cynthia. "We know how now."

"But we don't have the ingredients," said Blauwitz, "and I have yet to hear a plan compelling enough to risk a trip back to the mainland to get some."

"Immortality," said Russia.

"Immortality with the chance of adult-onset congenital disorders," said Lyle.

Cynthia shook her head. "The chances of that with a single dose are infinitesimal."

"But we could get another dose from anywhere," said Lilly.

Shorey shook her head. "What we really need is a genetic record of each one of us now, in our current bodies. If we run into trouble later and get contaminated with chimpanzee DNA or some other nightmare scenario, we can change back."

"Not all of us are happy with our current bodies," said Cynthia. "I'm almost sixty—if I'm going to reset myself I want to do it in something a little younger."

"So use Lilly," said China.

"Hell no," said Lilly.

"Lilly needs a new body, too," said Cynthia. "If we do end

up farming the island almost everything we can grow here will kill her."

"I'm perfectly happy the way I am," said Lilly.

Cynthia shot her a withering gaze. "That's because you're stupid."

"If we need genetic stock that's just one more reason to hit the Connecticut coast," said China. "Not to raid it, but to find people who want to join us willingly—people that actually know how to farm, or fix broken equipment. Hell, we're going to need equipment."

"We could be attacked by other looters," said Samoa.

"We're not looting," said China, "we're surviving."

"The danger of the mission makes it that much more important to preserve our DNA before we go," said Mexico. "ReBirth clones can recover from everything, up to and including gunshot wounds."

"That's a very dangerous way to look at it," said Lyle.

Blauwitz looked at Dr. Shorey. "How much do you have?"

"The government sent us thirty-four grams," said Shorey.

"That's huge," said Samoa. "We could do any of the things we've talked about, and more."

"You didn't let me finish," said Shorey, and the look on her face spoke volumes by itself. "They sent us thirty-four grams, but we've used or destroyed most of it in tests. I'd have to check the vial to be certain, but I think we have two grams left. Maybe two point five."

China's eyes went wide. "You didn't conserve it?"

"Why would we conserve it?" asked Shorey helplessly. "They told us they were making more."

"Two grams is barely any," said Lyle. "We can save the dying guy, but not much more than that."

"Forget the dying guy," said Cynthia. "This is our only sample, and I don't want to waste it on someone who can't even communicate with us."

"So we just let him die?" asked Lilly. "Is that a precedent we want to set for what is apparently going to be the start of a new civilization?"

"It's a precedent of conserving resources," said China. "New people we can get, but this is all the ReBirth we'll ever have."

"We don't need new people if the ones we have are immortal," said Mexico.

"Are ethics a renewable resource?" asked Lilly. "Because if we let people die for being inconvenient we might run out pretty quickly."

"We're not letting him die," said Cynthia, "we're just not fixing his ankle. We have antibiotics—he'll live."

"The odds are strongly against that at this point," said Shorey.

"Think about it this way," said Lyle, trying to think back to his days at NewYew, tricking the executives by appealing to their self-interest. "If we don't use ReBirth, and somehow he lives, he'll hate us. He'll have gone through months of unnecessary suffering, and he might not even be able to walk. He'll just be one more person on the island desperate to get the ReBirth and fix himself by any means necessary."

"That's hardly an issue if he doesn't live," said Cynthia.

"We save him," said Samoa, rising up to his full, imposing height. "I don't want his death on my conscience."

"Then let's do it now," said General Blauwitz. He hesitated for a split second. "I'll go to the lab with Dr. Shorey to make sure nothing happens to the ReBirth along the way."

Shorey scowled. "Now you don't trust me?"

"Alone at the end of the world with an elixir of immortality?" asked Cynthia. "I don't trust any of you. And you'd be fools to trust each other."

61

Lyle was suddenly, painfully aware of how many guns were in the room, and how close each person was standing to each of them. Mexico's assault rifle was sitting on a table, maybe five feet from both Mexico and the general. The general's own gun was farther away, but close to China. Cynthia's handgun was probably in her purse, which she pulled slowly closer. Lilly's submachine gun was somewhere around, but Lyle wasn't sure where. Did one of the scientists have it? They looked just as tense as the delegates.

The scientists will side with Shorey if this turns into a fight, thought Lyle. *There's four soldiers on the island, too, out patrolling the coasts— will they side with her, as well, or with the general? Or will it all be over before they can get here?*

"I want to go, too," said China, and looked pointedly at the general. "To *help* make sure."

"And who'll make sure of you?" asked Mexico. "We should all go."

"Not a chance," said Shorey. "That's not just a storage facility, it's an active lab for studying extremely contagious diseases. We're on an island because those diseases are so deadly it's literally illegal to store or transport them on the mainland. A group this size could destroy that lab's security and kill every one of us with something as simple as a misplaced foot." She paused. "Dr. Broadus is in the lab—let me call him, and he can bring the sample here."

"Or you can warn them," said Samoa, "and they'll use it before we can get there."

"Let me go with her," said the general again. "You can trust me—I'm a sworn servant of the American people."

"Some of us aren't American," said China.

The was a silence in the room, and Lyle watched each person's eyes dart back and forth across the group, sizing them up, gauging their own distance to the weapons, to cover, to the door, to the cars outside. If the peace fell apart, what would he do? He might be able to reach the general's rifle, but he would almost certainly lose if he had to fight China or the general for it. Mexico's gun was closer, but not as close as it was to Mexico. He could maybe get Cynthia's purse, but then what? He'd be making himself a target against better-armed foes. He looked at Lilly, and saw that she was just as scared as he was.

Come on, Lyle, he told himself, *you've got a backbone now. Use it!*

Lilly looked back at him, and he saw something else under the fear in her eyes. Determination. She held his gaze for a moment, Lyle trying desperately to hatch a plan, but they both looked up in shock when Cynthia spoke:

"Send Lyle."

The general scowled. "What?"

"He's already a clone," said Cynthia. "He won't use the sample on himself, and he's the one who's most insistent on saving the Libyan. We can send him for the lotion because we know he'll bring it back safely."

Lyle frowned, more scared by Cynthia's unexpected help than by the other people's suspicion. *Why is she supporting me? What does she want?*

"He could betray us for other reasons," said China.

"I say we send Lilly," said the general. "She has a deadly disease—she's not going to clone herself, either."

"She has a disease she's determined to live with," said China. "She might very well clone herself so she can at least stay young forever."

"Cynthia, then," said Samoa. "She's not young or healthy, so she's even less likely to clone herself, and she supported somebody else instead of trying to go herself. That's selfless."

There's nothing selfless about it, Lyle almost said, *she only supported me because she knew it would make you suggest exactly that,* but he realized that anything he said to cast suspicion on her would also cast it on him, as the person she'd supported. He looked at her with a subtle shake of his head, and she rewarded him with an even subtler smile of triumph. *She outsmarted us again.*

"Send them both," said Mexico. "Lyle and Cynthia."

"So they can work together?" asked China. "They're the ones who created it—they've known each other for years."

"And they hate each other," said Mexico. "Anyone who's spent any time observing them can see it—look at the look he's giving her now. They won't collude against us, and if either of them tries to do anything on their own, the other one will stop it."

The room was silent a moment while the group pondered. Lyle shot Lilly another glance, wondering what was going to happen—wondering what Cynthia was planning, and who was going to survive it. Lilly looked back, her eyes steady. Whatever it was, she was ready to face it.

I need to be ready, too.

"I agree," said Samoa. "Send them both."

"I agree, as well," said the general. He looked at Lyle and Cynthia. "You go with Dr. Shorey, you get the sample, and you bring it back—and make sure that it comes back. We'll cure the dying man and keep the rest here, where we can all watch it together, while we decide what to do with it."

Lyle nodded gravely, watching as Shorey walked to the door and Cynthia followed, purse in hand. She obviously had a plan. He needed a plan of his own, and he had only a short car ride to put it together. They jogged through the afternoon light—still bright, but night was coming soon—and piled into Shorey's truck. He rubbed his hands together in the cold, and thought through the situation as they drove to the lab in silence.

Both of the women looked as concerned and pensive as he did. Dr. Shorey looked extremely nervous.

What does Cynthia want? Lyle asked himself. *She wants power. How will this sample of ReBirth help her to get it? Immortality could be a major trump card, but not for years—if we end up trapped on the island for generations, the deathless matriarch would eventually, inevitably, be the ruler. But she doesn't want to be herself forever, unless that was another layer of misdirection. Will she try to steal Shorey's DNA? Will she wait until we get back to the living quarters, and try to steal DNA from one of the other women?*

Will she try to steal mine?

Lyle looked at Cynthia's purse, gripped tightly in her hand and still, he assumed, containing her handgun. Had she been able to reload it since the UN building? Would she try to use it? Immortality wouldn't help her much if she forced the issue and stole the lotion brazenly—as soon as they rejoined the others they'd know, and they'd throw her in the sturdiest makeshift prison they could create. Or they might just kill her outright—it wasn't hard to cause enough trauma that ReBirth's accelerated healing couldn't keep up with it. She couldn't regenerate a head. No, whatever Cynthia tried would be subtle and insidious.

The lab loomed before them through the trees, a two-story building with a curving, red-brick front. Several wings and courtyards sprawled out behind it; three tall towers stood in the distance, the local gas tanks, and near them was the recirculated water system that made the island an unlikely Eden. A single army jeep was parked out front. *One of the guards?* Lyle wondered. *Or are the vehicles communal, and that's what Dr. Broadus drove today?*

"I told the soldiers to keep an extra eye on the lab," said Shorey, parking by the jeep and opening her door. "Looks like that was a good idea."

"We're not going to do anything," said Cynthia, climbing out behind her. "We're here to get the lotion and take it back, just like they said."

"You're the one who told us not to trust you," said Shorey.

"I'm here because I'm the only one you *can* trust," said Cynthia. "Of course I want the lotion, but I want it under specific circumstances that can't be filled at the moment. It's in my best interest—more in my interest than in anyone else's—to preserve the lotion in pristine condition for as long as possible."

"You really want to steal somebody's body?" asked Shorey.

"Just the blueprints for it," said Cynthia. "I don't know where the real one's been."

Shorey grunted and turned to the front door. *She doesn't like her,* thought Lyle, *but now she trusts her, at least a little. Is that phase one of Cynthia's plan? To give her word and keep it until the rest of the refugees let their guard down? But let their guard down for what?*

One of the island's four soldiers was waiting in a small, sealed reception area, but Lyle didn't risk the assumption that he was the only soldier in the building. Shorey showed her ID and filled out the various visitor check-in forms, but did not, Lyle noticed, explain to the soldier why they were there and what they were retrieving. *That might be because she trusts us more now,* Lyle thought. *She's not immediately telling the guard to arrest us, which is a good sign.*

It might also be that she doesn't trust the guard, Lyle thought, *which is a very bad sign. If she's worried that the man with the gun might do something rash, maybe she doesn't have the sway over them that I thought she did. That would make one more faction on this already precarious island.*

Lyle grimaced and shook his head. *I'm just being paranoid. She's not being tight-lipped as part of a big crazy plot, she's being tight-lipped because we're here to remove a contagious substance from the facility, which is probably against every rule they have. There's no sense volunteering that kind of information.*

The guard let them through, and Dr. Shorey brought them to a staging room where they suited up in translucent yellow plastic, including elastic-rimmed bags for their hair and small masks for their mouth and nose. Lyle was pleased that he put it all on more quickly than Cynthia—he'd been in clean labs before—but Shorey stopped him before they proceeded and pulled the hatband down over his ears.

"You don't want anything getting in your ear canals."

Lyle frowned. "Is anything likely to?"

"At this level of 'what's the worst that could happen,'" said Shorey, "your threshold of overzealous protection should be set to 'remotely possible.' If we get all the way to 'likely,' you're already dead."

Lyle paled. "In that case I want eye protection, too."

Shorey pulled out three pairs of plastic glasses and handed them around. Last of all they pulled on plastic gloves and booties, and Shorey opened the door to a long hallway. "This is a polarized floor," said Shorey, leading them forward. "It's going to pull any lingering particles off your feet and legs, and the walls will be doing the same to your upper body. We'll pass through a similar one on the way out, plus a chemical trough and a shower that I suggest you treat very seriously."

Lyle realized he was holding his breath, as if he could avoid breathing the entire time he was in the building. ReBirth might be the most prominent threat in the building, but it was far from the deadliest.

Is that Cynthia's plan? he wondered. *Would she really risk taking anything else out of here? Nobody's that power hungry.* He noticed her purse was gone, left back in the changing room. *Does she still have the gun?*

They left the sterilizer and entered the building beyond, walking through a series of corridors and going down a pair of staircases to a storage room underground. Dr. Shorey paused in front of the door. "I don't suppose I can convince you to wait out here?"

"We promised the group we'd go together," said Cynthia. Lyle only nodded in agreement, feeling his stomach twist itself into knots. Shorey sighed and opened the insulated door; Lyle felt a soft puff of cold air wash out of the blackness before a motion sensor clicked on a series of bright fluorescent lights. They followed Shorey inside, and she led them past rows of flat metal cabinets. Inside of each metal door, Lyle knew, was a powerful contagion, packed and sealed and cushioned and protected from every possible form of disaster. Except, of course, for the disaster they were about to create on purpose. Dr. Shorey opened the drawer marked REBIRTH, and reached for the sample vial inside.

Cynthia put her hand on the doctor's.

Lyle stepped forward, reaching out to stop whatever was about to happen, but neither woman moved. Dr. Shorey looked at Cynthia. "What are your intentions, Ms. Mummer?"

"What are yours?"

Shorey's eye narrowed. "I'm going to take this sample back to the others, just like we said."

"And after that?"

Neither hand moved. Neither woman blinked. Lyle looked back and forth between them, wondering if he should step in. Was Cynthia still armed? Was this her big move? Did she know something about the doctor he didn't?

"There are only two options left," said Cynthia. "In the first, this is a nightmare we wake up from. The world we fled manages to put itself back together, worse for wear but repairable in some form. We go home, we rejoin the government, we carve our new niche in whatever power structure replaces the old one. I do not think this scenario is likely, but I'm too careful to count it out."

"Careful or paranoid?"

"That's our best-case scenario," said Cynthia. "If planning for the best-case scenario is paranoid, we're in a lot more trouble than we've dared to admit."

Shorey said nothing.

"In the second option," Cynthia continued, "this is it. Lyle's hellfire and damnation sermon was correct, and we're stuck on this island for the rest of our lives. The extreme measures we've proposed to deal with that situation are no longer ridiculous but necessary to our survival. We start a new colony here, self-contained and self-sustaining, and it will be generations before we can even think about leaving. The power structure here will be smaller than the one in option one, but it will still exist, and it will affect us more directly, and we will be able to climb much higher in it. Do you know who will control that power structure?"

The doctor's eyes had lost their ferocity; Cynthia's cold presentation of the facts had affected her. She nodded. "The power will go to whoever controls this lotion sample."

Cynthia mirrored her nod. "And what about option one? Who controls the power structure in that scenario?"

The doctor thought a moment before responding. Her breath puffed out in nervous clouds. "Whoever controls this lotion sample."

"Exactly," said Cynthia. "Now here's the biggest question of all, and I want you to think very carefully: Who controls this lotion sample?"

"Realistically?" asked Shorey. "Whoever has a gun."

Cynthia's other hand appeared from behind the open drawer, holding her small handgun—not aiming it at anyone, just holding it. Lyle stepped back. "The purest form of power," Cynthia said, "and at least one-tenth of the law. What are the other nine-tenths?"

"You don't need to treat me like a child," the doctor snarled.

"I want to treat you like an ally," said Cynthia, "but I need you to give me something first. I'm not going to use it, I'm not going to steal it, I'm not going to do anything the group doesn't agree on. But I am going to hold it, and that, as we've discussed, is the only thing that really matters."

The doctor looked at her, and at the gun, and slowly removed her hand from the lotion sample. Cynthia picked it up with a small smile. "Thank you, Doctor. I hope this is the beginning of a long and fruitful relationship."

62

The dying man was unconscious, wracked with fever; his broken ankle was swollen and discolored. Cynthia held the sample vial carefully, the lid open, and the room full of refugees watched in anxious silence as Lyle dipped in a Q-tip, dabbed it on the man's skin, and waited. Inside the fat white drop a million tiny retroviruses scanned his DNA, copied it, and spread it like a plague to each of their neighbors, over and over in a growing cascade. A tiny invisible cataclysm. A moment later Lyle touched the Q-tip back down on the dying man's skin, smearing it around, rubbing it deep into his tissue, and in that instant the man became a fallen god: eternal, immortal, and changeless, and damned. Lyle wiped the man clean with a thick rubber glove, and sealed both glove and Q-tip in a hazardous materials bag from the lab. Cynthia closed the vial and tucked it safely in her pocket.

"It's done," said the general. "Let's get back to work."

"Work if you want," said Lyle. "I'm going to sleep." He left the room, walking quickly back to his own. Cynthia called after him, but he ignored her. He didn't want to hear her, he didn't want to see her, he didn't want to see anybody.

Why didn't I stop her? he thought. *That's why I was there. To stop her from abusing the lotion.*

But she's not abusing it; she's just holding it.

Or is ReBirth really so powerful that simply holding it is enough?

He'd once told NewYew they were irresponsible, doing

something so bad it was like giving guns to mentally disabled children, but he'd been wrong. He was the mental case here— he was the idiot, the half-wit, the brain-damaged fool who'd found a technology he couldn't understand, and used it wrong, and ended the world. Now there was nobody left but the carrion feeders, Cynthia and the general and everybody else, snapping at the carcass and ripping it to shreds until there was nothing left but bones and skin and maggots.

He reached his room and slammed the door, standing in the center of the floor and breathing. Thinking. Trying, at least, to think of something positive.

Someone knocked on his door, and he turned around to see Lilly push it open and peek through the gap. He sighed, feeling hollow and defeated. She opened the door a little farther.

"You want to talk?" she asked.

"No," he said, but stopped her before she could leave again. "Come in, though, please. I don't . . . I don't know what I want." He rubbed his eyes, exhausted, and laughed drily. "I want to go back in time and stop this. Destroy my research, burn down my laboratory, whatever it takes."

"My mother always said you can't change the past," said Lilly. "The best you can do is learn from it."

"That's very easy for your mother to say," said Lyle. "What'd she do that was so horrible, kill a guy?"

"My father," said Lilly. "The court ruled self-defense."

Lyle forced himself to close his mouth. "I'm sorry. I mean, I'm glad she's okay. I mean . . . All of a sudden I feel like kind of a huge tool." He winced and grabbed a chair. "Do you want to sit down?"

"I'm fine," she laughed, "this is all ancient history. I've dealt with it, I've learned from it, and I've moved on."

"Sit down anyway," said Lyle, and grabbed a chair for himself. "I feel like I've been dragged behind a semi for . . . I don't know, nine months?" He laughed again, small and sad. "Forty-two years?"

She stepped into the room, revealing from behind her back two bottles from the food supply: a year-old Coke, and a bottle of spring water at least twice that old. She handed him the Coke and sat down. "Normally I'd prescribe ice cream for depression, but we have limited resources."

"They're going to be really mad at us for drinking these," said Lyle, but he took the bottle anyway.

"We're going to put it back," said Lilly, dismissing the protest with a mischievous smile. "We've got the greatest water reclamation system in the world, here, right? Just drink it up, hit the restroom, wait a few days, and boom, it's back in the tap and ready to refill the bottle."

Lyle laughed, not defeated this time but amused—the first time in days that he'd laughed with genuine humor. "I don't think mine will be quite as fizzy by then."

"You 'think' it won't be?"

"Well, you can never be sure."

"That concerns me." Lilly screwed off the cap and took a swig from the bottle. "There's, what, twenty of us on the island?" She pointed at him in mock seriousness. "I fear for the future of the human race if five percent of the surviving gene pool has carbonated urine. You've been keeping secrets from me."

Lyle laughed again, and opened his own bottle. It was tepid, but the carbonation bit his throat, and the taste and feel of it was almost shockingly comforting after so much chaos. "No," he said, swallowing and shaking his head. "I don't have any secrets left. I'm Lyle Fontanelle—you probably met at least ten of me before we ever even knew each other."

"Five at the most," said Lilly. She paused, and said her next sentence with her eyes fixed on the floor. "None of them was half as interesting."

Lyle paused, the bottle halfway to his lips. *Did she say what I think she said?* He didn't want to look stupid, or eager, so he brought the bottle mechanically to his mouth and drank, all the while wondering what she had meant, and what she was feeling.

When he allowed himself to look back at her, he saw she was looking at him. He wiped his mouth with his hand, feeling self-conscious, and looked at the bottle because it was easier than looking at her.

He leaned forward, playing with the bottle in his hands, looking at her feet instead of her face. "I feel like I barely know you."

"You don't."

"So tell me about yourself." He looked up, caught her eye, and held it this time. She seemed to smile not just with her mouth or her eyes but her entire face. She was more beautiful than she'd ever been, because each new scrap of understanding showed that she was kinder, wiser, funnier than he'd ever imagined. But she was still a mystery. "I want to know everything."

She opened her arms wide, as if encompassing the entire world. "We've got plenty of time." She took another sip of water, and made a beckoning motion with her hand. "Hit me. What's your first question?"

"What does your illness mean to you?"

"It means I can't eat pizza."

"I'm being serious," said Lyle. "You have a genetic illness that has warped your health, your diet, your social life, your entire existence, into a daily struggle just to get by. ReBirth could have solved that problem in a heartbeat—a few thousand dollars, four months of nutritional supplements, and you'd never have to worry about your health again. You could eat pizza, hamburgers, cake, candy bars; you could drink Coke; you could live a normal life again. And yet you never did it."

"I like being me."

"I don't doubt that," said Lyle. "I imagine everybody likes you. But nobody works that hard to accommodate a curable disease unless the disease itself is an integral part of who they are, or at least of who they think they are. Who they want to be. I don't think you like yourself in spite of celiac sprue, I think you like yourself because of it."

Lilly looked at her water bottle, twirling it in small circles and watching the liquid swirl around inside. "That's . . . a little deeper than I was expecting this conversation to be. I think the thing is . . ." She took another drink, a long, slow guzzle that gave her time to gather her thoughts. "I'm not gorgeous."

"Yes you are."

"I'm a professional model, Lyle. I know the difference between pretty and gorgeous, and I'm pretty. In any other social circle I'd say I'm very pretty, though I hate saying that because it makes me sound conceited, but on a shoot with a bunch of supermodels I can't help but feel self-conscious. Especially because I'm usually 'the black girl' they brought in to round out the demographics."

Lyle felt a pang of guilt. He'd been a part of those demographic hiring conversations too many times.

"For a while," she continued, "my first few months in the industry, celiac was my excuse. 'I can't be as pretty as her, I can't have her body, I can't follow her exercise program, because I'm sick.' It made me different, and being different made me feel better, but it doesn't take long for 'I feel better than you do' to turn into 'I feel better than you *are*.' Celiac became my consolation prize—my snide little triumph that maybe you never ate bread, but I never ate bread or else I'd *die*. Maybe you had a strict diet, but I had an even stricter diet with my life hanging dramatically in the balance. Maybe you were prettier than me, and featured a little more prominently in the group poses, and got more shots overall in the final magazine, but I was a martyr an inch away from the hospital. It made me feel better about my insecurities; I had something that nobody else had."

Lyle shook his head. "I don't believe you."

"You don't think I'm that shallow?" She raised her eyebrow. "Or you don't *want* to think I'm that shallow?"

Lyle smiled thinly, looking down at his Coke. "Nobody that self-aware is shallow. Which, conversely, makes me the most shallow person in the world." He laughed drily. "Maybe literally, at this point."

A hint of Lilly's playfulness crept back into her voice. "How can someone who's met himself ten thousand times not be self-aware?"

"Out there," said Lyle, gesturing toward the front of the barracks, "earlier tonight, when Cynthia suggested that you could get a new body you almost punched her. Which I kind of wish you had, actually." He puffed out a long, slow breath. "That . . . fierce protectiveness, that zeal to defend your disability. Celiac's not just something you lord over the other models." He looked her in the eyes. "I think celiac makes you who you are because it threatened to make you something else, and you didn't let it. You're not a victim, you're not a patient, you're not a dropout or a charity case or anything like it—you're a happy, healthy, successful woman, not because life made you that way but because you, personally, overcame everything life put in your way to stop you. You love it because it's the mountain you climbed to become great, and now that you're standing at the top you can see farther, and be greater, than you ever could before."

Lilly stared back at him, holding his gaze without ever looking away. "That might be the most romantic thing anyone's ever said to me."

Lyle looked at her, warm in the dim light, tired and disheveled and wonderful. He stood up, still looking her in the eyes, and she practically leaped across the room. He held her in his arms and kissed her urgently, hungrily, and she kissed him back with the same fierce desperation. She pressed him back, two steps toward the bed, until his legs knocked against it and all he wanted to do was to fall backward, to pull her down with him, to bury himself and his problems and the entire world in one moment of pure physical perfection. She pressed against him, hot and ravenous, but it was wrong, and he was wrong, and she was wrong. He felt corrupted inside, like he was already dead. Spoiled meat. He pushed her out to arm's length. He was gasping for breath.

She looked confused. "What's wrong?"

"I can't just forget," he said.

"Sometimes we need to forget, just for a minute."

"Here at the end of the world, trapped on an island, locked in a building, alone in a room—are we just closing our eyes to it? To everything that's gone and everyone who's died and . . ." He shook his head, gripping her shoulders, cursing himself for doing anything other than kissing her again. "I want this, and I want you, but I don't want it to be a concession. I don't want it to be the . . . going-away party for human civilization. Does that make any sense at all?"

"You want to celebrate life instead of hiding from death."

His rush of a breath was like a sigh of relief. "Yes, that's it exactly. Are you . . . ? Is that okay?" He wanted her, but he wanted it to be *right*. "I don't take a lot of stands, but this one seems important."

"That's fine," said Lilly, and took a deep breath. "I know exactly how you feel, actually." She looked down, sighing, then looked up again quickly and pulled him in for another kiss, longer than the others, deeper and more passionate. Lyle felt himself melting, almost ready to throw his stand out the window and throw her down on the bed, but she pulled away. "If we're waiting I can't stay here." She rolled her eyes and hurried to the door. "I'll be in my bunk."

She closed the door behind her, and Lyle stared at it. "What did I just do?" He sat down, still staring, and took a long pull on his bottle. It was sweet and acrid, and he wished it were booze.

The start of a new world, he thought. *Not just the end of an old one. There has to be more—I thought the world was over, but it's not. For all her amazing qualities that's the single most amazing one, hands down: she convinced me the world isn't over. We can make a new one.*

I just don't know if we can make it here.

Cynthia was a terror, determined to hold power by any means necessary, and she wasn't the only one. The general was just as power-hungry in his own, less Machiavellian way—he'd been the man who'd destroyed São Tomé, after all. He didn't have the plans Cynthia did, but the plans he did have he would pursue with a single-minded ferocity. The three delegates were simultaneously useless and terrifying; their solutions, on the rare occasions they had any, were vast and sweeping and completely insane. All three of them had been willing to turn the entire human population into seven billion copies of the same person, the biggest eugenics crime Lyle could even imagine. How long before they came up with something even worse?

Worst of all was Dr. Shorey—not who she was, but who she was becoming. Lyle had watched her closely in the lab, in the truck on the way home, in the front room as they treated the dying man. She'd promised to watch Cynthia carefully, and in a way she had, but it was more focused than that. She wasn't just watching Cynthia, she was watching Cynthia's hands. She was watching the lotion. Lyle had even caught her staring at Cynthia's pocket, obsessed with the ReBirth sample, her thoughts obviously focused on it constantly. As careful as they'd tried to be, they'd brought another plague with them from the depths of the lab: Shorey had become infected with suspicion and greed, and she would spread it to the scientists and the soldiers and everybody else. Even now, in the silence of the living complex, Lyle felt like he could hear them—half a dozen little factions, whispering and scheming, plotting their moves and staking their claims on the glorious throne of a windswept rock barely half a mile across.

"We have to leave," Lyle whispered. "I don't know where else we can go, but we can't stay here."

The trouble was that Plum Island really was the perfect haven. It had modern amenities, stored food, and that irreplaceable clean water system. As long as nothing dangerous got into it, they could recirculate their water for generations, and never have to worry about the ReBirth that tainted the rest of the planet. The only other alternative was to find a place the lotion hadn't touched, but where? It was everywhere. That's why they'd come to the island in the first place.

"The islands," Lyle whispered, and he felt his heart race with excitement. *The Samoan delegate wanted to go to the islands, to the*

Bahamas or Bermuda or the Caribbean. Somewhere so small no one else wanted it, and no one else has touched it, just me and Lilly alone on the beach. We could fish, and eat coconuts and bananas and anything we want. Most of it wouldn't even have gluten—she'd never be sick. We could do it. We could live. We could take Cynthia's boat and disappear forever.

But only one of us would live forever.

Lyle stood now, pacing the room, searching through the variables to find a way through them. *We could leave, and we could sail south, and we could get to our island, but I'm immortal. I'll spend sixty years with Lilly, watching her age and die, and then I'll spend a thousand years alone. Ten thousand. I can't do that. What good is a paradise if it ends in death, and emptiness, and maybe even suicide?*

The answer, Lyle knew, was in Cynthia's room, in Cynthia's pocket, in a tiny glass vial. It would be easy—Lilly wouldn't even have to know at first. He had her water bottle right here, with her DNA on the mouth and floating in the leftover water inside. *All I have to do is drop the lotion in it, just a tiny drop, and let it drift around and pick up her DNA code. And then she can drink it, and become a clone of herself, and stay young and healthy and beautiful forever. We can be together forever.*

All I need is one drop.

63

THE END OF THE WORLD

Lyle opened his door. The hall was empty and dark. He crept through the corridor carefully, quietly, watching for shadows in the corners and doorways, and listening for any other sound of human life. The building was as silent as a tomb. Lyle walked slowly to Cynthia's room, forcing himself to be patient. If he could slip in while she was asleep, if he could take what he wanted without waking her, without anyone knowing, then they could slip away in the night. He could wake Lilly and they could run.

Lyle put a hand on Cynthia's doorknob, cold and rough from ancient use. He turned it, slowly, warily, using just enough pressure to test the lock. It was open. He turned it farther, hearing the mechanism slide, hearing the bolt scrape across the rim of its housing, an inaudible whisper that seemed to scream in his ears like a freight train. He turned it farther, felt it open, pushed the door gently and held his breath, waiting for the squeak of rusty hinges. The door opened smoothly, silently, not alerting a soul to his plans. He looked inside.

The room was empty.

Lyle frowned. He slipped in, looking behind the door, searching the closet, and his spirits plunged as he realized Cynthia was gone—she had left, or someone had taken her. Lyle raced back to the hall and looked around wildly, his heart racing. Someone had come for her! One faction or another had already made its move, and the lotion was gone. He ran to the front room and looked outside. All the vehicles were still there. He looked in the storage room, in the bathroom, in the empty bedrooms. He looked in the kitchen and saw a slim, skeletal shadow in the corner, sitting at the cracked kitchen table.

"Lyle," said Cynthia. "I never guessed you would be the first."

"The first?"

She clicked on the light, and Lyle blinked his eyes against the sudden glare. As they adjusted he saw the vial on the table, a tiny glass monolith a few inches from Cynthia's hand. Lying next to it was her handgun, black and gleaming.

"The first to make a play for the lotion," said Cynthia. "I knew someone would try it, maybe several someones. You won't be the last tonight, I assure you, but it surprises me that you're the first."

Lyle found a second light switch and turned the lights back off. "Lower your voice," he whispered, "they're probably all still awake."

"How very noble of you," said Cynthia. Lyle heard the gun slide across the worn Formica. "Protecting me from the others' schemes. What's your own scheme, Lyle? Is it equally noble?"

She already knew, so Lyle saw no sense in waiting. He walked toward her slowly, wary of the gun. "I want to save Lilly."

"Disappointing," said Cynthia. "I was hoping for something original, but I suppose you only have two settings: 'Don't use ReBirth ever, for any reason,' and 'Use ReBirth to save the girl I'm currently lusting after.' That didn't work out so well for Susan, did it?"

"This is a selfish motivation, and I admit that," said Lyle. "I'm going to live forever, and I want Lilly with me. All I need is a drop—nobody else has to know." He shook the water bottle, hearing the liquid slosh. "I have her saliva, it's as good as a mouth swab."

"And by then we can concoct some other plausible scenario," said Cynthia, as if she'd known the plan all along. "We can pretend it happened before the fall, in the UN, perhaps, or we could feign ignorance altogether." Lyle saw the outline of her grim smile in the darkness, and felt a chill. Somehow, no matter what he said or did, he always felt like he was following her script.

How had she gone so quickly from surprise to control? Was it all an act? Was she really that smart?

Or was she just evil?

"She'll still have celiac sprue," said Cynthia.

"Celiac causes the body to damage itself in the presence of gluten," said Lyle. "ReBirth will undo the damage. She'll destroy herself and heal herself at the same time—she'll still get sick when she eats it, but she won't die from it." He cleared his throat. "And you and I keep the secret, and nobody ever knows. If she doesn't get injured, Lilly won't even know."

"Wait," said Cynthia. "Lilly doesn't know?"

"I . . . thought that was obvious."

"Of course it wasn't obvious," Cynthia sneered. "But." She nodded. "I can see why you thought it was. Because you're the great Lyle Fontanelle."

"I'm not great."

"You were always the smart one—always the self-righteous one. That's all you ever wanted, isn't it? To make other people's decisions for them. You didn't just tell us how to use your products, you told us the morally correct way to use them. The correct way to run the company. To use ReBirth. To save the world. Even in the UN you treated everyone like foolish children, because you were always right, and if only the whole world would stop arguing and listen to you, then all our problems would be solved."

She stared at him, and he stared back in silence.

"You were always spineless, Lyle, but that was never your biggest problem, and now that you've learned to stand up for yourself your biggest problem is bigger than ever: you want to make the choices for everyone else. The only difference now is that you're brave enough to go through with it."

"I'm trying to save her life," said Lyle.

"And what will she think of you when she figures that out?

When Lilly cuts her finger or breaks her leg or never ages—
what will she think of you when the secret is finally out? The
others will lose their trust in you, but Lilly—oh my. Lilly will
hate you. You'll be the monster who corrupted her, who made
the biggest decision of her life without even asking her permission. Knowing exactly what she wanted for herself, and
denying it to her forever."

"Maybe she'll come around," he said, trying to convince himself as much as her. "Forever is a long time."

"Then why not wait until she does?"

"Because it has to be—"

He stopped himself, but it was too late.

"It has to be what?" The sneer was gone from her voice, and
that ice-cold analysis was back in its place. She was putting together the pieces.

Lyle didn't dare to answer.

Cynthia's words slithered out like a snake. "You're leaving."

"No."

"You're leaving," she said again. "It has to be tonight, because
you won't be here anymore."

"Just give me the lotion," Lyle growled.

"Never."

He stared at her, and at her gun. There was nothing he could do.

Cynthia stared back, and after a moment she smiled at him,
cruel and cold. "Do you see what I mean about power? Do what
I tell you to, support me in our meetings, and someday I'll give
you what you want. Oppose me, and I tell everyone what you
tried to do here tonight. I tell Lilly." She spread her arms wide,
as if embracing the entire island. "I have ReBirth, which means
I have ev—"

Lyle lunged forward, and she couldn't bring the gun back to
bear on him in time; he caught her arm mid-swing, and when
she pulled the trigger the shot went wide. He shoved her backward, knocking her off her chair, and as she fell she grabbed the
edge of the table. It fell with her, and Lyle's heart leaped into

his throat as he watched the glass vial of ReBirth arc through the air in a terrifying parabola, up and over and down to the hard floor.

The sound of it shattering rang louder in his ears than the gunshot.

Cynthia screamed.

Lyle unscrewed the cap on the water bottle in one frenzied twist, and dipped the lip of it in the pale white smear on the floor. Some of the water spilled out, mixing with the lotion, but he ignored it and slammed the cap back on. Cynthia fired her gun again, and he ran.

"Help!" Cynthia shouted. Her voice echoed down the hall. "Lyle attacked me! He's stealing the lotion!" The doors that flew immediately open proved that very few people were actually asleep. The general stepped halfway into the hall, frowning at the noise, and Lyle shouted as he dodged around him.

"Cynthia's gone crazy. I went for a drink and she started shooting." He didn't wait to see how the general would react, for now Lilly's door was open, too, and she stood wide-eyed in the doorway. "Grab your coat," he shouted. "We're going!"

"Going where?"

"Away!" He bolted past her into the room, shoved her coat into her hands, and found her shoes. "You can put these on in the car."

She stood in the room uncertainly, but another gunshot from the kitchen made her flinch in fear, and after a moment's hesitation she started pulling on her shoes. "What's going on?"

"They've gone crazy," said Lyle, "we're going to take the boat and go."

"Where?"

"We'll figure that out when we're safe, let's go!"

Another gunshot. Lyle didn't know if the others had tried to calm Cynthia and she was defending herself, or if they were fighting over the ReBirth on the floor. He stepped back toward the hall door, then thought better of it and simply went to the window, unlocking it and shoving it open. The air outside was bitter cold, and he shivered as he leaped through. Lilly threw her room's wool blanket out after him, which he wrapped around his shoulders while she crawled out behind him. They ran to the trucks, praying that the keys were still in them; the gunshots had turned now to shouting, and Lyle ran from vehicle to vehicle. The front door flew open. Lyle found keys in the fourth vehicle, a fat white van, and yelled for Lilly. He turned the key— the engine revved once, twice, three times in the cold before finally turning over—and then Lilly was in and he peeled out, ignoring the shouts behind them.

"What's going on?" Lilly demanded.

"Do you trust me?"

"I wouldn't be here if I didn't."

"I tried to get a drink of water from the kitchen," he said, using the same lie he'd given the general. "Cynthia was in there, and she thought I'd come to steal the ReBirth, and she shot me."

"Did she hit you?"

Lyle shook his head. The drive to the docks was short, barely a mile on the tiny island, and he screeched to a halt. There were already headlights behind them. Lyle and Lilly ran to the sailboat—*Mummer's Hoard*, with a dark green Yggdrasil painted on the bow—and a soldier stepped out of the guardhouse, confused.

"Is everything okay?"

"There's been an outbreak!" Lyle shouted, pointing wildly at the headlights. "Don't let them get close!"

The soldier's eyes went wide with terror, and he turned toward the approaching trucks with his assault rifle leveled, spraying a short burst of bullets as a warning. The trucks swerved at the unexpected attack, the beams of their headlights dancing wildly through the darkness. Lilly fired up the onboard motor while Lyle untied the boat. The trucks were stopped, the people in them crouching low and shouting at the guard to stop. The soldier backed toward the boat, firing another burst every time their pursuers poked their heads up, keeping them expertly pinned down.

"What do they have?" he asked. "Can we catch it from here?" He turned toward Lyle, but the boat was already fifteen feet from the dock, now twenty, now thirty. The soldier screamed in fear and fury, raising his rifle as if to fire on them, but turned back toward the trucks. He looked back and forth a few times, unsure what to do.

"We couldn't stay," Lyle whispered. "You have to believe me—there was nothing left for us but madness. You heard the plans they were coming up with: raiding the coasts for food and women. They were ready to kill each other over hand lotion."

"*You* have to believe *me*," said Lilly. "I'm glad to be rid of them." She steered south, around the tip of the island toward Block Island Sound. "Will they chase us?"

"Can you really sail this?" asked Lyle. "Without the motor, I mean?"

"Through good weather, yes."

"Then they don't have anyone with the skills to chase us." He looked behind them, but saw nothing. "I say we head south, and find an empty island in the Caribbean. We can hug the coast—at a safe distance, of course—and follow the GPS. We won't even have to stop: we don't need gas, and we can't trust the food on the mainland anyway."

"That's a long trip," said Lilly. "There's supplies belowdecks, but I wish we'd brought more water."

"I got one bottle," said Lyle, holding it up. He held it toward her with a trembling hand. "It was the best I could do."

She drank it, and Lyle threw the empty bottle in the sea.

———

The coast was on fire.

Lyle and Lilly sailed past in silence, watching from a distance as smoke rose from the husk of America, now in billows, now in slow, smoldering fingers. At dawn they saw movement on the shore, but they simply turned farther out and passed by on the open ocean. They saw no other boats or airplanes. They heard nothing on the radio—no broadcasts, no warnings, no pleas for help. They dined on the champagne and canned caviar from Cynthia's luxury hold, toasting the night in case it was their last.

The weather grew warmer as they fled to the south. They almost stopped in Florida, but a creature on the shore scared them off—tall and simian, with tusks and human breasts and arms that hung well past its knees. They tried again in the Abacos, but a group of twenty identical women watched them with silent, somber eyes, and they steered away again.

The next day a black storm rumbled on the horizon.

"Can ReBirth get into the rain?" asked Lilly.

"Maybe," he whispered. "Nothing we can do about it now."

64

10 DAYS SINCE THE WAKING OF THE PEOPLE

Ket had been watching the white thing all morning, trying to decide if it was growing bigger or simply getting closer. None of the People had ever seen anything like it, and they were scared, but Ket was not scared, and he was not surprised. None of the People had ever seen *anything* before, for there had never been anything to see. They awoke at the birth of the world, granted a wisdom beyond the other animals on the island, and everything was new. They had food and water; they had tunnels to nest in, and a sky full of lights. They had everything they needed. There was nothing else.

But now there was a white thing on the water.

Ket tapped his spear against the ground. His sister Chirt had begun to make the spears on the eighth day of the world, and now on the tenth nearly everyone had them. They made it easy to catch the insects and mice the People lived on, far easier than catching them with teeth and claws. New things like this were happening almost every day, and Ket had to wonder if the world was offering them new ideas, or if their own capacity to have ideas was expanding. He wondered, for a moment, if his own ability to wonder was a new development, as well. The People were becoming smarter by the day, growing larger, and there were other changes, as well. He looked at his paw. He did not remember having these fingers in this shape when he awoke ten days ago. The mice and other rodents didn't have them. Only the People. He wondered, and not for the first time, if the People had once been like the mice, and if their transition into something else was still happening.

What, he pondered, *will we turn into?*

The white thing was definitely closer to the shore now. It was enormous, the biggest thing he'd ever seen beside the island itself. He peered closer and saw with shock that there were creatures on it. Was it another island, floating up to theirs? More of the People clustered around him now, Chirt his sister and Tsit his brother, a dozen or more. They watched the white thing slide close to the shore, and the two creatures who rode it jumped down in the shallow water.

"They have arms like us," said Tsit. "Arms and legs and hands."

"It almost sounds like they're laughing," said Chirt. "Are they People?"

"They're too big to be People," said Tsit. "They're as tall as the trees. And they have no hair on their bodies, only a tiny tuft on the tops of their heads." He cocked his head to the side, watching closely. "Like leaves."

"I do not think they are trees," said Chirt.

"Look what they carry," said Ket, and the People grew silent. The creatures in the water were pulling objects out of the white thing now, miraculous things that none of the People had ever seen before, and yet Ket could not help but compare them to the spear in his hands. *We built this,* he thought. *Did they build that? And that?* Their objects made a massive pile on the sand. *Who are these creatures that build such great things?*

"I think that they are Gods," said Ket.

Chirt's sharp eyes looked at him. "What are Gods?"

"Gods are People," said Ket, "only bigger, and smarter. They have everything the People have, but they have more of it. Their size is greater, and their deeds are greater." He looked at the Gods' hands, saw their fingers in the same shape as his own. He wiggled his fifth finger, the one that gripped against the other four. The one the animals didn't have. He looked back up. "We should approach them," he said. "We should ask them for their gifts. Perhaps, with their gifts, we could become like them." He paused. "Perhaps that is why they are here."

"We will give them our gifts, as well," said Chirt, and the People picked up their spears and their broad leaf platters of meat, both mouse and insect. They crept out of the bushes, out of the tall grass, and onto the sand—dozens now, nearly a hundred. The full group of the People. The Gods were touching each other, in what Ket was almost convinced was a kiss, and they didn't see the People until they were only a few short hops away.

The Gods screamed and moved back. They babbled, and their voices were loud, but Ket couldn't understand them.

"They can't speak," said Tsit. "They can't be smarter than us if they can't even speak."

"Maybe their language is greater," said Ket, "like their objects are greater." But he had his doubts. As confusing as the words were, the feeling seemed clear; he could hear it in their voices, and see it in their eyes.

They were afraid.

"A God should not be afraid," said Chirt.

The larger God was clutching a giant spear, but a strange one; instead of tapering to a sharp point it flattened into a broad, flat leaf. Ket wondered what type of creature the Gods must hunt to need a spear so powerful. Tsit hopped closer, his eyes narrowed and suspicious, his spear held at the ready. The darker God—the female, he thought—hid behind the lighter one, and the male brought its spear down on Tsit with a great rush of wind. Wet sand flew. Ket had never seen such strength.

The God raised the spear. Tsit was a bloody mess in the crater it had made.

"These are not Gods," said Ket, shocked at the attack. "They are not great." He looked back at the People behind him, saw the fear in their eyes. The rage. "Animals have died before, and insects, but never the People. They have not brought us gifts, but death." He turned back to the Gods. "They are afraid. They have great things, but they are not great. We would be better Gods than these!" He looked at the People and roared in righteous anger. "We will take their gifts! We will eat their meat! And we will become new Gods!"

The creatures screamed, and the People charged.

Acknowledgments

I started writing this book in early 2010, when I was working on a different book and got bored with it and decided to watch TV instead. *The 6th Day* was on, and it came to a scene where Schwarzenegger's character comes home and sees himself through the window of his house, talking to his wife and playing with his kids, and he is suddenly and irrevocably faced with the reality that he is not unique. That the fundamental individuality of each human being, one of the foundational tenets of our entire way of life, is no longer true. He is not the only him, and he never will be again. The movie is okay, but that scene hit me like I've rarely been hit before. I dropped my other project then and there, and started working on *Extreme Makeover: Apocalypse Edition*.

The first person I should thank, then, is Arnold Schwarzenegger, along with Cormac and Marianne Wibberley. I've never met any of you, but you inspired me when I needed it. The next person I should thank is not so much a person as the entire health and beauty industry, in which I worked for eight long years between college and full-time authorhood. I knew that I wanted to write about cloning, see, but I also knew that I wanted to write something new about cloning, and that meant combining it with a branch of science no one had ever really combined it with before. And what branch of science did I have eight long years of experience writing about? Health and beauty, baby. I came up with the idea of a hand lotion that overwrites your DNA right then and there, sitting on the couch during a commercial break, and I never looked back. Thanks, vast array of heartless beauty companies. I couldn't have done this without you.

Once I had the core concept, the help just poured in from every side. I told my writing group about it and they practically exploded with amazing ideas. Brandon and Emily Sanderson, Karen and Peter Ahlstrom, Ben and Danielle Olsen, Alan Layton, Ethan Skarstedt, Kaylynn Zobell: you're the best. I told Howard Tayler about it and he extemporized a microbiological backstory on the spot; I told my wife, Dawn Wells, and she gave me an amazing list of horrific ways in which the technology could go wildly and amazingly wrong. At this point I knew I needed to do some actual research, so I talked to one of the health and beauty industry lawyers I used to work with, Allen Davis, and picked his brain about each and every one of those doomsday scenarios: if X thing existed, and Y thing happened, what would be the repercussions? How would the company react? How would the company defend itself? Everything I got wrong in this novel is 100 percent my fault, but everything I got right has its origins in one of these and many other conversations with people who are smarter than I am. Thanks to all of you.

At some point in every creative project, life inevitably intervenes. *Extreme Makeover* was bigger and weirder and more ambitious than anything I'd ever written before, and as such, it kept getting back-burnered while I worked on other projects that could actually pay the bills. I wrote the Partials Sequence, and a new John Cleaver novel, and started the Mirador series, and moved to Germany, and had two more kids, and did a thousand other things that ate up all of my time, but whenever I had a free minute or two I'd come back to *Extreme Makeover* and write another chapter or scene or paragraph. When I finally finished the book, it was wonderful and glorious and messy and unfocused and enormous, but my amazing editor, Whitney Ross, performed the single most amazing feat of long-form editing I have ever personally witnessed, and together we chopped that book by more than 35 percent—that's almost 70,000 words cut, which is more words than my first novel had all by itself. Whitney and the rest of the Tor team did an amazing job, and deserve all the thanks I can give them: Amy Stapp, Alexis Saarela, Patty Garcia, Irene Gallo, and a ton of other people behind the scenes. I must also thank, as always, my incredible agent, Sara Crowe, for being incredible. She's the best business partner I could ever ask for.

Thank you to JD Luckesen and Mike Woolf for bringing me fried chicken.

Last but not least: one of the themes I tried to focus on in this book was the idea that nobody is unique, and that doppelgängers appear everywhere, and that certain ideas and actions and names, and even people, will repeat themselves endlessly throughout our lives. Where common author wisdom tells you to make your character names unique and identifiable, I made them confusingly similar on purpose; when I needed an actor for my main character to try to impersonate, I chose Dan Wells because how awesome is that? And thus it is only fitting that, six years after I created the blond twenty something intern in the book, I would end up hiring a blond twenty-something assistant in real life. I promise it's not her. Thank you, Kenna Blaylock, for helping to get this book off the ground. I'm sorry you got shot to death by future chimpanzees on the roof of the UN building.

And thank you to *you* for reading. This is my *Gotterdammerung,* and I hope you enjoy it as much as we all enjoyed bringing it to you.